The Blooms That Broke Us

A NOVEL

ASHLEY DILL

Copyright © 2023 by Ashley Dill

All rights reserved.

No part of this book may be reproduced in any form or by any electronic or mechanical means, including information storage and retrieval systems, without written permission from the author, except for the use of brief quotations in a book review.

*To those grieving invisible losses—you are seen.
To those fighting for love—fight on.*

AUTHOR'S NOTE

Please note this book has a trigger regarding motherhood that is handled with as much care, sensitivity, and validation as possible.

PROLOGUE

The people who claim love is enough—they're flat out lying.

If it was, I wouldn't be alone.

If it was, we'd blossom. We'd be an abundant garden.

But it's love that's crushing me.

Trampling my heart. Withering my spirit.

Tiny pin pricks all over my body. That's what the water feels like. I need to turn down the temperature, but I can't drum up the strength to move. I let the scalding water scorch my skin. The sting feels good. Distracts me.

The floral aroma of the soap I used mingles with the rising steam. The steam's so thick, I wonder if it's possible to drown in it.

He knocks on the door. His voice is barely audible over the pounding of the water against my body. "Hey, you okay in there?"

I swallow the bitterness in my tone. "I'm fine."

"Can I come in?"

I don't answer. Because I don't care.

I've already cleaned up all the blood. Weeping in agony, I did it myself.

That's the part he should've been here for.

The door cracks open.

He says, "I have to head out. Are you going to be okay?"

"Yes."

"Do you need anything?"

I need you.

"No."

"Alright. I'm going to go then. Call me later, okay?"

The door clicks shut.

I don't know how long it takes for me to drag myself out, but when I finally do, the water is cold. It cooled my blistered skin, dissipating the steam. I wrap a robe around my tender shoulders and slowly make my way to bed.

He left a vase of flowers on the nightstand.

Fresh tears fill my eyes. The mix of cut carnations and daisies and greenery are an outrageous substitute.

I reach the window sill and pull. Freezing night air rushes into the room, nipping against the nakedness under my robe and chilling the wet roots of my hair.

I push out a corner of the window screen and tug until it tumbles two stories and lands on the concrete driveway. I grab the bouquet. Squish the blooms down to make them fit through the opening. Then I let go.

Glass shatters, penetrating the quiet of night.

Looking down, I think the shards and scattered flowers look familiar.

ONE

Miranda

I hated spring. The season of newness felt like a slap to the face because nothing new or good ever happened to me. While everyone welcomed the warm April weather and prepped their flower beds, I tucked my tail. Tried not to do anything the universe might interpret as a dare. Chaos had a way of finding me. If circumstances didn't screw me over, I usually found a way to do it myself.

Self-inflicted suffering has always been my preferred mode of delivery. When you are the bonehead causing problems in the first place, it's easier to swallow. You grit your teeth and handle the consequences. But when other people cause the suffering? The result is an onion. There are layers to process. The whys, the grief, the betrayal. And after you've gone through every layer, the sting lasts a long time.

I ended the call on my phone, despair wrapping its tentacles around my midsection. I deep-breathed once, then twice. Fighting to stay calm.

Kacey ambled to where I sat on the porch steps, holding a clover flower up to my face. "Dis is for you, Mommy!"

"Oh, thank you. It's so beautiful." I sniffed and tilted my head to the side, attempting to keep my tears from spilling over. Three-year-old Kacey had grown so aware of my feelings the past few months. It was becoming difficult to hide my ever-present watery eyes or conceal the tremor in my voice. "Can you find me some more? I want a bouquet."

"Sure!" He ran off. I frantically wiped at the escapees, soaking them into the underside of my sweatshirt. I prayed the bouquet task would buy me thirty seconds to get my crap together.

Anxiety roiled through my stomach. I hadn't expected the representative from the Cincinnati women's shelter to turn Kacey and me away. I could tell it pained her, but the apologetic tone of her voice didn't help to soften the blow.

She'd said calls were at an all-time high.

There were no beds. None at all. Only a big, fat waitlist.

And I was *sick* of waiting. Truly sick. As the days went by, it felt like I was being ripped apart from the inside. Like my body was slowly dying alongside my heart.

I had made plan after plan after plan. But there was always a hole. Always a problem—usually money or a place to land. Everything I owned belonged to my boyfriend, Chris. My home and everything in my wallet besides my license. It was an unfortunate reality he never let me forget.

My dear cousin, Tag, had offered for us to come live with him in Texas on the ranch he inherited from our grandparents. I spent every summer there growing up. As much as I loved the ranch, moving there was an option I hated from the depths of my being. The place was one grocery trip away from bankruptcy. Tag promised that no matter what happened to the ranch and his home, we'd figure it out, that our safety was the most important thing. He was right, but Kacey and I would only be extra mouths to feed and I couldn't stand the thought of burdening Tag more than he already was. But, what choice did I have?

I wished things were different with my mom, but she was wrapped up in her own life. Definitely didn't care to be bothered with mine. Her life was all about her man. She'd stopped being a safe option long ago. If I went to her, she'd keep us for a few days then encourage me to go back to him no doubt.

If I was ever going to leave Chris behind, Texas just became the final option.

I could not—*would not*—keep staying in Ohio.

I raised my voice so Kacey could hear. "See the clover patch near the fence? Go get those!"

He shrieked in delight and ran off. I sniffed hard, determined to get through the evening. Kacey needed me, and Chris would be home anytime now. I could sink into hopelessness after everyone was safely asleep.

Before I could dry my face, the unmistakable low rumble of the Challenger's souped-up engine jerked my attention down the street. I turned my head away, stuffing the phone in my jeans' pocket. I rubbed my nose then pressed on my cheeks.

I stood, strolling toward the driveway. If I didn't greet him, he would wonder why.

Chris parked and the loud bass speakers clicked off with the engine. He stepped out, flashing me the poised smile that fooled many unsuspecting people with its charm. His eyes were concealed by mirror-like sunglasses. I couldn't read him when he wore those. He said, "Hey, sweet thing."

"Hey, baby."

He pulled me into a hug. His clothes reeked of beer.

So much for the job search.

"Any luck out there today?"

"Nah." He draped his heavy arm over my shoulders. "Nobody wants to pay anything worth it these days."

"Not many are worth the pay."

He stopped, frowning down at me. The ripple across his lips made my mouth dry as his fingers barely tensed around my upper arm. "What do you mean by that?"

I smacked his chest and produced a fake giggle that usually worked in my favor. "Oh, you know I don't mean *you*."

He relaxed, his lips softening into a neutral expression. "Hope not."

"Maybe we could watch a movie tonight," I suggested in an attempt to change the subject.

"Yeah—" He stopped his meandering toward the front door and turned my shoulders to face him. I averted my eyes in Kacey's direction. Chris moved his glasses to the top of his head, squinting at me. "What's wrong?"

My stomach tightened. We'd been together too long.

"Nothing's wrong," I lied.

"Yeah, there is." His dark brown eyes roved over my face. "Look at me." I didn't at first so he grabbed my chin to force the action. "You've been crying. Why?"

"Just feeling a little bit emotional today." My shrug wasn't sufficient to dislodge his grasp.

He didn't roll his eyes, but they lifted toward the sky a bit. Like he'd been-there-done-that. "Who did you talk to today? Was it *Tag*?"

I shrugged again, wracking my brain for a way to change the conversation. I couldn't admit to calling shelters and making plans to flee to Texas. Why was I such an open book? Even my thoughts couldn't have a smidge of privacy. Like a hound on the trail, Chris couldn't resist the urge to sniff around when I had something on my mind.

He sighed, "Miranda, we've been through this." He let go of me and took a step back.

I played along, pretended vacation was all I wanted. "I know you have to keep looking for work, but what if Kacey and I went by ourselves? We'd visit for a ten days or so then come right back."

"It's not safe for you to travel alone like that."

"I can drive fine."

He scoffed, his agitation swelling.

"What? You don't think I can drive to Texas? We'd have Tag once we got there—so we wouldn't be alone." Arguing with Chris wasn't a great tactic, but I had to make some sort of case.

"You haven't seen him in years, why now?"

"I miss him." When his jaw ticked, I realized I probably should shut the heck up and stop pushing.

"You *miss* him." He wanted me to confirm.

"Yeah?"

He crossed his arms, daring me to ask him. "What would you need from me?"

"Nothing."

He cocked an eyebrow. "Nothing?"

"I—just gas money."

He threw his hands up. "Unbelievable!"

The unfairness of the situation made my chest clench. Chris was the unappointed gatekeeper in my life, and I hated him for it.

"So, let me get this straight. You want to use money we barely have to go see another man?"

My jaw dropped and I faltered for a response. "Chris! What are you insinuating?" I needed to dial in my emotions, but his audacity! "You do realize Tag is my *cousin*, right?"

"Still it isn't appropriate for you to go see him like that."

"Besides my mom and stepdad, who I don't care to ever see again, Tag is my only family."

He rolled his eyes full-on this time. "Do you not remember anything? You were abandoned. When you needed help, I was the only person there for you. Not Tag." He grabbed my shoulders again, turning me toward Kacey this time. He leaned forward and his yeasty breath moved the hair around my ear. "*We* are the only family that matters, Miranda. The rest of them left you—high and dry."

The vision of my son swam. Chris wasn't wrong.

He continued facing me toward my one treasure. Kacey was throwing specks of grass into the air as the wind lifted beautiful curls off his forehead. The sweet baby had no idea all the turmoil his venture into this world had caused. I never wanted him to find out.

Chris' grip tightened, and I squirmed. "You wouldn't have him without me. Better not forget that."

He let go, and I stumbled forward a step. Had he pushed me? I couldn't tell.

He climbed the front steps. "You know what? I think I'm gonna go watch the game at Devon's house." I didn't turn to look at him because tears were streaming down my face. Watching Kacey play was safer. "I spend the whole day trying to get a job to make sure I can keep a roof over your heads, and you want to leave?" I jumped when Chris kicked the screen door and strung together some choice words. "An ungrateful bitch is what you are."

My hands wouldn't stop shaking. I tucked them under my chin.

A few beats of silence passed. I took a deep breath through my nose, pressing my lips together. I didn't know what time the game started, but I hoped it was soon.

His footsteps descended down the stairs again. "Look at me, Miranda."

I turned. Brave face activated.

He shook his head when he saw the tears. His voice was softer, and some of the rigidity had melted from his posture. "Listen, sorry for losing my temper. You can do whatever you want. It's your life. But two things you won't be taking." He lifted his fingers as he counted them off. "Any of my money. I won't financially support a stupid vacation." Then he nodded toward my son. "Or him. After everything I've done, he's as much mine as yours."

When the screen door bounced behind him, I collapsed onto the front steps, forcing down waves of nausea.

Chris was right; he'd done everything for me and Kacey. We would be lost without him. But in exchange for his provision, I'd unknowingly sold my soul.

I couldn't need Chris anymore. I had to make my own way.

As terrifying as it was, Texas was my only option left.

And I didn't need Chris' permission.

It wasn't a stupid vacation.

TWO

Miranda

Chris' obsession with credit card offers drove me to the brink of insanity nearly every day. Between collection agencies and automated text messaging systems, my phone rang constantly. He used *my* number on the sign up forms. There were probably some rich bank men on a beach somewhere, sipping margaritas because of suckers like Chris.

But tonight, one of Chris' stupid cards would be the answer to my problems. I'd found one in the back of our junk drawer. A quick phone call proved it was active and not maxed out yet. Five hundred dollars was plenty of money to make the nine-hundred mile drive to Texas, as long as nothing happened to the Corolla.

While Chris was at Devon's house, I'd packed everything. Clothes, extra food, toys, charger. All our necessities were ready.

Except the credit card.

I silently pulled it from the junk drawer and stuck it in my pocket on the way out at two o'clock in the morning.

After two days of prep, my plan was officially underway.

It was unnaturally cold for early April. About forty-one degrees. My teeth chattered as I buckled half-sleeping Kacey in. His groggy voice whined about the cold. I glanced at the front door, whispering, "Shh, Kacey, it's okay."

Idling the car would be stupid, so I grabbed an extra blanket and tucked it around Kacey. When I pulled the keys out of my pocket, the credit card clattered to the ground. I hissed a curse, fighting the adrenaline surging through me. Couldn't leave without the credit card, but every moment I delayed risked our discovery. I collapsed to my hands and knees, peering under the car.

Where was that thing?

I'd barely breathed the last few hours. Wouldn't feel better until I was crossing state lines. I'd looked over my shoulder a hundred times and fully expected my schemes to be hacked to pieces at any moment.

After patting around the cold concrete, I chanced pulling out my phone and flipped on the flashlight. Two seconds with the light and I'd found my ticket to freedom, standing up to get in the car and make my escape.

A figure stood at the rear of the car.

I gasped.

Chris.

My heart nearly stopped.

This cannot be happening.

"Where are you going?"

"Uhm, the hospital." I tried to be quick on my feet, force my voice to sound normal. "Kacey has a fever."

I couldn't see his face, but Chris' stance softened a little. "Oh, why didn't you tell me?"

"I—I think it's pretty contagious. Didn't want you to be laid up in bed tomorrow." My brain frantically searched for a way out as my lungs tightened.

It would be a sheer miracle if this didn't end in tragedy.

He stepped closer. His voice was soft, inviting. "Miranda, you know I'm not worried about that kind of thing. Let's move him to my car, and I'll go with you."

"That's okay, he's sleeping. The hospital's not far."

Kacey whined, betraying me.

There wasn't much light. I hadn't turned the floods on. But there must've been enough from the street lamp down the road, because when Chris approached me, he looked at my hands.

I realized my mistake too late.

His one true love was clutched in my fingers. On full display.

"Whatcha got there?" He nodded toward the credit card.

"Oh, uhm"—I shrugged and stuck it back into my pocket—"Kacey's Medicaid card."

And that was all it took to awaken his suspicion.

The light came from behind him, contorting his figure into a dark silhouette. I couldn't see his face, but I could imagine the slip in his expression as he squinted his eyes and pressed his lips together.

"What's really going on here?" The icy chill in his tone made my stomach flip and panic sweep through my body. I couldn't draw a full breath.

"Nothing. He's just sick—"

"And you weren't even going to tell me?" He cursed and his words grew in intensity, rumbling in his throat. "Miranda, you've got my boy sitting in a freezing car."

My boy.

My heart balked at his claim.

The quiver in my words was impossible to hide. "I didn't want to disturb your sleep."

"Give me the card."

"What? No."

"I'm taking him."

"I want to do it. They will probably give him some Tylenol, and he'll be fine."

"*Give* me the card."

"It's okay. I will let you know what the doctor says when we get home."

He stepped forward and I retreated, feeling my backside press against the frigid metal of the Corolla. He whispered, verbalizing his deepest fear. "You're leaving me aren't you?"

"Chris—no, of course not."

"Then give me the card."

"This is silly. I—"

He didn't let me finish. He lurched forward, and I yelped. One hand jerked me forward by the arm and he thrust the other inside my jeans' pocket. Once he found the credit card, he let go and pulled out his phone, tapping the screen to illuminate it. He cussed. So loudly I winced.

"What the hell are you trying to pull?"

"Nothing, I think I grabbed it by mistake."

His voice was growl-like and angry. "You liar."

He turned on his flashlight, shining it into the car. In the backseat next to Kacey were diaper boxes full of clothes. I didn't have tape, so the flaps were open, advertising their contents.

"Clothes?"

"For Goodwill."

He shook his head in disbelief. "You must think I am some kind of idiot."

"Chris, I—"

"Where do you think you're going?"

I didn't answer.

"*Where?*"

I managed to suck in a deep breath, mustering courage. "The *hospital*."

With the speed of a viper, he reached up and grabbed the back of my neck. His fingers pressed deep into my muscles, and I grunted in pain, attempting to twist away. "Ow—Chris! Let go!"

He stepped forward, pressing his body against mine, trapping me on the side of the car. He squeezed, forcing my face upward to look him in the eyes. My own stung as I tried to push him away. He was like a brick wall. My size put me at a distinct disadvantage with Chris who had eight inches on my 5'3" stature.

He hissed, nose to nose. "You're going to Nashville, aren't you? Back to him."

"What?" I should've expected he'd accuse me of this again. "*No*. I swear I'm not!"

I whimpered, moving my head from side to side. He pressed his forehead against mine. All ease had melted from his expression. His brows cut angry slants over his eyes. He whispered into my face, "You aren't going anywhere—especially back to Nashville—with my money or my kid."

"I'm—I'm not going to Nashville."

"Texas?"

I considered throwing a punch at him—I knew how, but ultimately he'd overpower me and there would be hell to pay as is.

I nodded and tears spilled out of my eyes. "I just want to go see Tag." Words scraped out of my tight throat. "I'll come back. I promise."

His thumb rolled over the tendons in my neck, and I cried

out. With his free hand he groped around my other pockets until he found the car keys and my phone.

"Shh!" Spittle hit my face, and he glanced over his shoulder to make sure we hadn't caught any attention. "You want to leave? Fine. But you're leaving without Kacey." He let go of me and yanked Kacey's door open before shoving my stuff into his sweatpants.

My world spun.

There was no way I'd leave without *my* son.

Chris leaned to unbuckle Kacey, murmuring, "Poor little guy. Momma made you cold, didn't she?"

I was paralyzed. Now what? My plan had failed. Chris tucked Kacey against his shoulder and headed toward the front door. "Let me know when you get to Texas. Don't want to worry about you."

His long strides took him through the front door in record time, and I flinched out of my haze, hurrying after them. Right as I neared the threshold, it slammed in my face. The slide of the deadbolt penetrating the quiet night.

"Chris!" I tried the handle. "Chris!"

Nothing.

"Chris, open the door." I beat on it with the heel of my hand. "You can't leave me out here!"

I paused to listen.

He won't leave me out here, will he?

Panic gripped my vocal chords. "Chris! Please!"

Surely, he didn't realize he'd locked me out. My teeth chattered. I had no phone, keys, or money. I only had a thin sweatshirt between me and the chill of the wee morning hours.

Tears raced down my cheeks as a flush of anger so heavy and thick heated my body. Hurt feelings and furious words spilled out of me. After five minutes, I plopped down on the steps, my hands throbbing from banging on the door.

I lifted my face, glancing across the street. A soft glow illuminated my new neighbor's window. A dark shadow stood against the blinds, cracking the slats open. When I looked up, the crack disappeared and the shadow backed away.

Great. Now the neighbor knows we are dysfunctional. Yellow glow from our own windows lit the porch and the barren garden beds alongside the walkway. The front of Chris' house was ugly—lifeless. He'd never bothered to beautify it, so neither did I. But gardening fascinated me. I'd always wanted to have a garden of my own. To toil for a harvest seemed a romantic task. But it required trial and error. Mess-ups and dead plants. Problem-solving and fixing. Dedication and commitment.

And I was *way* too tired for all that.

So the beds stayed bare. I hated them.

If things had been different, maybe we'd have tulips and daffodils sprouting. Maybe I'd have perennials bursting to life with the newness of spring. Maybe I'd have a wide-brimmed hat to wear in the sunshine and a teensy pair of gloves for Kacey. Maybe we'd plant tiny seeds and learn about how they grow. Maybe it'd become the safest place in the whole wide world.

Chris' figure passing through the house jerked my attention back to the door. I jumped up, slamming my fists against it. "Chris!" I kicked the door to protect my stinging hands.

I shrieked, "Please!"

His shadow hesitated a moment.

But the lights clicked off and darkness overwhelmed me.

THREE

Jack

I pushed into the Moores' kitchen via the side door. Inside, my frazzled sister had one of the girls in a carrier on her chest and was bent forward, tapping the tops of cupcakes in the oven with one hand and protecting the baby with the other. Her eyes lit up as she looked over her shoulder. "Jack! My savior!"

"Oh no. What's wrong?"

"You picked the perfect day to be early." She nodded toward her other baby who sat in a swing, red-faced in protest. "Do me a favor and grab her so she'll stop fussing."

I scooped the angry baby into my arms. "What's wrong, Winter?" At six months old, Winter and Woods looked so similar. But I was getting it down. Winter had droopier cheeks. I held her pink onesie-clad body against my chest and lightly patted her back. "What do you need, sis?"

"Mostly someone to take care of Winter. The twins have been fussy today and have barely napped, so I am super behind schedule." She glanced at a gray clock on the wall and swiped a strand of hair out of her face. "Pat is dealing with an unhappy client, and Sunny is going to be home from therapy in about an hour. A few of her friends are coming to game night." Her smile contradicted her eye roll. "They demanded cupcakes like a bunch of five-year-olds."

Her cupcakes were still in the oven. Piles of dishes wrapped around her kitchen counter and clean laundry was all over the couch. For a mom of twins, she was doing great. But in terms of game night, she was behind. Horribly so.

I chuckled. "Give me the other backpack thing and I'll help."

"Oh! That's a good idea."

A few minutes later, Jules was securing Winter into a cocoon-like pouch on my chest. She giggled as she tightened a strap on my side. "Aw. She looks tiny on you." At 6'3" most people looked tiny next to me. She pulled a strap, making the carrier fit. "Hopefully, she will fall asleep."

Looked like we would have no problem there. Winter's cheek landed against my chest as her eyelids grew immediately heavy. Her twin, Woods, was completely passed out in Jules' pouch. I reached in and rubbed the patch of brown hair on her head. Couldn't help but smile.

Thirty minutes later, we'd cleared the sink and couch, swept her floors, moved chairs near the fire pit on the deck, and had flash-chilled the cupcakes in the deep freezer.

"I could not have done this without you." Jules spread a glob of frosting over a cupcake. "Pat usually helps me get ready for game night."

Speak of the devil. The door opened, and Pat, my brother-in-law, walked in. Jules abandoned her task to greet him at the door.

He leaned forward to quickly kiss her, but held her at arm's length. "Hold up, baby. There's grease all over me." His gaze bounced around the clean-ish house. "I'm so sorry, Jules. I meant to help you with all this."

"Don't worry. Jack saved the day."

"Jack, thanks so much man."

"No problem. It's been fun." Recently, being home meant being alone. Which made house work while streaming nineties boy bands a pleasing alternative.

"You need to go shower so you can pick up Sunny."

Pat and Jules disappeared down the hall.

When I was alone, I paused my cupcake decorating to look down at Winter. Lightly snoring, eyelids fluttering, her face was smooshed against me, pushing her rose-bud lips into a triangular shape. I swiped my hands against a dish towel and reached in to poke her cheek. A soft chuckle escaped my throat as I pressed a kiss to the top of her head. She smelled sweet like berries and clean like she'd just had a bath.

Winter and Woods were something else. When I learned my twin was pregnant with twins, I was excited. But the extent of the love I felt for my nieces had completely blindsided me. And not just the twins—Sunny, too. Even though Jules had adopted Sunny, she might as well have been blood.

When I picked up another cupcake, the floor creaked. Jules was hiding behind the door frame, but held her phone upright, trained on me.

"What the heck are you doing?"

She said nothing.

"Why are you taking a picture of me?"

She came into full view, shamelessly snapping a few more.

"Because this"—she gestured toward me—"this hot guy holding a baby and decorating cupcakes thing is the stuff of women's domestic dreams."

"Gross."

"Calm down. Not *my* dreams." She stepped closer. "Here. Do this." She demonstrated a face.

"It looks like you tasted a lemon."

She laughed. "I don't know how to do it—you know, like a smolder face."

"You're insane."

"Just once."

"Absolutely not."

"Fine. I got some good ones anyway." She plopped onto a bar stool and started scrolling. "I'm going to send these to Katelyn."

My skin prickled. The conversation had taken a bad turn. "No, you aren't."

She smiled, thrilled beyond reason. "Nothing—and I mean nothing—says, 'please have my babies' more than *that*." She turned the phone around to show me, and I snatched it out of her hands.

"Very funny." I shoved it into my back pocket, rolling my eyes.

"I'll send it to her later." She hopped up and went to the fridge. "Want a drink?"

In the Moore house, *drink* meant a coke or sweet tea. Alcoholic beverages never crossed over the threshold. Jules said their demons still paid visits.

"Sweet tea. Thanks."

She pulled the pitcher out. "By the way, where is Katelyn? I thought she had Friday nights off."

I'd been putting this off for months. Probably time to spill the beans though so Jules wouldn't send Kate that stupid picture after she got her phone back. "She does."

A thoughtful frown crossed over her face as she raised her voice over the ice dispenser. "Is she busy today then? I haven't seen her in forever."

"About that—"

Jules stopped.

"We—"

"Jackson, no." She paled. "Don't even say it."

I stopped explaining and watched a wave of anguish cross her face. Her matrimonial hopes and dreams for me were being dashed to smithereens. Yet again. Without me even divulging the details, Jules knew. Irritation flashed in me. Felt my jaw clenching.

And here we go.

Her voice was breathless as she melted back onto the stool. "When?"

"Beginning of January."

"That was three *months* ago!"

I scraped the last bit of frosting from the jar as she sat there, mouth open.

"Why didn't you tell me?" she pressed.

"Didn't feel like talking about it. Still don't."

She smacked her forehead with her palm. "I feel like an idiot! I texted her two weeks ago and told her we missed seeing her around. No wonder she didn't text me back!"

"Sorry about that."

"I liked Katelyn! Why did you dump her?"

"Why are you automatically assuming *I* did the dumping?"

"Because it's always you."

I scoffed at that. Not *always*. Not when it mattered.

"Can we stop talking about this?"

She ignored my request. "I can remember one time in the last four years that a woman did the dumping. Women fall hard for you."

"Not that hard."

"Come on, Jack. Yes, they do. Remember Bree?"

I couldn't forget her if I tried. Bree was a whole other level of obsessed. I opened my mouth to respond, but Jules cut me off.

"My point is the women who date you are serious and then you dump them!"

It was true. I was a chronic dumper. The one time I was dumped—she honestly beat me to the punch. No woman could meet my very specific standards. How was I supposed to pick and settle for a second best when I'd experienced the best? There was no way Jules would understand.

"I'm picky." I dropped the knife in the sink and finished lining the cupcakes on a tray.

"You're breaking hearts, Jack."

A frown pulled at my face. Wasn't fond of the accusation. "That makes me sound like a womanizer."

"I know you're not." She shook her head. "But Katelyn was into you. *Long term* into you."

Couldn't argue with her there. I'd had three nasty break ups. Kate's ranked at number three. I'd seen worse, but that one was rough.

"I thought Katelyn might end the streak," Jules whined. "What happened? She seemed so sweet. She was gorgeous and ambitious and had good tastes and—"

"And also didn't want a family."

Her shoulders fell. "Really?"

"Not kids anyway."

"Oh."

"No point in being together if we don't want the same things."

"How did you not know that?"

I rolled my eyes.

"What?"

"You haven't been in the dating scene since high school."

"Pat and I dated."

"Whatever you two did was *not* dating."

She huffed but didn't argue.

"There are unspoken rules. You don't ask 'how many kids do you want' waiting for the appetizer." Jules had long ago abandoned my glass of sweet tea, so I finished the pour myself. "Katelyn had talked about settling down. Like an idiot, I assumed she meant family. What she *actually* meant was that she wants to be a pampered wife and own a dog in a nice house in Franklin."

Jules grimaced. "I'm sorry."

How many times had Jules and I had this exact conversation? Jules felt like every girl I took to dinner could be wife material.

"Yeah, me too. I know you guys are probably ready for me to stop hanging around."

She sat up straight, intensity furrowing her brow. "Don't you dare say that."

I smirked. Knew that would get a rise out of her.

"You are always welcome here." She rolled her shoulders, adjusting the baby carrier strap as silence settled between us. "Are you okay?"

Such a dumb question.

"It's okay to not be okay, you know."

That response had Pat written all over it. If I remember correctly, we were raised to be tough as nails. I tried for sarcasm. "Moose Tracks and Days of Our Lives help me cope."

"Jack."

"Of course I'm fine."

She paused, tapping her fingers against the granite. "So three months single, huh? Anyone else on the horizon?"

An emphatic *no* spilled over before I had the chance to check my tone.

Jules' eyebrows lifted. "Well, we have a great new picture

for your dating profile. It will communicate *family* loud and clear."

"I'm done with apps."

"They've helped you make some decent matches. Granted, not *the* match, but still."

"I'm sick of trying."

She squinted at me then slowly rolled her eyes like I was a lost cause. "I wish you would just admit it."

"Admit what?"

She shook her head. "That you dump everyone because you want—"

"We've talked about this. That is not the reason." How many times did I have to tell her?

"There are other women out there, Jack. You're throwing your opportunities away."

I'd done a good job not getting totally pissed off, but now Jules was pushing.

She continued, "You haven't let her go. And I wish you would so you can move on and be happy and not be alone forever."

"Can we *please* talk about something else?"

Her posture softened as she leaned back in the chair. A look of pity washed over her and her voice lowered. "You'll find someone else, Jack. You will."

Would I? I'd been on the hunt a long time. I wasn't alone for lack of trying.

To my relief, Pat re-emerged and distracted my sister from my love life.

Game night was always a good time. Pat and Jules called it one of their "anchor points." They'd said anchors in their schedule helped them stay consistent for Sunny and forced them not to isolate when things were hard. And the Moore family dealt with a lot of hard. But game night carried on nonetheless. Two Fridays a month.

After Pat creamed everyone at Scattergories and my team won Pictionary, we called it quits and moved out to sit by the fire pit. I sat back in a porch chair and watched. Sunny and her friends were charged, and slap-stick comedy abounded from the other side of the deck. The twins were in bed. And Danny, the elderly neighbor, had joined Pat, Jules, and I around the fire.

Pat and Jules' chairs were pulled close together. He had his arm around her, and she was tucked into his side. They sat like that every chance they got. Jules radiated contentment around Pat. He had highlighted wonderful sides of my sister I wasn't even aware existed. She was peaceful, calm. Not chasing a high anymore. Seemed fulfilled.

If anyone was due some genuine happiness, it was Jules. I was glad for her, but couldn't ignore the pinch in my chest. The Moore family was a sight to behold. They were blossoming together. They'd had a winding journey, but had found their place. The sense of belonging surrounded them like a thick aura.

It's funny. I'd been better, faster, and greater at everything Jules and I ever did in life. Twin rivalry is sibling rivalry on steroids. Especially when you grew up in a house like ours—where nothing but A-game was accepted. But Jules spent her childhood years in my shadow. I had the upper hand in grades, social circles, parental favor, sports, the arts, opportunities, strength. You name it. I gloated about it too. Like an idiot.

I'd never been jealous of anything she had.

Except this.

My ribbons and accolades didn't keep me company. Certainly didn't keep me warm at night. I went home to an empty house, an empty bed. No sounds but the AC clicking off and on and the ice tray emptying occasionally. I stifled a sigh at the thought.

I'd outdone Jules in every way except the only way that mattered.

Here I was, going on thirty-four years old, and I'd yet to start a family of my own. I had one failed attempt under my belt, and I hated the failure more than I hated being alone.

Flames licked the darkness, pushing back the night. I found myself staring into them, lost in what-ifs and could-have-beens. My phone vibrating jerked me back to reality.

I unsnapped it from the clip and glanced at the screen. A Chicago number? Didn't really get calls from that area ever since I moved to Nashville years ago.

"Hello?"

"Hi, is this Jackson Barkley?"

"This is him. Who's this?"

"I'm Sarah, a nurse from Northwestern Memorial Hospital in Chicago. I'm afraid I'm calling with bad news."

FOUR

Miranda

I huddled on the front porch, waiting for the mail. Cincinnati temps were in the mid-fifties. If left up to me, I'd be inside, under my afghan with a romance novel, but Kacey was dedicated to the outdoors. Rain or shine. Thin with age, the sweatshirt I wore offered little warmth. Chris lavished me with nice clothing, so it drove him crazy when I wouldn't let the decade-old sweatshirt retire. I pulled my palms into the oversized sleeves and shivered.

I tucked a strand of hair behind my ear, wincing. Forgot how sore my face still felt. I was physically recovering from my altercation with Chris. But emotionally recovering was a whole different ball game. I shivered again. Less from the cold this time.

I'd spent almost two hours outside our front door that night. I'd checked every window and pounded on the door until my toes hurt and my fists bruised. My face was so cold I couldn't feel my lips. Just when I decided to wake the neighbors, the door opened. Chris pulled me in, apologizing, claiming he hadn't known he'd locked me out. He wrapped a blanket around me and started a warm shower. Hot tea waited for me on my side of the bed and he'd started a heating pad for my feet.

He fell all over himself. Calling me his "sweet girl" and acting like he cared. His remorse was so convincing that I felt sorry for him. I knew the truth—his actions were intentional. But I doubted *he* knew the truth. Delusion seemed the only way to explain such cruelty.

Honesty was the second big mistake I'd made that night. After being thwarted, threatened, and left to freeze, my fury forced everything out without permission. I called him delusional. Accused him of doing it all on purpose. I admitted my plan to leave him, and said I wouldn't be happy until I was free.

I didn't have mental clarity around Chris. It's hard to see things as they are when you're around someone who weaves his own version of reality. But the veil lifted, and I'd spoken with more clarity than I'd felt in years. But that one lucid moment had morphed nice Chris into destructive Chris.

He hit me.

Backhanded me across the face so hard, I fell backward and broke our slatted closet door. Of all the crap Chris has done, he had never hit me before.

The only way I'd been able to deescalate the situation was to apologize. Tell him I was wrong, reassure him of my love, and thank him for taking care of me. To snuggle into bed with him. To let him hold me. To stroke *his* wounds.

I humored him. Holding down waves of nausea. Fighting the flight response. My stomach clenched so tight I couldn't draw a full breath. But I did it. I made my wrongs right. Just like I always did.

Now, a few days later, I huddled on the porch, trying my best not to relive it over and over. Kacey played with his Hot Wheels in the yard. The cap I wore was pulled low over my forehead, and my make-up almost covered the bruise on the right side of my face, but not quite.

Kacey shrieked with delight when he heard the mailman coming down the street. "Mail! Can I get it, Mommy?"

"Sure, buddy. Go ahead." He scampered up to the fence. I reminded him, as mothers do, "Say thank you."

The mailwoman stopped at our fence when she saw Kacey standing there with his hand reaching up. She smiled, greeting Kacey with the enthusiasm of a party princess, and handed him a small stack of envelopes over the top of the fence. She'd grown used to seeing him standing there and seemed to enjoy his pleasure in the menial task. His interaction with other human beings was so limited. The service people who rumbled down the street were his heroes.

He deserved better than what I was giving him.

After she left for the next house, Kacey brought the mail, chattering his little head off. He handed it to me as I strolled over to our big trash can on the driveway. I shuffled through the stack—mostly credit card offers. As I was lifting the lid to drop the junk in, our new neighbor exited her house with her little dog and a huge purse slung over her shoulder.

"Hi!" She waved as she descended her porch steps. Kacey ran down the driveway, waving back. Wished he wouldn't have done that. I ducked my head, crossing my fingers she wouldn't see the bruise. My swollen eye would make a great first impression, huh?

"I've been wanting to meet you guys!"

"Hey." I faked a smile.

"My name is Sherri."

"I'm Miranda and this is my son, Kacey. It's really nice to

meet you. Are you guys getting settled in?"

She nodded. "I think so. We used to live in the countryside, so the noise is something we have to get used to."

We talked for a few minutes about her old place. Apparently, they'd moved into the city so her husband, Ed, could be closer to the hospital. Lots of health issues. Her dog was named Muffin and loved the attention Kacey bestowed on him.

She glanced toward our front door. "Is your husband home?"

"Yes, he's napping right now. He's my boyfriend actually."

Sherri was middle-aged with silvery streaks in her dark hair. Big, brown eyes behind her red rimmed glasses gave her a smart look. Her smile never faltered. "Do you guys have a security system or any cameras?"

Taken aback, I stumbled for words. "I'm sorry—*what*?"

"I have something to give you, but wanted to make sure there wouldn't be any footage."

I shook my head. Who asks something like that? "Yeah, uhm, no." My pulse shot sky high—what person asks that? "We—we don't have any cameras."

She reached into her purse and handed me a business card. She lowered her voice, like she was afraid someone might overhear us. "I'm sorry to creep you out." Her smile melted, and tender concern lines drew her eyebrows together. "Muffin wakes up to go to the bathroom early every morning. So I was awake and heard commotion the other night. Saw what happened." She shook her head. "I probably should've come out and done something—helped you somehow—but I got scared for some reason. Pretty silly, honestly. And I'm sorry I didn't."

A hot, sticky flush slowly climbed into my ears.

"My first husband was a very cruel man. We had a few

children together and, well, when he started being cruel to them, I knew it was time to go. Past time, actually." She shrugged. "I wanted you to have my cell number, work number, and I wrote my work schedule on the back. If you ever need help or want to leave, I'll help with whatever I can."

I opened my mouth but no words came. My face was on fire.

"I'm sorry if this was too personal—"

"No, no. It's okay, Sherri." I resisted the urge to fan my heated face. "Me and Kacey...I'm embarrassed, but I also really appreciate it."

"Don't be embarrassed." She pressed her lips together, blinking tears back. "I've been there." She changed her tone back to peppy and looked at Kacey. "Well, sweetheart, Muffin is going to hate me for this, but I got to go to work."

"Kacey, can you say bye-bye to Muffin?" I urged him as my throat tightened with emotion. "He has to go home now."

He leaned to kiss Muffin's head. "Bye-bye, Muffin!"

We exchanged goodbyes and she left.

My mind whirled from our conversation.

I had settled onto the front steps when my cell phone vibrated in my hand. I frowned at the screen. A Chicago number? Probably a collection agency. I ignored the call and examined the business card in my lap.

Sherri knew. Mortification and relief competed in my chest.

I stiffened as the screen door creaked. I shoved the card underneath my sweatshirt, lodging it deep inside my bralette. Just as I slipped my hand out, Chris settled next to me on the steps. His ash brown hair was mussed. "It feels amazing out here."

"I've been shivering."

He put an arm around my shoulder and pinched my sleeve.

"It's 'cause you're wearing this old thing. Why won't you get rid of it?"

He was baiting me to bring up Tag again. He asked even though he knew full well I loved this Schrute Farms sweatshirt because Tag got it for my birthday one year.

My phone buzzed again. Same number.

"Who's that?"

I shrugged. "Stupid sales call." Chris entwined his fingers with mine, and we sat in silence, watching Kacey run around the yard.

He moved to the step below me and turned to look into my face. I tried not to grimace when he leaned forward to kiss me. Forced my lips to kiss him back. Last thing I wanted was to rock the boat. He lingered with the kiss, placing his hands at my sides. His lips sweeping over mine made my stomach turn. It was all I could do not to push him away.

To any onlooker, we were a happy couple enjoying an intimate moment on the porch.

He forcefully deepened the kiss. I knew rejecting him would make my night harder, so I played along as best I could. But when his hands snaked under my sweatshirt and grabbed my breasts, I had to push him away. Couldn't risk him feeling the jagged edges of Sherri's card beneath fabric.

"Chris!" I backed away and crossed my arms over me, faking a smile. "Not in front of Kacey."

He smiled and winked. "Later."

"Sure." My voice was flat, and I swallowed hard, looking away.

I didn't know how I'd get through "later," but it would be the last time. I would make sure of it.

Somehow, someway, I would make *sure* of it.

A notification alert buzzed. The Chicago caller left a message.

FIVE

Miranda

A few days later, I peeked out the blinds and dialed Sherri's number, watching Chris' Challenger disappear around the street corner. We had talked in my driveway every day and yesterday finalized my plan to leave Chris. I knew exactly what to do. It was now or never.

Hope surged. As much as I dreaded driving all the way to Chicago, the meeting could change my life. I had no idea why Nathaniel Barkley included *me* of all people in his will, but when the attorney's office called and said Nathaniel requested his beneficiaries be present for the reading of his will, I accepted the invitation. Nathaniel was a very wealthy man and whatever he had for me could change my entire situation.

Heck, a mere five hundred dollars would change everything.

She picked up. "Hello?"

"Hey, Sherri. Do you have a cup of sugar I can borrow?" It was our code.

Two minutes later, Sherri was in my house, quietly packing my things and Ed was in our driveway, filling my motor oil. Sherri had said we needed to use codes and keep talk to a minimum in case Chris had more surveillance going than I realized. The notion scared me. I'd never seriously considered the possibility. She told me to discard my phone and buy a prepaid one before I made it to my final destination. Just in case he looked up my coordinates.

My heart hurt for Sherri. She must've been through so much.

In record time, we had my car packed and ready. Kacey was buckled in.

My lips trembled as I faced her. "I'm—I'm scared."

She wrapped her arms around me and started to cry. "I've been praying for you all night. For some reason, I know you guys are going to be okay. You're going to find the next step." She held me back to look at me. "There's lots of possibility out there. And it's better than this. I promise."

I nodded, swiping the tears off my face.

She thrust a piece of paper with an address and hand-copied directions on it. "Don't look up Brenda's address on your GPS. Just follow the instructions. It's pretty straightforward."

Brenda, Sherri's best friend, lived in Milwaukee. She had graciously taken Sherri in after her ugly divorce and agreed to open her doors for me and Kacey, too.

First stop, Chicago. Destination, Milwaukee.

It was more than I could've hoped for.

Ed shut my hood after checking all the fluids. They gave me a hundred dollars for gas and lunch. Sherri cried that they couldn't give more. But Ed's hospital bills made it difficult to pay their mortgage and keep the lights on.

I assured them they'd given me hope—more than I'd had in a long, long time.

If everything went according to plan, I'd be in Milwaukee by nightfall.

Two hours into our drive, Kacey had fallen asleep and I listened to a mixed station. I checked my review mirror with the manic persistence of an insane person. I fully expected to see the Challenger on my rear or have police cars run me into the ditch on an Amber Alert call. My hands ached from the way I was gripping the steering wheel.

What if Chris found me? What if the meeting in Chicago didn't go the way I hoped? Would Jack travel from Nashville to be there? Surely, he would. Was he informed I was coming? I *really* didn't want to see him.

What would I do—what would our life look like in Milwaukee? I didn't know the first thing about Milwaukee.

I caught myself biting my nails.

I tried to push the thoughts out of my head and force some deep breaths. I needed to focus on getting to Mr. Paul Ruben's office. According to the directions Sherri provided, I'd arrive around 2:45 p.m. Right in time for the three o'clock meeting.

SIX

Jack

John Haskins shook my hand. "Good morning, Jackson."

"Mr. Haskins?"

"That's right. I'm your father's successor trustee. You can call me John." His smile was genuine and kind. He turned and made introductions with Pat and Jules. "How are you all holding up this morning?"

Jules adjusted the purse on her shoulder to shake his hand. "Just fine, sir. Thank you for asking."

"Funeral was beautiful. Fitting ceremony for a man like your father."

That must've been John's way of saying no expense was spared. The funeral was lavish and attended by many—mostly colleagues, investment partners, and long-time clients. I nodded.

"That it was."

The lobby in Mr. Ruben's office reeked of luxury, decorated with plush burgundy chairs, a beautiful painting of downtown

Chicago, and plants of all sizes. A Starbucks coffee machine lined the wall—the kind that ground fresh beans on the spot.

"When will you all be heading back to Nashville?"

Jules answered first. "We have a flight out in a couple hours. We have three daughters to get back to."

Pat, Jules, and Mr. Haskins talked about the girls. I couldn't help but notice how peaceful Jules looked—even after something like a funeral. Pat held her hand and only talked when spoken to.

"And, Jackson, you're staying in Evanston at the lake house for a day or two, correct?"

"Yeah, Mr. Ruben's secretary called me and said we'd have a few days to gather any personal items."

"Right. Good. Glad you'll be doing that."

John waved us toward the coffee. "Well, please make yourself comfortable while we wait for Paul and the other beneficiaries. Feel free to have some coffee then I'll show you back to the meeting room."

Jules and I exchanged a curious glance.

I figured there would be others named on Dad's will. Made sense. Not like Jules and I had been an active part of his life the last ten years.

Still, I couldn't help but wonder who else would inherit my dad's fortunes. The four of us made small talk while we each selected our preferred roasts. A low grinding sound filled the room and the machine spit out my nice, steaming cup.

After an awkward beat of silence, John eyed me. "Your father said you were an officer. I have real respect for the Blue—especially nowadays."

That made John completely different from my father, and I started to wonder how they even became friends. My father had a deep respect for law, but not so much law *enforcement*. He was pissed when I blew off law school—to put it lightly.

Before I could respond, the door flew open and my Aunt Marge walked in. She wore her usual look of disgust and regarded each of us with a curt nod. Her blue eyes and icy expression were so like Dad. "Morning, Jackson. Julia. Mr. Haskins."

John directed her through the coffee routine before we proceeded down the hall to the meeting room. He glanced at his watch. "Mr. Ruben should be with us shortly. We are waiting for him and one other."

Now that Aunt Marge had arrived, the conversation grew tense and uncomfortable. It was no secret she hated me. Hated Jules. Hated everyone who hadn't lined up to kiss Nathaniel Barkley's butt. And I had stopped doing that at twenty years old. Her memory was in working order, apparently.

I was glad Jules was with me. As teens, we used to play a game at Thanksgiving called let's-torture-Aunt-Marge. One year, Jules put a scoop of Jell-O salad in her Gucci bag. Another year, she intentionally let our affectionate nickname "Aunt Barge" slip while gathered around the turkey dinner. I could always count on Jules to do something impulsive to make us laugh for a few decades. She was probably too mature for stuff like that now.

As we took our seats at the large mahogany table, she mouthed, *"Aunt Barge,"* and waggled her eyebrows, shooting me a look that said, *should I do it?*

Guess she wasn't too mature.

I pressed my lips together, suppressing a laugh. Shook my head. Although I'd pay to see it, she better not.

A man came into the room. His receding hairline and sunken cheeks gave away his age. Late sixties, like Dad. "Good morning, I'm Paul Ruben, Nathaniel's attorney." He shook hands around the room. "I know Nathaniel would appreciate each of you traveling out."

As he settled into his seat at the head of the table, the door opened one more time. Air left my lungs like I'd taken a punch to the solar plexus. The last person I expected to see walked in. She had a white cap pulled low over her forehead, and long blonde hair spilled over her shoulders. She bit her lip as she shook John and Mr. Ruben's hands. When she glanced around the room, our gazes connected. She timidly tucked her chin, and John waved her into the seat next to mine.

My world spun.

I shook my head in disbelief, a myriad of emotions muddling my thoughts.

Nothing could've prepared me to see her. What was she doing here?

A deep warning surged heat through my blood. A sense of doom, heavy as a rock, weighed on my chest. I was about to be duped. Didn't know how or why. But her presence was an intentional slap to my face.

SEVEN

Then

Jack

"And the last time you saw her was?"

The young guy, Samuel Taggart, shook his head and twisted the rim of a cowboy hat in his hand. Worry lines creased his forehead. He was doing his best to keep his emotions in check, but a potential missing person put everyone on edge. He stammered, "I'm not real sure. Three hours ago, maybe?"

My partner, Chaves, jotted answers onto the report while I asked questions. "She didn't tell you where she was going?"

"No. But she's walks everywhere. Her car is here, so I'm figuring that's what she did. I told dispatch that the GPS on her phone is hovering right above the neighborhood pond or lake—whatever it is."

"You checked her phone's GPS?"

"Yes sir. We share a cell plan so I called to have them check."

I nodded. Chaves' walkie clicked as she called for backup.

"And you expected her home at a certain time?"

"Well, she was planning on making homemade pizza for dinner. So, she acted like she was going to be here."

"Okay, have you checked with neighbors, friends, that sort of thing?"

"No, sir. I don't live here. I'm visiting from Texas. I don't even know who Randi talks to."

"Randi?"

"Oh, I'm sorry. That's Miranda's nickname."

"No problem, Sam. We have backup coming. We are going to start by taking a drive around some of the nearby roads, and you need to keep your phone on."

He nodded, looking like he was about to be sick.

"Go ahead and describe her one more time. Do you remember what she was wearing last time you saw her?"

"Yeah, she's about 5'3", long blonde hair, wearing a maroon Schrute Farms sweatshirt."

He went on, and my gaze flitted back and forth to the neighbors' houses. Two other squad cars had parked on the street in front of the house, making a grand total of five. We were ready to launch a search.

Right at that moment, a feminine voice yelled from up the street. "Tag?"

Sam whipped his head around.

"Tag! Oh my gosh!"

"Randi?"

Weaving in and around the fleet of vehicles was a woman with long honey blonde hair. She was a petite but curvy little thing. Her eyes were wide with fear as she ran up to Sam, clutching an angel figurine to her chest. She wore an oversized sweatshirt that almost hung to her knees.

The woman, who I could only assume was Miranda, launched herself at Sam, hugging him. "Tag, are you okay? What's wrong?"

He held her back at arms' length, looking her over. "*Where have you been?*"

She frowned in confusion, her pink lips ajar. "I was—I was at the—"

"I've been worried sick about you!"

She glanced around, still not understanding. "Why are all these police here? What happened?"

He was incredulous. "We were looking for *you*."

Understanding dawned. She slapped a hand over her mouth as a deep wash of pink spread across her face. She glanced at me. Golden brown eyes danced with humor.

Miranda was adorable.

Her shoulders shook once.

Sam cursed and growled at her. "Don't you *dare* laugh."

They shook again. Soft laughter escaped from under her hand. The pink morphed to red—tomato red. Her words were muffled as she scanned the cars surrounding her front yard. "Y'all were looking for me?"

"Duh, Randi! You've been gone for three hours."

"Tag—" She said his name on a laugh. Her hand had finally left her face and I got a glimpse of deep, identical dimples right in the center of each cheek.

"GPS shows your phone is in the daggum lake!"

"The lake?" She was laughing and talking at the same time, trying her best to hold it all in. She pulled her phone out of her pocket. "It's dead. I took some apple crisp to the neighbor's house. They are the sweetest elderly couple."

"For three hours?!"

"They were telling me all about Utah."

"Utah."

"Yeah, I lost track of time."

Elderly neighbors, apple crisp, Utah.

Were Sam and Miranda together? Surely.

I came across plenty of beautiful women in my job, but Miranda was radiant, lively. Pulling my eyes away proved difficult.

Miranda tried her best for his sake, but she dropped her forehead against his bicep, shoulders silently shaking. Her inhale was sharp—a wheeze of laughter. "I'm—I'm so—so sorry."

If they were together, Samuel Taggart was one lucky son of a gun.

He muttered, "I should'a known."

"Yes you should have! I *told* you over the phone, doofus." Squeaks of laughter peppered her words. A couple tears leaked from her eyes. She held up the angel, hanging onto his arm to keep from collapsing. "But they gave me this—they said—they said I'm their—their angel."

I found myself chuckling and agreeing wholeheartedly, too. A three-hour social call to older folks definitely *made* her an angel, and the blonde hair falling down her back made her *look* like an angel.

Should I fish?

The two of them bickered about half a minute before she turned back to me and Chaves. "Oh my gosh, I'm so sorry."

I decided to fish.

"We're just glad you're safe. Your boyfriend here"—I nodded at Sam—"was pretty worried."

She patted his chest. "Cousin, actually. And he's *always* worried."

Relief filled me. As well as frustration.

Getting her number would be against protocol.

I inwardly cursed myself for fishing.

I forced my brain back to the task at hand while Chaves dispersed the forming search party. "We're going to need your statement before we head on."

"Sure." She stepped forward, wiping the moisture from her face with the inside of her collar. As she recounted everything and answered a few questions, she laughed all over again. I was mesmerized.

She pressed her palms against her cheeks. "I've never been so embarrassed in my life."

"Don't be. Misunderstandings happen all the time."

"I'm sure you get weird calls."

I chuckled. "Oh, you have no idea."

She crossed her arms across her chest, openly checking me out. She hesitated and nibbled her bottom lip. "You have a lot of stories?"

My blood churned.

Walk away.

"Dozens."

Miranda glanced at Chaves then trained her gaze on my face. "I'd love to hear them sometime."

"I'd love to share them. It would fill a whole evening."

Chaves frowned at me and snapped. "Barkley."

Get lost, Chaves.

She smiled, but backed off. "Well, thank you, Officer Barkley."

"We're just glad you aren't in the lake."

Miranda walked away, giggling, and I glowered at stupid Chaves.

Two days later, when I came in from patrol, a container of

apple crisp was on my desk with a note. The swirly feminine handwriting read:

Officer Barkley,

I would love to hear your stories. I work at Sal's BBQ House. Come by sometime.

Miranda

I couldn't believe my luck.

EIGHT

Then

Miranda

I tried to look extra nice. I had twisted my hair into a low bun with long pieces hanging out, did my make-up using dark brown mascara and eye-liner that matched my brown work t-shirt, and picked a pair of light blue jeans that made my short legs look longer. Just in case he came.

Officer Barkley was hands-down the finest male specimen I'd ever seen. And he was into me. He dropped the boyfriend comment like a complete novice. It was the cutest thing.

Section two was slammed because a lot of regular customers asked for me. Great for my tips, but stressful when I hoped a sexy cop would walk in any second and ask for my section. Something in my gut told me he would come. Which was why I upset the kitchen staff more than once. My game was off.

I told my coworker, Jennie, all about Officer Barkley. Big

mistake. She was more excited than I was. Between our whispers by the kitchen door, my constantly checking the hostess stand, the orders I beefed, and the constant teasing and poking, the line cooks were raging at us.

When he showed, I didn't recognize him at first. No uniform this time. Jeans and a light jacket.

I panicked.

Come on. I don't even have a free table!

Jennie rounded the corner from the sevens, eyes wide. "Girl, is *that* the guy?"

I felt breathless. "Yes."

She hummed her delight, smacking me on the butt with her stack of menus. "Have fun with him, sugar."

His eyes scanned the restaurant and landed on me. He smiled then lifted his hand in a little wave. Almost turned me into a puddle on the floor.

A few minutes later, the hostess found me. "Uh, there is an extremely hot dude waiting for one of your tables to open."

"He's waiting?"

There were open tables in lots of other sections, but he was waiting for mine. I swooned. After that, I nearly ran. Doing my best to get someone—anyone—out of their *stupid* table. Didn't offer desserts or extra drinks like a proper waitress. Even dropped off checks before people were finished.

When Officer Barkley finally sat down, my nerves tingled with apprehension. He looked huge with his arms crossed over the table top. I'd noticed in the driveway how big he was, but something about the way his broad arms and shoulders dwarfed the table made my mouth go dry. I cleared my throat and put on a smile. "Officer Barkley."

"Miranda." His eyes were deep blue, sparkling with pleasure.

"Thanks for coming."

"Thanks for inviting me." He quickly looked me up and down, making me feel a little self-conscious for being in an apron and having sweat on my brow. He didn't look too disappointed though. "How long until you get a break?"

Hot blood scorched my veins. "I've already had it." My level tone surprised me.

"And you get off..."

"In about an hour and a half."

He nodded, thinking a moment. "I'll wait."

"You'll wait?" I squeaked.

"If you don't mind me hogging up your table."

"I don't mind. Most of my tables will be clearing soon anyway." I placed a menu on the table. "Can I get you something to eat or drink?"

He ordered an ice tea and said he'd wait to eat with me.

I fluttered through the next hour and a half. He watched me and my face flamed red the entire time. Could hardly force my awareness on anything besides him. By the time I clocked out, the kitchen was petitioning for my termination.

Something happened when I joined him at his table.

Magic. That's the only word there is.

I was immediately swept away. We shared questions, stories, history, laughter. Officer Jackson Barkley brought out my talkative side. After a late dinner, we continued on to a Starbucks, where we talked for one more hour before they kicked us out to close up shop. We meant to go home, but ended up sitting on the tailgate of his truck in the dark parking lot. After our five hour date, we knew quite a bit about each other.

It felt so right.

When we were for real saying goodnight, he asked if I kissed on first dates.

I said no.

He softly chuckled. "As much as I hate to hear it, it's a good answer."

As I drove away, I kicked myself. Tonight was so much more than a *first date*.

NINE

Miranda

I wished I could've picked my own seat. Definitely wouldn't have put Jack on my right side. My concealer couldn't hide my darkening bruise. Even though I let my hair hang, surely he would see. Heat rushed to my cheeks, and I felt sticky red rising up my neck.

The half-second glance I threw his direction answered my first question. He was *not* expecting me.

I sat down, grateful for the chance to hide half of me under the table. I placed my coffee on a coaster and eased into the swivel seat, hoping the high-end furniture could make me look less pathetic somehow. I forced myself to breathe in. Then out.

Despite my desire to evaporate, I squared my shoulders and lifted my chin. I could do this.

John stood, introduced himself, and explained the role he played in the meeting. I didn't hear. Didn't care. If I didn't focus on quietly breathing, I'd pass out.

Jack stared at me. But he didn't deserve my acknowledgement. So I pretended not to notice his attention.

This is for Kacey. This is for Kacey.

The kind receptionist offered to let him sit with her and do some coloring pages. His attention span for coloring was about five minutes. I didn't tell her that though and just crossed my fingers he wouldn't run her ragged.

In my peripheral, Jack rubbed his forehead and ran a hand over his head. He leaned my direction an inch and whispered, "What are you doing here?"

His voice.

How many times had I imagined it? My throat tightened with suppressed emotions. Everything was riding on this meeting, and I couldn't look him in the eyes without becoming unglued. Kept my eyes glued to John Haskins and Paul Ruben.

He sat back in his seat.

John spoke. "It was Nathaniel's wish you all could be here and have any questions answered. I know he would appreciate each of you taking the time to be here during your grief. Being an incredible attorney himself, Nathaniel left no stone unturned. This whole process should be smooth, quick, and hiccup-free—for the most part." John shot an uneasy glance my direction with those final words.

What did that mean? Hiccup-free except for the fact that I shouldn't be here?

He spent the next twenty minutes listing some of Nathaniel's assets and explaining how a living trust worked. I didn't understand most of it. According to him, the items in trust had already been retitled. A lot of his assets were going to charity, and the rest would be divvied out among the beneficiaries according to his wishes.

"Marge, Nathaniel wanted you to have some of his investment accounts outright." He passed her a sheet of paper. "Here's a list for you of what is included. These accounts are ready for your signature. Mr. Ruben's assistant can help you with that at any time, although there is no rush. I understand this is a heavy time.

"Nathaniel wanted Julia and her husband Patrick to receive the beach house on Sullivan's Island outright"—John scratched his chin and shifted in his chair—"and the lake house in Evanston is to go to Jack *and* Miranda. There are some, uh, stipulations on that allotment though."

Breathe, Miranda. Breathe.

"Wait." Jack's chair squeaked as he sat forward and crossed his arms over the table. "When was this will made? There must be some mistake."

Jules nodded in agreement.

"Miranda and I got divorced over four years ago. Dad knew that."

My stomach dropped.

I am an idiot.

Of course I was contacted in *error*! And here I was, thinking Nathaniel was trying to be nice.

"There's no mistake. Nathaniel was specific in his requests and added Miranda as a beneficiary recently."

"Recently?" Jack was incredulous. "Why?"

"He didn't leave a detailed explanation of his reasoning, unfortunately, but there is more you need to know about your portion." John shifted again and fiddled with the pen in his hand. "He didn't want you to receive the house outright. It is contingent on, uh, your marital status."

My lungs felt stuffed. Couldn't exhale.

"Marital status?" Jack's voice was tense and clipped. "What does that mean?"

"Nathaniel requested that you and Miranda be married prior to receiving the lake house."

Wait! Married?

"To each other?" Jack asked.

"Yes." John's face was apologetic.

I stole a glance at Jack as my heart spiraled into hopelessness. His face was hardened, cheeks ticking, as anger pushed into his expression. His voice was nearly a growl. "You've *got* to be kidding."

"That is unless Miranda has already remarried."

Every eye in the room turned to me. I swallowed hard, my brain fuzzy and swirling. On instinct, I tilted my head toward the table, trying to find my tongue. "No, I'm—I'm not married."

What shocked me was that Jack hadn't remarried. He and Miss Long Legs hadn't tied the knot? My brain urged me to confirm. I used my peripheral vision to double check his left hand. No ring.

John continued. "A remarriage was the only loophole. If you both were still single, he wanted you to marry for no less than sixty days before signing the trust documents and receiving the house. After that, you could sell it, keep it, whatever. Although a couple buyers have been breathing down Nathaniel's neck for years—"

Jack stood, his chair rolling back. "He is forcing me to get remarried to Miranda?"

"Once you have met the sixty day mark, you will be able to sign the papers and the deed will be in *both* of your names." John shrugged.

Jules' fist was pressed against her lips as she watched quietly, eyes wide. "This is so extreme. I don't understand why he would do this."

"I do," Jack muttered.

"Why?"

"He..." Jack shook his head, the words dying off on his lips. "This is just like Dad!"

"It was his wish that—"

Jack smacked the table with his palm. "To hell with his wish!"

The reality of my stupidity hit me like a ton of bricks. Why, oh why, did I think someone was going to write me a check here in this office today? My desperation made me foolish. A crack in my determination caused my shoulders to drop and I sunk down into the chair. The one thing that could save Kacey and me from destitution was contingent on something that would never happen again.

Marriage. To *Jack* of all people.

"Still controlling me from beyond the grave. Unbelievable!" Jack ran his hands over his head again. "This cannot be legal, Mr. Ruben."

"I know this is upsetting to hear, but Incentive Trusts are very legal. Some parents use it to encourage what they feel are wayward children onto the right path. Some require marriage or a college education or even financial classes before their children can inherit. Now, I'll be honest, Nathaniel *was* pushing his legal bounds by naming a specific spouse for you." Mr. Ruben shook his head and sipped his coffee, unfazed. He probably had conversations like this one every day. "I discourage my clients from making moves like this, but he was a very stubborn man, as I'm sure you know."

I peeked in Jack's direction again. His handsome blue eyes blazed, wide and fiery. His fists were clenched. He was angry, and honestly, he had every right to be. I should've known Nathaniel would have something up his sleeve, devising a way to control one more time.

My phone vibrated in my pocket.

Once. Must be a text.

"The good news," Mr. Ruben added, "is there's an expiration date on that requirement. If you choose not to marry, you can receive your portion outright in six years."

Jack's tone was coming unhinged, quaking under years of expectations. "Six years? I can't believe this! You said he was pushing his legal bounds. Could we fight this in court?"

"You are welcome to get an attorney and contest the will. There is a chance you could be successful. But be advised, will and trust cases are very lengthy and costly."

Jack deflated back into his chair, and the woman across the table spoke for the first time. She lifted her chin. "Nathaniel had strong convictions about marriage. He warned Jack marriage ties are not easily broken. My brother held marriage in the highest regard—which is why he was faithful to Bonnie even beyond her premature death. He likely sees Miranda as his daughter, the same way he saw Cameron as his son. Daughters and sons go on wills. Makes perfect sense to me."

Jack made a grunting noise, and Jules shook her head as a frown pressed into her brow.

Jules pushed. "Are you sure this isn't a mistake, Mr. Ruben? Our Dad never even sought a relationship with Miranda or my late husband, Cameron. The idea that he saw them as a son and daughter is a bit far-fetched. I'm sorry, but Miranda shouldn't have half of Jack's inheritance."

My face heated and my eyes brimmed with instant tears. Why was I such a freaking idiot?

"No mistake." John shook his head. "Nathaniel had her added. It's—ironclad."

"But why—"

"He didn't give a reason and wasn't required to."

The older woman looked smug, like she had the answer the rest of us were clamoring for—was it as simple as she made it sound? Based on my limited knowledge of him,

Nathaniel seemed stuck in a permanent superiority complex. Maybe he thought this scheme was a way to flex his values.

Jack leaned back in his chair, rubbing a hand down his jaw. My thighs were clenched so tight, I was trembling. I tucked my hands into my lap and swallowed down the lump in my throat. Last thing I needed was a total meltdown right here, right now.

My phone vibrated again.

Jack shook his head. "I know exactly what he's doing. Dad wanted me to be him, and I've done nothing but disappoint. He's not going to give me the fortunes he worked for when I haven't lived up to his standards. My divorce was just one way I fell short."

Hurt rolled off Jack's countenance. At one point, I would've rushed to Jack's defense. Would've lashed anyone who dared to call Jack a disappointment. Funny how years change things. Now, I felt he deserved it. I'd watched Jack take the coward's way out time and again. Maybe Nathaniel thought his son was a coward, too.

I knew my ex-father-in-law was a bit traditional. Was this Nathaniel's way of punishing Jack for getting divorced?

The meeting continued awkwardly as Mr. Ruben went through some last minute instructions. As soon as we were dismissed, I shot out of my chair. I didn't want to talk to anyone. Especially Jack. Because I would *not* get married. No way in heck. I didn't bother shaking John's hand when he extended it. I rushed down the hall to reception and snatched Kacey from the secretary's desk.

The decision to high-tail it was a good one. As I tugged little Kacey out the front door, tense voices flitted down the hall behind us.

Once we were safely in the car, I checked my phone.

Sherri: Something horrible happened. Brenda's daughter went into labor way earlier than expected and she lives in Washington. Brenda is on the first flight there. She gave me a phone number to her friend we could call. They may be able to put you up until Brenda gets back...

The text went on. Detailing all of my fears. What would I do? I wasn't even comfortable going to Brenda's because I didn't know her. I mean, I barely even knew Sherri. Now, it felt like Kacey and I were being passed to the friend of a friend of a friend. My stomach twisted.

Chicago *and* Milwaukee failed me? Nothing was going right. I mentally ran through every possible option. I needed a place to crash for the night while I sorted it out. But that hundred dollars Sherri gave me wouldn't take me terribly far. Certainly wouldn't get a hotel for the night.

Tears stung my eyes and nose. Marriage was the last thing I expected to hear today. Jack and I couldn't get remarried. I would never subject myself to the loneliness I felt as Jack's wife ever again. I closed my eyes against the resurging memories of the desperation and pain. Of the months I'd spent immersed in the depths of depression after he abandoned us.

No. I'd find my own way.

I sank into the driver's seat, letting my head tilt back. My life was a train wreck. A complete and utter wreck.

Homeless, penniless, stranded. All my nightmares come true. I was a big, desperate idiot toting an innocent child from state to state. What would happen to us now?

TEN

Jack

Storming out into the parking lot, I understood two things: my father intended to humiliate me and Miranda had to be in on it. Each of them made it no secret they hated my guts. My father had made my life a living hell since my seventeenth birthday and my ex-wife told me to go there the last time I saw her.

All I'd ever tried to do was the right thing. So much for that.

My muscles tensed with anger at the injustice of it. I was angry at Dad for orchestrating this madness. And though I couldn't believe Miranda had the gall to come stake a claim, I had to admit, I didn't hate seeing her.

Dad wanted us to get remarried. As angry as I was at Miranda for divorcing me in the first place, I'd be open to remarrying her for the lake house. I wanted money from the sale. But based on our last encounter four years ago, I figured she would likely choose death over remarriage. She had some choice words for me that day, and we hadn't spoken since.

I scanned the parking lot for her. She'd had a few minutes head start on me, and I could only hope I wasn't too late. Had to talk to her. I scanned the lot for a few beats, hoping to see her between the cars somewhere. Nothing.

Giving up, I hopped into my truck. As I buckled, a Corolla zoomed down the aisle, heading toward the main drag. White ball cap behind the wheel.

She's still driving that Corolla?

My gaze followed her car. As she turned right onto the highway, something small tumbled off the top of her vehicle.

I threw the truck into drive.

At the stop sign, I jumped out to retrieve the item. A wallet. Long, gray, with little pink and purple designs on it. My pulse quickened. Part of me wanted to chuck the stupid thing into the hedges and flip off her fading rear end. But another part of me—the dumb part—was excited to possess something of hers.

My natural instinct was to follow her. But doing so would approach *psychotic ex* territory. As much as I had loved her, I'd never gone down that path. Didn't really want to start now.

But, she needed her wallet. She was miles from Ohio.

Before my brain fully granted permission, I was depressing the gas, trying to catch up.

I tried her phone a couple times. It went straight to voicemail. But not before her voice left instructions. "Hey, it's Miranda. Knowing me, my phone is probably on silent and MIA. But if you leave a message, I'll call you back whenever I find it." I swallowed hard as my heart squeezed. Ridiculous how much that voice affected me. Couldn't believe she still had the same number.

Same car, same number. I wondered if anything about her had changed.

While idling at a busy intersection, I flipped open the wallet. Miranda's I.D. stared back at me. She had a Ohio address and her last name read *Howard*. Her maiden name. As sucky as those DMV pictures typically were, hers took my breath away.

There was nothing else inside. No cards, cash, change. Nothing at all.

I frowned.

I dropped it onto the console as Miranda pulled into the turning lane. I still remembered my way around Chicago and knew she was heading straight for the ghetto.

"Where are you going?" I muttered.

My phone buzzed. I glanced at it.

Jules: I cannot believe Dad did this! Please call me. We are on our way to the airport. I'll have about two hours. I'm worried sick about you! I feel like this was my fault.

I ignored the text and tapped my turning signal.

Ten minutes later, we were deep in the bowels of Chicago. Barred and boarded windows, trash piles on the sidewalks, and loitering individuals were the tamest things you'd see here. Nashville had its own version of the hood. And I'd seen enough images to last a lifetime.

In my twelve years as a police officer, my gun stayed in its holster more often than not. I hadn't gone into the business out of a desire to fire at humans. But because I'd seen plenty of situations go sideways, the glock 22 at my side never hurt.

Especially now that my ex-wife's car was smoking.

You've got to be kidding me.

What started as a tiny gray strand of smoke turned into a full-on billow in about thirty seconds. Her emergency flashers came on and she pulled into the parking lot of a boarded-up gas station. She tumbled out of the car and ran to the front to open the hood. She waved a hand in front of her face and coughed.

In true form, she didn't see me park behind her and step out of the truck. Great to know my lectures about situational awareness made such an impact.

I called out so as not to startle her. "Miranda!"

She looked around the popped hood and her mouth fell open. "Jack?"

"What are you doing out here?"

"Are you *following* me?"

Her hair surrounded her face like a curtain—leaving only a sliver exposed. The hairdo and hat screamed *hiding* and my skin prickled.

I fought the explosive anger charging through my veins. "You shouldn't be out here. Are you lost or something?"

She crossed her arms and stepped back. "No! I'm not lost!"

I pushed past to look into the engine. "Did it overheat?"

"I—I don't really know. I wasn't paying close attention."

"That's a shocker."

She scoffed.

"It's going to catch fire if you keep driving."

Her head tipped downward. Between the hair and the hat and our one foot height difference, the only thing I could see of her was the top of the stupid hat.

"I'll wait. It will cool down."

"How much further do you have to go?"

She shrugged. "A few minutes?"

"Well, you won't be driving this thing. You need to call for a tow."

She said nothing.

"I'll wait with you."

"No!" She shook her head. "Go on. I don't need help."

"I'm not leaving you out here by yourself."

She made no move to call.

"Fine! I'll call." I pulled out my phone and searched for tow companies. She shifted in discomfort, the aging asphalt crunching beneath her feet.

As I dialed a number, I asked, "Where do they need to tow you?"

The top of her head moved side to side and she gently lifted a shoulder.

"Miranda? Where do you need to go?"

"I can't afford a tow, Jack." Her tone was bitter, frustrated. She turned her head toward the oncoming traffic. "Even if I could, I wouldn't be able to afford whatever is wrong with the stupid thing. No doubt it's colossal. I haven't really kept up with maintenance the last few years."

"Yeah—okay." I ran a hand over my hair. "I can pay for it."

"No way."

"Then I'll take you where you need to go. Once you're off the side of the road, you can decide what to do."

"You don't need to help me!"

"So what? You're just gonna camp out here?"

"No."

"What's your plan then?"

Her head shook again.

"That's what I thought. Get your stuff and I'll take you."

"You never answered my question!" she accused with a wobbly voice. A voice etched into my memory. My stomach clenched.

Please don't cry.

"What question?"

"Were you following me?"

"Yeah and thank goodness I was!"

"But why?"

I pulled her wallet from my back pocket and handed it to her. "You left this on top of your car. It fell."

Her shoulders sagged. "Oh."

I sighed, conflicting feelings that I *hated* pressing against my ribcage. "Listen, Miranda, you need help." I moved to close her hood. "I know you hate my guts, but I'm not leaving you on the side of the road to fend for yourself."

"I remember how."

I couldn't help but chuckle at that. I'd taught her some self-defense and for her size? She was pretty good. "You might be able to throw some decent punches, but in a place like this—that's not enough."

She squeezed her arms tighter around her torso, looking up the street one more time. She shivered and my heart tripped.

I'd noticed her physical condition in the meeting, but now I let my eyes truly linger on her.

Something was off.

Big time.

My brain threw red flags right and left.

Part of me wanted to take stuff out on her. Blame her for the insanity that went down in the meeting. But the wind left my sails. A twisting feeling in my midsection shut my mouth.

Her clothes were nice, although incongruent. She wore a pair of dress pants, a white button up shirt, and a white ball cap. The business formal and casual styles clashed. But it wasn't her clothes that bothered me. She looked...sick. Unhealthy. Not like the woman I used to know.

Miranda had been round and curvy with beautiful legs and a pert behind. When we were married, I'd tease her by saying her 5'3" stature packed a punch. Now, she looked thin and frail. Her clothes hung off the parts of her that used to stretch material.

I knew from too much experience Miranda outright refused food when she was stressed.

Couldn't help but wonder what was going on in her life.

And the way she was hiding behind her hair and hat…

I'd been berating her. Decided to soften my tone a bit. "Please. Let me drive you."

Innate intuition has always been one of my most valuable assets. Has saved my life a time or two. But no amount of sixth sense could've prepared me for what I heard next.

ELEVEN

Jack

A sharp, high-pitched screech sounded from inside the Corolla. For the first time, I peered past her tinted windows. A little boy with tousled blonde hair was kicking his feet like a maniac, screaming, "Mommy!"

Mommy?

For reasons I didn't fully understand, my blood ran cold. The dark windows didn't allow me to really see the boy, but from what I could tell, he was her spitting image. My heart pounded as I tried to process the new information.

She has a child?

My brain couldn't process the idea of Miranda being a mother. Felt my mouth hanging open. I shouldn't have been surprised. A ton can happen in four years.

But hearing those tiny cries from the backseat baffled me.

How?

It didn't seem right or fair.

Miranda's voice pulled me from my trance, and I directed

my attention back to her in time to catch her saying, "I can call a cab. I have enough for that."

"Mommy! I hunn-gy."

She opened his door and unwrapped a granola bar, handing it and a sippy cup to the little guy. She cooed, "Here you go, buddy."

He pushed the offerings away. "I want to get out!"

"Shh. It's okay." She offered him the cup again.

Miranda was a mother? It seemed unreal.

"Walk! Walk, Mommy, please?"

"We, uhm..." She looked over the top of her car toward the traffic yet again. "Not right now, okay?"

I shook my head, urging—forcing—myself to close my mouth.

She was uncomfortable, and I made it worse. Last thing I wanted was for Miranda to feel uneasy. I felt uneasy enough for the both of us. Man, those red flags were soaring. If she thought I would hop into the truck and bid them farewell, she was sorely mistaken.

Not only did we have to discuss the fact that we were co-heirs, there was something weird going on. I was getting all sorts of bad vibes from her. Vibes that had nothing to do with the lake house.

Regardless of our history, I still cared for her well-being. Wouldn't ever wish harm on her. Wouldn't ever abandon her if she needed me.

She had her head tipped so low, I couldn't even stoop and see the tip of her nose anymore. The hair of my neck stood on end. Her demeanor was nothing like the bubbly, beautifully-happy Miranda Howard I fell in love with ten years ago.

Why was she hiding?

I tried not to let my mind entertain reasons too long. I was already scrambling to keep my head on straight. If someone hurt her, I'd...

My chest constricted and my fists clenched.

Before my brain had even filed through the ramifications, I ordered, "No cab. I'm taking you."

She opened her mouth to protest.

"If you call a cab, I'm getting in with you."

That stopped her.

"You can't get rid of me at the moment, so save your money."

"There's a lot of stuff." She motioned to the trunk.

"Open the trunk and I'll get it. You get your—" I fumbled for words. "The, uh, kid."

She nodded, silently moving to the front of the car while he screamed. I got a better look at his face with the door open. Blonde curls, round face. Miranda's child through and through.

Boxes of clothes and blankets were stuffed in the trunk. There was a ziploc bag of toy cars and a jumbo box of pull-ups. Then there were about thirty grocery bags of shelf-stable processed foods.

Looked like they robbed a Dollar General.

I moved the things to the back of my truck, breathing harder with every step. My blood coursed through my veins as unbidden what-ifs bounced in my brain.

"Is that everything?" I put the last grocery bag in the backseat of the truck. "Anything left behind will encourage a break-in."

She nodded. "Just need to buckle his car seat in."

"I can do it."

"You know how?"

I shot her a look. "All emergency responders do." She should know that.

A minute later, as Miranda leaned to grab her son, he bolted off. The Chicago wind sent the white cap flying through the air behind her as she sprinted through the parking lot after him.

The hat landed at my feet.

It was my chance to see her. Really see her.

She turned back to me with the kid on her hip. The wind whipped around, throwing her blonde hair in all directions. She held a hand to the right side of her head in an attempt to keep the hair down.

I picked up the hat and held it out.

In order to take it, she had to let go of her hair.

She hesitated.

But when she did, my breath caught.

A bruise covered the entire right side of her face, and the corner of her eye was a bit swollen.

An expletive rushed out of my mouth.

Off-color make-up was thinly smeared over the bruise. Still purple-blue, I guessed the injury was only a few days old.

Could this situation get any worse?

The bruise. The empty wallet. The nervous behavior. The furtive glances over her shoulder and up the street. The weight loss. The deep, dark circles under her eyes. The smoking car with a spare tire.

She grabbed at the hat, but I moved it out of her reach. Rage boiled in my veins until I couldn't draw a full breath. "Miranda." I tried to keep my tone even keel, but it rumbled with anger. "Who did that to you?"

She stomped her foot, hanging her head behind the kid's, refusing to look at my face. "Give me my hat, Jack!"

"Absolutely not. Tell me who did that."

She raised her voice. "No one! I fell."

Did she think I was some kind of idiot? "That is not from a fall."

"It's none of your business!"

"I think it is! You're on the side of the road and it looks like someone beat the crap out of your face!"

"Why do you care?" She spat.

It was a fair question. I tried not to think too deeply about what I was seeing. She wasn't my responsibility. I didn't have to care. I knew that. And yet...

I did.

So much, I must've officially lost my mind.

I'd intervened in plenty of domestic violence situations. It doesn't take a rocket scientist to spot a victim. Miranda had the classic signs.

I softened, lowering the hat to her level.

Miranda snatched it and jerked the cap down over her forehead, spinning away so I couldn't watch as she adjusted her hair. She leaned to buckle the boy into his seat. I rounded the truck to the driver's side, fighting the urge to punch something.

She had navigation pulled up on her phone.

Five minutes to go until her destination. 8 Milford Street.

"We have a lot to talk about."

She lifted her chin up and toward the window, her arms folded over her torso. "I am *not* talking to you."

"Well, whether you like it or not, we have business to discuss."

Her voice quaked. "I'm not getting married ever again—to you."

Not sure why the clarification stung as badly as it did.

"There. Business discussion over." She sniffed and swiped a hand across her cheek.

We drove in near silence, except for the occasional whines from the boy and Miranda's soft reassurances.

And the tiniest, almost inaudible, sniffling.

Miranda kept her face turned toward the window. She was crying.

The knowledge gutted me.

I didn't know what to do. What to say. I had no clue how to help her. I took a deep breath, sighed. My conscience nagged me. Forced me to feel responsible for the situation she was in. Was I the reason all this happened to her? Could I have prevented this somehow?

My hands ached around the steering wheel. After coming face to face with an elephant, the silence was torture. Do I ignore it? Drop them off and call it good? Wait six years for the inheritance and hope they find their way?

I glanced at the GPS, anxiety rolling through my gut.

One minute left and we were still in a bad neighborhood.

A big structure came into view. Looked like a church but wasn't. Lots of folks loitered around the outside of the building with carts and strollers full of possessions. I rolled into the parking lot and squinted to read the faded sign by the door.

It was a freaking homeless shelter.

You have got to be kidding me.

Apparently, this situation could get worse.

I fought to keep my voice calm. "You want me to drop you two off at a *shelter*?"

She said nothing and didn't look my way, but her chest was heaving with her breaths.

"Miranda." I ran my hand over my head, wondering if I

was about to wake up from a nightmare. "You have to start answering some questions. Do you have anywhere else to go?"

Her throat worked, her voice a whisper. "No."

I cursed under my breath.

Then did a u-turn in the parking lot.

She sat a little straighter. "Wait. Where are you going?"

The truck jerked as I cut the turn too fast. This was pure insanity. "*We* are going to the lake house."

TWELVE

Miranda

My stomach muscles clamped so tight they throbbed in pain.

Jack ran a hand over his forehead. "I can't—this is—this is crazy, Miranda."

He fumbled for words as I fought the urge to defend myself.

"Places like that aren't safe."

Safer than home.

I wanted to smack myself for calling Chris' house *home*.

Kacey and I didn't have a home. We never did. Chris' house was supposed to be a temporary landing place. Nothing more.

I felt like the worst mother on the planet. I had no plan. How was I supposed to *make* a plan when I had no home, car, money, or job? When Brenda was across the country and my only friend lived across the street from my abuser? When my only other ally was nine-hundred miles away and had as much in his wallet as I did? When the father of my son had rejected us?

I swallowed. "The women's shelters are a lot nicer. They all have waitlists though."

"That's not what I meant." He flipped his turning signal on as we merged onto a highway. Warm air blew from the vents. The high-pitched hum of tires against asphalt and the occasional bump filled the silence that had engulfed us. Kacey was quiet. I hoped he fell asleep. Between the busted tire, late lunch, and crossing into another time zone—he was probably exhausted.

"Is no one there for you two in Ohio? I could buy you a plane ticket home. You can take some time to think things over."

I scoffed. Did he honestly think I would remarry him after what he did? "There's *nothing* to think over."

"Okay, fine. Obviously, you don't live in Chicago though and you need help getting home."

Even Jack was using the word *home*. Which, why wouldn't he? Four years ago, he made it crystal clear our home wasn't together. Bitterness stirred in me every time I remembered.

"We aren't going back to Ohio."

"Do you talk to your mom at all now? Could you call her?"

I shook my head.

"Okay," Jack sighed, hesitating over his next words. "I'm—almost afraid to ask...are you running from someone?"

I blinked, the motion sending a couple tears down my cheeks. I swiped them with the back of my hand. My throat worked conflicting jobs. Let the words out, keep the sobs in. "Yes, we are."

I hoped the knowledge would gut him. Hoped he'd feel a fraction of the pain I'd shouldered the last four years. Hoped it would stir a flicker of regret in his stone-cold heart.

"From the person who hurt you?"

"Yes." I took a deep breath through my nose, fighting to still the tremble in my lips. Was the emotion fear? Indignation? Heart-shattering grief? I couldn't decide. I gripped the side of the passenger seat as my thighs bounced with tension.

Jack stayed silent for a few beats. My ex-husband was anything but an idiot. He knew how to read a situation when there were hardly any clues. He probably had me figured out while we were still sitting in the meeting. I glanced his direction only long enough to see his fingers flex around the steering wheel. When he spoke, his voice was low, scraping with intensity. "When did it happen?"

I'd always known Jack was gutsy, but he obviously had no speck of conscience left. My question burst out of nowhere. "*Why* do you care all of a sudden?"

He frowned, his head jerking backward in disbelief.

"You can't just swoop in and pretend like you give a crap, Jack. Why on earth would you of all people deserve answers from me?"

He made a frustrated noise. "Because you wanted me to drop you off at a *homeless* shelter and the side of your face is..." He squeezed the wheel again. "Of course I have questions."

"Well, can them! I'm not interested in being prodded to satisfy your curiosities like I'm some kind of circus sideshow. You burned our bridges a long time ago. The only reason I'm here right now is I have literally *no* other choice." My voice broke over the last word, but I quickly pulled my composure upright. I continued on my tirade, thankful to have a minute to lash out. How long I dreamed of this. "And I have a little boy back there to take care of. If it were just me—I'd gladly pick the homeless shelter over sitting here with you." I scoffed and a tear leaked out of my eye. "But *good* parents put their *kids* first."

"Damn. Sorry for wondering."

His sarcastic apology made me roll my eyes yet again. The things I would say if I wasn't so desperate...

"Look. You hate me. I get it. But, I'm on leave from work right now. I'll be at Dad's lake house for a couple days before I have to go back to Nashville. You can stay there. Maybe take some time to figure things out." He puffed in agitation. "Don't worry. It's got three floors and is plenty big enough. We'll hardly see each other."

I tucked my arms over my stomach. Why, oh why, was Jack my *only* option at the moment? We had come full circle and the irony was maddening.

And heartbreaking. So very heartbreaking.

My jaw clenched as I wrestled the anger, resentment, hopelessness—whatever it was—back down into my heart.

"Dad had all his affairs taken care of—down to his cars, furniture, and who is going to dust the house." More trees dotted the drive as the Chicago metropolitan melted into wealthy suburbs. "John said I'm allowed to take personal items, like photos and old stuff from the attic, so I might venture up there and grab a few things. Otherwise, I don't have much to do here. I'd rather be at home in Nashville anyway." He paused before adding, "I'll do whatever I can to help you and your son, Miranda."

Your son?

It took all of my strength not to lurch over the console and throttle the man.

How could he say that? Boy, Jack had some nerve. I spoke through a clenched jaw. "His name is *Kacey*."

"Okay—I'm sorry."

I almost laughed. Here Jack was. Still using *sorry* like it was a magic band-aid. Wielding the word like a spell that instantaneously healed mortal wounds. If I had a dime for every time

Jack has used the word *sorry,* I wouldn't need Nathaniel's inheritance.

A minute went by. Jack said, "At least humor me a little. Is someone looking for you?"

I shrugged, wanting to deny him information. "No clue."

"Come on, Miranda. I need to know if you're in danger."

"I don't know!" Stupid tears pushed against my eyes again. I wanted to appear strong, but it was hard when feelings kept squeezing my throat. "I have no idea. He—he might be looking for us. I can't write off the possibility."

"So a man—your boyfriend or something."

"*Ex.*"

"Fine. Do you think your *ex* will come looking for you guys?"

Most likely he was. I just shrugged my shoulders. "Not sure."

"Hm." Jack tapped the wheel. "Do you still carry?"

"No."

I could almost hear him thinking. Jack was going into defender mode. It was one of the reasons I fell in love with the man. But apparently he preferred defending the public—perfect strangers—to doing his actual duties.

So much for Jack's innate sense of justice and honor.

I tried to call him off the trail. "We are far away. We should be fine now."

"What's his line of work?"

"Unemployed at the moment."

Jack grunted, shifting in the driver's seat. "From everything I'm seeing, he doesn't sound like the type to let go of his woman and son so easily."

His son?

The blood in my veins froze.

Chris' son?

All the animosity I felt drained like a torrent as if someone had pulled a huge plug in my heart.

My stomach flipped. The pads of my fingers came to my lips—holding back a surge of panic welling in me.

What was Jack talking about?

Kacey was *not* Chris' son.

But Jack knew that.

Didn't he?

Blood rushed from my face. A light-headed sensation skittered across my nerve endings and my heart jumped to my throat. I couldn't swallow. Couldn't breathe. Could hardly think.

He does know that? Doesn't he?

For the first time since I'd walked into the meeting, I looked—really looked—-at Jack's face. His dark brows were furrowed with deep thought while his eyes scanned the roadway. He shot me a fleeting, curious glance. The lines etched across his forehead were concerned, inquisitive. The hardness I expected to see there was nowhere to be found.

It was as clear as day. Jack didn't know.

"Kacey isn't Chris'—" The words escaped on a breath.

"Chris? That's your ex's name?"

I think I nodded. My soul felt distant from my body as shock radiated through my limbs.

Jack continued as if my entire life and existence hadn't just shattered into oblivion. "Oh, I just assumed."

Every defense I'd erected for my heart crumbled. My entire reality—everything I'd clung to—took flames. For four years, I thought he knew. I thought he moved on.

Inhale. Inhale.

"Who's his dad? I mean, is he still in the picture? Someone you could go to?"

My gut twisted so hard bile filled my throat.

How did he not know the answer to that question?

I felt more than heard myself murmur as a buzzing sound crowded out my thoughts. "Jack, please. You have to stop the truck…"

He must've caught the message because a second later rumble strips on the side of the road jolted me.

My fingers reached for the door handle, and I stumbled out onto the shoulder of the road, dry heaving.

Then

The warm air inside the Nashville Police Department made my pores tingle, and I pulled my oversized rain coat tighter around me. Lots of the people here knew who I was. Jack had been there eight years. Long enough to gain some seniority. Long enough to have dragged me out to countless parties and gatherings.

The raincoat was way overkill. It was only drizzling, but I was thankful for the bit of weather providing an excuse to cover up and hide from prying eyes. We could've talked in a safer place, but Jack brought this public-ish confrontation on himself.

If he would've called me back, we wouldn't have to do this. But now, I was fully aware why he hadn't returned my calls.

He'd been busy.

Mighty busy.

I couldn't let my brain come anywhere close to the topic of *her*, or I'd have a panic attack. Right here on the department floor. An officer I didn't recognize sat me in a chair while he phoned back to Jack's desk.

Jack answered on the other line—meaning he was there. Coming was a gamble. I could guess when he'd likely be in, but would never be certain. Knowing I was about to come face to face with him turned my insides to jelly.

This would be the first time in almost four months. My lips trembled and I pressed them together, tapping my swollen eyelids and pinching my blotchy cheeks one final time. The two-hour sob session before walking in didn't put me in prime condition.

After my run-in with Miss Long Legs, I doubted he even deserved the truth...but I needed to give him a chance to do the right thing.

The officer put the phone down. "He said he's coming down."

I nodded, my tongue sticking to the roof of my mouth.

Waiting for a minute or so felt like eternity. I kept my eyes trained to the door across the lobby area, expecting his broad uniformed shoulders to appear any minute.

When my gaze landed on his face, I wanted to vaporize. His dark brows were slanted, blue eyes flaming, jaw set. He saw me and the tenderness I'd come to expect there was nonexistent. His regard was cold, hardened. He crossed the room in half the steps it would've taken me. "Miranda."

I stood, summoning all the strength I had left. "Jack."

"*What* are you doing here?"

"What do you *think* I'm doing here?"

He huffed, looking back at the two officers at the front desk, shamelessly watching us. "Do you want to go somewhere private?"

"No. We'll do this right here."

He took a deep breath, folding his arms over his chest. "Fine."

My lips trembled disobediently. "I take it you got the letter."

He nodded once. "I got it."

I looked at his eyes, unable to read his expression before my view got blurry. I blinked, my anger faltering as something worse—much worse—crowded my heart. "I figured you'd want to be involved...or at least help me financially."

He widened his eyes in disbelief, shaking his head like I was a dummy.

"You don't have anything to say?"

His jaw fell open a little and he shrugged his shoulders. "What do you want me to say?"

That you want us, Jack.

He sighed. "It was the last thing I wanted to hear. But it's a consequence *you* have to deal with."

"Me?"

"Yes, *you*." He ran a hand over his head. "Miranda, I am sick of you calling and texting. I blocked your number because I"—he held his hands out, spreading his fingers—"I can't handle you anymore."

My forehead prickled with heat as his words struck an off-key chord in my gut. I ground my teeth together to keep from collapsing.

His frozen gaze stared me dead in the face. "This"—he jerked his index finger back and forth between the two of us—"is no more. I've completely moved on and so should you."

I sucked at the air, trying to fill my lungs. "So, that's—that's it?"

"Why shouldn't it be?"

"Because we are a unit—a family, Jack!"

He gave a mirthless laugh. "Pretty sure I remember you *begging* me to sign your papers. You didn't want to be a family. There's no *we* anymore, Miranda." He took a little step back, shaking his head. "I'm over this." He looked me dead in the face. "Over you."

My spirit went limp.

The heel of my tennis shoe squeaked once against the tile as I backed away. The pressure growing in my throat was unbearable. A sob leaked out without permission and my hand flew to my mouth to block any more. When I glanced around, a few officers watched us. I turned, ready to run out of the lobby before delivering my parting words. They hurt my throat, ripping through my trachea with an intensity only grief can fuel. "Go to hell, Jackson Barkley!"

I mustered the last bit of fight I had left to lift a middle finger in his direction and scream two more.

THIRTEEN

Jack

I felt cheated.

The stupid lake house and my dad's scheming occupied my mind. But only for a little while. Spending the evening with Miranda and Kacey shifted things. Inheritance and remarriage concerns now paled in comparison to my concerns for them.

As I laid in bed, I couldn't think of anything but *their* situation.

Things with Miranda were strange. I didn't know what to make of it. One minute, she was seething, spitting fire at me in the truck. And the next, she was pressing her lips together—which could only mean she was fighting down a wave of emotion as big as a tsunami. She used to bite the inside of her lip to keep from bursting into tears.

I had no doubt that's exactly what she'd done when the bedroom door slammed behind her.

After I unloaded the truck earlier, I brought a few bags to

their chosen bedroom and rapped on the door. "Miranda? I have your stuff."

One quick sniff then her scratchy voice replied, "O-okay. Just leave it there."

Yep. She'd been crying.

Hours later, images of them being abused and neglected by some absolute piece of garbage continued to torture me. I'd worked myself into a sweat over it and tossed the covers off. Getting sleep was mission impossible at this point. I lay, bare-chested, under the gentle breeze of the fan, listening to the pull strings clack together.

Seeing Miranda again sent me into a tailspin. I'd always assumed I was over her. It was the line I fed myself—and Jules—over the years. But the sight of her—like *this* especially—did something to my insides I hadn't anticipated. To say I was unprepared would be an understatement.

Her every move, every sigh, every word. How was it I was still so aware of her? I thought most ex-spouses hated each other. But here I was, doing my best not to torture myself on memory lane. Wondering what happened to her.

Marriage seemed like a half-way decent idea, if for no other reason than to save them from whatever was happening in their world. But Miranda had made it very clear she had no intentions of getting married—so I guess I'd be waiting six years.

I hoped they were comfortable. That suite she chose had a nice tub. Miranda used to love baths. I wondered if she still did. Maybe she was able to take a bath and have a nice evening.

My imaginations—or rather my memory—wandered too long in that regard.

Traitorous brain.

What was wrong with me? I'd brought her here, hoping

to give her a night to make a plan then send her on her way. But after one evening, it was clear how difficult that was going to be. I'd coaxed her into taking Kacey for a walk and played with him at the lake. It took about sixty seconds for the little guy to get covered head to toe in the loose mud. He'd had the time of his life as we chucked rocks into the lake.

Miranda had stooped down to teach Kacey how to skip a few, gently curling his little finger around the rocks and helping him flip his wrist. One had skipped twice, and Kacey squealed in delight. She'd done all the work, but cradled his hand in hers so he felt like the hero.

I couldn't help but be amazed at her.

The walls of her life were crashing in, and she was still showing up for her son.

Proof she was every bit the mom I knew she would be.

That afternoon, when I asked how old Kacey was, she said he turned three in March. I automatically launched into the mental math on the last time Miranda and I were together. Didn't time out.

We'd tried so hard for a family.

Some lucky son of a gun made a beautiful family and—from the looks of things—was doing a pretty poor job taking care of it.

I couldn't help but imagine what she looked like with a rounded belly, what labor was like, and if motherhood was everything she dreamed of. Wasn't my place to ask. There were more pressing issues at hand anyway.

Typically, I considered myself pretty good at reading people, but I couldn't read Miranda. After the meeting, she seemed agitated with me. But after she got sick on the side of the road, she acted afraid. Withdrawn. Skittish, even.

Allowing myself to wonder what she'd been through sent

my brain into a spiral. Made me feel ready for a ten mile jog, not sleep.

After we emptied her stuff out of the truck, I noticed the Schrute Farms sweatshirt. She'd been wearing that thing since before I met her. Still looked as cute as ever in it. The sweatshirt fell mid-thigh and the sleeves bunched at her wrists. She could even tuck her knees into it without stretching the belly.

Watching Miranda tie the sweatshirt around her slim waist ten years later caused desire to hit me out of left field. A longing for our simpler, happier times filled me until I struggled to breathe.

She forgot it; left it draped over the back of the couch once her and Kacey retired to their suite. Because I'm an idiot, I did something stupid I'd never be able to come back from. Something that launched the moments flashing through my brain into full body experiences that filled me with craving. A craving for my old best friend. For everything we used to be. For everything we shared.

I smelled it. Knowing full well the fabric would smell like her.

Did it ever.

It was nostalgia and novelty meshed together, creating an intoxicating aroma. The citrusy smell was new. But the earthy-sweet scent was agonizingly familiar, flooding my head with countless memories of us.

I replaced it on the couch, only to come back fifteen minutes later and take it to bed with me.

As I laid beneath the spinning fan in my old bedroom, I took one more deep breath of her and promised myself it would be the last.

Traitorous, *traitorous* brain.

Jules accused me last week of not being over Miranda. I'd rolled my eyes, flat out denying it.

Yet here I was, lying in bed, tormenting myself with desires that would only hurt again. As much as I wanted the lake house now, letting Miranda back into my life would be a mistake.

What am I doing?

My skin turned clammy under the spin of the fan and my mouth was dry. I slid out of bed, slipped on my sweatpants, and headed for some ice in the kitchen. As I was rounding the wall to the dining area, I heard the tinkle of a glass.

Miranda.

How many times had we made each other glasses of ice water at night?

I let out a loud whisper before stepping into the kitchen. Hopefully minimizing the inevitable startle. "Hey, Miranda?"

She gasped softly.

I came into view and her shoulders slacked. "Dang, you scared me."

"Sorry. I needed some ice water, too."

"Old habits die hard, huh?"

"Yep." I filled a glass with ice then asked, "You couldn't sleep?"

"Not a wink."

"Me either."

"Too much to think through."

"Same."

She paused, setting her glass on the granite counter. Her voice was low, sad. "Jack, I realized as I was getting into bed you did so much for us and I never even stopped to give my proper condolences. I'm sorry—about Nathaniel."

I shrugged. "It's okay. You know we weren't all that close."

"Still."

"I appreciate that."

She picked her glass up and strode over to the dining room

picture windows. Huge and facing the lake, no blinds or curtains hindered the moonlight. "This place is beautiful."

No, *she* was beautiful. Standing next to the window, the soft white light of the moon illuminated her features. Standing on her left, I got a full view of her high cheekbones, the glow highlighting the curves of her face and the length of her dark lashes. As tired and run-down as she looked, she was stunning. Miranda had always been knock-out gorgeous, a ten in my book.

Still was.

It was impossible to be around her again and not notice.

A thrill ran through my midsection, making every cell in my body buzz with awareness of her. This was not good. Miranda and I were done. Over. We'd closed the door, which made my imaginings all the more frustrating and inappropriate. I ran a hand over my head, forcing my gaze to the lake. My dad had a rep for crazy—but this—forcing my path to cross with Miranda's was cruel. "It certainly is luxurious."

"How much did it get appraised for?"

I took a long swig. "Guess."

She bit her lip in thought.

I silently thanked the darkness. It lended to the first easy conversation we'd had since the meeting. Had it been daylight, she would've continued hiding.

"How about one point five million?"

I chuckled. "Try three."

"*Three* million?"

"Just shy of it."

She continued, slow and soft, like I might run from her if she spoke. "Sorry I'm not remarried yet. Not many men want a frumpy mom."

An explosive response pressurized in my throat. Took all my effort to hold it in. Frumpy mom? Nothing could be further from the truth. She had no idea how desirable she was. Without even a drop of effort. I'd seen this woman in many forms—there wasn't a single one I didn't fantasize about.

The idea of another man...or men...I forced my jaw to unclench, letting my cheeks puff with an exhale. Those were thoughts I usually needed a few beers to help bury. Water wouldn't do a single thing to shake those images. "You never answered my question about Kacey's dad. Is he still in the picture?"

She bit her lip, looking down at the glass in her hands. She rubbed her thumb over the condensation, "No, he—he's not."

Oh. The revelation was less satisfying than I thought it would be. "What happened there?"

"It was a"—she blinked rapidly a few times—"one night mistake."

I didn't know what to say. What we had tried so hard for was granted with a "one night mistake?" Didn't seem fair. To her, to me, or to Kacey.

Silence washed over us. To my surprise, she didn't turn to leave. She stayed, training her eyes to the waves lapping the shore below.

"Let me ask you—do you happen to know why Dad included you on the will? That was a bit unexpected."

"I don't know." She shrugged. "I feel uncomfortable even talking about it. I shouldn't have claim to any of this." She gripped her glass with both hands, elbows pulled into her side. From the moment I'd seen Miranda yesterday, she'd been tucked in. Her arms and hands never moved far from her core. But back when we were married, her hands always came out to dance—right along with her facial expressions. "You—" she faltered. "You didn't deserve what Nathaniel did." She pressed her lips together, as if the admission pained her.

"It's not your fault. I should've figured he'd have some sort of catch or fine print. He's always tried to stick it to me." I took one more drink, the ice crashing to the bottom of my cup. "Sucks because I don't really want to wait six years. I could use the money from the sale."

"I mean, who couldn't?"

"True. I bought a house a while back. It needs some updates. Like HVAC and new roof." A humorless chuckle spilled out of me. "Not to mention the Nashville area is getting stupid expensive. Be nice to not have a mortgage."

She harrumphed. "Everywhere is getting expensive."

"I actually turned down a promotion to lieutenant last year. I'm regretting that now."

She frowned. "You'd never be happy doing a desk job."

A smile played at my lips. She knew me. Katelyn said I should've taken it.

She must've realized her confidence because she backpedaled. "Oh—I'm sorry. Maybe that's your kind of thing now. Not like I'd know."

"No, you're right. I wouldn't like a desk job."

An awkward beat of silence passed over us before I changed the topic. "I'm assuming marriage is out of the question for you, but maybe it's a way we can help each other...and I want to help you." Even as I said it, my brain screamed *why*. She left me. She walked away. She broke off the marriage I wanted. But standing here, watching her, made the anger I'd felt feel like a million miles away.

Her chest rose with a deep sigh. "Jack, marriage is..." She shook her head at a loss for words. "You don't need to solve my problems. I've made a lot of terrible choices—I don't even know where I'd start." Her fingers traced lines in the condensation again. Her hallmark. Miranda always fidgeted when she felt uncomfortable. "There's so much clean up to do in my life."

Like Kacey's dad?

It was just an assumption. But I couldn't help but imagine Miranda with some dead-beat guy moments after running from my arms. I had wanted her. Tried to fight for her. I gave my head a hard shake as unwanted images sneaked in again.

There was Chris. And the one night stand guy. Maybe more.

Someone along the way must have programmed her into believing she was a problem. She apologized to me at least a hundred times for the most minor things. Like Kacey whining, or not finishing her slice of pizza, or for making a lot of noise. Stuff I wouldn't have thought twice about until she fell all over herself for it.

The Miranda I used to know lived unapologetically. She made more hasty mistakes than anyone I ever met. But I used to love that about her. She made messes out of things then laughed at herself until she collapsed.

If I ever came face to face with the person who hurt her, I'd capitalize. I had to take deep breaths to release the tension in my fists.

She continued, not waiting for my response. "Plus, if I recall correctly, four years ago, you said it was better for us to deal with consequences on our own and go our separate ways."

I swallowed, regret wrapping its fingers around me. "I think I did say that."

"Oh, you definitely did."

We'd gone our separate ways and fate threw us back together. "Well, we are both here now. And you need an ally."

She stayed quiet.

"Can I at least help you fix your car?"

"You've already done too much. I don't feel comfortable taking anything else from you."

"It's not a big deal. How about I offer you a trade. I help you fix your car, and you help me go through the crap in the attic?" We'd had the car towed to a mechanic who was running diagnostics.

The deep dimple on her left cheek made a brief appearance as she fought a smile. "That is *not* a fair trade."

I couldn't tear my eyes away from that almost-dimple. "You haven't seen the attic."

"Pretty bad, huh?"

"Last time I checked." It was like fifteen years ago, but still.

She said nothing, just bit her lip.

The urge to really see her welled up inside me until I felt like I would burst. She had been strategic. Always keeping me on her left side. But suddenly it wasn't enough. I wanted to look her straight in the eyes. To show her I saw it all. To prove I was on her side.

I must've been suffering from a head injury. Memory loss or something like that. Jack plus Miranda had equaled trouble from the start. But—for some reason—I didn't care.

I whispered, "Miranda. Will you look at me?"

Her head tipped down toward her glass. Her lips worked with a swallow.

"Please."

She bit her lip to still its tremble.

"I've already seen it. You don't have to hide."

Her voice was raspy, a scrape of swelling emotion. "It's humiliating, Jack."

"I know." *And I want to kill him.*

Unable to rein in my desire, I reached out and touched her hair. Feather light, hardly enough for her to feel it. But she drew a breath. She felt it.

The muscles low in my torso clenched.

She turned and looked up.

Her brown eyes were full of pain. They took me in. Roaming my face, wide and searching. Moisture in the corners glistened in the moonlight. The moment stretched out between us. It was the first time we held eye contact since the day she showed up at the department all those years ago.

I'd been telling myself I didn't care about her. That we chose our paths and moved on. But locking gazes with my ex-wife couldn't be anything but eye-opening. I might be able to keep lying to everyone else, but lying to myself would be difficult from here on out.

Her irises were dark with anguish as a tear slipped down her cheek. Without my permission, my thumb swept it off her soft skin. I let my hand linger near her face, and she didn't pull away.

She whispered, "Thank you. For all your help."

I said nothing when she turned away. Just tried to steady my breathing. As she walked to the kitchen and placed her glass in the sink, she said, "You said something earlier today. That—that I hated your guts. I want you to know, I don't hate you, Jack." Her voice broke over my name.

As she disappeared up the stairs to the second floor, I grappled with the obvious.

The answer to her problem was right in front of us, and we hadn't slowed down to truly consider it as an option.

But the more I thought about the ins and outs, the more I liked the idea.

Convincing Miranda would be the real challenge.

FOURTEEN

Miranda

My heart slammed in my chest as I descended the stairs. Jack asked me to come down once Kacey was asleep for the night. Said he wanted to discuss something. I had no doubt he was going to try and convince me to marry him. But fear pressed into my heart—maybe he already sniffed out my secret.

Please not that.

Everything I believed about Jackson Barkley had gone up in flames. I spent the entire last day tied in knots. I coped by keeping to the suite, pacing across the Persian rug. Moving forward would require herculean effort. I doubted I had it in me. Doubted I had the gumption to handle all these new revelations.

The universe must have plotted against me because I did the right thing way back then. My final plea to Jack was seared into my brain. I relived it, thinking through every last detail. It couldn't have been one big misunderstanding. There was more. There *had* to be more.

The defense around my heart was constructed in bitterness. For four years, anger was the only thing protecting me from life-shattering heartbreak. But my foundations shook. A crack in my shield threatened the little safety I enjoyed. The danger to my heart loomed, more imminent and real than ever before.

To make it worse, Jack was being kind. Too kind. Before, I would've relished in it, claiming he owed me some kindness. But now, I wracked my brain, wondering how *I* had managed to fail *him* so badly. Nothing I could do would make it right.

Every imposition Kacey and I made on him stacked against me. I ran my hands over my face, dreading the moment it all came to light. Part of me wanted to blurt the truth right there in the truck, but before I got the chance, the gravity of the situation hit like a boulder to the gut.

Right now, Jack was the only person I had. The only thing standing between us and a homeless shelter or nights in the car.

What if the truth made him think I schemed this? Made him think I purposefully hid Kacey from him? Would he throw us out? Ship us straight back to Ohio?

I know enough about Jack. He wouldn't handle the news well. Then again, who would? I nibbled my bottom lip, placing myself in Jack's shoes. Inevitably, he would be furious and hurt. So hurt. And he'd have every right to feel that way.

We had always wanted children. A fear imbedded itself inside my head. My palms grew moist. When Jack knew the truth, would he try to take Kacey away from me? Would he take me to court? It would make sense for him to claim custody.

I pressed on my lips, drawing a deep breath through my

nose. Panic started to close in, waiting to pounce on me. Keeping my head on straight was the most important task. I could not become unhinged right now. I had a bigger picture to consider and needed to place my fears aside.

My legs felt like jelly as I came into the living room area. Jack stood by the gas fireplace. It glowed with warmth. The lights were low. Only a lamp, the fire, and a candle on the mantel cast light around the room. It almost looked... romantic?

What the heck?

"Uh, what's going on here?"

Jack spun around. "Oh, hey, yeah—" He ran his hands over his head before they landed restlessly on his hips.

Was he...nervous?

What is happening right now?

He waved toward the couch. "—sit down."

"Okay," I responded slowly, easing myself down onto the cushion.

"Look, Miranda, I'm going to cut right to the chase." He dropped down onto the chair a few feet away and propped his elbows on his knees. His gaze bore into me. I shifted, unsure I was capable of looking into his face at the moment.

My thrashing heart made it difficult to focus.

"I've been thinking about this since last night. Try to hear me out."

I nodded. So it *was* the marriage thing. Had we had this conversation the day before, I would've angrily shut him down. But I didn't know how I'd respond now. I was heartbroken and desperate all over again.

"I think we should get married."

"I figured you'd say that."

"I think it would solve a few issues."

"While simultaneously causing a few issues."

"Not necessarily."

"Jack, we've done the marriage thing. Do broken hearts and divorce papers ring a bell?"

He shot me a look. "You said you'd try to hear me out."

"I didn't say—"

"You nodded."

"Fine." I waved him on, granting him permission to continue.

"A few things to consider. We both need the money from the sale of the lake house. And you need to get away from your ex. Without a place to live, a job, money, or a car, that's basically impossible without someone helping you."

I scoffed. Hated to admit how right he was.

He stood and started pacing in front of the hearth. "Sixty days married, we list the house, it sells, and we're both millionaires."

"Foolproof, clearly."

The sarcasm felt like an old friend I hadn't seen in years. I was never verbally combative with Chris. Not even in a joking way. He would strike me down. His words were the one punch knockout that left me reeling long after a fight had ended.

But Jack took it in stride. "I know you never would have chosen this, but think about it, Miranda. You could go anywhere you wanted. Buy a house and a car and never have a payment again. You'd never have to be saddled with someone out of necessity." He sat in the chair again, lowering his voice. "I want that for you."

"Jack! I can't let you marry me because you're worried about my ex!" I shook my head. "That is so something you'd do."

"It's not just about you. I told you about my roof and HVAC."

"Come on. You're telling me you'd get *married* in order to

have better air conditioning?" Even as I said it, I realized plenty of people would get married for a million dollars. And Jack would be able to do a lot more than fix his AC.

"My point is I have things I need money for too."

The idea was despicable, but my brain decided to poke it—test its structure.

"So, what? Would we get divorced after we signed for the sale?"

"If that's what you wanted."

"Wait, is that not what *you'd* want?"

He blinked, talking in a rush. "Of course we'd get divorced." He added more slowly, "We've done it once before. We can...do it again."

I nodded. We could do it again.

Granted, I doubted I'd live to see another day when it happened the first time, but I survived, despite all odds.

But Kacey.

I shook my head. "This won't work. I have a son to think about."

"I think Kacey's the reason you should do it."

But Jack didn't know everything. What would happen when the truth spewed? Would he call off the deal? Take me to court and make me look unstable and desperate?

Jack continued, "A couple months of this and you could give him a different life."

But a different life. It *was* appealing.

"Mr. Ruben said we could take it to court. Maybe we'd win. Then we wouldn't have to get married or wait six years."

"Yeah, I've been doing some research..."

"Oh no."

He shook his head. "We're talking a lengthy, expensive process."

"How expensive?"

"Five to ten thousand. Starting out."

I knew Jack didn't have much. Sure, he always paid his bills and had a bit in savings, but law enforcement wasn't the career for people with lofty financial goals.

"We could contest the will, spend all that money, and still potentially lose."

"Exactly."

"So…if we got married, would we live together?"

He rubbed the top of his head again. "I mean, I kind of assumed we would. It sounds like you don't have another place to go."

"Yeah, I don't."

"I have a second bedroom." He shifted in discomfort. "It's not like it'd have to be a real marriage or anything."

He didn't have to expound. I knew what he meant. My breathing shallowed at the memories. Back in close quarters with my old husband. With all the old problems. And all the old desires. Those desires were alive and well. I could see them in his eyes and feel them in my belly when he was near. They had never fully died.

My hand came to my collarbone as I tried to sort up from down. Felt like my heart was reeling.

"John said there were buyers lining up for the lake house," I remembered out loud. "The sale would probably be fast, we'd get the money, and our arrangement would end pretty quickly."

"True." He set to pacing again.

A few moments of silence passed as we considered it, suffering a brief lapse in sanity and common sense.

"If we did this—got married—when would we?"

He thought for a moment. "When we get to Nashville? Considering it's a timed thing, it makes sense to do it sooner rather than later."

"What about essentials? I don't have any way to support us. I'm thinking about groceries, nighttime diapers, that kind of thing…"

"Things aren't *that* tight. I can take care of your essentials."

"I'd pay you back."

"That wouldn't be necessary."

"Yes, it would."

He rolled his eyes. "Okay, fine. You can pay me back for two months of diapers and the *four bites* of food you eat per day."

I stared into the flames.

This would change everything.

My mind and heart were officially on overload. Felt myself dazing out, watching the blue flames flicker behind the fake log and listening to the hollow *whoosh* of the gas. How did my life end up in such a chaotic spiral?

Jack broke the silence a few minutes later. "We should sleep on it."

"Yeah, for sure." I stood to go.

He stopped pacing and turned toward me. Our gazes tangled and the thrill running through me didn't go unnoticed. His blue eyes searched my face, and I couldn't help but search his too. For a brief moment, my brain recalled Jack strolling into the kitchen last night, half naked. His broad chest and hardened abs on full display. Jack was too handsome for his own good. Still, ten years later, I wondered how someone so fine wound up with someone like me.

My mouth dried.

Marriage would be a *dangerous* game. Our hearts the stakes once again.

FIFTEEN

Then

Jack

It was her birthday. June third.

After months of prep, the surprise evening wasn't landing the way I hoped. So far, everything had gone according to plan, except Miranda wouldn't look me in the eye and had only picked at her meal. We made it through the candlelit dinner at a high-end restaurant with almost zero conversation. I started doubting my decision to do this tonight. My neck broke out in a sweat as we silently left the restaurant.

I considered abandoning the next part of the plan, but I already told Miranda we had another destination, so I kept driving toward Old Hickory Lake.

There was a private drive with lake access a friend of mine owned. He let me use it for tonight. We drove down the pitch-black driveway toward a dock. Soft twinkle lights penetrated the darkness and Miranda sat forward in her chair, squinting.

"Oh, this is really pretty."

It was the only thing she said on the twenty minute drive.

I parked and helped her out of the truck to the special spot I had prepared a few hours before. I'd laid a few blankets and pillows spread out over the dock for a cozy spot and packed a cooler with her favorite wine. Two glasses were already set out. Flower petals and twinkle lights around the railing graced the whole scene.

Visually, the space turned out better than I thought it would. But a brick sat on my stomach. I couldn't give Miranda her birthday present. Not when she seemed so distant and sad. I had to figure out what was wrong first.

I swallowed hard as I led her down the dock. I hated dealing with this sort of stuff. Was seriously considering calling it a night and taking her home.

Miranda soaked everything in. "You did all this for my birthday?"

"Yes ma'am, I did."

I sat on the pallet of blankets and pulled her down beside me. She snuggled beneath my arm. We sat in silence, watching the lake waves as my anxiety ramped. When I couldn't handle my beating heart anymore, I popped open the cooler. "We have some Chardonnay. Can I pour you a glass?"

Her chest shuddered with a deep breath and she looked at her hands in her lap. "No, thank you."

I leaned down and kissed the top of her head, squeezing her into my side. "Miranda, you said you're fine, but you aren't fine. You barely ate, you didn't drink anything." I fingered her gorgeous blonde hair, twisting a lock around my finger. "You haven't even smiled."

She turned her face from me and her shoulders shook once. My insides ached.

No, no, no. Please don't cry.

"Miranda, talk to me." My hand came to her cheek, and I gently guided her face to mine. "Please." She didn't look me in the eyes, and a tear trailed down her cheek. I swiped it away with my thumb then placed a kiss on her forehead.

Her brown eyes slowly lifted to meet mine. Her voice was breathy, scared. "I'm—I'm pregnant."

My world spun.

Pregnant?

Did I hear right? The word felt foreign in my mouth. "Pregnant?"

She nodded as she bit her bottom lip.

"Wait, wait, wait. You're—you're having a baby?" Energy drained from my body and shock radiated through my limbs.

She nodded again.

"I'm going to be a dad?"

"Yes," the word slipped out with a sob.

Brand new emotions flew through my chest.

We are having a baby?

Heat pricked the back of my eyes and I blinked the feeling away, taking a shallow breath that left me feeling lightheaded.

My smile finally broke through the shock and a laugh came right behind. I gripped her face with both hands. "Miranda, you're telling me we're having a baby?"

Her eyes frantically searched my face, and her jaw quivered against my palms. "I found out today."

"And you're sure?"

She nodded, pressing her lips together. My gaze roamed her beautiful face as I processed the fact she was going to be the mother of my child.

My child.

It was the last thing I expected tonight, but my heart beat with a fullness I never knew. Pesky heat pricked my eyes again.

"Jack, I've been worried sick all day you'd be upset or angry." She sniffed. "Please say something."

My thumbs moved to dry her cheeks. "Angry? Are you kidding me?"

"You're—you're not upset?"

"No!" A laugh bubbled up as I watched the worry lines on her face ease. "I can't remember the last time I felt this happy."

Her mouth fell open a little, and she blinked.

"The woman of my dreams is—is carrying my baby?"

"Jack!" Fresh tears sprang into her eyes, but her lips wobbled into a smile. "Does this mean you want the baby—want us? I was afraid you might not."

"Not want you?" I shook my head in disbelief. Why would she even think that? A laugh escaped her throat along with a sob as she came to terms with my reaction. "Miranda, there is nothing I want more."

With those words, she collapsed into my chest, the tears freely flowing. I sunk my fingers into her hair and rubbed her back. My heart raced out of control as a million thoughts flooded my mind. A child with Miranda. It was what I wanted, I just never expected it this soon.

After a few moments, I pushed her back enough to sidle around in front of her. Wanted to look her straight in the eyes. I spread my legs and pulled her between them, wedging her as close as possible.

"Miranda Howard, look at me." Her teary eyes met my face. "I could never not want you. Being with you makes me the happiest man. Since the first time I met you, I knew you were it for me. Knew I wouldn't be complete without you. You have nothing to worry about because I've been dreaming of a family with you for a long while now. You're the only woman I want that with." Her emotions continued to spill out as I tugged her closer, our foreheads meeting in the space between us.

I whispered softly, "Marry me, Miranda."

She shook her head vehemently, not registering the velvet box I pulled from my pocket. "No, I don't want you to rush into marrying me because of the baby."

"I'm not." When I flipped open her birthday present, she gasped.

Miranda's eyes barely connected with the ring before bouncing to the twinkle lights, the petals, the wine. "Wait. You brought me out here to—to propose?" The question was a squeak, eeked out around the emotion in her throat.

I nodded as I lifted her hand to my mouth, gently kissing her knuckles. "Please say you'll marry me."

"Oh, Jack!" Her voice swelled with relief and joy. A laugh bubbled out of her as she shrieked, "Yes! Yes!"

Her arms came around my neck and I pulled her into my lap. Her legs wrapped around my waist while I kissed her fiercely. After a few moments, she released me and we fell back onto the blankets together, breathless and overwhelmed.

"You want to see your ring?" I opened the box again.

"Yes!" She wiggled, excitement written in her every movement.

I lifted the box for her to see.

"It's so beautiful."

"Let's see if it fits." I pulled the tiny ring out and slipped it onto her finger.

"It's perfect, Jack."

She scooted closer and threw one arm and one leg over me, snuggling her head onto my chest. I massaged the slender arm across my rib cage as we watched the stars and listened to the gentle lake waves lapping against the shore. We talked for a long time, deciding to get married sooner rather than later. Miranda said she just wanted to be with me. To get our home ready for our baby.

When silence settled over us, Miranda looked out at the dark lake, a devious smile unfurling across her lips. "You know what? I could go for a swim right now."

"Seriously?"

She flashed a daring grin and jumped to standing. She stood at the edge of the dock, pulling her dress off over her head.

I fell in love with her all over again.

The water was cool on our bare skin, tugging us together. We laughed and splashed and acted like two kids. We were giddy—drunk on love and high with excitement. I pulled Miranda against me, our warm bodies colliding under the water.

I whispered into her hair, "I love you so much."

"I love you too."

"You make me happy. And so does our baby."

Her cheeks smiled against my chest. "I'm happy too, Jack."

SIXTEEN

Miranda

I was coffee desperate.

My tossing and turning coupled with Kacey's nighttime moaning was the perfect storm. I downed a cup with my nose pinched. I needed the caffeine, but apparently Nathaniel was too practical for things like caramel creamer.

Between Sherri and Chris, my phone was blowing up. Sherri hadn't stopped calling and texting since she'd learned Brenda couldn't take us in. Despite trying to help me make arrangements with Brenda's neighbor friend, the truth was, the idea of staying with a stranger was hard enough. Staying with the potentially unwilling friend of a stranger felt unbearable. Sherri didn't know how long Brenda would be in Washington. It could be a while, and I couldn't risk the good will of strangers indefinitely.

I tried to act like I wasn't freaking out to make Sherri feel better. But I was. The constant barrage of insults from Chris made it worse. I made a grave error and texted him back to tell him Kacey and I were *fine* and *please* stop texting me. I wasn't a rookie when it came to Chris' ways, so the mistake was just plain stupid.

My phone lit up like I was in a group text. He sent message after message. Insults, threats, pleadings. How would I find the money to get a burner phone and be rid of Chris for good?

The unknowns in my life clashed together like an off-beat cymbal. I had no bearings, no anchors. No way to plant my feet, find gravity, or sort up from down. I shoved the phone into my pocket, resisting the urge to growl in frustration.

Forging a new life away from Chris wouldn't be easy, but I needed the stars to align. Needed something to work out for me. Everything in me revolted against the idea that my stars *had* aligned. That maybe the only real answer to this predicament was Jack.

Jack! Of all people!

Breakfast was a quick affair. Cereal and fruit. Jack came out for coffee then disappeared into a room, saying he needed to do some stuff. I didn't know what to do with myself, so when Kacey whined to go down to the lake for the thousandth time, I relented.

When I located my sweatshirt draped over the back of the couch, I put it on. A familiar aroma flooded my senses, and I froze with the sweatshirt halfway over my head. My pulse charged into overdrive as I grappled with the chill bumps rippling across my skin.

I pulled it off, mussing my ponytail in the process. When I held it to my face and took a sniff of the worn fabric, Jack's scent hit my brain with a host of memories. It was as known to me as if I held him in my arms only moments ago. Tears pooled in my eyes as chills still danced all over my skin.

What on earth? Why did it smell like him? Surely, it

wouldn't smell this way just from being near him. And he couldn't have *worn* it.

Had this happened a couple days ago, I would've made a bonfire and turned the sweatshirt to ash. But it didn't. It was now, when I was defenseless and the most confused I'd ever been in my life.

I glanced over my shoulder, leaning to peer down the hallway. Making sure he wasn't nearby, I held the sweatshirt up to my face and took a long, deep breath. I pressed my lips together as my nose and eyes tingled. The scent was a touch of spiciness mixed with something uniquely him—belonging to his skin, his hair. I had breathed it in at the crook of his neck many times.

Tears blurred my vision. Taken aback by the surge of emotions, I tossed it back over the couch with shaking hands. An ache of nostalgia overtook my spirit, as painful as childlike homesickness. I drew an agonizing breath, exhaling through my nose. The feelings stirring in my gut were new, yet familiar—unbearably familiar.

And I should not feel that way. Should *not*.

I swallowed down the tangle of conflict tightening my throat and forced thoughts of him out of my mind.

Opted to go without a sweatshirt. If I was chilly, so be it.

I tried to play with Kacey, but Jack occupied my mind. In some ways, marrying Jack would solve a lot of issues. I could probably stay off of Chris' radar longer. We might get a minute of stability at Jack's. Life with Chris had been a mesh of chaotic and mundane. We were trapped there. Stuck in a cycle of same-ness, yet living on a precipice, wondering when our lives were going to explode. I did my best to shield Kacey from the turmoil.

Guilt set in for the millionth time. Stuff could've been so different.

Jack said we could divorce and go our separate ways after we got the money. Although I dreamed of freedom, I knew it wouldn't be that simple. At some point, Jack and I would have to discuss the truth.

Then our ties wouldn't be severed so easily.

Years ago, I was madly in love with Jack. But things change. He hurt me in ways I never dreamed possible. He distanced himself from me during my most vulnerable moments. I would never forgive him for that.

If I had a lick of common sense, I could've predicted our marriage would end the way it did, but I didn't realize until the damage to my heart was already done.

Jack handled the difficulties in our marriage with self-preservation and avoidance. He was programmed that way.

A deep sigh pressed into my chest.

Gracious, we used to be so in love.

I blinked back the rise of tears in my eyes. If only things hadn't gone sour so quickly. Our relationship took fire before it even had the chance to bloom.

Could I live with Jack again and escape emotionally intact? I didn't know if it was possible. I already lost my heart to Jack. Was there more I could lose? As the question filtered through my mind, the answer blasted my heart like a bombshell to my only decent option.

My son.

Jack could decide to fight for custody. Maybe even *full* custody. My track record wasn't all that great. It would be too easy for an attorney to make me look unstable, unfit. And Jack? He was the epitome of perfection. Serving in the police force for twelve years, an upstanding citizen, money in the bank, a homeowner, no crazy exes breathing down his neck...

As opposed to me—the homeless mom on the run with a

couple boxes of clothes and a trunk full of processed food. Who had "kept" a little boy from his father for four years.

Jack's voice from up the hill jerked me back to the present. "Hey! I figured I'd find you guys down here."

"Kacey's first word this morning was 'lake.'"

Jack let out a deep chuckle. At one point, it was my favorite sound in the world—leaving me breathless and awe-struck.

"I had to take care of a few things and make a few calls. But, after lunch I'm going into the attic to look for pictures, albums, and stuff like that." He turned toward me, furrowing his eyebrows. "I called the mechanic."

"I'm almost scared to ask. What's the damage?"

He shook his head, denying me an answer.

"You're not going to tell me how much I owe you for the car?"

"Per our agreement, you *owe* me cleaning out the attic."

"I did not agree to anything! I can't let you pay for my car."

"Too late. I already did. If you back out of attic-duty, I'm going to be ticked."

The breeze picked up, lifting the stray hair around my face. "I guess I'll help when I put Kacey down for naptime. You really shouldn't have done that."

After a few minutes, I found my manners. "Thank you. Seriously, Jack. I don't have anything to give you in return."

I shouldn't have picked up my phone. I was in the groove clearing out boxes in the attic. But when I felt it vibrate for the hundredth time, I glanced at the screen. A string of text messages and missed calls from Chris covered my home screen. He knew what time Kacey napped and was probably trying to wear me down into calling him.

I opened my messages, quickly scrolling through.

Chris was pissed, grabbing onto anything he could find. Apparently, he came to terms with the fact I left him for good and wasn't too happy about it. His texts were a string of curse words and ugly names, listing reasons I was a horrible mother and detailing my inadequacies in the bedroom.

My cheeks flushed and instantaneous tears rushed to my eyes.

Why did he always resort to embarrassing me?

I swiped at my cheeks, drying them with trembling, smudgy hands. Thankfully, I was on my knees, labeling boxes behind a wrapped Christmas tree, so maybe Jack wouldn't see my complete humiliation.

I considered blocking Chris, but decided against it. If he started throwing threats, I wanted to be able to see them. His "packing my bags" text was the first, and I figured there would be more. When we left this richy-rich neighborhood, I would ditch my phone. Get a prepaid like Sherri had suggested. If only I had some money.

I sniffed and straightened up as I heard Jack walking a box toward the "done" corner. Jack had been right. The attic was huge, disorganized, and disgusting. Boxes were open, mislabeled, or unlabeled. Dust covered everything. Nathaniel's meticulous way of handling things obviously did not extend higher than the third floor.

We searched and labeled boxes for forty-five minutes and were halfway done. Making decent time, actually. Out of all the junk in the attic, we only found two boxes containing personal items. Like yearbooks, letters, and pictures. There wasn't very much proving a family had once lived here. The lack of old toys, baby clothes, or anything belonging to Jack's mother shocked me.

All the Christmas decorations were glass. Nothing homemade or sentimental. Ninety percent of the items would go to the estate sale, never to be seen or missed again. The reality made me sad for Jack and Jules. He'd often told me their house stopped being a home when his mother got sick. Said Nathaniel turned it into an upscale barracks. He wanted functionality and nothing more. There was no room for memories in the Barkley household.

"I finished on that side. Now we just have the boxes in the middle," Jack called out as he set the box in the far corner and brushed his hands down the front of his faded jeans, returning to the opposite side of the attic.

"I have two more in the mostly-Christmas section." I avoided looking at Jack's face as he passed by, hunched over from the attic's low clearance.

My phone buzzed in my back pocket. I couldn't help but pull it out and look again. I told myself I needed to read them to "stay one step ahead" but maybe I was just a glutton for punishment.

My stomach twisted into knots. Chris was threatening to kill himself if I didn't come back. The message was graphic, conjuring up images that made my eyes sting yet again.

As self-centered as Chris was, I didn't want to see harm come to him. I took a few deep breaths, forcing myself to remember the articles I read when I researched a plan to leave. Many domestic violence websites said abusers threatened to commit suicide as a way to manipulate.

He just wants me back.

Still. I couldn't breathe. Couldn't move. I couldn't shake the mental image his text painted. I held my hand against my rib cage as my heart clenched so hard, I wondered if it stopped beating for a few moments.

How could he think a death would make me happy?

I texted him back: *I'm going to call the police to come check on you if you keep threatening to kill yourself.*

With that, a string of frantic text messages and calls flew in. Angry, mean, spiteful.

Chris: *Go ahead and call the police.*

Chris: *I'll tell them you abducted our kid.*

I slammed the phone face down on the plywood floor beside me. One way or another, someone was going to try to take my son. Chris kept me very familiar with a list of ways I was unfit for Kacey. Those reasons, and many more I'd added to the list, filed through my head at lightning speed. Someone was going to eventually see how I'd mishandled things. Realize how little I had to give a child. And then what would I do?

I wanted to fly away. Wrap my one treasure in bubble wrap and disappear forever.

My vision blurred as I pulled the razor knife over a thin layer of tape on a box labeled "law books," frantic to occupy my anxious mind. Searing pain ripped through my left hand, and I jerked it back with a small cry. I blinked a few times in order to see clearly. Blood was spilling over the top of the box. On instinct, I wrapped it in my t-shirt. I cut it good.

Jack's voice was muted by the maze of boxes and layers of insulation all around. "You okay?"

"Yeah," I yelled back. "Got my hand with the razor."

"You bleeding?"

I squinted at the pad of my thumb. The quiver in my voice couldn't be hidden. "Yes, pretty bad."

"Hang on." Jack quickly disappeared down the attic steps, and I was left alone, sniffling and huffing, doing my absolute best to clear my face with the sleeves of my shoulders. But, the cut turned on a faucet. All of the stress of the last few days, all of the emotional turmoil, all of the problems in my life, all of the questions...the stupid razor had cut much deeper than my skin.

My heart was bleeding and crying, too.

Jack's footsteps ascending the ladder amped up my efforts. I lifted my collar and pressed it against my wet lashes and cheeks. If I was trying to hide the fact I was crying, I was going to fail miserably.

He came around the Christmas tree with a first aid kit. So like Jack. I'd have just run some cold water over it and called it a day. But he loved procedure.

He pulled a box up beside me and sat on it. "Here, let me see."

I let go of my t-shirt and held my hand out for him. He took it, bending close to see in the dim lighting. "Yikes"—he shook his head and laid my hand face up in his lap—"that looks rough."

I was embarrassed for throwing a wrench in our work time. "I'm sorry. I was rushing."

He tore open a couple gauze and an antiseptic wipe. "Don't apologize. Could've happened to anyone, especially with the bad lighting in here."

I caught his familiar smell again and my heart plummeted. Was there nowhere I could go without my heart taking a beating? I turned my head away from him, hoping to gather in a deep breath of the stale insulation and cardboard instead.

My phone buzzed on the plywood. I startled.

Jack glanced at me. "That thing has been going off all morning."

The crimson washing over my face burned. "Yeah."

"Your ex can't take a hint?" He gently dabbed the wipe onto the cut.

I winced but said nothing.

"We have to buy a new phone."

"I don't have—"

"I'm buying."

"No, I can't let you—"

"Stop." He squeezed my palm and looked into my eyes. Our gazes tangled. His was so serious. "You're getting a new phone *today*."

I sighed. Couldn't respond. How could I refuse help I so desperately needed?

"Miranda," Jack spoke slowly, like he'd been rehearsing and was afraid he might miss a line. "You wouldn't have to worry about him in Nashville. You'd be safe."

"I know. I was thinking about it all night long."

My finger throbbed. And my head, come to think of it.

"Did you decide what you want to do?"

As if on cue, my phone started buzzing again. This time I picked it up and read a few of the texts on the home screen. Full of threats. Full of obscenities. Full of insults that made me wish someone would bury me alive.

A deep sigh pushed against the pressure forming in my throat. How did I allow myself to grow so desperate?

"Marriage is the best option I have on the table right now. But I don't want you to destroy your own life in order to fix mine."

He secured a bandaid around my thumb. "Trust me. One and a half million dollars won't destroy my life."

A tiny laugh escaped. The money was the one silver lining for both of us. How pathetic.

My awareness melted to Jack's lap, fully honing on the warmth of his hands around mine. My finger was long bandaged, but he still cradled my hand and wrist. A gentle movement—almost imperceptible in its tenderness—tickled the back of my knuckles. My heart was off to the races.

His voice was low, a gentle pleading. "I want you to be okay. Kacey, too."

"I"—I swallowed, silently cursing the conflict in my heart—"I know you do."

Why did Jack affect me this way?

I should pull my hand away.

"I need to go home tomorrow."

"I know."

The tiny pleasure I was experiencing was not lost on me. Jack's big hands around my own were the best thing I'd felt in a long time. Our little arrangement would be for money and nothing more. There wouldn't be second chances. There *couldn't* be. We used to have love for each other, true. But we had lacked all the important things that make a marriage work.

And Jack? He left me. Alone. Many times. I'd be an idiot to give him my heart again.

But as a moment of silence stretched between us, Jack's attention flicked to my lips. My heart jumped. Hell-bent on stupidity, I reciprocated the action, checking out *his* lips. They were perfect. His lightly stubbled cheeks and jaw tapered into his chin. A whisper of smile brackets remained on his serious expression. His lips were sloped along the sides into a mild cupid's arrow, pink and full. And I knew from experience how skilled they were.

My cheeks grew warm again, and I tore my gaze away before he noticed.

Suddenly, I realized we'd been here before. Sitting in an attic, a decision looming before us. Dusty from boxes and so filled with desire for each other that the tension was electric, palpable, vibrating between us. How on earth were we here again? And better yet—why was I thinking of pressing him into the plywood floor right now?

The brief moment ended as fast as it began. Jack gently squeezed, jerking me back to the present. "What do you say then?"

What other options did I have?

On cue, my phone vibrated.

I couldn't go back. Only forward. Right now, forward was Jack. It could only be Jack. I had zero other feasible options.

"I guess—I guess we should do it."

Jack nodded once, pressing his lips together and offering the tiniest of reassuring smiles. "Okay then."

We finished up the attic and made dinner plans then interacted little for the rest of the day. When we did, it was tense, slightly awkward. We were getting married for money. To stuff cash in our pockets then get divorced. It seemed so shallow, yet it wasn't a light decision. Not in the slightest. How do you have a chill conversation with all that on the table?

You don't.

So we avoided each other.

But yet again, I couldn't sleep. I was thinking about Jack. Not how much I hated his guts and how angry I was he abandoned Kacey. Because—despite the muddy details—I came to terms with one thing: he didn't abandon Kacey. Not *knowingly* anyway. I wasn't recounting past wrongs and failures. I wasn't remembering how it all went off the rails.

I simply let myself realize how homesick I was for Jack. I protected my heart from this emotion for four years. Entertained bitterness instead when it pressed in on me. But with every passing hour, the fortress I created weakened. And the wistfulness and pining for my old best friend overtook me.

Past midnight, I crept down the stairs with wet cheeks and swollen eyes, foolishly determined to test the limits of my torture by taking that sweatshirt to bed with me. When I tried to fetch it from the back of the couch, it was gone.

SEVENTEEN

Miranda

"Do you, Miranda, take this man to be your wedded husband and do you promise to be faithful to him as long as you both shall live?"

I couldn't think. Couldn't breathe. My heart was coming out of my chest, and my hands went clammy. It was hard to focus with Kacey bumbling around on the chairs only ten feet away. Red flush washed my face. I must've looked ridiculous. I glanced down at the simple green dress I had on. Wished I would've had something nicer.

Breathe. Why can't I breathe?

Jack lightly squeezed my hands, and I looked up into his face. His blue eyes roamed over me, his brows knitted with concern. He mouthed, "You okay?"

The officiant prodded. "Miranda, it's your turn."

I swallowed hard, and my tongue stuck to the roof of my mouth. "I'm sorry."

"It's okay." He smiled. "Do you, Miranda, take this man to

be your wedded husband and do you promise to be faithful to him as long as you both shall live?"

"I—I do."

"You can repeat after me now."

I nodded, determined to pay better attention and not faint with anxiety. I fumbled through the prompts. "I, Miranda Leigh Howard, take you, Jackson Nathaniel Barkley, to be my wedded husband…"

It felt like a concrete block was on my chest, and my lip trembled. Jack saw. His thumbs glided over my knuckles in encouragement, and he gave another gentle squeeze.

It's not a big deal. I can do this.

"…for richer, for poorer, in sickness and in health, to love and to cherish, till death do us part."

For sixty days actually, but who's counting, right?

A crash sounded, and we all turned to look at Kacey who had simultaneously rolled three Hot Wheels off a chair onto the floor. Jack's handsome smile appeared yet again, those dimpled brackets on full display. I wondered how he could appear so confident at a moment like this. I kept wondering if we were making a huge mistake. All for some money!

This will change your life in a good way, Miranda. Buck up.

I took a deep, slow breath. Jack wouldn't hurt me. Not physically anyway. I was safe. Yet the impulse to run through the courthouse doors and throw myself off the front steps surged through my veins.

This was wrong. It was desperate, deceptive, and selfish. What-if's plagued me. What if the house didn't sell? What if Chris found out what I was doing? What if Jack regretted this later?

"Now, who has the rings?" The officiant—I forgot his name—shattered my thoughts.

"Uh, we don't have any." Jack explained, his tone even and calm. "I didn't get a chance to tell you."

It's not like we'd sat down for a premarital consultation with the guy. My twenty-four hours back in Nashville had been a whirlwind. We'd driven both our vehicles back from Chicago and settled Kacey and I into the upstairs bedroom of Jack's house. Today we'd waited hours for a marriage license, reserved a time block with an officiant and—*bam*—here we were. Who had time for conversations about rings?

"Oh, no worries. Lots of people get married without rings. We will say the vows still if that's okay with you."

"Sure."

"Jackson, you may repeat after me."

Jack's throat worked with a swallow. Maybe he was more nervous and worried than he seemed. He followed the officiant through the phrases, never taking his eyes from mine. My heart skipped under his gaze. Jack's intensity was too much. He was going to sell this as the real deal to the officiant. I glanced past him at the brightly lit windows, at Kacey, at the floor, at our hands. Anywhere but his intense blue.

The look in his eyes was reminiscent of the one he had on our *actual* wedding day. Promising and serious. Flamed with desire and radiating a level of tenderness most women only dream of. I'd always loved that about him. Tough around everyone else but tender for me alone.

But this wasn't real. Not this time. This was a game we were playing to win the millions. An emotionally dangerous, life-altering game.

I needed oxygen. He was unfairly handsome. Time had done nothing but lend additional ruggedness to his masculine features.

His thumbs traced my knuckles. The pitch of his voice was low, throaty. "Miranda, I give you my heart. I promise from this day forward you shall not walk alone. May my heart be your shelter, and my arms be your home."

Then it was my turn. I stuttered a few times and mixed a couple words around, but I did it. I said them, and we were almost done.

The officiant rambled on about a couple things, and I wished he would hurry. Every passing minute made me feel hotter and stickier. I wished I could collapse into a chair. Was my make-up running? I hoped not.

"And with that, inasmuch as you, Jackson, and you, Miranda, have announced the truths that are already written in your hearts, by the power vested in me by the state of Tennessee, I now pronounce you husband and wife."

We hadn't discussed anything, really. Least of all the ceremonial kiss. Jack did say it didn't have to be a real marriage, but I wasn't sure how this part would pan out. My insides clenched.

"Jackson, you may kiss your bride."

Jack's expression was almost apologetic. His dark brows slanted at the sides as he leaned down without a smile. This was purely obligatory. My heart raced with a cocktail of anticipation and dread.

His large gentle hand came up to tilt my chin upward, and I instinctively rose on tiptoes, grabbing the lapels of his coat for balance. To my surprise, he didn't go for my lips. His thumb guided my face a hair to the side, and he kissed my cheek at the corner of my mouth.

Just my cheek.

My breath tumbled out of my lungs as I dropped down. A cheek peck. I could live with that. But disappointment shot through me. For a delicious moment, I thought I'd get to taste his lips again.

Which was silly. Because tasting him would only complicate a situation that was far too complicated already.

But I'd be lying if I said I hadn't thought about kissing him since the attic two days ago.

Hot, sticky red erupted over my face, neck, and ears. I blinked back tears. All the feels in my body made me ache with confusion. This was officially the worst tease someone could think up. I was going to walk back into life with Jack—*family* life with Jack. It was the thing I always wanted. And here I was. Stepping into a dream I couldn't actually have.

What the heck is wrong with me?

I took a steadying breath as Jack straightened and the officiant said, "Congratulations Mr. and Mrs. Barkley, you're hitched."

Mrs. Barkley.

Never thought I'd hear that again.

EIGHTEEN

Jack

I poured myself a hot cup of coffee, eager to take up my neighborhood watch on the front porch. I loved greeting the day and usually took to the porch chairs much earlier. It was going on 9:00 a.m. Upstairs was quiet and absent of Kacey's tiny pitter-pattering footsteps. So I held the doorknob as I eased the door closed behind me.

According to Miranda, the upheaval of the last week had caused Kacey to sleep poorly. My guess was they had a bad night and were sleeping in a bit. It was only our second morning back in Nashville. Hopefully, the little guy would settle into a routine soon. The ceremony and wedding stuff made our schedule crazy yesterday, and he missed his nap. I suggested resting and waiting a day or two before tying the knot, but no, Miranda wanted to get our two months started as quickly as possible. She was determined not to waste a single day.

I stifled a deep breath and drew a too-hot sip of my coffee.

Burnt my tongue, which was a decent distraction. Two months would evaporate before our eyes. I didn't want to think about it.

Things had been awkward between us, as I imagined, but not as bad as they could've been. My hope was that Miranda would let her guard down. Maybe she'd relax here, sleep more, and look a little healthier. Maybe I could cook some things she used to like and coax her to eat—

My thoughts shattered as a familiar Altima pulled down the street. Panic coursed through my veins.

Jules.

I wanted to kick myself. Should've known ignoring her calls and most of her text messages would backfire.

I was not prepared to talk to Jules about all that had transpired. She'd have a million questions and would probably lecture me about how insane and stupid I was. Which, come to think of it, I *was* stupid. Because I knew my twin well enough to figure she would pull a stunt like this. She had sent me a few butt-hurt messages last night, like, *"Jack, I heard you're suffering from amnesia. I'm your sister, Jules."*

I should've dealt with it right then and there.

Avoidance nipping me in the behind once again.

She was sour because of the silent treatment. Who could blame her? Last time she saw me, I was storming out of the meeting after my ex-wife. I blew out a tense breath and rubbed the back of my head. Took a few long sips of coffee to amp myself up for the surprise visit.

Why hadn't I just called her and told her everything over the phone?

An even worse reality dawned in my mind. Poor Miranda would have no idea Jules was coming. What if she came downstairs while Jules was here? I didn't have my phone to warn her. I considered bolting for the bottom of the stairs and yelling at Miranda to stay put until Jules left, but they were already pulling in. At least Miranda's car was in the garage now.

I stood and leaned on the porch railing as they parked the car. Pat and Jules got out, leaving the car idling. Jules approached me with a scowl.

"Hey sis." I said. Tried to keep my voice light. "What are you guys doing out this early?"

She cocked an eyebrow as she climbed the porch steps. "I wanted to make sure you were alive."

"You didn't have to make a special trip."

She held out her arms, and I pulled her into a hug.

"We didn't make a special trip. The twins have a doctor's appointment in Nashville, and I wanted to swing by and force you to talk to me. You didn't tell me any of your thoughts after the meeting, and I've been worried sick."

"I'm sorry I haven't been in touch. It's been"—I shook my head—"more hectic than you would imagine."

Pat stepped up behind her.

"Well, we aren't staying long. The girls are sleeping in the car." Jules plopped onto a porch chair and Pat settled in next to her, wrapping his arm around the back of her shoulders. "I'm willing to overlook the fact you have refused to talk to me if you start explaining right now."

Suddenly, the front door swung open, and Kacey barged out onto the porch. The door slammed behind him. Jules' brows knit in confusion. Kacey took one look at everyone and turned to go back inside. He struggled with the door handle for a second or two, whimpering, "Mommy!"

"Hey, come here." I called to him, hoping to side-step the impending meltdown. But as I did, the door gave, and he rushed back inside.

Jules turned to me, mouth agape. "*Mommy*? Did you hook up with someone last night?"

"No, it's not what it looks like—"

The door opened again. This time, Miranda strode out onto the porch with a cup of coffee, Kacey clinging to her leg. Her hair was pulled into a low ponytail, and the bruise on her clean face was in full view, now yellowing and greenish from the passing of time. The sweatshirt swallowed her. We'd been playing this fun game where she'd wear it during the day then leave it on the couch. I took it to bed with me every night and placed it back on the couch before she rose in the mornings.

Well, *I* was playing that game.

She gave a soft gasp and moved like she was going to tuck her tail and run back inside. She quietly apologized.

I stopped her. "Miranda, you're fine. You can stay."

Jules' mouth hung open as she watched Miranda take a porch seat close to me and pull Kacey into her lap. She held up a hand. "No, Jack, no." Jules shook her head back and forth.

"You need to let me explain before freaking out."

"You did *not* get remarried."

I glanced at Miranda. Color had drained from her pressed-together lips.

I spoke, mustering up convincing confidence. "We did. Yesterday."

"I cannot believe you!" Her eyes were wide. "How is remarriage a good idea?"

Pat squeezed her shoulder, grounding her.

"Well, considering the house, we felt like—"

"Who cares about the house! You can't just get married to someone all wrong for you—for money! I mean, I didn't think you would actually do this."

Miranda timidly chimed in. "It's only temporary. The money could solve some of Jack's and my financial issues."

Jules whipped her head to me. "Financial issues? Jack! You never said anything about financial issues."

Miranda patted Kacey's back and told him to run and fetch some cars to play with. He scampered into the house, probably eager to show them to Pat and Jules.

"You couldn't have just waited six years?" Jules' voice grew with emotion and disbelief as Kacey disappeared. "Does 'temporary' mean you're going to divorce when you get what you want?"

My chest tightened. My reasons were a lot more important than money. But I couldn't discuss them right here, right now. "Listen, Jules. It might seem crazy, but it wasn't your decision to make. Dad didn't leave us with many options."

Miranda's face flushed crimson and moisture gathered in the corner of her eyes. Anger flared in me. Jules was not entitled to barge into my home and upset Miranda.

"But another divorce? You still haven't moved on from your first divorce, Jack." Jules wasn't yelling, but her volume was uncomfortable for the close seating arrangement of the front porch. "Miranda broke your heart! She toyed with you."

Pat shifted in discomfort, quietly said Jules' name.

I didn't want a fight, but that's exactly what Jules was asking for. I avoided looking at Miranda. Clenching my jaw with a tight swallow, I answered, "There was a lot more to our divorce you know nothing about."

"Enough to know that doing it all over is a recipe for disaster, and you're going to get hurt again. The divorce tore you up! She—"

"The circumstances are different now. You heard Miranda. This is temporary, and we both agreed."

"This is insane!"

"I don't need your approval to get married, Jules."

"I can't believe you let Dad manipulate you like this!"

I scoffed, fighting to keep my voice level. "Manipulate? What do you know about that? Dad required so much less of you!"

Her jaw dropped. "You have officially lost it. We had the same—"

Pat forcefully rubbed Jules' knee. "Hey, baby, you and Jack should table this. Talk more about it later."

Miranda's small voice interjected, low and humiliated. "It's fine. I can leave if you want to talk now." I didn't want to look at her, but couldn't help myself. A tear had trickled down her cheek.

I was officially pissed off.

I ground my teeth together before speaking. "You're out of line, Jules. There's a lot you don't know, and I don't appreciate you making my wife cry."

Miranda's head turned toward me, probably because I called her wife. Fleeting embarrassment muddied my thoughts for a moment. Wasn't sure why I said that. Sure, I was thinking of her that way, but didn't want Miranda to know it.

Jules narrowed her eyes, staring me down. Her gaze cut to Miranda then back to me. Right when she opened her mouth to reply, Pat stole her opportunity. "We need to head out before the girls' appointment." He turned to Jules and grabbed her hand. "Look, you and Jack have phones. Let's get out of here, and you guys can talk it out when you're in a better state of mind. Conversations like this never help anyone."

Jules glowered at him, but stood and disappeared down the steps and into the front seat without another word. Pat lingered behind and introduced himself to Miranda. "Didn't get the chance to meet you in Chicago. I'm Pat."

"Thank you. I've heard a lot about your family."

Pat turned to me. "You can give Jules more details later.

My guess is there's some layers at play here." His gaze roamed from my face to Miranda's then back to mine. I wondered if he was suspicious of Miranda's bruise. The way she tipped her head down told me she was wondering the same.

Kacey barged onto the front porch with an armful of cars.

"I'm sorry. I didn't mean to upset her like this. I should've talked to her sooner. I've just—I don't know. Been putting it off, I guess."

"It's okay, man. Just talk it out with her soon. It's been a big, emotional week and she'll feel better once the two of you are synced again. She's been worried sick with you not picking up." He shook his head. "You Barkley twins are protective of each other. Still nursing some wounds in that regard." He rubbed his midsection with a gentle smile.

I couldn't help but chuckle. I'd knocked him flat on his back right before he and Jules made their relationship official. Thought he was another trashy guy taking advantage of her. Turns out he's ten times the man I am. "We're still talking about that?"

"Never gonna stop." He extended his hand to me, offering a firm shake. "Congratulations are in order, I reckon. And ah, I hope...everything turns out as it should." He nodded at Miranda. "Nice to meet you and your son."

Thank you, Pat.

He'd saved Miranda from more embarrassment. She didn't deserve to be collateral damage in any dispute between me and Jules. Pat saw that. Saw how the conversation would have blown things to a new level. I gave them a wave as they pulled out of the driveway.

Miranda's cheeks were splotchy red, like she was ready to burst with tears at any moment. She tucked her chin and tried to direct Kacey back into the house, coaxing him with promises of food. She didn't want to stay out here with me. Didn't want me to see her cry.

I stopped her. "That shouldn't have happened. I'm so sorry."

"You shouldn't be." She said from the doorway, keeping her face turned away. "This is your house, and she's your sister."

"But you were put in an awkward situation."

"I can't say I blame her for freaking out."

"Guess we seem a little nuts."

"A little." She huffed as she wiped her eyes dry. "Well"—she nodded toward the toddler zooming cars down the handrails—"it doesn't look like Kacey's having any trouble making himself at home." She changed the subject. "Have you eaten? I need to make Kacey something. I wouldn't mind—"

"No, Miranda." I held up a hand to stop her. "You don't have to cook meals or do anything for me."

"Oh." Her gaze followed her son through the yard. "What if I *want* to? Might be fun to cook a little. It's been so long."

"You don't cook much anymore?"

"Um, no. Chris liked eating out."

Everything I heard about that idiot made me hate him more. "Make yourself at home in the kitchen then. I won't be the one to stop you."

A small chuckle spilled from her. I made sure to watch—didn't want to miss the dimples that made infrequent appearances.

"Speaking of food"—I pulled out my phone—"I need to order some groceries."

"Don't buy anything special for us. We aren't picky."

Fat chance. Had to get some meat back on her. I shrugged, "I say we make some old favorites. I don't cook since it's just me. So it'll give me a reason to get back in the kitchen, too."

Miranda and I were both knowledgeable chefs and had shared many fun—and intimate—moments in the kitchen. I tried not to think of the latter. The woman could out-cook me any day of the week. Something I'd never complained about.

Although she claimed my breakfasts were better. Probably because I'm the morning person between the two of us.

"Any particular meals sound good to you?"

"Not really. Whatever you want."

I took a deep breath. I wanted the *old* Miranda. The one who would've launched into a description of a four course meal she saw on Food Network. The one who would've browsed the dairy cooler for fifteen minutes trying to decide on a new, disgusting creamer for her coffee. The one who would've waltzed into the kitchen, insisting we play the tasting game. The one who would've lit a candle at every meal because the glow made things look special.

I hoped that Miranda was still there. Somewhere.

"That's fine. I'll just add the basics."

It would be so easy to forget this situation was a mere business arrangement. To forget the alluring woman and likable kid in my home weren't mine. It would be so easy to pretend the years between us were a blip on the radar. Easy to pick up where we left off as if nothing happened.

Easy for me, I should say. Not for her. When she left me, she made it very clear I failed her. A pain settled in my gut.

I might not be able to reverse time. But this was my chance. And I planned to take full advantage. It was the closest thing to a do-over I would ever get.

As I added items to a grocery order, Kacey came and drove a car down my thigh and shin. He made tiny zooming noises then took the car back up my other leg. I smiled at him. "Kacey, that's a cool car."

He handed a red one to me. "You be dis one."

I took it as my heart flipped.

I turned the tiny toy over and read the bottom. "Oh, this one's name is *Twin Mill*."

Kacey's eyes widened—they were soft brown, like Miranda's. "Dey have names?"

She watched us.

I shifted. Why was I nervous?

"They all have names. Let me see that one."

Kacey gladly relinquished his blue car.

"This one is *Bone Jigger*."

Kacey giggled, repeating the name. "Bone Jig-gah, Mommy."

"That's so neat, buddy." Her voice wobbled, and she tucked her hands beneath her chin.

Pretty soon, cars were piled in my lap. I was reading off names and Kacey was doing his best to memorize each one of them. After a minute or two, Miranda stood. She wasn't looking at us, but fidgeted with the edge of her sweatshirt, the emotion in her voice apparent. "I need to make him some food. Come on Kacey, let's go in."

I hoped I hadn't done anything wrong.

Kacey whimpered and laid his head against my knee.

That was something. A smile tugged at my lips. "I don't mind staying out here with him for a few more minutes."

She hesitated at the door then slowly nodded her consent before going inside. I scooped the little guy up to sit on my lap. He started babbling to me about his cars, which ones went the fastest, about the one with a broken tire, and had me read off the names again. He was a good talker. I understood every word. The breeze lifted his hair, and I caught his scent. Kacey smelled sweet and fresh. Like my nieces, Winter and Woods, did. As we chatted, he leaned against my chest and absentmindedly tapped up and down my arm with his chubby fingers.

When Kacey asked to go in, we found Miranda at the stove, working with a spatula. She'd taken off the sweatshirt and wore a fitted white t-shirt and blue jeans. Despite the incredible aroma, I felt my mouth go dry.

Yep. Way too easy.

NINETEEN

Jack

"I'm honestly surprised you picked up."

"Yeah, well, thanks for calling. Pat was right per the usual. I needed to cool off. Sorry for everything I said. I didn't mean to make Miranda cry."

"It's okay." I stretched out on my bed. "I'm sorry for not keeping you in the loop."

She asked, "Do you feel like you can talk now?"

"Yeah."

"Same." She hesitated a beat. "Any ideas why Dad put Miranda on his will?"

"He was pissed at me maybe? He's been giving me crap since I was—what, maybe twenty? He's kept a growing list of reasons. I got rebellious as a teen, I blew off my perfect GPA, I dropped out of college for the police academy, I followed you and Cameron to Nashville, and I'm not a hoity-toity lawyer like he was. To top it off, I got divorced—the failure of all failures."

And I didn't take the shot.

It was the moment his disappointment truly began.

Jules tsked. "Gracious. Yeah that's a lot of ways to piss Dad off. But I don't think that's the reason."

"Any other ideas then?"

"Yeah, I—I actually have something to confess, and I'm scared you're going to be mad at me."

"That doesn't sound good."

"Well, you know Dad and I talked—I mean, really infrequently, but a little here and there."

"Yeah, I know."

"I talked to him maybe six weeks ago. He asked how you were doing and if you were seeing anyone and had any marriage prospects on the horizon..."

My pulse kicked up a notch. "And?"

"Well, I told him you were dating someone who I really liked, but I doubted it would go anywhere because you would probably dump her just like you have every girl since Miranda. I told him I felt like you were still in love with her even though you keep on denying it."

"What? Why would you tell him that?" I fought the anger surging up in me.

"I don't know! I have felt *awful* about it since the meeting. I hope him adding Miranda wasn't my fault, but I totally feel like it was. He wouldn't have done that if he didn't know your relationship status." Her voice faltered. "I'm so sorry."

"Wait, so you're saying you think that was Dad's convoluted way of helping us get back together?" I shook my head. "I think that's far-fetched."

"Is it? Think about it. He knows you're a cop and don't make tons of money so he probably figured you wouldn't take this to court. It's the perfect scenario for him to devise to his heart's content."

"By making sure that what—I get a happily-ever-after?" I scoffed. "I doubt Dad cared that much."

Jules made a soft humming noise. "Dad did care. He didn't know how to show it, but he did care. If there is one thing Dad understood, it was never getting over a woman." She choked up. "Dad never remarried. Never even entertained the thought. Last time we talked, he told me he still pretends to have coffee with Mom every morning. I told him he needed therapy."

"Wow."

"I don't know, Jack. Maybe this was his really screwed-up version of doing something nice." She sighed. "But I guess we'll never truly know." She sighed. "Dad aside—I'm worried about this arrangement with Miranda. Exes are exes for a reason."

"There's a lot you don't know, Jules."

"Fill me in then."

I told her everything I knew about Miranda's *current* situation. Left the past in the past.

"She needs the money. And I want her to have it. She deserves better than whatever life she's living right now."

"So she's staying at your house then?"

"Upstairs."

"I do feel bad for her, but it sounds like Miranda is coming out with the better end of the deal here and that's not fair." Jules listed, "She's taking half of the inheritance which should be yours, getting a free place to stay for her and her kid while she waits, and gets to walk away into whatever life she wants after she's trampled your heart for a second time."

Jules wasn't wrong, but the need to defend Miranda cropped up in my chest again. "Little bit harsh, don't you think?"

"It's not harsh! I try not to hold grudges, but Miranda up and left you."

I didn't feel like explaining the details of my divorce. Unfortunately, it was more complicated than that. Jules never got the full picture.

"I have zero expectations for this. It's a business arrangement. That's all."

"You are a decent liar, but I'm your *twin*. Can we just talk honestly?"

I shrugged even though she couldn't see me. "What do you mean?"

She sighed into the phone again.

"Seriously, what?"

"You've never gotten over her."

"I'm completely over her."

"I swear. Pat is the only emotionally intelligent man I know. No offense."

"None...taken?"

"I understand why you did this, but you and Miranda splitting the first time wrecked you. What if you get attached to having her close and suffer all over again when she walks away?"

It was the question keeping me up at night, but I denied it. "That's not going to happen."

"Come on, Jack. You've dated some amazing women the past few years but haven't made any commitments. You aren't scared of commitment; you're just in love with Miranda."

"I'll be fine. You need to stop worrying."

Frustration laced her tone. "I know I'm right, but whatever. I have something more important I want to talk about." A beat of silence passed before her tone shifted. "Are you sitting down?"

"Yeah?"

She gathered a deep breath. "Is there any chance that little boy is yours?"

She was only doing the mental math I did myself. Still, the idea pulled the air from the room, making it hard to breathe. "No, I've already thought it through. It doesn't time out." I rushed to add, "Plus, she would've told me. Also he looks nothing like me."

"He does look like you."

"No. He's the spitting image of Miranda!"

"True, but it's minor things. The shape of his head and his shoulders. The way he walks. His lips are like yours, too."

"I don't see it." I shook my head. "And the timing's all wrong. He's recently three."

"Did she say that?"

"Yes, his birthday is in March."

"I think she's lying."

"Miranda wouldn't lie."

"Well, maybe she would!" She murmured to Pat in the background and I heard a door open and close. "Sorry, I stepped outside onto the deck for a minute. I worked in special education, Jack. I'm pretty familiar with childhood milestones, fine motor skills, and normal growth patterns. He seems big to me. I wish I could've heard him talk some more. That would've helped. Is he using a lot of words?"

My stomach twisted. "Yeah."

"Like what?"

"I mean, I haven't memorized his vocabulary, but you can have a conversation with him and he speaks in full sentences."

She hummed. "I have my doubts, Jack."

My wheels turned.

"Your divorce was final in what?"

"January four years ago."

"But you guys had been separated since I think... November maybe?" She continued working the details around. "If the last time you were together was November that would make him pretty close to four already—hmm." She made a frustrated noise. "He doesn't seem quite that old."

Miranda threw the flowers out the window and left me a few days after that Thanksgiving. It was when we separated but it *wasn't* our last time together. Our last time was a memory I revisited almost daily. Didn't really want to share it with my sister though.

She went on and on, verbally processing through different timelines and theories. Driving me crazy, honestly.

"Sis. Stop."

"What?"

I sighed. "Our last time together wasn't that November."

Then

I drained the last beer while I sat on the front porch. It was Friday night, biting cold. Felt good for some reason. I came to dread nights off. I was never much of a drinker, but the last couple months, something about beer hit just right.

I told myself I liked the taste. But if I was being honest, I liked the numbing effects. Pretending life wasn't so bad for a couple hours was kind of nice.

Just when I was about to go inside, a car pulled into the driveway. Miranda's Corolla. I hadn't seen her in weeks. Our sole communication had been through an attorney. It made no sense for her to be here. The divorce would be final in mere days.

The flutter in my chest was stupidity. Excitement was completely inappropriate. But I smoothed my hair and walked to the porch steps. A foolish surge of hope rippled through my body.

I'd left the porch lights off when I came out. I cleared my throat so she wouldn't be startled. "What are you doing here?"

She didn't look up as she climbed. "I forgot a box of my stuff in the spare room."

The nearest streetlamp was across the way, providing just enough light to see her. Miranda was like an angel ascending the steps. Her soft, blonde hair tied into a sloppy bun at the top of her head, with tiny wisps brushing the skin of her neck. Despite the early cold of January, she was coatless and only wore skinny jeans and a long sleeve shirt with a scooped neckline. It was *well* fitted, allowing for a generous tease of her body in multiple places.

The goddess in front of me was still my wife.

I cleared my throat again for entirely different reasons. "What stuff?"

"Old crap. Like letters, papers, and junk. I can't find my social security card, old letters from Tag, and a few other things. You mind?"

I motioned toward the front door. "Go right ahead."

She proceeded into the spare bedroom and jerked open the closet doors. Only two boxes there. Neither held the desired items. I followed her around as she searched every closet in the house. I couldn't keep my eyes off her. That shirt was…and she knew it. The longer we searched, the more convinced I was she came dressed like that on purpose. Like she wanted to torment me. Like she wanted me to haul her off to the bedroom.

"We'll have to search the attic." She stormed into the hallway and reached for the ladder string she couldn't reach. She looked at me, arching an eyebrow, arm stretched upward.

"It's not up there."

"How do you know?"

"Because you can't get up there without my help. And I haven't opened this attic door in…"

"Just open it!" She stamped her foot in frustration, her blonde brows furrowing.

I pulled the string, guiding the creaky ladder steps to the floor. Did my best to fight my smile back. Bossy and angry Miranda was…extremely sexy. But I always pissed her off when I enjoyed it too much.

Her tough expression faltered as our gazes tangled. She tried to look strong, hold her chin high, but I saw. She was one poke away from crumbling. One touch away from falling into my arms. Why she was insisting on a divorce would remain a mystery to me. I waved her on. "After you."

Up we went. We rifled through boxes for a long time. When the last one had been checked, I sat on a random old chair. "I think this box is a figment of your imagination."

She shivered. My insides were so tight. I couldn't be around her and not feel her presence—be aware of her every move, every sigh. It took all my power not to ogle her and to allow her some personal space.

She plopped down on a plastic tub. "Yeah, me too."

When our gazes tangled again, I thought I'd see anger and coldness in her expression, but I didn't. Her big brown eyes looked sad and lonely. Mirrors of everything I felt, too. She chewed her lip, shifting uncomfortably. "Thanks for helping me look."

"No problem."

We made our way down the ladder and back out to the porch. My heart plummeted. I did not want her to go. Anything but that. I took a few deep gulps of the night air, my trachea burning with the deep cold, searching for my bearings.

She hung her thumbs on the back pockets of her jeans. "I guess I'll get out of your hair."

Barely scraped out a response. "Okay."

But she didn't leave. She stood there.

"What's wrong?"

"Nothing." She waved me off with a hand and turned toward the stairs.

I reached out and grabbed her elbow. "That look isn't nothing." I searched her face in the moonlight. "Was there something else you wanted?"

I wanted *her*. In every way.

A long pause followed. She was thinking hard—her twisting lips and furrowed eyebrows were the dead giveaway. When she spoke, the words, laced with emotion, were barely a whisper. "I wanted to tell you I'm moving to Ohio. Trisha lives there now and has a place for me."

The statement knocked the wind out of me. If meeting with an attorney didn't feel final enough, Ohio certainly did. I tugged her closer. My voice was pained as I swallowed the emotions pressurizing in my chest. "Please don't do that."

She shrugged, struggling to hold her own emotions in check. "I need a change. Need to leave Nashville for a while."

"Please." I lifted my hand to move a strand of hair off her face. She drew a sharp breath when my fingers brushed her cheek. Shivered violently again. "What can I do to convince you to stay?"

"Nothing." She caught my hand in her own and held it against her freezing cheek. "I'm so sorry, Jack."

I hadn't touched my wife in months. To say I missed her would be the understatement of a lifetime. Yearning was more like it. Not just physically. She was the perfect companion in every way. Separation was a constant wound.

Miranda's touch affected me right down to my toes. It was

always that way with her. Our love was explosive right from the start.

"Miranda," I whispered back. "I miss you so much."

I ran my fingers down the slope of her neck, and she tilted her face up to mine.

"Come back inside. We can talk for a while. You don't even have a coat on."

"I—I forgot it."

"Come in. Please."

"I shouldn't." Her palms flattened across my chest like she was going to push me away. But she didn't.

"None of this has to be final."

"I—"

"We still love each other."

She shook her head, averting her eyes.

I held her chin steady with my hand. "Look at me, Miranda."

She did.

"Look me in the eyes and tell me you don't love me."

"Jack—" She stifled a sob. "I do love you. So much, but—"

"Don't go then."

"—but sometimes that's not enough."

Even as she said the words, her gaze fell to my lips. That simple act of wanting was all the permission I needed. I laced my fingers into the hair behind her ears, cupping her head and neck with my hands. Her eyes fluttered closed and her fingers flexed into my shirt. Her breathing became ragged.

I whispered, "Please stay."

Her hands slipped around the back of my neck.

Our lips crashed together. Hers were freezing against mine. I meant to only kiss her.

But she kissed me back, intense and provoking. Her lips quickly warming as I encouraged blood to flow into them. The kiss was angry and hurt. But the building heat and suppressed desire were undeniable, unavoidable. She opened her mouth and tensed her arms around my neck, allowing me to lift her. When her legs locked around my torso, our fate was sealed.

We collided. Eager mouths, starving bodies, and bleeding hearts.

I awoke the next morning holding Miranda under the sheets. Assuming she was still asleep, I snuggled in behind her, careful not to shake the bed. I drank in her smell, and my hand meandered up and down her smooth side.

In my deluded sleepy haze, I figured our night together meant something. Surely, she knew it wasn't too late. We could turn back. We could cancel everything and work out whatever was between us. We were better together. A perfect match in every way. Meant to be from the start.

As the late morning sun peeked through the blinds, I convinced myself she would wake up and agree with me. That we'd drive over to her friend's house, pack up her stuff, and bring her home. That she'd wake up and want me again.

After a long time holding her, I leaned forward to brush my lips against the top of her shoulder. She stirred.

"Jack?" Her raspy morning voice was beautiful. One of my favorite sounds.

"I'm right here." I tightened my hold around her waist, nestling in and allowing my lips to find her skin again.

But she bristled.

"What's wrong?"

Her shoulders fell with a long sigh. "I'm so stupid."

My heart dropped.

"I shouldn't have come last night. We're getting divorced, Jack."

How could she still want that? "We don't have to follow

through with any of those plans. Nothing has changed for me. I want to be together."

She said nothing.

"We can talk. Figure out what's between us. Fix it and move forward—"

She sat up on the bed, swung her legs over the side, and faced the wall. The clock ticked as a long moment of silence passed. Finally, she ran her fingers through her hair and tucked her arms over her bare chest. When she turned to look at me, her brown eyes were brimming with tears. Her lip trembled, and her forehead creased with hurt. "How can you possibly say that?"

She reached for my t-shirt and slipped it on. It was a dress on her.

"Figure out what's between us?" She shook her head and tears escaped down her cheeks. "Jack, how do you not know what's between us? After all this time?"

I opened my mouth to speak, but the words didn't come.

A soft noise escaped her throat and the tears freely flowed. "We've lost so much, Jack. So much. But you don't care about any of it. First Cameron then—"

"You always say that! I do care! I care a lot." I sat up, facing her.

"No, you say, 'loss is a part of life,' like I should just forget them. You've told me verbatim 'we have to move on, Miranda.'" She stood as the memory fueled her tears. They turned angry, her face menacing and her words clipped. "I can't and I won't move on. And *that's* what's between us, Jackson Barkley."

"I've never asked you to move on."

She laughed in disbelief as her jaw dropped. "What planet are you living on?" She stepped into her lacey undergarments and gathered her clothes from around the room. "We might be great together in every other way, but this right here is why we can't go the distance. You refuse to see, Jack! You refuse to acknowledge how you have hurt me." Her voice broke with a sob and she turned away.

And in that moment, I knew. The final nail drove into our coffin. All my hopes for reconciliation spun down the drain. Was I broken or something? I had to admit she was right. We had talked and I apologized for the stuff she said I did. But I didn't see. I did not see how those things broke us. How those hurts snowballed into this moment.

When she replaced her clothes from the night before, she said, "I'm sorry I came. This was a huge mistake. I don't know what I was thinking." She plucked her shoes from the floor and said as she walked out. "Please don't call me."

But it was Miranda who couldn't hold up to that demand. Day after day *she* called *me*. And texted me. And constantly touched base until I blocked her number two months later. It pained me to do it, but I couldn't handle the off and on communication. I couldn't handle hearing about her new life in Ohio. It kept me up and sent me into a rage on more than one occasion. I couldn't move on with the lines still open.

It drove me mad because I *loved* her.

I didn't want to be a friend. An old pal. A confidant. Or a texting buddy. I wanted to be her *husband*. Nothing—*absolutely nothing*—less.

Every time I heard her voice proved how much she loved me too.

I wanted Miranda totally. It could only be all or nothing.

So it was nothing.

"Jack, what? Tell me!"

I sighed. "We hooked up right before the divorce."

"What?" Jules shrieked into the phone. "I cannot believe you! Who does that?"

"Come on, it's not like we planned it. And we were still married for crying out loud." I ran a hand over my face, wondering what mess I got myself into.

"I am in total shock." She took a deep breath. "Like, wow."

I sighed.

"Okay, so let's do this math. If your last shenanigans with Miranda was in January sometime, that would mean the kid—"

"Kacey."

"—if he's yours, was born around September. That's assuming Miranda had a normal pregnancy and carried him to term."

Normal pregnancy? The possibility felt foreign.

"And that would put Kacey at three years and eight months or so, which makes more sense to me."

"More sense? Does seven—eight months make a huge difference?"

"In three year olds? It does!"

I shook my head. The need to defend and deny coursed through my veins. "There is absolutely no way Miranda wouldn't have told me. We got divorced, but she would never keep my son from me."

Right?

"Plus, Jules, kids are all so different. Maybe he's advanced for his age or just a big kid."

"That's true so it's possible. But let's say his birthday really is end of March like she claims..." Jules counted under her breath. "Was she already with someone so soon?"

"No, she said it was a one night mistake."

"So, sleeping around?"

"Yeah—yeah, I guess." I hated that possibility too.

"People who aren't in a good place emotionally can make bad decisions. I know better than most. When did she get with the psycho guy?" Jules reminded me of Nancy Drew and fighting the temptation to hang up on her made my jaw ache.

"I don't actually know."

I didn't like the way any of this looked. Either she was keeping my son from me, she played the field pretty quickly after our divorce, or Kacey was Chris' son. She vehemently denied Kacey was Chris', but maybe she was lying? The idea Miranda and Kacey could be permanently tied to that abusive piece of garbage was plausible. My fists clenched. Fierce protectiveness quickened my breathing. I'd take any explanation over that one.

Jules continued. "Look, I'm not going to tell you what to do or think. But, as your sister, I'm letting you know...something feels off about Kacey." She took a deep breath. "You are the most intuitive and observant person I know. But you're blind here because you want to believe the best about Miranda. The Miranda we used to know would never do anything crappy or spiteful, but situations aren't always what they seem. And life has a funny way of changing people. For the better or for the worse."

I said nothing.

"You there?"

I sighed. My swallow was painful and my lungs couldn't fully expand. "I'm—I'm here."

"I made you sad." Her words were soft and apologetic.

"No, no. You didn't."

"What's wrong?"

So many things. Jules and I had hit a couple rough patches

in our adult life. But we recently promised to be honest with each other. Which was difficult for both of us. In order to be honest with each other, it meant being honest with ourselves first.

The truth squeezed out of my tight throat. "I do—I do care about her, Jules."

"Aw, Jack." Emotion swelled in her voice.

"You're going to worry about me now I've admitted it."

"You didn't have to admit it. I knew."

"Maybe I should be angry at her, but when I saw the bruise, and the way she kept looking over her shoulder…"

Jules sniffed.

"I wanted to do whatever was necessary to make sure the two of them were safe. But I feel like a big idiot now. Maybe I should've left it alone. She's made her choices."

"No." Jules' voice wobbled. "There's nothing wrong with loving her, Jack."

Despite our history, nothing had changed for me. I'd been in love with her since the apple crisp. Felt good to admit it.

"I'm being cautious because I love you. I want you to have your eyes wide open and know this might not end the way you want it to." She gave a mirthless laugh. "You want to hear what Pat said, though?"

Between the three of us, Pat was the Sage. We both knew he was right a grand majority of the time. "Definitely."

"He said this was your second chance, and he'd lose respect if you didn't capitalize."

TWENTY

Miranda

I sucked down a glass of water like the earth might be running out. I let it thunk on the counter in front of me and swiped at my cheeks with the back of my shaking hand. I pressed the glass against the lever on the fridge and a spew of water filled the night's silence once more.

Until I heard a door open. Jack's.

I rolled my eyes, sniffing hard. He had just made an appearance in my nightmares as my opponent in a courtroom, fighting for my son. And now, he was strolling into my moment of peace. I needed a second to regain my composure. Not strike up conversation.

"You okay?"

I didn't turn to look. Just answered quietly. "Yeah."

"Couldn't sleep?"

"Nightmare."

"That sucks."

I nodded. "Sorry I woke you."

"You didn't. I was up."

I took a swallow of water, really wanting him to go away. The past few days had been the weirdest of my life. Didn't need his presence in the wee hours to complete my twenty-four hour cycle of regret and confusion.

I glanced his direction and wished I hadn't. He was shirtless and his body was as solid as it had always been.

"Do you want to talk about it at all?" He moved to get his own glass from the cabinet.

"No."

But I did. So badly I did. I wanted to ask him if he remembered the day I came back to Nashville. Ask why he turned the two of us away. Ask how this all could've happened. I had been willing to come back and try. To make it work for our child.

It was *Jack* who said no.

But I couldn't ask those questions now. What if Jack got angry with me and called off our arrangement? What if he *truly* didn't remember for some reason and thought I'd hidden Kacey from him all these years? Any normal person would be angry and upset. Any admirable man would fight for his son.

Jack was certainly admirable. He had his flaws. But none a court would take very seriously.

My eyes filled with tears again as my brain replayed the stupid dream. For the first time ever, I was on the brink of being able to support my son *on my own*. All because of Nathaniel.

I couldn't talk to Jack now. I'd try to wait. Keep my distance until I could provide a stable living for Kacey. Then we'd talk. Then, if Jack took me to court, I'd be prepared.

"Jack?" My voice sounded hoarse.

"Yeah." He leaned against the opposite counter top, fully facing me.

I averted my eyes from him.

"Do I—seem unstable?"

"Hm." He thought for a moment then spoke slowly. "Unstable, no. But really hurt and afraid, yes."

I nodded, emotions choking off my response.

He rushed to add, "And you have every reason to feel that way."

Jack thought I was thinking about Chris. If only it were so simple.

I quickly glanced at him. Darkness shrouded his face, but he was watching me. The heat of his gaze caused my cheeks to burn.

"Can I ask you something?"

I bristled. "Uh, sure."

"How long were you with your ex?"

A humorless, bitter chuckle escaped my lips—fueled by disbelief at myself. "Almost four long years."

"But Chris isn't Kacey's dad?"

He was starting to wonder and it made the breath in my lungs freeze. I squeezed out, "No."

"Why were you with him so long?"

"Necessity I guess." The most basic of answers.

"Did—did he hurt you often?"

My fingers picked at a loose thread on my pajama bottoms. "No, that was his first time hitting me."

His low voice was throaty. "There are lots of ways for a man to hurt a woman, Miranda."

He didn't have to say more. I knew what he meant.

A need to defend my honor propelled my answer. "It takes two."

"Not always."

"I consented."

"Coercion isn't consent."

"Why are you assuming I was coerced?"

He said nothing for a moment and ran a hand over his head. When he responded, the edge in his voice gave me chills. "Because I'm having a really hard time believing you ran out and fell in love again so soon."

His words squeezed the air out of me. Of course it looked that way. Not like *he* was one to talk though. I knew for a fact he shacked up just as quickly. Anger surged through my veins as I remembered her. Tall, long-legged, auburn hair, and dark eyes. Gorgeous. She had opened Jack's front door wearing *his* t-shirt.

My breathing grew labored at the horrible memory. It had crushed me. "Oh puh-lease. Don't act like you didn't test drive other women that fast."

He was taken aback. "Miranda..." He shook his head. "I didn't."

I wanted to rip him a new one for lying. But every moment I spent in Jack's home was acting out a lie—and my lie was *so* much worse.

"Why are we out here"—I glanced at the digital clock glowing from the oven—"at 2 a.m. talking about my sex life?"

"Sorry," he growled.

Adrenaline scorched my veins. Anger peaked. I wasn't sure if I was angry at Chris for manipulating me into intimacy so many times, angry at myself for letting him, or angry at Jack for sniffing it out and acting like a saint when I *knew* he wasn't.

"I need to get to bed."

I stood to go and he grabbed my forearm. "Wait."

When I stopped, his hand slid to mine, grasping my fingers.

"I'm sorry, Miranda." His thumb glided over my knuckles. "That was way too personal. I'm just—working through a lot of questions I guess." He gave my hand a soft squeeze.

"It was too personal. Thanks for apologizing."

His hand dropped to his lap. "Okay, well, goodnight."

On my way up the stairs, I noticed my sweatshirt was gone. I left it in the same spot every night. And each morning, I slipped it on, even if I wasn't cold. The renewed Jack smell on it was enough to get me out of bed each morning. He could lie till he was blue in the face. But I knew the truth. He was taking it to bed with him each night. Doing exactly what I was doing each morning.

The fact it was missing now proved it.

I should discontinue the game. It was silly.

I really should wash it.

I snuck downstairs as late as possible. I put off taking Kacey down for breakfast because I was still trying to recover from the embarrassing conversation last night. He was starting to ask questions and I needed to avoid confrontation until I decided how to handle the answers.

But by the time my head thumped with the need for caffeine, Kacey was whining for cereal. Today was Jack's last day off. Part of me was glad to see him go to work. Kacey and I would have a little more free rein of the house, and I'd be less anxious every moment of my existence.

Jack's house was nice. Two bedrooms, a spare upstairs, the master downstairs. The furnishings were basic, which didn't surprise me. Jack, like the total neat freak he was, kept the place as neat as a pin. I did my best to clean up after Kacey so we didn't disturb the aura too much.

I poured Kacey a bowl of cereal and myself a cup of leftover coffee from the carafe. The light had clicked off, but the joe was still hot-ish. Jack probably had his cup over two hours ago. I doubted he had creamer, but I peeked in the fridge anyway.

Front and center sat a Cinnabon creamer. A flavor so ridiculous and extra.

He must've put that on the grocery order.

Why were tears coming to my eyes?

I blinked hard a few times as I added the creamer to my cup. Right as Kacey and I sat down at the table, the front door opened.

A sweaty Jack walked in, still panting from a run.

Good gracious.

I swallowed a hot gulp a bit fast. Stared straight into the cup.

I glanced back at him. Just in time to see his perfect smile as he said, "Good morning." His hair was mussed from the exercise, the long sleeve spandex shirt pulling tight across his chest. A slight dark shadow graced his jaw.

Can't say it was only the bad dream keeping me awake. I'd thought about his shirtless chest until I worked myself into a tizzy. I didn't know how I could be so angry at him, so afraid of what he might do, and yet still so drawn to him. It made no sense.

My confusion wasn't my own fault. Jackson Barkley was just far too handsome for his own good. It's a wonder there wasn't a line of ladies at his front door. The fact he stayed uncommitted for the past four years was beyond me. Something told me there were probably some broken hearts involved. Like Miss Long Legs.

Even as I chided myself for admiring him, Jack stopped at Kacey's seat and said, "Kacey, I hope you're saving some of that for me."

Kacey giggled. "No. I gonna eat it allll."

The slow melt of my heart and pull of a smile was impossible to prevent. The simultaneous twinge in my gut and burn in my eyes was too.

Jack made a silly frowny face, and Kacey giggled some more.

He finally looked to me on his way into the kitchen. My pulse doubled. "Did you get back to sleep alright?"

"Took me a while. You?"

"Same." He filled a glass of ice water at the fridge.

My imagination ran. Was he up thinking of me?

Stop, Miranda.

I cleared my throat. "Uhm, the creamer is amazing."

His lips tilted into a tiny smile as he dropped into the chair next to mine.

"Thank you—for remembering such a small thing."

He met my gaze. His deep blue drew me in, a sparkle dancing in them. His throat bobbed with a swallow. "There's not much I've forgotten about you, Miranda."

The breath in my lungs froze.

What was that supposed to mean?

I didn't have the chance to respond. He ran his hands over his head. "I need to apologize for being so nosy last night. I'm not sure what I expected. You don't owe me any explanations."

I nodded like I agreed. But I didn't. I owed him lots of explanations.

"It's no big deal." I waved a hand.

"It is a big deal. I want you to be able to trust me, and me trying to pry information out of you to satisfy my curiosity is crossing a line."

"I—I really appreciate that."

And it was obvious he appreciated *me*. His eyes left my face and worked downward, lingering a few moments on several places. And it wasn't the first time he openly checked me out. When he met my gaze again, he arched a dark eyebrow. Like he meant for me to see. Meant to make me squirm.

Warmth spread through me as my imagination started misfiring. Did Jack like what I was wearing? I'd pulled on a pair of skinny jeans and pink tank with an unbuttoned chambray shirt over the top to keep myself warm in his freezing house. The idea I might be a tease to him was oddly satisfying. Kind of wanted to drive him crazy.

Why, Miranda? That's horrible.

I shifted, changing the topic. "So, how far did you go?"

"About six." He said it like running six miles was a walk in the park. He asked, "Do you have plans today?"

"Uh, well, I think I'm going to look for a job."

He raised his eyebrows. "You know you don't have to do that."

"Of course I do! Why wouldn't I need to provide financially for my *son*?"

He held his hands up in surrender. "You're right. Sorry. What type of job?"

"Something I can do here. Answer calls. Virtual assistant. Something like that."

"That's a great idea." He stood, kicked his tennis shoes off, and picked them up. "Is it going to take you all day?"

"No, I'm just researching some ideas at this point."

"Good! Because today we are going to make sure you remember how to shoot a gun—"

"Jack! No."

"I'm going back to work tomorrow. Have to know you'll be okay here by yourself."

"A gun seems like overkill."

"It's absolutely not overkill. Thought we could go to the

mall and make a fun day of it. We'll hit up the family-friendly range that's just outside of Nashville."

When I opened my mouth to protest, he said, "Kacey, do you want to go to the mall?" Jack eyed me, knowing full well he just won.

Kacey squealed.

TWENTY-ONE

Then

Jack

We were finally together again. Huddled in a tree stand, waiting for the big one.

Our first date had been one for the books and I thought of Miranda constantly since the moment it ended. I mentally cursed the weird hours I worked that kept us from seeing each other again. But, at last, we found a time that coincided with our busy schedules. Granted, I should've been sleeping. But it was an easy sacrifice to make.

Since it was the start of open season, Miranda wanted to go hunting on a friend's property. Her cousin took her hunting lots of times and she called herself a "pro." Made all the legal arrangements, got supplies, and everything.

I lied and told her I'd never gone before.

We sat in a deer stand, whispering in the crisp early morning. She had all the garb. Looked like a tree trunk with a smear of orange spray paint. Cute as can be. I, on the other hand, wore something dark green and a brown jacket. She said it was fine.

For the first two hours, nothing happened. We just sat, whispered, and sipped coffee.

I leaned back on our bag. "This is kind of nice."

She frowned. "You're supposed to be watching."

Trust me. I'm watching.

"I am."

She squinted at me, reading my expression. A smile warred against her fake frown. "Not watching me. Watching for deer."

"Oh. Sorry."

She giggled into her hand. "You have to stop making me laugh. I am not a quiet laugher."

"I've gathered."

She set her thermos down and blew into her hands.

"Cold?"

"A little."

I reached out, heart thumping, and grabbed her hand. First time I'd openly touched her, minus the hug she gave me that morning. Her hand was receptive, curling around mine. I tugged her a little closer to me. "I can keep you warm."

She laughed. "Jack, you are worthless when it comes to hunting."

"I'll be your personal heater then."

She pressed her lips together, her big dimples shining in all their glory. "Okay, fine."

I put an arm around her. She scooted in. Her tiny body pressed against my side was perfection. Complete perfection. Her hair smelled so sweet. Yep. I was useless—that was the honest truth. There was far too much to pay attention to right here in the tree stand.

We fell silent as we watched through the trees.

As the sun was lighting up the field, a few deer stepped into the clearing.

"Jack! Look!"

We both sat up and grabbed our rifles.

She shook my arm and hissed, "A buck! There's a buck!"

I looked through the scope, counting. "Ten point."

She elbowed me. "You take the shot."

I looked through the scope again and swallowed. My aim was good. I would take him down if I pulled the trigger. My finger rested, held back by some invisible force. My pulse kicked into overdrive. My view through the scope wavered. I tightened my grip to steady my aim.

Take the shot, son.

I hesitated, clenching my teeth through the adrenaline surge.

Thirteen years had proved that I still found hunting undesirable. Guess most people thought when they saw a big guy like me that I enjoyed shooting and killing things or blowing crap up.

I didn't. Not in the slightest.

Through the scope, I saw magnificence. A life I wanted to protect. Not something I wanted on my wall. If my family was starving for food that would be different. For sport felt barbaric.

I took a deep breath, humiliation seeping through my veins. Felt my throat constricting and prayed she didn't see the heat washing over my face.

I'm a cop for crying out loud.

"Come on. He's going to get away."

My finger twitched.

Take the shot, son.

Against the internal voices shouting at me, I lowered the rifle. Miranda frowned in confusion, her eyes searching mine.

"What's wrong?"

I shook my head, angry at myself. "I'm an idiot."

"Why do you say that?"

"I lied to you." I sighed. "I've been hunting before."

"Oh."

"I went when I was ten. We were invited by one of dad's attorney friends for a father-son hunting weekend, and I embarrassed my dad."

Her shoulders fell. "What happened?"

"There were two other dads and two boys about my age. I was the only one who'd never gone before. So when the first opportunity came, they urged me to do the honors." I kept my gaze on the field, not wanting to look her in the eye. "Couldn't take the shot."

"Were you afraid?"

"Yes and no. I knew how to shoot a gun, so it wasn't that. I didn't want to kill it. The death is what scared me. My mom died the year before. Maybe that's why. And then knowing something so beautiful would be killed for fun." I shrugged, the explanation sounding stupid to my own ears. "My dad was pissed. He cold-shouldered me the rest of the day and when we were out of ear-shot, he let me have it."

She reached out and touched my forearm. "You were only ten. That's not fair."

"Well, I'm twenty-three now and apparently not much has changed."

Her fingers tightened around my arm.

The buck meandered toward the edge of the clearing.

"When I blew off college to go to the police academy, he laughed at me and brought up the hunting trip. Said I didn't even have the balls to shoot an animal."

I glanced at Miranda. Her eyes were teary, unmoving from my face.

"But by then he was bitter for all sorts of reasons. Mainly because I screwed up his dreams of my becoming a defense attorney like him. I didn't want to be anything like him, so I picked law enforcement. It sent him over the edge to say the least. He brought the hunting thing up to make me feel pathetic. He was a pro at that."

Miranda's fingers slid down the palm of my hand and intertwined with mine. "That's terrible, Jack."

"It's not a big deal."

She frowned and her bottom lip poked out a smidge. It was the thousandth time I wondered what that bottom lip might taste like.

"Did you even want to be a police officer?"

I thought for a few seconds. "I don't really know. I'm glad I am one, but I can't say my reasons were only for the greater good."

She let that soak in.

A beat of awkward silence fell between us. I laughed, trying to lighten the mood. "I'm oversharing. Sorry."

"There's no such thing here. Always overshare with me."

Her round brown eyes were misty. No one in my entire life had invited me to speak openly and responded well when I did.

It sent my heart into a free fall. Fast and hard. No brakes to slow the descent. No pads to soften the blow. My heart was hers. I was all in from that moment on.

She squeezed my hand.

When I glanced back at the field, the buck was gone.

"Miranda, I'm sorry. I ruined your hunt."

"No, you didn't."

"You probably regret bringing me."

She laughed then. Full on. Not trying to stay quiet.

She leaned in, a sultry look in her eyes.

"The *only* thing I regret is telling you I don't kiss on first dates."

I swallowed hard. "You regret that, huh?"

"Most definitely."

She slid her hand up and over the ridge of my shoulder. My breathing quickened. I whispered, "We can fix it."

"I hope so." Her gaze was on my lips like mine was on hers. Sweet, pink, full. Framed by porcelain cheeks and dimples.

The breathlessness in my voice surprised me. It's not like Miranda was my first kiss ever. "Do you—kiss on second dates?"

She nodded, wetting her lips.

Her chest heaved. My hands slipped around her neck, thumbs caressing her face. When her lips meshed against mine, we got lost.

She owned me. Heart, mind, body, and soul.

When we left the tree stand, the sun had warmed the November morning and the cold dew was long gone.

TWENTY-TWO

Jack

I plunged a corkscrew into the wine bottle, twisting it deep. Soft voices wafted from upstairs and the bath water was running. Kacey whined occasionally. Miranda agreed to come back down after she got him tucked in. Hence the wine. My body practically hummed with anticipation.

I should've been tired. That phone call with Jules kept me up all night.

I stared at the spinning fan until the wee hours of the morning as I considered every possible angle on the Kacey situation. My conclusion was this: Kacey *couldn't* be mine.

Miranda and I had sour history, sure, but she never would've kept my son from me. I had to assume what she said was true—Kacey was the product of a hook-up. As sad as it made me, it was easier to swallow than the other two possibilities. And grasping onto the easiest explanation was the only way I was able to embrace a wink of sleep.

Miranda never had big goals or ambitions. She was happy

with normal things. Wasn't pursuing a career or chasing dreams. She just wanted to be a mom, have a family. She liked things like reading novels and going on walks. Enjoyed being outdoors. Baking and having get-togethers. She even talked about homeschooling one day. Miranda's goal in life was *togetherness*. It was one of the things I loved about her.

And it was something I was happy to provide.

But we tried. Again and again we tried. And every time we lost a baby, I lost a piece of my wife, too.

It's why Kacey's existence stung. How could a one night stand give her the one thing we both wanted?

If I was the man I should be, I'd be happy for Miranda. But I wasn't ever what I ought to be. The sting of jealousy crept in, no matter how hard I tried to fight it. She left me all those years ago, made terrible choices, and now here I was helping her. I wanted to be the one to make things right for Miranda. And Kacey. Despite the conflict raging in me, I would give her anything. She could take everything I had.

I didn't know if that made me a stupid idiot or a fool in love. "In love" sounded *crazy*, but I didn't know what else to call it.

Watching her enjoy her creamer and meandering around the mall together solidified my second conclusion: I was a fool.

Through and through a fool.

As much as I hated to admit it, Jules was right. I was going to get my heart trampled in the worst possible way if this all ended the way we agreed it would. It would kill me to sign papers a second time.

Every moment I spent with Miranda made "in love" sound less psychotic. There were endless things to love about her. She could turn the most anxious expression into a blooming smile when Kacey called for her. She could go from chewing her finger nails to singing the "Itsy Bitsy Spider" in two seconds flat. Her commitment to him was—straight up hot, to be honest. Maybe one of the most selfless displays I ever witnessed.

Speaking of hot, I also forced her to buy a holster at the outdoor store for one of my 9 mms. She picked one that would cradle the gun right below her left breast. Like a true glutton for torture, I watched her try it on over her pink fitted tank top. The young guy selling them was watching too, which made me want to tear his face off.

She was absolutely oblivious to how sexy she was—yet another thing to adore.

When we visited the shooting range, I was disappointed to learn that Miranda hadn't forgotten a thing about guns. Meaning, she didn't need my help or any refreshers. Meaning, I wasn't able to get as handsy as I would've liked.

But whenever I could, I placed a gentle hand on her back, her arm, her side. Anywhere and anytime I got a subtle chance. Accelerating toward the brink of insanity with every touch.

And Kacey was a really sweet kid. I lifted him up onto the rocks at the edge of the big tank at outdoor store, and we looked at fish for fifteen minutes. He talked my ear off then cried when we had to leave. He felt better when I offered to let him ride on my shoulders.

I pretended to bump into the walls and display tables until he laughed so hard I was afraid he might puke on me. But Miranda laughed, too. A sound I would gladly take some puke for.

We got dinner out and let Kacey run at the restaurant's playground. He scarfed down nuggets and waffle fries and scampered off. Miranda ate three nuggets, and had half a medium fry. It was more than I'd seen her eat before...but still not enough.

When we left, Miranda had to sit in the backseat of the

truck and sing songs with Kacey to keep him awake for bath and bedtime. He told us about ten times it was the best day he ever had. Which made me laugh. But made Miranda cry.

As they sang, I stewed. Tried to figure out how I could get her to eat more. She wasn't getting enough and never looked relaxed while she ate. When she was tucking Kacey into bed, it dawned on me. I fished the bottle of red wine from the kitchen cabinet and pulled the cork.

It took a little convincing, but she agreed to stay downstairs and watch Food Network with me. It almost felt like old times, and I was delighted. It was a habit we started while dating. We both loved food so much, it just made sense.

A niggle of conscience pricked me as she settled on the couch a few cushions down. I wanted to pretend we were something we weren't—a family. Me, Miranda, Kacey. Three mere days under my roof and I was smitten.

I am a fool.

After she tucked a blanket around her legs, I handed her a glass of red wine.

She frowned, not moving to take it. "What's this for?"

"I have a hunch."

"Which is..."

"That it's anxiety keeping you from eating. You hold your stomach like it hurts. So, I thought maybe a little nudge toward relaxation would help you eat more than three bites at a time."

She blinked, staring at the cup.

I swirled it in my hand. "Do you not like merlot anymore or something?"

"I do—it's just been a long time."

"Sip slow then."

She took the glass, examining it. "So—you think this will help me eat?"

I lifted a shoulder. "It's worth a shot."

We turned our attention to the TV. Despite her efforts to keep it on the down low, I sensed her crying. A few shuddering breaths were a dead giveaway. A twinge of guilt settled in my midsection. I didn't mean to make her cry. Almost apologized a few times, but decided against it.

Twenty minutes into our show, she set her empty glass on the coffee table; her head tilted back onto the couch.

"So what's the verdict? Feel like you can eat?"

"Yeah—I honestly do."

A smile spread across my face. It was exactly what I hoped for. I came back to the couch a few minutes later with some crackers and peanut butter, a Yoplait, and a banana.

"Jack." She pressed her lips together. "You're being too nice to me."

"Good. It's about time someone was nice to you."

"But this"—she waved at the small offering before her—"this is too much."

"It's processed snacks."

"It's more than that." She shook her head. "I don't deserve all this."

Surely, the beautiful woman in my living room did not think she deserved whatever that world class piece of dirt was giving her.

I brought my knee up to the cushion, facing her. "You deserve a lot more. Eat."

She dutifully grabbed a cracker. We sat back and watched a head chef cuss out participants in a cooking competition. She quietly laughed a few times. I could hardly focus. My brain was preoccupied with her every move, every bite.

Pride and possessiveness unfurled in me. My plan worked. She ate the whole time. Every crumb.

Then she curled into a tiny ball and fell fast asleep.

I flipped the TV off, shamelessly scooting toward her. I stopped a couple inches away and watched. My heart was coming out of my chest. The bruise on her face looked better by the day. But each time I saw it, it reminded me how much I cared about her. How I never stopped caring.

The warmth radiating from her sent a tremor through my body and shallowed my breathing. Disbelief swelled in me. How was I still this affected by Miranda?

I touched her shoulder to wake her, but changed course, allowing my hand to slide down her arm. My brain lost the privilege of commanding my arms and hands. They moved of their own volition, wrapping around Miranda's limp body and gently pulling her flush against my chest. I knew I woke her because she stiffened briefly then melted back, her hands finding a place over my forearms and squeezing.

She let me hold her and held me back.

Her sleepy hum made me draw a shaky breath.

My blood burned. I dropped my face to the top of her head. Kissed her hair and buried my nose into it. I shouldn't have, but I lingered there several minutes, breathing in her scent and relishing in the fact she wasn't pushing me away.

This was *way* better than the sweatshirt.

Need cropped up in me, until I felt like I was going to rip into a thousand pieces. I decided to test the waters. I moved my hands to her shoulders and gently twisted, leading her body around to *face* me. She turned and brought her knee up onto the couch between us. Her eyes, sleepy and hooded, met mine.

I whispered, my vocal chords taut. "Let me hold you."

Her nod, almost imperceptible, was permission enough. I slipped my arms around her back and pulled. She came. Soft and molding to my chest. Her head landed against my sternum. Instantly, it was not enough. We were sitting, leaning, with inches between us.

Because I loved torture, I pulled her legs over my lap, tightened my hold and scooted down to the recliner seat on the couch. I pulled the lever and leaned us back.

She sank into me. An arm draped over my torso. Her legs parallel with mine and her head still resting on my chest. I snaked my arms around her body. She hummed again as she cozied in, wiggling around to get comfortable.

"Jack?"

I said nothing, just waited.

"I was hungry. Thank you."

Those words sent a blend of feelings storming into my chest. Anger she'd ever known stress to such a degree. Relief my plan worked. And debilitating longing for so much more.

I reached up and tenderly ran my fingertips through her hair. Down her arm. Over her back. Anywhere she would let me while still remaining appropriate. Any rigidity left in her body dissolved as my palms rubbed tension away. We stayed like that for a good long while. Me massaging, her melting.

She was...falling back asleep?

I stilled, listening to her breath. It had deepened. I hadn't planned on sleeping here, but I wasn't going to be the one to make her move. I arched my back, slowly bringing the recliner down a few more inches, until it was completely flat.

I reached, grabbed my phone off the end table. Tapped on my alarm. I adjusted my arms, tugging her a little higher onto my chest so that her forehead was right under my chin.

Then I closed my eyes.

A gentle vibration woke me. I pulled my eyes open. Miranda was cuddled next to me. Cocooned between the arm of the couch and myself. She had her knees drawn up, a perfect little ball I had formed my body around. My big arm and one leg caged her in.

I reached over and tapped my alarm off. Never hated an early morning as much as I did right then. I lingered as long as I could, but when my third snooze alarm went off, I knew I had to get going.

I swiped her hair back. "Miranda?"

Tried again.

Her froggy morning voice was adorable. "Yeah."

"We need to get you into bed."

"What time is it?"

"Four-thirty."

"Crap." Miranda abruptly sat up, her ponytail flopping to the side and her face reddened with pressure scars. She stood, nearly stumbling into the coffee table. I grabbed her elbow to stabilize her.

"Careful."

She pushed a strand of hair out of her face. "Sorry I fell asleep last night."

"Don't say sorry."

She made her way around the couch and to the steps, hurrying—out of embarrassment I thought. On the third up from the bottom, she tripped, catching herself on the railing.

"You're going to break your neck." I caught up in a few quick steps, deciding to spare her the trouble of walking. Scooping her into my arms was as natural as coming home.

She gave me a drowsy swat. "Jack, I don't need help."

"Well, too bad."

Surprisingly, she didn't argue with me. Her arms slipped around my neck and she leaned in as I climbed the stairs. I pushed open her door and walked her to the side of the bed, wishing the walk was much longer. When I stooped to place her on the mattress, she squeezed my neck, causing me to falter a step. "Thank you, Jack." Her voice wobbled as she whispered in my ear. "For—for everything."

I didn't respond as she lifted the covers and climbed in.

Before I closed the door, I looked back. Two blonde heads snuggled close together. Little lumps under the covers. They had no place to call their own. No one watching out for them. Their only safety was each other.

Something behind my breastbone burned.

Knew it would be a long time before that image left my mind.

TWENTY-THREE

Miranda

Compared to Chris' tiny yard, Jack's was a paradise. By the time we came down for breakfast, Jack was long gone. So we had a quick bite and went out to explore. The backyard had a chain link fence and a few large maple trees rustled in the breeze.

The person who lived in this home prior to Jack must've put their fair share of time into the yard, because beautiful shrubs lined the back fence. Some of the branches needed to be clipped back. Jack admitted he did nothing in the yard besides mow.

An old swinging bench sat in the far corner by two raised garden beds. The beds grew grass and not much more. Kacey ran through them, and went to jump on the bench.

"Kacey, wait!"

He slowed up and looked back at me.

"We need to make sure that can hold you. It's probably very old."

We drew closer and tested its structure. Looked sturdy enough. I swiped my hand over the worn wood, green with pollen. When we carefully eased our weight onto it, the bench creaked, but rocked and held us up. I made a scared face as the wood groaned beneath us, and Kacey giggled. After that, we rummaged through the shed in the back. There wasn't much to see except for paint cans in the corner and two old garden rakes. I figured they belonged to the former owner.

As Kacey ran off to play, I sat on the bench again and pulled out my phone to restart a job search. But a peppy whistling jerked my attention into the neighbor's yard. An elderly man hobbled out his back door. He was tall, thin, and bent forward. A straw hat and overalls gave him a farmer-like appearance.

Being the social butterfly he was, Kacey ran up to the fence. He stuck his hand through the chain link and waved. "Hiiii!"

The man looked over. "Well, hello there young man!" He regarded me, his voice raspy with age. "And you, young lady."

I hoped he wouldn't linger, but Kacey immediately launched into a story about his Hot Wheels. The elderly gentleman slowly strode over to the fence to hear Kacey's story. A soft sigh escaped my lips as I rose and headed into the conversation too. I wished I bothered to put make-up over my fading bruise since I was going to be forced to talk to a stranger.

The man was kind. He listened to Kacey's rambling for several minutes before he turned to me. "My name's Richard."

"Nice to meet you. I'm Miranda."

"And what's your name?"

Kacey held up a car. "His name is Bone Jig-gah."

Richard looked confused.

"Tell Mr. Richard *your* name."

"Oh! Tacey!"

"It's Kacey," I confirmed.

Richard smiled. "Well, pleasure to meet you Kacey and Miranda." He pointed toward Jack's house. "Jack is a nice fella. He's helped this old geezer"—he patted his chest—"now and again." Dark brown eyes studied my face and the temperature in my cheeks raised a few degrees. Hoped my bruise wasn't too noticeable. "Are you two family?"

"Uh, well, we are..." I stammered for words, unsure how to answer that question. "Friends, actually. He is letting us stay with him a while."

Richard nodded.

Changing the subject, I pointed toward his garden. There were flowering shrubs, vegetable beds, and climbing flowers on trellises. "You have a lovely yard. It must've taken years for it to look that way."

"That it did. The magic maker was my wife." He winked at me. "She passed four years ago, but I'm still reaping the benefits."

"I'm sorry."

"Don't be. She gave me sixty-one wonderful years and five beautiful sons. Now I have fifteen grandchildren."

Sixty-one years? That number seemed almost incomprehensible. "Wow. sixty-one years. You must've been married young. You don't look a day over fifty."

He gave a hearty laugh. "That right there's flattery, but I'll take all I can get. We got hitched at eighteen and nineteen. My parents picked her out and boy, was she a keeper."

"Your marriage was arranged?"

"Well, arranged makes it sound too formal." He adjusted the straw hat on his head. "We met at church and our parents thought it fitting."

"That's incredible."

"She had a real eye for beauty. Everything you see behind

me is ultimately her doing. She started it and the harvest goes on with just a little tendin' here and there."

I thumbed over my shoulder. "Did the homeowners prior to Jack garden?"

"Yes. But Phil got real sick after a while and wasn't able to tend anymore. Been nigh a decade—maybe eight years since those beds have been tended."

I let my eyes roam over Richard's lush plants. "Yours are certainly alive and well. Looks like you have dozens of varieties."

"That we do."

He said *we*. It brought moisture to my eyes.

"Come on over and I'll show you around our space."

Our.

Good gracious. She lived on in his heart, and it was clear how smitten he still was. Sixty-one years, a husband in love, and a family to carry their legacy. I blinked back the emotion it stirred in me.

Kacey and I came around the fence and boy did we get the tour. Early spring flowers like daffodils and tulips grew at the base of every tree. Forsythia and quince shrubs were in full bloom. He rattled off names of plants as we passed them. A stone path wove through the beauty.

Richard said his wife had requested they make a path and they did it together. Stone by stone. It was finished right before her ten-year off-and-on battle with cancer began. She worked less and less in the garden. Some days she'd only make it out to the patio chair. But he tended it. For her. Because she loved her garden and he loved her.

He showed me early spring crops he had going. Lettuce, kale, snap peas, broccoli, and onions.

When we came to a section of dark green flowerless shrubs

tied to a lattice, I looked closer. Thorns on the stems, oval leaves. "Are these roses, Richard?

"That they are. They won't start blooming until late spring though." He came over and smiled. "Her name was Rose."

"Your wife?"

He nodded.

"Richard, you're determined to make me cry."

"Go right ahead, young lady. I don't mind."

I chuckled and dabbed at my eye with my t-shirt. "I've always wanted to learn to garden."

"I'd be happy to teach you."

"Really?"

"Well, it'd be my pleasure."

"Jack has a couple garden beds, but they are filled with grass." I waved toward Jack's yard. "Maybe we could go buy some seeds or something."

He chuckled. "You could, but it's a mite early for that."

"What do you mean?"

Kacey drove his car over a pile of mulch near Richard's shed. He hobbled to a bare spot in his vegetable bed and waved at the dirt. "First gardening lesson is this—most gardens don't do real well."

"How come?"

"Because folks are so excited about gettin' a harvest, they don't take time to work on the foundation."

"The soil."

He nodded. "That's right. It's the most important part of your garden. If your soil's depleted or infested, the harvest will suffer until it eventually dies off completely. Lots of people stick seeds or transplants right into a foundation that's far from ready and wonder why things didn't pan out."

"That makes sense."

Richard showed me his routine. Every morning, he brought

his coffee grounds, one banana peel, and one egg shell out to the garden and buried them. Then he opened his shed and brought out soil test kits. Before I even had time to register what I was undertaking, we were in Jack's yard, testing the soil, stripping out the grass, and wheelbarrowing some of Richard's compost over to the beds. He brought fertilizer and other things too. Gave me a pair of gloves and a few garden tools. The prospect of a fresh garden plot and teaching a newbie made Richard so happy. He shared his knowledge and resources with excitement rivaling kids on Christmas. It was precious and selfless.

My heart warmed for my new friend and thankfulness unfurled like a hug to my spirit.

Before I knew it, Kacey and I were covered head to toe in dirt and it was high noon. I learned about nitrogen, phosphorus, and potassium. How some plants deplete the soil and how others replenish. About organic matter and the cycle of death and life in the garden. About oxidation, worms, and composting raw material.

"Death makes the soil stronger in the long run," he explained. "Without some dyin' now and then, the soil will deplete. You can always dump in some manufactured chemicals to give it a boost, but nothing strengthens the foundation like a good dose of dead plants. Brings about new life."

Richard talked with such passion, teaching as we went. Referencing his dear Rose many times. It was fun for Kacey, but deeply inspiring and emotive for me. Something about Richard and Rose made me want to dig in—create something to span the ages. The way Richard spoke, you would think the plants were eternal. Truly life-filled. And I felt that. Right to the depths of my bones.

His old hands dug into the soil alongside mine as we churned the new into the old. His were hardened with deep wrinkles and raised veins. He worked alongside his wife until her final days. I wondered for a brief moment what Jack's hands would look like forty years from now. Entertained the what-ifs of us.

I shouldn't have, but I let Jack hold me. And it felt better than I remembered. Jack's gentleness defied his size. His hands had always been exceedingly tender. The memory of how they moved across my back and shoulders made me tear up on more than one occasion today.

Kacey cried for food, jerking my thoughts back to reality—I was only here temporarily and this summer garden I was planning with Richard would be abandoned. It hurt my heart, but I pushed the concern away. This was my chance to learn, if nothing else. Maybe Jack could enjoy the harvest himself.

I was pretty sure he wouldn't mind us working the beds. Maybe I should've asked first...

"Richard, I need to take Kacey in for lunch and nap."

"Not a problem. If you want, we can talk tomorrow about what to plant."

"That sounds great. Thanks so much for being willing to teach us."

"The first occupation granted to humans was gardening," he said with a shy smile. "My Rose didn't take that lightly. She felt it was a skill to pass on, and I'm happy to do it."

Later, I prepped some chicken strips and salad. Jack would be back from work about five o'clock or so and I wanted to make sure dinner was ready. As I washed and chopped the store-bought lettuce, I thought of Richard's garden for the millionth time and wondered what I could plant. "Hey Siri?" I called. "Can you read a list of summer vegetables for planting zone..." I faltered, wracking my brain for what Richard had said. "...seven."

Siri rattled off a list and I let myself dream. I could make some fresh salsa with the things she listed and my heart soared. No matter that we might not be here. What if we *were*? Or what if we stayed close by after the divorce? Surely, Jack would want to see Kacey, so I could stay close and come by to pick.

I knew it was optimistic, but I didn't care. I could use a smidge of optimism in my life.

When Jack got back, he talked to Kacey in the living room for a few minutes before finding me in the kitchen. "Hey," he said. "Smells good."

"Hey! Thanks!" I smiled. Genuinely.

"Uh,"—he ran a hand over his head—"just making sure you know...you don't have to make dinner."

"Kacey and I have to eat too."

"Yeah, I know. Just don't do it for *me*. Don't want you to feel obligated to have dinner on the table when I come home."

I looked at him and let my eyes rake down his body. His black uniform was as sexy as it had always been. He appeared large and commanding all the time–but something about the uniform kicked his look up a notch.

"I don't. I'm happy to make you some dinner." Breathing became difficult and I tore my eyes away, focusing on the chicken in the pan and wrestling a few vivid memories away. He usually wore his badge and utility belt home. I did the honors of removing them many times.

His gentle nod and slow smile made the kitchen labor very worth it. "I won't lie. I'm definitely hungry."

"Ten minutes till it's ready."

"I'll go clean up then."

He turned to go and it required all my effort to keep my thoughts from following him to the shower.

TWENTY-FOUR

Jack

After another long shift, I came home. Something I now looked forward to. But the house and kitchen were completely quiet today. So much so, I wondered if Miranda and Kacey were sleeping. I kept my voice low just in case. "Miranda?"

Waiting for a response, gentle laughter floated in from the back yard. I went to the back door and peered out. Miranda and my neighbor Richard knelt next to the garden beds. Kacey was doing something—waving his arms around and flopping into the grass repeatedly. They were laughing at him. I chuckled too. He was a really cute kid.

I strode out to the porch and leaned against the railing, just watching.

My heart ached for a moment. The sound of laughter alone was enough to send my thoughts into a spiral. I loved having Kacey and Miranda in my home. I was on a mission to convince Miranda to stay; to somehow give me a second chance. Our problems weren't water under the bridge by any means. They loomed large. But there had to be a way to fix things. If I only knew where to start.

She wore that pink tank top again and khaki shorts. Her hair fell out of the messy bun on her head in wisps. She had always complained about how fine her hair was because it slipped out of whatever hairstyle she attempted. But the tousled look was beautiful on her—and drove me crazy.

As if on cue, she removed her garden gloves and reached up to gather her hair back into a ponytail. She arched her back and stretched her arms behind her head, raking her fingers through the spun gold as she conversed with Richard. Man, I certainly loved to torment myself because I watched the whole time. Shamelessly enjoying my chance to admire her undetected. She twisted the rubber band around and pulled her hair through. It would only be a matter of time before she had to repeat the routine.

Jules' words had haunted me a hundred times a day since our phone call.

Just know it might not end the way you want it to.

I'd been called passionate. Determined. Very little would get in my way when there was something I wanted. And I wanted Miranda with me forever. This whole arrangement would end the way I wanted. I would make sure of it.

Miranda must've sensed my presence because she looked toward the house. She smiled at me, and I smiled back. For a moment, our gazes held. Her eyes widened right before she tore them away—she realized I'd been watching her. She searched the grass for a few seconds, trying to locate her gloves. Which were right in front of her, draped over the edge of the garden bed. My attention typically had this effect on her. She'd lose her cool—her voice would falter, she'd get distracted, or flutter around for a few moments.

There was heat between us. We'd look dumb trying to deny it. Every night, we watched Food Network and she'd end up sitting close. We hadn't fallen asleep in each other's arms again, but I held her hand one brief time. Her signals were mixed though. Hot then cold. Some nights she was easy to draw in, and some nights she kept her distance.

After she pulled her gloves on, she looked up again and waved me out. My feet obeyed without question.

Kacey waved and ran up to my side. "Hi, Dack!"

"Hey, buddy." I swiped grass off the top of his head.

He grabbed my hand and pulled me to the garden beds. "Yook what we panting!"

Richard and Miranda greeted me as Kacey launched into a detailed explanation of the tiny transplants all around. Tomatoes, peppers, basil, cucumbers, squash, and marigolds.

Miranda smiled. "We're just getting started. Want to help?"

Could I say no to her?

She had apologized to me yesterday for not asking first before using the garden—as if I would've been upset or something. She didn't realize she could have whatever she wanted.

"Sure!"

Richard showed us how to gently remove the plants from the tiny plastic containers. He had grown all these from seed himself.

"This is the most exciting part of planting a garden. Newness. The beginnings." Richard didn't look as nimble as the last time I saw him. He rambled on about the plants, absentmindedly smoothing the dirt while he talked. "It's the part everyone skips to, but few are prepared for. See, these little plants are tender." He brushed his hand down the side of a tomato seedling and sniffed his fingers. "Right now, they're weaklings. Too much water, a cold snap, heat waves, and any number of things can kill them off pretty quick."

Miranda stuck her shovel into the dirt, making a little hole.

Richard cleared his throat, though it did nothing to clear the rasp in his voice. "They haven't had time to root. Lots of folks make the mistake of sticking 'em in the ground, tossing some water on, and hoping for the best. They think the hard part is over." His chuckle was low, knowing. "They get what they work for, and so will you. Neglect will affect the bounty. You might get *some* harvest, but it won't be nothing to write home about."

I stifled a snort. Richard was very serious about this business. I glanced at Miranda and she grinned from ear to ear, thoroughly enraptured. She loved older people and clearly ate this up. She chattered with Richard and kept pulling Kacey into the tasks, letting his little fingers fumble through the process of fishing the tiny plants out. She had always been so easy to please. This type of stuff—simple things—is what Miranda lived for. I loved that about her.

Felt myself grinning, too.

We got all the plants and some okra seeds in the ground. He showed us how to water. How different types got watered differently. It shocked me when he watered the tomatoes for several *minutes* then instructed us to let them dry out for a week.

The man knew his stuff, I'd give him that.

Once we ripped open a bag of natural mulch, he showed us how much to pack around the bottom of each plant. "This will help protect the little plants from the heat. The sun comes and sucks the moisture right out of the dirt. The mulch is a small barrier, but at least it's something."

I couldn't help but slide glances Miranda's direction as she leaned into the garden. We were working side by side and her tank top kept riding up on her hips. I didn't understand how a few inches of skin could make me lose my head, but I was well on my way to half-mad, my thoughts spinning a thousand miles an hour.

A good dose of mulch had gathered on her bare thighs. I reached over and ran the back of my hand down her thigh, knocking the mulch into the grass. She froze, a handful cradled in her gloves. Her soft skin made me ache. I flipped my hand and did it one more time. Because...mulch. Let my thumb dust the top of her knee before pulling away.

Her brown eyes roamed my expression, trying to read. She saw how much I adored her. She had to. I doubted I could keep it off my face.

I winked, and she snapped her attention back to the garden, a gentle pink touching her cheek bones. I bit my bottom lip to keep from laughing.

With so many hands in the garden, we finished quickly. Kacey was filthy and was packing the plastic containers with mulch just for fun. He was a good listener and had done a great job when Richard handed him a tiny watering can.

Before I knew it, we were all heading inside, Miranda rattling off some dinner plans.

I couldn't even comprehend how a mere two weeks ago I was coming home to an empty house. Fixing dinner and spending free time alone. Felt like a completely different life.

TWENTY-FIVE

Miranda

I dumped a load of laundry onto the couch and got to folding. The hot fabric scorched my fingers. Jack reassured me over and over that I didn't need to do stuff for him. But I liked helping. Folding a bit of laundry here and there or making dinner made me feel part of a home. Maybe it was stupid to play pretend like that, but I couldn't seem to help it.

A week had flashed by before my eyes. Jack worked odd hours. Sometimes through the night, sometimes he left midmorning. He had enough seniority to pick better shifts, but he liked keeping things exciting. Before he left, he would stand out on the front porch, looking up and down the street with his hands on his hips before getting in the truck. He was worried and told me multiple times to keep my gun close. To pack my firearm if we went anywhere.

His vigilance made me feel safe.

Despite the turmoil of my life, I relaxed. My guard melted. I couldn't help it. After months—well, years—of staying on the alert, it felt nice to let someone else look out for us. Without being asked, Jack hogged the protector role. The natural defender in him rose to the occasion.

Looking over my shoulder, deleting calls and texts on my phone, pretending to be happy constantly, apologizing to avoid conflict, and tip-toeing through a mine field...I was all too happy to stop doing those things. And once my defenses cracked, they crumbled.

If it was anyone else, I wouldn't have been able to relax so quickly. But it was Jack. And I knew Jack. He wasn't perfect—I knew more than anyone—but he wouldn't hurt us, and we were safe here. It was why I was sleeping and eating better than I had in years.

Chris receded from my daily worries like a bad dream. He popped into my brain occasionally and I'd do my best not to dwell. My new life was here. In Tennessee. I was never going back. Never going to contact him.

Although it pained me to say it because I left everything I owned in his home. Even my scrapbooks. I should've grabbed them when I was moving out, but for some reason, I packed essentials only. Dumb.

Kacey and I stayed close to Jack's house. I had no desire to go on any adventures. I went to the store a handful of times for an ingredient here or there. And I put in a few hours a day for my new virtual assistant job.

It wasn't much, but one of Jack's coworkers also ran a side gig on social media. She had told Jack she was swamped with the never-ending list of things to do. Of course, Jack said he knew the perfect person to assist her. She was the nicest lady and we hit it off. The pay was only $150 a week. But the shot in the arm it provided was worth a lot more.

Kacey and I spent hours outside. Either in our garden or in Richard's. We watched buds emerge and our little seedlings steadied on. I soaked in every word Richard said. I was determined to be a master gardener by the time our arrangement ended. Plus, he was a dear friend. Whenever I had to move on, it would break my heart to say goodbye.

When Jack was home at night, he made the wine a routine. He would put something emotionally non-draining on the TV then bring me a glass of red and a plate of food. I ate more in a week than I had in a month. And I was feeling *so* much better. The constant ache in my mid-section waned.

Which might be why I found myself in a freaking emotional spiral. Feeling things for Jack I shouldn't. Mixing up left from right. Many times, I almost blurted the truth about Kacey to Jack. My heart was ready to have the conversation, but my brain said wait.

My body was a whole other problem. Jack was so unfairly handsome. His white teeth, blue eyes, olive skin, and dark facial stubble were a perfect contrast of color. He stretched every shirt he wore and could fill out a pair of jeans quite nicely. Whatever he did made the muscles in his forearms twitch—something I was oddly obsessed with. In fact, when we were married before, I made him play thumb wars with me so I could watch that sexy twitch.

All those minor attractions were just the starter pack.

He was so much more.

And the sweatshirt? I still hadn't washed it. Every night it disappeared then magically reappeared the next morning.

Except for once. I came down after he was already gone for work, and it took me several minutes to locate it. When I found it, I cried. It was in his unmade bed by his pillow. Seeing it crumpled up where he laid his head was too much. He must've been running late that morning, because Jack never left his bed unmade.

I had the sweatshirt on when he came home that evening.

The look in his eyes flamed with desire. The charade was up. We both knew the other knew. But we said nothing and continued passing it back and forth without a word.

How do you continue like normal knowing someone desires you that way? You don't. Which is why the heat blazed between us. We were on the precipice of being consumed by it.

I'd let him hold my hand and wrap his arms around me a few times. My imagination was wild. I wanted to scoot onto his lap and brush my lips against his slow smile. And a thousand other things. Fighting those crazy urges was like fighting a fire while dumping kerosene on it.

An idiotic task. Dangerous.

It was way too easy to forget what was between us. What had happened in the past. Why we broke in the first place.

Right when I would convince myself to keep my distance, Jack would do something unintentional, flinging me back into the war between my heart and mind.

Like two days ago. Jack worked an overnight shift and slept a portion of the day. After working through Kacey's nap, I flipped on cartoons and dozed off myself. I stirred around 4:30 p.m. to soft voices. Jack, with his hair still messy from sleep, was lying on his stomach on the floor while Kacey drove cars over his body. They were whispering about which of Jack's shoulders was the gas station. I pretended to be asleep so I could watch them.

Then yesterday, he threw Kacey onto the couch so many times I thought he was going to be sick from giggling.

Jack was far too easy to get comfortable with.

And my sweet baby loved Jack. Loved his *dad*.

The knowledge broke me.

Then

I bit my nails to the quick waiting. My stomach rolled and I lost my breakfast before walking in. The queasy feeling wasn't new. I came to expect it with all my pregnancies, no matter how short-lived they were.

But a unique cocktail of emotions churned in my gut. Heartbreak, fear, hope.

So much hope. Too much.

A soft knock sounded on the door and I snapped into an upright position, swiping my fingers against my jeans.

A maternal fetal medicine doctor stepped in. "Miranda? Hi, welcome back. I'm going to look at your chart real quick." He typed a few things on the computer before he sat on the rolly stool and swiveled toward me. He smiled. "I have some good news for you."

Hope swelled.

He took a deep breath, "Your prognosis looks good. We can't say what will happen for sure, but given your ultrasound and blood work results, we can tell you a few things." He started counting on his fingers. "The baby has a heartbeat and looks on track for fourteen weeks gestation. Your progesterone levels are healthy. There's no sign of hematomas. I think your chances are really good. But, given your history of miscarriage, the fact that you're experiencing some spotting now, your bicornuate uterus, and the fibroids, you need to be on bed rest."

The air left my lungs in a rush.

Bed rest?

"I think this baby can happen, but I wouldn't do anything to encourage contractions or labor. We already know your risk of miscarriage is high, but pre-term labor is too."

He smiled like he didn't throw a bomb into my life.

"All this is great, wonderful even, but I'm single and have a job. I'm a waitress. It's all I've ever done."

"I understand, but if you want to up your chances, I would consider doing something else for the time being. The lifting, the being on your feet all day"—he shook his head—"if it were me, I wouldn't do it."

I was planning to wait and see what happened to this pregnancy before rushing to tell Jack. But he would want to be a part. The thought of facing him again made me shift in my seat. But I knew he would want this. He'd do what he could to make us work. He'd help me rest to up the baby's chances. He'd give this family another shot.

After all, a family is what we tried so hard for. But, ultimately, the failure broke us.

Maybe a baby—our long awaited baby—would fix us.

How couldn't it?

As nervous as I was, I called him that very night.

TWENTY-SIX

Miranda

Jack worked late. I was already watching Food Network when he came home. Well, kind of. I was actually reading a digital book on my phone and Food Network was on in the background. Honestly, the TV was a cover. I only half-way watched. Pretty sure I just used it as an excuse to linger on the couch before bedtime.

And so did Jack.

After a quick shower, he joined me on the couch.

His eyebrows shot up when he saw the glass of wine I'd poured myself and a box of chocolates on the cushion beside me.

"Don't judge."

He huffed in amusement. He was pleased—thrilled even.

"Kacey ran out of his diapers, and for some dumb reason Russel Stover's candy was 40% off. And"—I lifted the glass—"I'm getting spoiled."

A crooked grin pulled at Jack's lips. "Being a little spoiled isn't bad."

"When it leads to eating way too much candy, it is."

He plopped down on the other side of the cardboard box and grabbed the little sheet, naming the varieties. I snatched it out of his hand. "How dare you!" I crumpled it up and tossed it across the room. "We don't do that here."

Jack's jaw dropped, incredulous, his grin incongruent with his furrowed brows. "I'm sorry! I like to make informed decisions."

"Nope. This is my chocolate. And the rules are—eat too much and take chances."

He squinted, his eyes cutting between me and my wine. "Is that your first glass?"

"Uhm—no."

"Wow."

"But first pour was like legit two ounces."

"Legit two ounces." He repeated me, skepticism dancing in his eyes.

"Yep."

"Su-ure."

"If you play by the rules, you can have some."

"Fine." He picked up the box and set it in his lap. His huge frame bent adorably over the tiny box. He surveyed each one with laser-like focus. Slowly plucking one out, he said, "This is the one."

"Go ahead."

He popped the entire thing in his mouth. I watched him chew for a minute. Funny how his strong jaw and thoughtful frown made something like chewing attractive. I fought the stupid smile on my face and tried not to gawk at him.

"Well?"

"It was a good choice."

"Was it caramel?"

He shrugged. "I have no idea."

I giggled. "That's no fun. Take a bite next time so we can see the inside."

We ate chocolate and talked for the next half an hour. He told me a few work stories. I told him about the garden. The TV was on but neither of us watched it.

Jack trained his gaze on my every move. I should've been nervous. Self-conscious even. But I wasn't. Maybe my ease was the wine talking. I laughed, licked chocolate off my fingers, and shoved Jack with my foot when he tried to count how many pieces I'd eaten.

The easiness between us felt so good. Like a pair of old jeans. Perfect fit, cozy, always a go-to. Something you never want to take off. It made sense. Jack had once been my best friend. Of course we'd stumble into companionship again.

I pushed the box away, moaning. "I'm going to make myself sick."

Jack patted his rock hard abs as if he had a candy belly or something. "Yeah, that was a lot."

I sat back, adjusting my feet on the couch, and melted into the cushions.

Jack's hand wrapped around my ankle.

I jerked it back but he held on. "What are you doing?"

He said nothing, but brought my foot into his lap. His thumbs moved across the sole of my foot.

It felt way...intimate.

"You don't have to do that." Even as I said it, I fought my eyes from rolling back into my head.

"I want to." His gaze was serious, intense. "Let it happen."

Couldn't fight him long. I loved foot rubs. His thumbs moved in circles until he stopped abruptly. "This is new." He gently rolled over a spot.

I winced. "Ow."

He softened his touch. "Oh, sorry."

"It's okay. I stepped on a nail two years ago. Went two inches into my foot."

"Is that scar tissue?"

I nodded, my voice breathless. "Still hurts."

He rubbed the spot with a tenderness that belied his masculine hands. My heart thumped. This man was doing things to me. Moments like this made me feel so undeserving. Like a fraud. Like a horrible person.

I wanted to stay away so we both didn't get hurt, but getting sucked into this vortex was inevitable. Had I ever stopped feeling so much for him? I thought I did...

What was it he just said?

This is new.

I let my eyes flutter closed for a second. Jack was the only person on earth familiar with the *soles* of my *feet*. My lips twitched as I battled cresting emotion. Squeezed my eyes tight and pushed the prickling sensation away.

A moment later, I stole a peek at him. He was watching my face.

"Why are you looking at me like that?"

He shook his head, denying me an answer.

I tapped his chest with my foot. "Spill."

"You just—are a lot more relaxed here than you were before." He smiled and shrugged. "You caught me noticing."

"I did have two glasses of wine."

"I mean in general. Without the wine."

"You're right. I am."

"Miranda"—he paused, frowning at my foot—"I'm glad you and Kacey are here. I'm glad we did this."

"Me too, Jack." I should've stopped, but more spilled out. "You make me feel safe."

His chest collapsed as air rushed out. "You have no idea how happy that makes me."

Silence settled between us as he continued rubbing my foot. I could think of nothing but his big hands, now rubbing my ankle. We both stared at the TV, but neither of us paid much attention. I knew because the contestant we rooted for the last several weeks got eliminated from the show. Neither of us said a word.

One of Jack's hands slipped up to the back of my calf. I did my best to hide how my breathing shallowed and heat erupted over my face.

How many massages had Jack given me over the years? They always started small. A hand, a foot, the top of my head. But he knew how to work down my defenses. How to melt me. How to touch me so I would move closer.

He was doing that now. The knowledge terrified me. But, I allowed it. Allowed him. Allowed my mind to entertain the thoughts I'd been fighting. Remember things I'd been blocking. But when his thumbs swept over the top of my knee, I panicked. I sat up, pulling away and he returned his hands to his lap with a satisfied smile.

I couldn't draw a breath. Prayed my struggle for oxygen wasn't too obvious.

I could just go upstairs—get away from him. But it was still early and I wasn't ready to leave him just yet. So, we watched the TV for a little longer and I gulped the last of my abandoned wine in one big swallow.

What we needed was a mood-lightener. Some fun. I knew the perfect thing.

"Hm." I frowned at his face.

"Now what?"

"I'm disappointed in you."

His head lolled slightly back. He had read my voice, and

figured I was about to give him a hard time. His tone was laced with sarcasm. "Oh great. What'd I do?"

I pressed my lips together then sighed. "You let your unibrow grow back."

His hand spread across his sternum and he exploded, laughing. "*What*?!"

"Yeah, I mean"—I grimaced—"it's bad."

"You are insane."

I scooted closer. "Here, let me count."

He pushed me back with his elbow. "Absolutely not."

"No, come here. It'll only take a sec." I leaned around his arm, giggling, pushing my pointer finger toward his face.

He swatted my hand away so I brought the other one up. I tapped the air in front of his eyes, counting as fast as I could. "One, two, three, four..."

He wrestled my arms down. "You are officially limited to one glass." His words were peppered with the most adorable sounds, laughter leaking out. "Your extra two ounces is making you see things."

I kept counting, jumping straight to the thirties to stress him out. "...thirty-one, thirty-two." I said it like it was a huge recurring problem. It wasn't. I plucked his eyebrows twice in the years we were together. But I had brought it up many times to watch his cortisol surge.

He pushed me back, breathless with laughter. "You're gonna give me a complex."

"Come on, let me pluck them."

"Why are you morbidly obsessed with crap like this?"

"It's fun."

"No."

"Have people been staring?"

He laughed fully again, his head tilting back. "Not for that reason."

"Wow! Cocky much?" The laughter was a key sliding into a rusty lock, opening a mysterious door of possibility. Felt so freaking good. I wanted to stay here forever. "Jack, seriously. You have a few hairs. It'll take me five seconds."

He sighed through his smile, long and loud. "Fine."

I bounded up the stairs to grab my tweezers.

He waited patiently for me as I settled in. I sat on my knees, facing him, nestling close. "Okay, now just relax." I shoved his head onto the back of the couch. "I'll be done in a flash."

I turned his face toward me, and he closed his eyes a whisper of a smile stuck on his face. I plucked the few stray hairs in under twenty seconds. But I pretended there were lots. Tapped the tweezers on his brow at least a dozen times. Then his forehead, along the sides of his eyebrows, a couple on his cheeks...

He opened his eyes, laughter dancing in them as he chided me. "Miranda." When I moved the tweezers under his nose, he snatched my wrist. "Stop that! What are you doing?"

I laughed, letting myself look into his eyes. The dark blue was enthralling, with white flecks like cresting waves. Huge mistake. I lost my cool as butterflies flooded my midsection. Suddenly the game had ended—the only reality left was him. His powerful body confidently spread on the couch before me, his heat, his unwavering gaze. I tried to smile. "Just messing with you. There were only like five."

I brushed the few hairs off his brow and cheek. One had landed above his lip. I brushed it away with my thumb once. But it stuck.

His gorgeous lips. I couldn't catch my breath. My chest felt hollow. My hand felt panicky as I reached to try again.

Finish and move. Hurry up. Hurry up.

When I swiped my thumb over his lip the second time,

Jack caught my hand and pressed the pads of my fingers against his soft lips.

My insides unraveled. Warmth spread through my veins at the simple act of tenderness. A breathy whisper escaped my tight throat as I watched him kiss my fingers a second time. "Jack."

His gaze was on my lips too.

Magnetic intensity existed between the two of us. And each second I resisted drained my reserve. At some point, I was going to give in to this man. The results would be explosive, catapulting the two of us back down the road we just traveled.

I tried to dig my heels in. Resist him.

But his hands came to rest on my hips, and he pulled.

Maybe I should've hopped up, walked away. Been done right then and there. Not let myself linger.

But desire to be held in safe arms melded me against his chest.

Every argument disintegrated.

My face landed in the curve of his neck, filling my senses with a scent I'd ached to inhale again. His hands splayed on my back almost spanning the entirety of it. We were pressed together, and it felt like home.

My eyes filled with tears as he dropped his lips to my hair. He kissed my head twice as his hands rubbed up and down my back.

We'd done this the night we fell asleep together. But this was different, more intimate. On the heels of an electric moment. We were closer than before. Our faces inches apart.

After a few deep breaths, my lips found his neck. Just one kiss to his neck and I would be done.

Or maybe two.

His voice was strangled. "Miranda."

I kissed him again. I couldn't help myself. It was that dang leg massage. I wanted to touch him. I drug my hands over his shoulders and onto his chest while my lips never left his neck.

I've missed you, Jack. So much.

So much for one kiss. Again and again I kissed him, afraid of what would happen if I lifted my face to his. We'd be swept away. Desire would overtake us like an angry storm surge—insistent, destructive, unrelenting. We'd drown in it.

It had been waiting for us for so long.

His chest expanded at an odd pace. His hands threaded into my hair. "Miranda..."

My hand glided along his rough jaw.

When he said my name a second time, I wrenched my face away from his neck, setting my forehead against his. He tightened his grip in my hair, stopping me as I moved to close the distance.

His brow was furrowed, his eyes closed. He swallowed hard. The scrape of yearning in his voice was impossible to miss. "I have to make sure this is what you want." I stopped, backing up as his eyes fluttered open, looking straight into mine. "You know what will happen if we kiss."

He didn't have to say more.

"We won't stop." He pushed some strands out of my face. "If we start this, I can't promise I'll leave it at a kiss."

I closed my eyes, nodding against his forehead. Had to think.

Jumping here would change our arrangement forever.

Did I want that? I wanted Jack, but we had a common goal here.

And it wasn't marriage.

It was money.

My heart withered. Died on the spot.

Why was our history so tainted? Why did everything go the way it had? I wanted to let bygones be bygones and make sweet love with this man. Throw caution to the wind. Cross my fingers and hope the second go-around would be less painful than the first.

But second chances don't work that way.

Jack gave me everything except the only thing I ever truly asked for. The one thing I needed more than anything else.

His presence.

Until he could share his heartaches and was willing to share mine, we had no foundation.

I felt like Mary from It's a Wonderful Life.

"Jackson Barkley Lassos the Moon."

Maybe so, but he had no idea what to do with hearts.

Because when mine broke, he did nothing.

He watched it bleed and did nothing.

TWENTY-SEVEN

Jack

Miranda wanted to kiss me. The knowledge put pep in my step for an entire week.

All this time, I had forced myself to believe my feelings were mostly one-sided. So when Miranda found her way into my lap, I was stunned. It was a welcome curveball. Took every ounce of my strength not to push her down on the couch and kiss her senseless.

We were just shy of three weeks into our arrangement, and Miranda already tried to kiss me. Granted, after thinking about it, she chose not to. But she *wanted* to. Pain etched her brows and slightly puckered her bottom lip. Her visible frustration was enough for me.

Maybe this situation wasn't as hopeless as I thought.

Considering the timeline, our trajectory looked promising.

But there were two problems. One, I could not stop thinking about her. Remembering all the intimate moments we shared before. Remembering details I loved about her body and longing to see how time had changed her. Remembering the feel of her skin against mine. If I had wanted her before, now I bordered insane.

Sleeping. Focusing. Not reliving those neck kisses over and over. All were impossible tasks. I did an okay job keeping myself in check. But when her hands moved across my chest, my resolve snapped.

The woman I longed for was my *wife*.

Not my ex-wife. My *current* wife.

That reality became the fuel of my desires.

Second problem: Miranda was avoiding me. She skipped the wine and Food Network routine ever since that night. I paced like a caged lion, hoping she would come down night after night. Each day at work, I wracked my brain, trying to devise a way to spend a little time with her.

And I finally had the perfect plan. The next day was game night. Jules had had a very full week and the girls weren't sleeping well, so she asked me to bring a dessert this time. So I picked up a gallon of strawberries from a farm stand on the way home. I should've been exhausted from my long day at work, but the sight of Miranda made my insides buzz with anticipation. The house was quiet because Kacey was in bed for the night. She was putting away dinner dishes when I came into the kitchen and cleared my throat. "Hey, want to help me make a dessert for game night tomorrow?"

"I doubt you need help with that."

"Not really." I shrugged. "But company to keep me awake would be nice though. My hours have been crazy."

"No kidding." A gentle frown scrunched the ridge of her nose. "Yeah, I'll help."

Perfect. Anything to keep her downstairs longer.

After scouring the internet for good recipes, we pulled out all the ingredients for a strawberry cake with buttercream frosting. A little extra for a game night, but I wanted the recipe to be complex and take a while.

She started the frosting, and I made the cake. We worked in silence for a while, making small talk here and there. Once we had the cake in the oven, I leaned against the counter. "I got an idea."

She raised her eyebrows, scraping the sides of the bowl.

"Why don't we play the tasting game while we wait?" It was my attempt to encourage her to let loose again. To restore the easy companionship we shared prior to our almost kiss.

She scoffed. "Heck no. I don't trust you."

"What? Why not?" I pretended like I didn't know what she was talking about.

"Because, like a monster, you put hot sauce in my mouth the last time we played." She propped her hands on her hips. "Remember?"

Oh, I remembered. It was cruel. Miranda hated spicy stuff. She cried.

"I apologized profusely for two weeks."

"That doesn't mean I want to play again."

I crossed an x over my heart. "Miranda Barkley, you have my word. Nothing spicy. I'll be nice."

She squinted. I knew she was plotting revenge, but I was willing to take my chances.

"You'll be nice?"

"I promise."

She perked up. "Okay, let's do it."

Oh yeah. Miranda didn't give up that easy. She had something up her sleeve.

A smile pulled at my cheeks as I drug a table chair into the kitchen. I waved her into the seat. "You first."

She plopped into the chair without argument.

"I don't know what to use for a blindfold, so let's just drape a kitchen towel over your face."

She leaned her head on the back of the chair, and I placed the towel across her eyes. But not before seeing her arch a single eyebrow in challenge.

"You look way too pleased."

She sat still so the towel wouldn't fall, only her nose and mouth uncovered. She smirked.

It took me forever to find something. Mainly, because I was distracted. Miranda wore a button up plaid shirt, knotted near her waist above her jean shorts. Her hair was down, hanging over the back of the chair.

"What's taking you so long?"

"Sorry." I forced my attention back to the contents of the fridge. I grabbed a jar of cherries and quietly shut the door. "Okay, I'm ready."

Her brave face vanished as her hands flew to her lips, protecting them. She squeaked. "I'm so scared."

"Don't be."

Her words were muffled by her hands. "That's exactly what you said before you touched a habanero to my tongue!"

I chuckled. "Open up."

She shook her head and her feet tapped the floor. "I can't."

"Quick, then it will be your turn to get me back."

She wailed, but very slowly opened her mouth. I leaned over her chair, my gaze riveted to her lips. It would be evil to kiss Miranda without her expecting it, but I wouldn't say it didn't cross my mind.

She squealed in anticipation, her hands pressing against her chin.

As soon as there was clearance, I dropped a cherry in.

She stopped in surprise and a sweet, sweet smile spread

across her face. "Aw. That was nice." Unhindered, I watched her lips as she enjoyed the cherry.

I pulled the towel off her face and her gaze met mine. My voice was deeper, more breathy than I intended. "My turn."

I took the chair spot and covered my eyes. I think she opened every cabinet and door in my kitchen looking for the perfect torture. She thought she was being quiet, but I knew exactly where she was at all times. After a couple minutes, she said with far too much glee. "Okay, Jack, open up."

I knew it was going to be horrible. But I dutifully obeyed.

Cold, sour liquid.

Freaking pickle juice.

She howled as I gagged and ran to the sink. I hated pickles. Anything pickled. She rubbed my back, laughing, as I rinsed my mouth. "I'm sorry, Jack!" she wheezed. "I had to."

"That was disgusting." I spat in the sink.

"Why do you have pickles if you hate them?"

"Pat and Jules," I croaked.

She quit laughing and replaced her hands on her hips. "Are we even now?"

I turned with a serious face. "Absolutely not."

Before she could process, I grabbed the sprayer on the sink and got her good. She gasped then dashed out of the spray zone. I grabbed the towel on my shoulder. "Miranda, there's no *even* after a stunt like that." I slowly flipped the towel around and around in my hands, turning it into a thin strand.

Her jaw dropped open as fear and realization dawned. "Jackson Barkley, don't you dare."

I moved closer to her, boxing her into a corner.

She started laughing and whining, holding her hand in front of her. Like she was taming a wild beast. "Let's talk about this, Jack. Be reasonable."

Once the towel was tightly wound in my hand, I snapped

one end letting the other hit a cabinet door with a loud *crack*. She screamed. I did it again, faster this time. She bounced on her toes in a clash of delight and terror, her brown eyes dancing and pleading. The stress and fun of the moment made her brows pull together and her hair fall in her face. "Jack, stop!"

I would never actually hit her with the towel. A damp towel could give someone welts. But she knew it was flex. All for show.

I snapped a cabinet for the third time, and she bolted from the corner before I could reload.

She was so cute.

Before I realized what she was doing, she thrusted her hand inside the bag of powdered sugar on the counter and held a fistful at eye level. We faced each other with our weapons. Her voice, wobbling with laughter, urged me. "You better think about what you're doing before—"

I let the towel fly and she threw white dust at my face.

"I cannot believe you." I laughed, reaching for the sugar bag myself.

In thirty seconds, we did substantial damage to the kitchen. There was powdered sugar all over the floor and counters, all over Miranda's shirt and face. She was laughing with wild abandon. I let the sound wash over me, warm me from the inside out.

If I ever entertained for a second that there was anyone on the planet for me besides her, I was dead wrong. Miranda was perfect.

If I was a schedule, she was the freedom.

The whimsical to my practical.

And the heart for my brain.

Everything I wasn't. Everything I wanted.

It's why no one else had ever been able to take her place.

I loved her before. I loved her after. I loved her now.

We had chased each other back around to the sink. She reached it first, flipped it on, and grabbed the sprayer. "Call a truce now or I'll spray."

"Fat chance."

Water hit my face. I wrestled it out of her hands and dragged her over to the freezer while she kicked. Holding her around the waist with one arm, I took a fistful of ice with the other. Down the back of her shirt it went. But I wrapped my hands around her back, holding the ice in place so it didn't fall out. She was laughing, screaming, beating my chest and trying to push away.

"Jack—Jack, please. Please! I can't handle it."

Her squeal turned into a distressed sound, and I immediately loosened my hold. Ice clattered to the floor and her shoulders dropped. She breathed heavily, a smile still on her face. "You—you are *so* awful."

Maybe I was awful.

Because the only thing I could think about was towing her to the shower and washing the sugar out of her hair. She was still pressed against me, my hands on her back.

"Okay, truce," I rasped.

"About time."

She looked up. "You are soaked." She swiped my forehead with her hand. I couldn't move, couldn't breathe. The game had escalated into something else entirely. My pulse was chaotic with adrenaline. The feel of Miranda's feminine curves was a provoking and torturous experience. My need for her was thrown wide-open, full throttle.

She squirmed. "You're not going to let me go?"

I shook my head, my insides clenching as I realized letting her go was absolutely not an option. "No."

Her gaze snapped to mine. She must've seen the desire

written there because she drew a quick breath, her footing faltering. Confusion shone in her eyes as she searched mine. Her lashes fluttered closed for a brief second as I reached up to push damp hair out of her face.

"Miranda," I started, having no clue where I planned to go with this. "I don't want to let you go. I shouldn't have let you go to Ohio." Courage swelled in me, the truth piecing together in my head as I spoke. "I should've followed you and camped on your doorstep until we got things right."

Her breathing quickened and moisture gathered in the corner of her eyes.

I let my fingers slip into the hair behind her ear. I guided her chin up, so I could look her fully in the face. Her hands flexed against my chest. "I've tried to move on and date around." I ran a thumb over her sugared cheek. "But every person I met only reminded me how great I had it with you. How perfect we were for each other. I know it's too soon and you didn't sign up for any of this, but I need you to know one thing. I believe without a shadow of a doubt there's only one person for me."

She pressed her lips together. I wanted to dive deep into her gaze, to somehow know what she was thinking.

"This second chance with you might be the only nice thing my dad has ever done for me. And I plan to take full advantage. I let you walk away back then, but I don't plan to let you go so easily this time."

A tear rolled down her cheek, leaving a wet trail in the splatter of white. Her gaze flicked to my mouth as the tension in the air around us crackled.

I leaned forward, whispering my next words over her ear. "And I'm going to kiss you now, because if I don't"—I huffed —"I think I may wither and die. Right here on the kitchen floor."

I honestly tried to take my time and not rush, but my breathing had frenzied, trying to keep up with the racing of my heart. I brushed my lips across that tear. Then I kissed her forehead. And her other cheek. The tip of her nose.

She grabbed handfuls of my shirt and stood, motionless, letting me caress her face.

"You, Miranda." I could hardly talk. "You're the only one."

Coming in easy was like frantically paddling upstream from a massive waterfall.

My lips found hers. They were just as sweet, full, and soft as I remembered. She braced her hands against my chest, like she was worried we'd get too close. So we just kissed. Chaste. Lips only, with my hands cupping her gently moving cheeks.

Using restraint against the force storming in me caused my hands to tremble against her face. Fire roared through my veins and heat spread through my body. Miranda was home to me. Kissing without proving how desperate I became for her would be impossible.

But after a few seconds, her hands softened on my chest. I stole the opportunity, slipping my hand back around her waist. I tempted the kiss just a bit, letting my tongue meet her lips and hoping she'd want more. She made a tiny pleasure sound and so did I.

The soft duet broke a dam. Her body said *screw it* and her resolve vanished.

It was a long awaited surrender.

We melted together in a sweet relenting.

Going to her tiptoes, she slipped her hands up and around my neck, stretching out against me. My hands pressed her in. As I swept my lips over hers, she angled her face to mine, opening fully.

A groan came up from the furthest place in my gut. I dove

into her, filling her and her me. It took about sixty seconds for the intensity of our kiss to climb to dizzying levels.

She tensed her arms. She wanted me to lift her. Just like we'd done hundreds of times.

I leaned down further, letting my hands slip to the back of her thighs. Hoisting her up was effortless. She ran her hands through my hair and gripped me with her legs. She squeezed me, her every touch firm and demanding more.

I held her steady with one hand and slipped the other beneath her shirt. Her hands traced lines down my shoulders and arms then plowed into my hair again. They left a trail of fire over my skin. I burned for her. Desperate in a way I couldn't remember being ever before.

I walked her into the living room, bumping into an end table, then let her back hit the couch. I left enough room for her to roll away, push me off if she wanted. But her ankles crossed behind my waist and pulled. Her clumsy, hurried fingers fumbled with buttons on her flannel.

I could not get close enough to Miranda.

"You." I trailed kisses down as buttons gave way. "You, Miranda."

A high-pitched cry joined us.

I froze with my lips on her chest.

Her hands stilled on the fourth button.

A loud squeal followed by a call for mommy flitted down the stairs.

Felt like I was going to explode with frustration.

Miranda tried to catch her breath, "May—maybe he'll be okay."

As if on cue, he wailed, gaining volume.

She pushed up on her elbows. We waited for a few seconds. I felt the moment slipping away from us and frantically committed her to memory. Her sloppy hair, the sugar smeared on her face, the rise and fall of her chest, the way her open shirt had slipped off one shoulder.

The crying wasn't stopping.

"I—I need to—to go to him."

We held gazes for a long moment. Anguish in her expression. Certainly a mirror of my own.

My whisper was hoarse, a needy begging. "Come back. Please come back."

She nodded and rolled out from under me. She buttoned her blouse on the way up the stairs.

I waited on the couch for a few minutes. Then I brushed my teeth. Lit a candle in my bedroom. Paced like a caged lion.

After thirty minutes, I cleaned the sugar off the kitchen floor and iced the cake. After an hour and a half, I took a cold shower, blew out the candle, and got into bed, feeling worse than I remembered feeling…maybe ever.

But I can't say I was surprised.

TWENTY-EIGHT

Miranda

As I worked in the garden, my heart bounced between desire for Jack and crippling anxiety.

Jack had to work early the next morning. Which came as a relief to me. I wasn't ready to face him, not after what happened between us the night before. Leaving him hanging was cruel. I wished I hadn't done it. But once I finished getting Kacey back to sleep, I couldn't go back down.

There was so much between Jack and I that sleeping together would be *wrong*. As much as I wanted to, our web was sticky enough as is. Intimacy would only make things worse. And I couldn't partake knowing full-well I harbored a secret.

But it killed me. I got into bed and sobbed.

I had to tell Jack about Kacey. Had to. I was a fraud to keep up the charade. Of course he would be angry, but the longer I kept the secret, the worse it would be. One more month of pretending felt impossible. There was no way I could keep the truth locked up that long.

Day after day, I hated myself for even agreeing to this. Was marriage truly the only way? Maybe I could've figured something else out. Something that wouldn't hurt Jack so much...

Because Jack would be crushed when he learned the truth. Honestly, the fact he hadn't put two and two together was shocking. Jack was meticulous, detailed, didn't miss much. It's what made him amazing at his job. Kacey and Jack didn't look alike necessarily, but they had similarities. And if anyone looked closely—or looked in the right places—they'd know the truth, too.

Jack hadn't even questioned me about Kacey's birth and timeline. He must've discounted the possibility I would deceive him. In his mind, it was off the table because he trusted me.

Harboring this information was betrayal. I was a traitor.

I thought I could keep lying. But I was wrong. My conscience wouldn't let me keep Kacey from him a minute longer. The fear of a custody battle had waned, now paling in comparison to the heavy guilt I felt from keeping the truth hidden.

I took a deep breath and swiped my cheeks dry, determination seeping into my spirit. I had to tell him. If I cared about Jack—which I did—I had to do it. Come what may.

Tonight.

My thoughts were far too optimistic. Maybe Jack would forgive me and want to make things work between us for our son. Maybe he'd be *happy* and we could pick up where we left off. Maybe we'd fix our brokenness and be happier than ever before.

I couldn't help but replay our last moments together on repeat. The man could flat-out kiss. I was pretty sure I would be remembering his white powdered face till my final, dying breath. He had always been so exceedingly tender with me. So committed to making me happy. So careful. I remembered and longed for our intimacy countless times since the divorce.

Chris was harsh. I only ever relented to him out of guilt.

Chris entered the picture for me and Kacey because I had no other options. I had no one to turn to, and I *thought* the father of my baby rejected us. Leaving Jack and somehow finding a path to Chris was, without a doubt, the worst thing that had ever happened to me.

I would've gladly stayed with Jack, despite our problems, had I known.

Then

I worked at the Italian restaurant for three months. My tips were fantastic. I had no clue what I was going to do to make it financially, but I had to find something else. The doctor told me waitressing was a risk to the baby. Nothing else mattered. Just my baby. Couldn't even entertain the thought of losing another.

I imagined holding a tiny bundle in my arms so many times. Smelling sweet baby hair, learning to nurse, rocking and humming to the little one, giving the baby a first taste of real food. My imagination would run until tears streamed down my face.

Jack was always a part of those imaginings, but not anymore.

Bitter, angry tears. Sad tears. Hopeful tears. All I did was cry.

I swiped my eyes dry before knocking on my GM's office door.

"Yep!"

I poked my head in. "Hey, Chris."

"Miranda, come in."

I shut the door behind me.

Chris was busy at his computer but swiveled his chair around. "What can I do for you?"

"Um, I hate to say this, but I need to quit."

His eyebrows raised in surprise. "Oh? You just started with us. It takes a lot of money to train new employees."

"I know and I'm sorry."

"It's nothing about the work environment here, is it?"

I shook my head, feeling fresh tears gather. "Not in the slightest. I actually love it here."

He cocked his head to the side, listening.

"It's just—just a personal thing."

He nodded slowly. I always thought Chris was quite handsome. He had a dashing smile, light brown hair, and chocolate brown eyes. He was young to be a general manager and was very good at his job. Most everyone blindly followed him due to his charisma and leadership skills.

"You're providing a two week notice?"

I took a deep breath. "No, I can't."

He spoke gently. "And that's because..."

A tear leaked out. I was so afraid. What would I do without a job?

I wiped it away as fast as I could.

"Hey, hey." Chris leaned forward, his eyebrows knit with concern. "It's okay. Just take a deep breath."

I took one, willing myself to calm down.

"We can talk about this. What's going on?"

"I'm pregnant," I blurted. "I've lost a lot of pregnancies and the doctor says I can't be on my feet all day or I could lose this one too."

Chris tsked in understanding. "Oh, I see. That must be so stressful."

"It is. Waitressing is all I've ever done. To make it worse, I moved to Ohio only three months ago. I was rooming with an old friend of mine, but her fiancé proposed and she's moving back home to be with him. So, I don't have a place to live now either." I sniffed, wiping a few more tears. Chris leaned forward, listening to my every word. "I know I can't give you two more weeks, but if you would still give me a glowing recommendation to any potential employers, I'd really appreciate it."

"Of course, I'll do whatever I can."

"I apologize for any bind my sudden leaving puts you in."

He waved a hand. "It's no biggie. Most important thing is taking care of your baby."

I gave a halfhearted smile through my tears.

"Do you mind if I pry?"

"Uh, no, it's—it's fine."

"Where is the father?"

It *was* a highly personal question, but Chris was the only person I'd talked to about it. Everyone loved Chris and talked about what an all-around good guy he was. So, based on the way he was listening and understanding, I figured he wanted to help me. And God only knew how much help I needed.

"He"—I looked at my hands on my lap—"he doesn't want us."

I wasn't watching Chris, but his chair creaked as he sat back in it. He muttered a quiet expletive. His voice was tender. "Miranda, I'm so sorry."

I shrugged. Couldn't talk or I'd cry.

"When is your friend moving?"

"End of next week."

"Hm. You know I own some properties, right?"

"I didn't know."

He sat forward, placing his elbows on his knees. "Yes and I have a duplex with an unoccupied unit right now."

"I don't think I could afford rent at a duplex. Not by myself anyway."

"But maybe we could work something out. I have to get $500 out of that unit to make the mortgage payment. Could you do that?"

I swallowed. That was very cheap. I nodded slowly, processing on the fly. "Uh, yeah, I think so—I guess it depends on where I end up finding another job."

"Well, take this week. Think about it. Look for a job. Have potentials call me and I'll give you a great recommendation. Let me know by about Monday whether you want to get in the unit or not. We won't even worry about the lease. Just go month to month, whatever you need." He smiled, and I was grateful for a friend.

"Chris, wow, thank you so much."

"Can you do all that and get back with me?"

"Yes, most definitely."

"Awesome." He reached over and patted my forearm. "It'll all work out. You guys will be okay, you'll see."

I stood to go.

"And Miranda?" He swiveled his chair back to the computer screen. "The guy who gave you up? He's an idiot."

For the first time since I left Nashville, it felt like someone was in my corner.

TWENTY-NINE

Miranda

My phone rang. It was Jack. I hesitated to pick it up, but he never called me from work, so I figured I should.

"Hello?"

"Miranda, hey."

"Hey...is everything okay?" It was awkward. But of course it was. I'd left him hot and bothered after a steamy make-out.

"Oh yeah, everything's fine. I was calling because there's been an abrupt change of plans. I know you weren't planning on going to the Moore's for game night, but Jules called and asked if they could actually do the gathering at our house instead."

Our house?

My heart hurt.

"Jules and Pat have been up all night every night with the girls recently. Jules said their house is a mess and they are too tired to entertain. Jules also said she was desperate for a night *out* instead of another night in." He cleared his throat. "I didn't say whether they could come or not. I wanted to ask you first... didn't want you to be uncomfortable."

"I appreciate that." It was thoughtful of him. "Of course they should come. Jules should get a night out."

"I figured you'd say that, but I wanted to be sure. Jules and I are having some food delivered around five-ish. I should be back by then."

"Okay. I'll make sure everything is ready."

"Thank you, Miranda. And hey, please know you're invited. You don't have to stay upstairs." He paused. "I want you with me, if you're comfortable with it."

I want you.

Those words were five years too late.

I closed my eyes, remembering the feel of his palms, hungry for my skin. How his weight pressed into me and his open mouth tasted my neck. For the thousandth time, I let my mind imagine what would've happened had I gone back downstairs.

He had said, *there's only one person for me.*

I shivered. Wanted so badly to believe it.

"Yeah, Jack, of course. I—I might not play games, but I'll at least be around for some cake."

My answer pleased him.

Around five o'clock, food was delivered for dinner and the Moores arrived, but Jack was late. I was so uncomfortable opening Jack's front door. Felt like an actress. Playing a part I was not ready for. Wishing someone was there to feed me my next line.

Sunny, Winter, and Woods were beautiful and charming. Pat was friendly and easy to talk to. Kacey immediately took to him and Sunny. But Jules was cold. She smiled and pretended to tolerate me.

I almost collapsed with relief when Jack returned. After he

greeted his family and Kacey, he turned his eyes on me. They were still flaming with desire and sent my belly into turmoil.

I felt his gaze all night. He watched my every move. The realization made me hot and flushed on more than one occasion. Jack wanted me and was doing nothing to hide it. I was certain everyone could see as plainly as I could. When we made eye contact, his slow smile turned my insides to mush.

I was all too glad when it was time for dessert and volunteered to serve up the plates, knowing the partial kitchen wall would hide me from view for a blessed minute.

But Jack was right behind me.

When I reached the counter, Jack stood behind me, placing his hands low on my waist. He leaned down, whispering. "You didn't come back last night." He brushed his lips across my ear, sending a tremor through me.

I said nothing.

His hands splayed on my hips. "I have thought about you all day." He kissed my temple. "Any chance you want to pick up where we left off last night?"

My stomach clenched. Heat exploded through me.

Yes. Yes, I do.

I nodded, my resolve completely worthless. Powerless to say no to him. His chuckle was gravelly and so very tempting. "Well, cut this cake then. We need to get these people out of here." Before he let go, he slid his hands to my ribs and leaned down to kiss my neck.

That was when Jules walked in the kitchen. She said, "Can I help with the cake?" But her expression was not friendly.

Jack straightened, sliding his hands down my sides one last time. Then he meandered out of the kitchen, unbothered by Jules walking in on our intimate moment.

Jules was bothered though.

When she turned her icy blue eyes on me, I wanted to

vanish.

She came close so she could speak quietly.

"Miranda, we used to be friends."

I froze, mid cake-cut, and looked at her face.

"I used to think you were an amazing person. Was so happy Jack found someone like you." She shook her head. "Jack is one of the smartest, most intuitive people I know. But right now"—moisture filled her eyes—"I'm watching his blind spot. He doesn't want to believe you would hurt him on purpose. But I know what's going on here."

The knife trembled in my grip.

"Kacey is Jack's. Pat and I knew the truth ten seconds after we met him. I gave you the benefit of the doubt, but tonight..." She pressed her lips together. "He shares so many of Jack's features." Her voice shook, picking up speed and emotion as she went. "What I don't know is *why* you would do this."

My vision blurred, and nausea pressed against my throat.

"I know you two have bad history, but Jack is an amazing man who deserves to be part of his son's life. The fact—the fact you're in his house, with his secret son, using him? For money?" A tear leaked out of her eye as her bottom lip trembled with a frown. "I just can't believe you'd do something like that."

I swallowed the sobs gathering in my chest.

Deep breaths. Deep breaths.

"And the worst part, when all this comes out, Jack is going to get hurt. It doesn't take a brain surgeon to see how crazy he is about you. He's never gotten over you, and you are going to break him *again*."

Hot tears streamed down my face.

"I thought more of you, Miranda. I really did." She wiped her cheeks with the sleeve of her sweater. "But this is...this is wrong. So very wrong."

"Jules"—I cleared the emotion in my throat—"you don't know what happened. I spent years—"

She held her hands out to stop me. "I don't need to know the past. Despite whatever happened between you two, there is *nothing* that makes this situation okay. You've been together for three weeks."

She wasn't wrong.

She sniffed, straightened, wiping her eyes again. "I'm going to tell him. If he doesn't know in two days, I'm going to call and tell him."

I couldn't breathe. My heart hurt so much.

"I used to be the type of person who would have just blurted the truth to a roomful of people. Even though you deserve that, I've changed. Two days is generous. I don't want to be the one to tell him, but if I have to, I will."

She walked out as I stood there, knife still suspended over the top of the strawberry cake. I'd been so excited about trying a piece, but as soon as I was done serving plates, I retreated to the upstairs bathroom, locking the door behind me. A bit of frosting was on my finger and I washed it down the drain.

Jack showered after the Moores left, and I hustled to get Kacey into bed. I needed to get him in bed and talk to Jack before Jules changed her mind. It had taken all my strength to come down the stairs to retrieve Kacey for his bedtime routine without disintegrating with fear.

I tried to talk Kacey into water in his sippy cup before bed, but he was a stickler for milk. He wasn't going to fall asleep without it. So I crept down the stairs, hoping—*praying*—Jack was still in the bathroom. I filled his cup, but as I was turning for the stairway, Jack opened the bathroom door. He came out, wearing only sweatpants and a towel draped around his neck. His smile was eager. Too sweet. Too much.

My eyes filled with tears again. They stung.

I am a horrible, horrible person.

He came and wrapped his arms around me. Which was the worst thing he could possibly do. My heart plummeted. Poor Jack. I didn't want to disappoint him a second time. Heat climbed my neck as Jack kissed the top of my head. My arms couldn't hug him back. There was no way I could delay another minute in telling Jack. I already felt like I was about to faint.

"You getting Kacey in bed?"

I nodded.

"Are you coming back down after?"

"Yes"—I gently pushed back from him—"but I need to talk to you about something."

He leaned back, alarmed by my tone. "Everything okay?"

Right as he asked, little Kacey came to the stairs, his toddler gait thump-thumping down the steps. "Mommy? Dack?"

"We—we're down here, buddy."

He joined us in the hallway. "Hi, Mommy." He had a devilish grin, knowing full well he was supposed to stay in bed. Then he looked at Jack. A delighted expression crossed his face as he approached Jack with his pointer finger outstretched.

I realized too late what Kacey saw.

Everything unraveled in slow motion.

Please don't, Kacey!

"Oh, Dack! I have one of dose too!"

He poked Jack in the side then lifted his own shirt.

Their birthmarks.

Two to three inches in length.

Like a brush stroke of brown paint over their right hip bones.

Nearly identical.

Jack stiffened and his hands dropped to his sides.

Fear paralyzed me.

He stared at Kacey for a few long moments as silence hung like dense smoke—smothering me. When he spoke, his whisper was strained. "Please tell me I'm making the wrong assumption."

Jack's chest heaved. When I looked at his face, moisture was in his blue eyes. His throat worked with a swallow. I opened my mouth to speak but words died on my lips. A choking noise came out instead as pain ravaged my heart. Kacey hung on my leg and whined for the milk. Jack finally looked at my face. The hurt in his gaze was more than I could bear.

He studied me for a few long moments. "Miranda? Say something!"

"I—" As I fumbled for words, his expression froze. The hurt and moisture receded and a gaze as icy as Jules' took its place. The muscles in his cheek rippled as he clenched his jaw.

He took a couple steps back from us and ran his hands over his head, muttering cuss words. He looked at Kacey again then back at me. His voice, hard and unfeeling, commanded, "Take him upstairs. I don't want to lose it in front of my—" He motioned toward Kacey then paced down the hall once more, running his hands over his head again.

My vision blurred as I ushered Kacey toward the stairs.

"Miranda?"

I turned back.

"You *are* coming back down tonight."

THIRTY

Miranda

"About damn time." Jack didn't look at me. I'd just come down the stairs from tucking Kacey in and he was leaning against the window sill, looking into the night rain.

"Say it."

I didn't answer, unsure of what he meant.

"Admit Kacey is my son."

I swallowed, fighting against the fear closing off my vocal chords. Despite the pep talk and reassurances I attempted to soothe myself with, I was shaking. The unknown terrified me. Even I didn't fully understand this situation. We would only be able to piece together the past if we worked together. The turmoil in my midsection told me this wouldn't be a peaceful conversation where we compared stories. I forced calm into the truth. "He—he's your son."

Jack hung his head down, using the sill to support him as he leaned forward. His back, now clothed with a red t-shirt, collapsed on a deep exhale. "You know, I feel like a real idiot.

Jules told me two weeks ago Kacey was mine. And I defended you. Said you'd never do something like hide my child from me."

"Jack—"

"I thought I knew you."

"You do! I—"

"No, I don't." He turned to face me then, his eyes burning with anger. "Because the Miranda I fell in love with would never do something like this." He gained volume. "I have missed *four years* of my son's life. While some abusive piece of shit has been taking care of him?" He motioned out the door, indicating Chris.

I blinked, clearing my vision. "There is so much you don't und—"

"What is there to understand? Nothing—*nothing*—makes this okay. You kept my son away from me and allowed him to be neglected and mistreated."

"Allowed it?" My voice was a squeak of emotion.

Jack's voice was uncomfortably loud for the small living room, his hand motions were jerky and broad. "I don't know everything about your ex, but I know enough. You wanted me to drop you off at a homeless shelter for crying out loud!"

"I had no other choice!"

He scoffed at that. "Dammit, Miranda! How about come *home*? Did you ever think of that? Did you ever consider that Jack—despite all the problems you said he had—wanted his kid?"

"I tr—"

"If I recall correctly, I was *begging* you to stay. Begging you!"

He wouldn't let me finish a sentence and I wanted to scream at him. But I choked on my tears. "Jack—"

"Do you like him better? Is he so great you thought you'd nestle up there in Ohio with *my* kid? Pretend like a family?"

Indignation poured into me. "Jack! There are things you know nothing about!"

"Apparently! Because I have a three year old son I met three weeks ago."

"I thought you knew!"

That stopped him for a moment and he scoffed in annoyance. "Oh, I see. This is another round of that game we used to play in our marriage. Where I have to *read* your *mind* and automatically know exactly what you're thinking, what you're feeling, and have the perfect response in all situations in order to keep you happy."

A sob escaped. How could he say that? "Jack, I have *never* asked you to read my mind."

He fake laughed. "Oh yeah? How about the months that went by where we didn't talk? Never spoke to each other and you had the audacity to claim I didn't listen to you. Like, what the hell? You weren't *saying* anything!"

He was treading on a tender place. "No, it's bec—"

"I tried to be nice, even brought you flowers, and you threw them out the window!" His eyes were wild, his muscles taut. "Is Chris better at reading your mind, knowing your needs without you having to actually communicate them? Is that why you've been in Ohio for four years with *my* son?"

Sobs shook my shoulders.

"Wait a sec." He held his hand up, thinking. "I was the 'one night mistake' wasn't I? A night with your husband, who loved you, and wanted a child, was the big mistake? I *loved* you. I have never stopped loving you. All the time we've been apart, I wanted you here with me. The past few weeks, I thought we had a chance—a do-over where we could make things right... but this?" He shook his head, running his hands over it.

Desperation edged into his tone. "We won't be able to come back from this, Miranda Howard."

Howard?

A knife to my heart.

"Please stop talking and let me explain!"

"Stop it. There is no *explain*. I don't want to hear about how hurt you were at the end of our marriage. About how I messed it all up and you were scared or couldn't trust me or whatever your reasons are. I've heard all that shit before and I'm sick of it. You know what?" He grabbed his jacket from the hook. "Screw this. I need to take a run."

This was why our marriage had died. When things got too tough for him to handle, he left. He disappeared and hoped the problems would too.

He charged out the front door and I followed him into the night. The cold rain had picked up speed, a freezing contrast to the warm April night.

He slipped his arms into the jacket as he walked toward the road.

"You can't just leave like this!"

"Why not? You did!"

"There is so much you don't know. Please stay!"

He barked a haughty laugh and whipped around to glare at me. "Stay! Oh, trust me. I'm staying." His eyes were fiery. "One thing you need to get comfortable with right now is this—I'm not going *anywhere*. He's mine, and I *will* be a part of his life."

Then without realizing it, he spoke my fears into existence.

"That little boy deserves to have a man in his life who actually gives a damn about him." He zipped up the jacket. "We'll talk custody arrangements later."

With that, he took off at a brisk pace down the rainy street and into the dark. As he disappeared, the rain seeped into my t-shirt and hair. I stood there, lost and alone, feeling my world shrink. The walls closed in.

What have I done?

For a brief second I missed Ohio. Would almost trade the fire in Jack's eyes for the instability of life with Chris. I shook my head at my own wandering thoughts. I couldn't go back. My life was permanently meshed with Jack's—for better or worse—because of Kacey.

We'll talk custody arrangements later.

The steady rain morphed into a downpour. I turned back to the front door, trembling.

"Miranda?"

I startled and whipped around to see Richard standing on his covered porch.

My heart almost jumped out of my chest. "Richard!" I raised my voice for him to hear me over the rain. "You scared me." As much as I loved him, I wasn't in the mood. What was he doing up so late anyway? Had he been watching us argue?

"Weather's looking bad." He yelled something else, but I didn't hear him.

"What?" I cupped my hand behind my ear.

He spoke slower, his voice barely carrying over the rising storm. It took a few tries, but I was finally able to catch it. "Too much rain will wash away your seeds!"

Too much rain?

What was I supposed to do about that? You can't protect a garden from rain. Tears pricked my eyes. The dumb garden was one more thing I ultimately had no control over.

THIRTY-ONE

Jack

"Man, I've never seen you do that many reps." Cass, a gym rat, huffed at me.

I grunted, but didn't bother responding. I broke quite a few of my personal records tonight. I wasn't a body builder by any stretch of the imagination, but I was strong. And tonight? Rage was my fuel.

My dad had preached about mountains and valleys to us on lots of occasions. I am not sure why he enjoyed that imagery so much, considering he wasn't an outdoorsy guy at all. But he reminded Jules and I that life was full of valleys, but to every valley there were dozens of peaks. We could keep our heads stuck in the valley, or embrace the suck to climb the peaks.

For my dad, expressing this truth meant when things got hard, he dug in. He pressed into the things he was good at. Like winning nearly impossible defense cases. He said those types of wins made the valley seem small.

I obliterated a few personal records, garnering way too much attention from people at the gym, but my valley didn't feel smaller. Not in the slightest. In fact, the opposite was true. It loomed bigger, sat heavier, with each quiver of my muscles.

The only thing the two hour work out accomplished was muting my rage by a notch or two. But as furious energy was spent, something else took its place. A feeling I hated and would much rather ignore.

After sitting in the sauna, I showered and headed to the truck. No clue where I was going next, but it sure wasn't going to be home. The rain had slowed to a fine mist and the night was warm. Surprisingly so. A huge storm system was passing over Middle Tennessee. Maybe the worst was over for the greater Nashville area.

My wandering brought me to a late-night bar I'd visited a time or two. Probably didn't need a couple drinks, but I wasn't sure where else to go at this time of night. The place was deserted as I talked with the bartender and the few people at the barstools. It was a weeknight, after all.

After the bartender poured my second, I paid my tab. Stomach was hurting.

He held up a remote at the sole TV showing baseball replays over the bar. "Hey, you guys mind if I flip to weather? Want to see what this storm is doing."

As he flipped channels, my brain traveled to Miranda and Kacey. I did my best to avoid thinking about them. A second drink hadn't helped yet.

Conflict roiled in me. On the one hand, I was relieved Kacey didn't belong to Miranda's ex. But...mine? She *lied*. She'd hidden him for four years. And for three weeks she had lied. And she had the guts to come play house for some money.

I thought it was impossible for Miranda and I to have kids. But we got our miracle and I wasn't even there to be a part of it. My fingers flexed around the lukewarm glass on the counter.

And then to further confuse me...I was glad. Thinking about Kacey made my chest so tight I could hardly breathe. I had a *son*. And he was an energetic, funny kid who looked so much like Miranda. I liked him a lot. The past few weeks had caused deep yearning for a child like him. To find out he was mine...

How could she do this? This wasn't like Miranda. She wasn't spiteful. I'd had some girlfriends who might pull a stunt like that—maybe Bree—but not Miranda. She was the most good-hearted person I knew. Incapable of pure evil.

Had I been too hard on her?

What had she said?

There are things you know nothing about.

I wondered what she meant. What type of things would justify something this terrible? I had ripped her a new one instead of hearing her out. A deep breath filled my lungs. She probably cried herself to sleep. The image churned regret in my midsection. I ran my hands over my head, wishing I could rewind the evening.

Or while I'm at it, the last ten years.

How had we gone from hot and heavy to *this* in twenty-four hours?

I glanced at the clock on the wall. One a.m. Need for sleep pressed in. I'd worked a long day, had it out with Miranda, and my muscles still burned.

A tiny voice in my spirit urged me to go home, make it right. But another voice—deep and booming—told me to focus on the peaks. The valley would always be there and I could deal with it later.

I pulled out my phone and picked up an 8:00 a.m. shift.

THIRTY-TWO

Miranda

My eyes were puffy and burned from last night. I pulled a hat low on my forehead to shield them from the sun. The storm knocked branches down and killed the power. The wind scattered patio furniture across the porches.

The backyard was a mud hole. Water stood a few inches deep in low spots around the yard. Kacey thought the puddles were glorious and splashed away.

As I clomped through the muck to the raised beds, my heart in my wet tennis shoes, I prayed Richard would stay inside today. I was in no mood to talk. Every throb of my heart pained me. Guilt weighed down my steps.

A quick survey of our garden showed how much work there was to do. Branches had crushed a few seedlings. Okra and green bean seeds were exposed, the dirt mounds we'd patted over them having been washed away. Mulch piled around the wooden barriers of the garden, pushed this way and that—not doing its job anymore. Ripples in the exposed dirt showed how the garden had been pounded, punished, by the rain.

As I stooped to pluck up branches and twigs, Richard called. "Good morning!"

I sighed, tried to smile. "Hi, Richard."

"Storm was something, wasn't it?"

"Yes sir."

He approached the fence, draping his arms over the top of it. "How's the garden faring?"

"Well, you were right. The seeds were washed away."

He grunted. "Yes, young lady. Figured they would be."

I thought about his odd comment during the storm. "Why did you say that last night?"

His brows knit in confusion. "What now?"

"Why did you say that about the seeds in the middle of the storm? That the rain would wash them away?" I tried not to sound upset, but I was. So angry and hurt I couldn't stand it. Jack didn't even give me the chance to speak. He thought I hid Kacey on purpose. A tingle in my eyes made me blink. "You can't protect a garden from rain."

Richard clasped his hands together, leaning his weight against the fence. "True, true. Sometimes the heavy rain visits 'fore the little seeds are ready."

"But why tell me right in the middle of the storm? It's not like I could do anything right then." My voice wobbled as I stooped to pluck branches out of the garden.

"Just making sure you were ready for the work cut out for you today." He grinned, the strangeness of his statement not computing.

My squash plants were gone. Bent and broken on the main stems. My nose stung with tears. I rubbed it and pressed my lips together, mustering strength for things I didn't want to deal with. Letting nature take its course crossed my mind. Who needs vegetables anyway?

"Well, I lost my squash and all my seeds. What do I do?"

"What do you think you should do?"

I loved Richard, but he could be awful cryptic sometimes. "Uh, start over?"

He shook his head. "Nah. That's going back too far. You got that good foundation in place. Just rebuild. Harvest might be delayed a bit, but you'll still get one. Some years, you'll have better, easier harvests than others. And that's okay."

Some of the seeds in my palm had already begun to germinate. "Do—do you have any more squash seedlings?"

"I certainly do. I always have extra." He disappeared and came back with two yellow squash plants. I met him at the fence. "Want help getting these in?"

I shook my head and didn't meet his gaze. "No, I got it."

He didn't release the plants when I tried to pull them away.

His brow wrinkled in a million places as he frowned. "You alright this morning?"

I couldn't lie. The truth pooled in my eyes. Figured he'd probably been around the block enough times to see plenty of women cry. I swiped my cheek, surprised at the honest answer coming out of my lips. "Not really."

He nodded. Still didn't give me the plants.

I continued, suddenly needing someone to talk to. "My life...my life is chaos, Richard. I'm not doing right by my kid. I'm not doing right by Jack. I have *no* idea how I got in the mess I'm in." We hadn't ever gotten personal about Jack and my situation. I doubted he knew we were married—presently or in the past. "Have you ever felt so lost you wanted to give up?"

He clicked his tongue. "Many times. Many times."

"What did you do?"

"The next right thing." He said it without batting an eye—as if it was so obvious.

I turned my head so he wouldn't see the flash of annoyance I couldn't prevent as I dropped my hands. "But what if you've done all the wrong things for so long that the next right thing isn't obvious? I have no idea how to fix what's broken."

He thought for a long moment. "Well, sometimes the next right thing is pluckin' out what you've already done. Righting wrongs. Cleaning messes. Like what you're about to do with those squash plants." He shrugged.

"Then what?"

"You just replant."

It was a pat answer, but at least he gave me the dang plants.

I hadn't seen Jack in three days. And it was the reality check I needed.

One thing I learned, loud and clear. There was something *wrong* with me. Trusting too easily was my fundamental flaw. I should've known by now what to expect. I *told* myself this would happen.

This was Jack. Who he was. How he responded. It was why we were broken beyond repair. Because Jack wouldn't ever stick around for the *repair* part. Something about brokenness scared the heck out of him. He wouldn't face it like a man. Never had. And I *knew* this about him.

But did I use my past experience to make smart choices and keep my guard up? Nope. Like a gullible idiot, I let him sweep me off my feet. Had Kacey not interrupted us, I would've let Jack take me to his bed—as if this wasn't convoluted enough already.

Stupid. Stupid.

I understood he was angry, but we had mountains to scale, and he wouldn't get back here so we could start the journey. He hadn't even let me get a word in about what happened.

I expected him to avoid me. But now, he was avoiding *Kacey*. Whether he liked it or not, he was a father. And conversations needed to be had. We had to figure out what happened in the past and do our best to fix it.

I thought about texting him the whole story and begging him to come back. But decided against it. I was pissed at him. He was being the same old, cowardly Jack. I wasn't going to spill my guts over text. If he wanted the truth, he could face me—head on. Like a freaking adult for once.

I'd let myself stew for days over his words, *we'll talk custody arrangements later.* Once I had my money, we could talk custody all the livelong day. Because I would get the best and be ready.

If he wanted to call off the marriage deal prior to the allotted time, I'd just refuse to sign papers. I was staying. Until I got my check, Jack was stuck with me. But when I finally did...I was starting fresh. Completely. Nothing could make me stay.

My garden might have a decent foundation, but this marriage never did. What I needed was a fresh start. A new life.

I'd heard Jack coming and going at weird hours, presumably to sleep and have a quick bite. But he was only ever home during sleeping hours, and I never caught him.

Didn't care to catch him anyway.

In fact, I was so pissed I washed the stupid sweatshirt. All of the desires we'd been playing with were a disaster just waiting to happen. I tried to ignore the pain in my chest when I pulled it out of the dryer and it smelled like detergent.

But on the fifth day of total and utter avoidance, I texted him: *This is ridiculous, Jack. Are we going to talk like adults or keep avoiding this conversation like we are in middle school?*

It wasn't until the end of the day that he texted me back: *When?*

Me: *After Kacey's in bed.*
Jack: *I'm working.*
Me: *Tonight. Make it happen.*
Jack: *Fine.*

THIRTY-THREE

Then

Miranda

We tied the knot after a two-month engagement. I was twelve weeks pregnant at our wedding and you couldn't even tell. The baby was kind to me and let me keep my body for a while. I didn't have the slightest bump yet and still looked pretty hot in a bikini. Jack marveled at my pregnant body though—enjoying the parts that *had* changed. The crazy man actually looked forward to watching me waddle around.

Because my morning sickness was manageable, we had a destination wedding, small and intimate, on a Florida beach. I promised myself to the only man I'd ever loved while a sea breeze whipped my nearly sheer dress around my ankles. The wind picked up Jack's short hair and rumpled his shirt sleeves.

He dipped me in a kiss then hauled me into the shallow surf for pictures.

My heart soared. Everything I hoped for—a doting husband, a child, a home, a place to fully belong—was coming to fruition. I'd given my heart to Jack over and over again. He was wonderful, perfect. And the life we were building together was better than my fantasies.

When our friends and family left, we laid in the sun for an entire week. It was the best week of my life with my best friend.

Going home didn't even suck. I couldn't wait to do real life with my husband.

While the plane idled on the tarmac at Berry Field Nashville Airport, I started cramping in my lower abdomen. In the lavatory, fear struck my heart.

I was spotting.

Those little tinges of pink on the tissue sent panic coursing through my veins. We got married sooner than we would have because of the baby. We picked a house to rent with an extra bedroom and had already mapped out the nursery. We talked late into many nights, discussing names and dreaming together.

Jack was *so* happy.

I was happy, too.

This cannot be happening right now.

I exited the lavatory with shaking hands and a twisting stomach. I tried to pull myself together. Tried to remind myself pregnancy spotting does not *always* mean a miscarriage. Tried to take a few deep breaths and not freak out.

But I knew. The life I was living was too good to be true.

I tucked my chin as I passed by the rows, returning to Jack who had an aisle seat. When his eyes met my face above the rows, his expression shifted, immediately reading mine. Somehow, my body accepted what was about to happen. And even though my brain wasn't convinced, my heart was already breaking.

The bleeding escalated so quickly we had to scramble, stopping at a store inside the airport for some feminine products. I was crying my eyes out as we picked through baggage claim, caught a transit, and found our truck.

Jack was a stone wall. He had no idea what to do. No idea how to comfort me or support me while my hopes and dreams shattered into a million pieces.

Within four hours, the baby was gone.

And so was the first piece of my heart.

I stared straight out the truck window, letting my tired body sway with the curves and turns. Jack drove. The quiet was heavy, smothering. The hum of the engine and tires suffocated me. I hoped he would break the silence because I didn't have the strength. I fisted a bottle of prescription strength ibuprofen and hospital discharge papers. Despite my attempts to distract my imagination, I couldn't help but wonder what they did with my baby.

After two weeks of spotting and a confirming ultrasound, I went in for a D&E procedure. The meds were wearing off and my head was clearing. I wished it wouldn't. Wished I could just sleep through the next few weeks.

I didn't want to mourn another loss.

This baby was nine weeks, so we hadn't told anyone yet. Jack said we shouldn't make *it* a big deal until we knew whether I'd have a normal pregnancy or not. The joy of new life wasn't even celebrated. His caution and hesitancy to get too excited protected *him*.

But it left my heart in open water.

Because I celebrated alone, I grieved alone.

Jack had one hand on the wheel and one on my thigh. It felt distant, cold. He was there but not really. His heart was far away. Just like it had been before.

For Jack, *vulnerability* meant an empty magazine.

When he spoke, I winced.

"We can always try again, Miranda."

Could we? Two in a row felt like a bad omen.

I blinked, turning my face toward the window so he wouldn't see the few tears leaking out. In our marriage, I learned sad tears made him uncomfortable. So, I swiped them away.

"It's going to be okay, you'll see."

Those were pretty words. I expected pretty words from the outside world, but not Jack. Not my *husband*. I was broken for weeks after our first. And when I slowly bounced back, a piece of me was missing. I would never be the same.

Jack didn't understand it. Or if he did, he didn't care.

"We've only been married five months." He shrugged. "We—we probably weren't ready for a baby anyway."

I ground my teeth. Now, the silence was preferable.

Shut up, Jack. Please just shut up.

"Wasn't meant to be, I guess."

Meant to be?

"Please, Jack. Please just stop talking."

He must've taken my desperate plea to heart. Because he stopped. Completely.

He asked how I was feeling once or twice over the next week.

But other than that, we never talked about the baby again.

He got busy at work, joined a marathon team, and life continued as normal.

For him. Just for him.

THE BLOOMS THAT BROKE US

Curled into the armrest of our couch, I clutched a heating pad to my belly, eyelids still swollen from the ordeal. This one was quick, five hours tops. Thirteen weeks gestation.

The doctors said I had an abnormal uterus which caused the loss of viable pregnancies. The only fix was surgery. One not covered by insurance. A miracle was possible, but certainly not guaranteed.

Jack was desperate to repair me. And I was desperate to repair us. My delusion was thick. I thought a baby would be our savior. So we tried again.

I was inconsolable when the bleeding started.

But no arm came around my shoulders. There was no chest to collapse into. No one held me or shouldered the burden.

Our third baby came and went. No one knew. No one except Jack.

The pain in my heart would've been more bearable if he didn't know. It would be less painful to suffer alone, than to have a partner and still suffer alone. After it was over, he tucked a blanket around me and made sure I had a few things —like the remote and ibuprofen. Then worked a twelve hour shift.

As the weeks rolled by, Jack became more and more scarce. Because suddenly the department was short-staffed. Or there was a work situation. Or he needed a run. Or there was a race coming up he had to train for. Or his buddies wanted another night out.

He was anywhere but home. With anyone but me.

He told me our family might take more time. That we'd be okay with just each other. That we need to move on.

And I honestly hated him for it.

The only way we had been able to somewhat hold our marriage together was to pretend to be okay. Jack couldn't handle my pain, so I said I was fine. And so did he.

THIRTY-FOUR

Jack

I got home late. The house was mostly dark, except for the front window. Miranda must've been waiting for me in the living room. I dreaded this all day. I didn't want to talk to her. My brain bounced from so furious I could punch through the wall to so distraught I wanted to drive straight back to work.

Work and the gym were the only two places I could get lost—forget that I'd missed four years of my son's life. Forget that Miranda, the woman I loved, kept him from me.

I sighed, doing my best to tamp down the conflict in my chest, and unlocked the door.

As I suspected, Miranda sat on the couch, TV off. She glanced over her shoulder at me, eyes bloodshot, and I felt my heart squeeze.

I avoided her for this exact reason.

I didn't want to see her cry.

Regret pooled in my belly. Stupid. She was the one who messed everything up, yet here I was, feeling sorry.

But her red eyes and pink nose made me feel like a giant jerk for being MIA for five days.

We didn't greet each other, which was awkward. But I hesitated to speak first. I hung my keys on the hook and stooped to unlace my boots. When I straightened, I finally asked, "You want me to shower first?"

"Go ahead."

When I returned to the living room with damp hair and sweatpants, Miranda had her head leaning back on the couch, clutching the blanket underneath her chin. Her eyes were closed. Thought she might be sleeping.

"Hey."

She startled, and her head came up.

"Were you asleep?"

She shook her head and swiped her cheeks. "No, just running my lines."

I snorted a half-laugh. Couldn't help it.

I eased down on the other side of the sectional couch. A few beats of quiet passed between us. Since she was the one who demanded we talk—I figured I'd let her start us off.

She fiddled with the fringes of the blanket. "Jack, we need to talk about what happened. Because—I promise. It's not what you think."

Her statement was like seeing a distress flare in the distance. A conflicting blend of dread and anticipation raced up my spine.

I leaned forward, propping my elbows on my knees, and nodded, probably looking a lot calmer than I felt.

"I have to tell you everything." Her voice shook. "My heart cannot keep it in any longer. But, I'm probably going to cry. Maybe"—she took a deep breath—"maybe even sob. Is that okay?"

Memories I'd rather forget played my mind. Like the times

she sobbed on the floor of the shower. How I'd left to pick up extra shifts because I couldn't stand the sound of it. I swallowed the lump in my throat. "Yes."

She picked at the blanket, fingers shaking.

"Are you afraid?"

She nodded. "Yes."

My lungs felt tight. "Of me?"

"Yes." She hesitated. "If you leave because I'm crying or walk away for some reason, it'll break me."

I didn't know if she was referring to something I did in the past. The flash of confusion in my head gutted me.

Break her.

Walk away from her.

I stuffed down the guilt cropping up and reassured myself.

I never left her. She left me.

"I'll listen. You have my word."

THIRTY-FIVE

Then

Miranda

After my doctor appointment, I called and left dozens of tearful messages. Even emailed him. Begging him to call me back. I wasn't going to tell Jack I was pregnant over text. That was the type of information you deliver voice to voice. Plus, he would have questions. Any normal person would.

I checked my phone over and over like it was a nervous tic. The fact he wasn't responding—surely, his phone broke or something. Jack wouldn't just ignore me, would he?

Things had gotten so sour between us, maybe he would.

Last time I saw Jack, we spent the night together. Like the two idiots we were. Last time we talked over the phone, Jack was tense. Said he "can't do this anymore." I wasn't sure what he meant, but now, a couple months later, I wished I'd asked him to explain.

He probably blocked my phone.

That possibility stung like peroxide on an open wound.

I tried calling Nashville PD multiple times, but they would never patch me through to Jack, even when I told them it was important. Without a doubt, Jack had instructed them not to. I wanted to kick myself. I contacted him too often after our divorce. No doubt he was sick of hearing from me and was simply trying to block off forms of communication.

Jack wasn't on social media, so I tried the last possible option: I wrote him a letter.

I hit the high points. Wrote that the baby was healthy and prognosis was good if I quit my job. Please call me, etc. Left out my emotional instability, financial crisis, and utter desperation.

A week went by without a word back.

I didn't have time to mess around. Every day I went back to work was a risk. I already asked coworkers to help me with the heaviest trays. Couldn't operate like this forever.

My hope diminished with each passing day. Maybe *I can't do this anymore* meant what it looked like. That he was fully over me. That I pushed too far and asked for too much and now he was done.

Really, truly done.

Depression loomed over me like an angry storm cloud. Took everything I had to keep my head above water.

Ten days after my doctor's appointment, I left Ohio and drove to Nashville.

I pulled onto our old street, my heart heavy. It sat in my chest like a rock. What if he rejected me? What if he got all the messages and just didn't want me or a baby anymore? The thoughts haunted me all through Nashville traffic. My neck hurt from the tension radiating through my body.

The sight of our old house was a stab to the sliver of my remaining sanity. I missed him. Missed Nashville. Missed this old rental with the tiny yard and the second bedroom with the peeling wallpaper that would've made the perfect nursery.

His truck wasn't in the driveway, but another vehicle was.

I'd already decided to go to the NPD if he wasn't home. But, considering the car in the drive, I figured I would knock.

Whose car is that?

Curiosity fueled me now.

I heard movement on the other side of the door. The deadbolt slid and when the door opened, my heart stopped beating.

The most beautiful woman I'd ever seen—auburn hair, tall, piercing brown eyes, flawless skin, infinitely long legs—stood there.

Wearing Jack's Chicago Bears t-shirt and sweatpants.

It felt like I'd been sucker punched.

Her hair was tousled like she just woke up. In fact, there was a sleep mark on her face.

I tried to inhale.

I mean, of course Jack wouldn't stay single forever, but she was—he was—so *soon*? Coming face to face with his rebound was like a nightmare.

Hell, actually.

A beat of silence passed as we stared at each other.

I couldn't form a coherent greeting as I imagined Jack with this model. As I imagined them tearing up the sheets together. As I imagined him touching her in all the ways he had touched me.

The hurt and rage unfurling in my gut was hot, nauseating.

No wonder Jack didn't call me back.

He had *her*.

Suddenly, I hated him. Hated him with every fiber of my being. He was too *busy* to be a dad. Why did he need us when he could have his pick of women? Jack had always turned heads. Had always charmed every soul he came into contact with. He didn't even have to try.

Of course my spot in the bed wouldn't get cold.

Maybe he didn't even miss me.

The nights I had spent mourning this man felt like a joke. There I was, thinking my life was over, and he was out picking up women?

A knife in my heart.

Recognition dawned in her eyes and she narrowed them, letting her gaze travel down the front of me, stopping on my belly.

I didn't have a big bump, but it was there nevertheless. My boobs were ginormous, and my tummy was growing. The combo made my v-neck too tight, accentuating my pregnancy.

"You must be Miranda."

Her eyes were soft, surprisingly unthreatened by my presence. Surely, my gaze shot daggers.

"Yes. And you are?" I wanted to take her down. Tear her limb from limb. Tie her up, light a match, and watch her burn.

"Bree. Jack's girlfriend."

An ongoing thing? The knife twisted.

I opened my mouth to respond, but no words came. What could I say? My cheeks and eyes burned. How in the world had my life come to this? Face to face with my ex-husband's plaything while pregnant with his son? Unbelievable.

Why do I care?

The question slammed into my heart and brought the

answer tumbling into my spirit like a ton of bricks. Painful, paralyzing.

Because I love him. I love him so much.

I loved him. I hated him. I wanted to wring his neck. And I never wanted him to be happy with another woman ever again. Why did I still feel this way? It made no sense.

What was wrong with me?

"I—I guess he's not here?"

She shook her head, pursing her perfect lips to one side. "No, sorry, Miranda." She leaned her shoulder against the door frame, standing in the threshold. Looked far too at home. "Are you here because of the letter?"

Air tumbled from my lungs. "He told—he told you about that?"

She nodded. "He was really upset when he read it."

"He was upset?"

"I mean, yeah, of course he was."

I grappled for a response. "Where—where is he?"

She huffed a sultry laugh. "You don't remember how hard your ex-husband works?" She shook her head, a smart tone rolling off her tongue. "He's at work, obviously." She smoothed the front of Jack's t-shirt like she wanted to call attention to the fact she was wearing it.

I tried to remember my fight was not with her. But the memory-jog didn't quell the mental image of grabbing and ripping patches of her lush hair out.

"Okay." I jerked my head, ready to dish it out. "What are *you* doing here?"

She looked at me like I was a stupid little idiot. Like she needed to let me down easy. "I live here."

I made some kind of noise. A choking sound? Did I gag? Did a sob escape? It felt like my soul left my body. Like I was watching this scene unfold from a distance.

This cannot be real.

At the end of our marriage, I was so hurt. So lonely. So angry at him. Nothing he did was right. Nothing he offered was good enough. Had I pushed him so hard he was just dying to get rid of me? Couldn't wait for me to be gone?

It's my own fault.

She continued. "I told him I'd help him watch his baby while he worked in case you two decided to split custody. But, I think he's just ready for a fresh start, ya know? Ready to leave the past in the past."

Her grubby hands on my child? I would die first.

Her audacity was unmatched.

I took a backward step, reaching behind me for the railing. She said something as I left, but for the life of me, I couldn't register what it was. I think I tripped over the last stair because my ankle started hurting.

A light rain had begun. I didn't even feel it.

When I went to the department, Jack closed the door on us. There was no *family*. There was no *want*. There was no *together*.

And I did it to myself.

I thought a baby would change things. But our miracle came too late, and I was alone now.

Completely alone.

THIRTY-SIX

Jack

I was up, pacing around the room, my chest so tight I thought I might crack a few ribs. My muscles twitched, itching to turn the couch upside down in a fit of rage. I was going to kill Bree. Why would she do that to me?

I ran my hands over my head. "I can't believe this."

"If you didn't know about me being pregnant, how did she?" Miranda's eyes were trained on me. The lights were dim, the brown of her irises dark—lending to the pained expression across her features.

"Because she's a bi—" I stopped, grappling for words that would help us both understand what was going on. "She was an emotional train wreck, and I absolutely would not put it past her to go through my mail."

"And read it?"

"Obviously!"

Miranda scoffed. "But why would she do that?"

"Bree was crazy!"

Her head lolled to the side in annoyance.

"I'm serious. She probably felt threatened by you, which is why she lied."

"Lied about what?"

"Uh, several things." I ticked them off on my fingers. "We didn't talk about the letter. She didn't live with me. And she wasn't even my girlfriend!"

Miranda's face was deadpan. "So, just a hooker then?"

"Miranda! No!"

I wasn't that guy. Why did everyone, even the person who knew me best, assume I was jumping into bed every chance I got? Even Jules had insinuated I played women to get what I wanted.

At one point, when I was young and dumb, I did. I was an idiot who thought satisfaction could be found in a moment. A notion Miranda had proved wrong every day. She taught me, more than anyone else, that something real—something *good* —was cultivated one moment at a time. Unfortunately, we learned everything good could be destroyed, ripped out by the roots, in the blink of an eye.

"She was *wearing* your *clothes.* She still had wrinkles on her face from the pillow. Sleeping till almost noon like she'd had a wild night." Her arms were crossed, and she wouldn't look me in the face.

I didn't have to defend myself to her. We were *divorced* and Bree was a young, selfish brat who rarely heard the word "no." I had more important things to talk about—like why and how I missed *four years* of my son's life because of her.

I ran a hand down my face, forcing calm into my tone. Forcing myself to slow down and explain for Miranda's sake. "There's a story. Want to hear it or keep on?"

"Fine."

"A coworker set me up with Bree because...I was struggling

after our divorce. We went on a few dates, talked a little here and there. But we never became an official couple. Bree acted like we did though." I shook my head, remembering a few things. Like how overly seductive she was. She wasn't my type at all. But I was lonely and made a lot of excuses to keep her around. "She was...she liked me more than I liked her, I'll put it that way."

Miranda was frowning at me. Why did this part matter to her? Why would it bother Miranda that another woman was in my life unless she was jealous?

"Anyway, that particular night, I had a few people over to watch the game and Bree came. I had one beer, but she had way too much. I kept telling her to stop so she could drive home. But by the time the game was halfway through, she was spilling crap. She dumped a bowl of salsa or something down the front of her shirt and pants.

"I planned to drive her home, but right as everyone was heading out for the night, I got called in. So, I told her she could crash on the couch and gave her some fresh clothes to wear. I didn't know how long she'd stay and obviously she never told me you showed up."

Her brow furrowed in confusion. "So, you assume this chick snooped through your mail, intercepted my letter, and lied to keep us apart?"

It did sound crazy. But yes, that's what I thought. I'd put nothing past Bree. I clenched my fists a few times to ease the tension building in my knuckles. Blew out a breath. "It sounds like something she'd do."

"She didn't live with you?"

"No. She never even spent the night."

"Why would she do all that then?"

I had a hunch and it twisted my stomach into knots. It made me want to march into the Blanton and Grayson insurance agency and wring her neck. The pieces of the puzzle clanged together and made my breathing shallow.

"Because...I'm pretty sure she was in love with me."

"In love?"

"We weren't even an item, but when I told her I wasn't interested in anything long term, she dragged her keys down the side of my truck, cussed me out, and sent nasty text messages for a month."

Miranda's jaw dropped open.

"Yeah."

But her expression quickly shifted. "But wait. When I came to the department—"

"I remember. You asked if I got the letter."

"Yes."

"I..." I scrubbed a hand up my jaw, the weight of what I lost settling on me, dragging me under. Desperation pushed me into a frantic explanation. "Man, I feel like an idiot. But I got so many letters from the credit card company, Miranda. You let the payments on your old card lapse and never changed the address. I couldn't change it for you since the card was in your name—I tried. There was a threatening notice, the interest rate and monthly payment were skyrocketing and your credit score went to crap—and it wasn't even great to start."

"You thought I traveled to Tennessee to talk about my credit card debt?"

"Yeah! You tried to communicate with me so many times."

"What?" She seemed incredulous, like she had no recollection of how often she'd hit me up.

"I ended up blocking your number because you called and texted me all the time about everything. One time you called to ask where your oil dipstick was located."

"I didn't have anyone!"

"I get that. But you *left* me." I opened and clenched a

fist near my face, trying to hold myself together. "You left while I was begging you to stay. I couldn't"—I dropped back onto the couch—"I couldn't keep the lines of communication open. It was killing me, Miranda. When you showed up, I assumed you were there because your credit score sucked so bad you couldn't get an apartment." The admission made me feel small. "Which is horrible, but I honestly wanted you to find your own way and leave me alone."

"But didn't I say I was pregnant at the department?"

"No, you definitely didn't."

"But we talked about the letter."

"You asked if I *got* the letter. You never repeated what it said. And then you mentioned something about me helping financially."

"Yeah, because I was about to be a single mom!"

"I didn't know that though! Try to see from my perspective. I thought you were *there* because you needed money."

She shook her head, trying to process. "I can—hardly believe it. How do I know *you're* not lying?"

She met my gaze, and I stared into those deep brown eyes. Surely, after everything, she could answer that one on her own.

"Do you really have to ask?"

Realization passed between the two of us and it stung. She wanted me to be there. She came back to give us a second chance. I would've gone to battle for that opportunity. And she knew it. We both knew it.

Four years. Four years we would never get back.

The thoughts flashing through my head were dizzying—enough to make any man want to go get lost in a bottle. My son, my wife, my stupid ex-whatever-Bree-was. Everything I had stewed over regarding Miranda got obliterated with one conversation. I had no reason not to believe her and had given her no reason to doubt me.

She pulled her gaze away and silence hung between us. I propped my forehead in my palms and took a few deep breaths. My skin turned damp as rage churned my blood.

Miranda softly sniffled.

Bree cost me my *family*.

My family!

"Miranda—" My voice scraped. "I never—" I swallowed, trying to clear it. Trying to find the words. What to even say? "I never would've turned my back on you or Kacey like that."

She didn't answer.

"Did—did you ever try again?"

She nodded, her sniffling growing more persistent. "Yes. So many times. I even mailed you pictures of Kacey months later, but they were returned to me. By the post office, I think."

"I moved. Bought this place." Silence fell, long and heavy.

Ultrasounds, doctor visits, his birth, first cry, first steps.

All the things I wouldn't share with my son.

Or my wife.

My chest heaved, my own eyes burning. I pressed my fingers into my eyelids, taking a few shuddering breaths.

Did she become a mom totally on her own? Who helped her? Who was there with them? I was afraid if I asked, she'd say Chris. And if she did, I would lose it.

"Why didn't you take me to court for child support? That's what anyone in your situation would've done."

She took three breaths, grasping for stability, before she spoke. "Part of it was money. Paying an attorney would've been impossible." She shifted, dropping her gaze to the blanket again. "The other part was due to my very complicated, very sticky relationship with Chris."

Of course. *Chris.*

She continued, twisting her fingers in her lap. "He reassured me that we didn't need you. That"—her voice broke—"that he'd take care of us."

The question threatened to burst from my vocal chords. I had to know, even though I didn't want the mental images burned in my brain. Didn't want the truth. My voice was taut, a painful rasp. "Was he there?"

"Where?"

"Chris. At the birth. After the birth. Was he there?"

Her long sigh was the only answer.

I jumped to standing and cursed. I paced toward the window, grinding my fist into my palm, stringing his name together with some choice words.

"I'm so—so sorry, Jack."

I stood, blinking against the sting. My head spun. I was shaking. "I—I need some space. I..." My words dropped off because I didn't know what I needed.

A time machine, that's what.

Something, anything to take us back.

She stood, her head tipped toward the floor. "I understand. Me too."

She silently slipped up the stairs and I watched her go, the weight of loss pressing into my chest deeper, more constricting with each passing second.

I glanced at the clock. 11:30 p.m. If Bree still had the same schedule, she showed up at the downtown Nashville agency around 8:30 a.m.

I'd be waiting.

THIRTY-SEVEN

Jack

B&G insurance sat right smack in the downtown hustle and bustle. I got there a little early, dressed for work, in case it took a while. Had to be at work by ten.

The receptionist on the ground floor of the high-rise building directed me to floor sixteen.

About twelve people crammed in behind me. I backed into the corner. Didn't like small spaces. Made me feel larger than I already did.

A loud hum filled the lift. I took a few deep breaths, gathering my thoughts once again. My eyes stung a bit—was dead tired. I wore ruts into my bedroom floor last night, not dropping to sleep until well after two in the morning.

My anger had cooled a smidge and been replaced with hurt. With a deep insatiable need to understand *why*. To make sure Bree comprehended what she destroyed. There wasn't a way to get justice. Nothing could ever be done to make things right.

I needed confirmation of what Miranda said. Tangible evidence it was true. That my son hadn't been *hidden* from me, but *stolen* from me. I needed to hear it.

From Bree.

And I wanted that letter. If she had destroyed it, they might have to call on-site security to haul the rogue officer out of the building.

Tension radiated through my body. I wanted to slam my fists against the close-door button. Dumb elevator stopped at every freaking floor.

My watch read 8:37 a.m.

When I exited the elevator, I found a receptionist who helped me navigate the maze and directed me to Bree's office. I was glad she had her own space and not a desk inside a common area. Maybe she'd been promoted.

She had her head bent over a schedule on her desk, chewing on the end of her pen. Fresh anger rekindled in me at the sight of her auburn hair. Beautiful, but only skin deep. I imagined her, tousled and sleep-faced, smirking at my heartbroken Miranda. Taunting my pregnant wife.

Maybe I shouldn't have come. If I didn't flip her desk, it'd be a miracle.

Bree must've found her happily-ever-after despite the havoc she'd wrecked on mine. I was surprised she could lift her left hand given the huge rock on her finger.

I took a deep, steadying breath before rapping my knuckles on her propped-open door.

She looked up and her mouth opened in surprise. "Jack!"

I nodded once, but didn't smile. "Bree."

"What a pleasant surprise!" She stood, straightening her tight skirt, and giving me a very obvious once over. "It's been years—you look fantastic."

"Do I?" I drew a deep breath. "That's a shocker because I'm pretty freaking pissed right now."

The smile on her face melted. Recognition skittered across her features before her jaw set.

I unclipped my cell phone at my side and tapped the home screen to illuminate a picture of Kacey and Miranda playing on the swing set at the park. I held it out for her to see. "You ever see that woman?"

She flicked her hand dismissively. "I don't know. Maybe."

"Don't lie to me. Do *not* lie."

She looked up into my eyes. The truth was there—on full display for me to read.

"Answer me."

"Sounds like you know."

"Say it."

A faint hint of a smile tugged at her lips. She made no move to speak, denying me information.

"That woman and my *son* have spent the last four years in hell, and I want to know if you're the one responsible."

I clipped the phone back as she crossed her arms over her chest. I refused to fill the silence. This woman was going to tell me the truth if I had to sit in her office till next week.

A few long moments passed before her jaw clenched with a tight swallow. "Fine. She came to your house that morning after the game. Remember?"

I nodded, my blood near boiling point. "And?"

"And I told her plain and simple. You were over her and she needed to move on."

"Bree, she was—"

"Pregnant?" She lifted her eyebrows. "Yes, I know."

"And you knew because you read my mail."

She gave a soft laugh. "Yeah, I've never been one to deny

my curiosities. One envelope in your gigantic stack of mail had an Ohio stamp…I knew your ex lived there. So, I opened it."

"Where is it?"

"The letter?"

"Yes."

"I threw it away." She scrunched her nose like the letter left a bad taste in her mouth. "Years ago."

"You had no right to do that." I drew a sharp, shuddering breath. Breaking my knuckles in the drywall would hurt less.

"But I did. What's done is done, right?"

"No. You injected yourself into the intimate details of my life, and stood between me and the *only* person I have *ever* wanted. I just met my son three weeks ago."

"All is fair in love and war, Jack. You should know that." She waved toward my phone. "Looks like you two found your way back together anyway."

I pushed the words out around a lump in my throat. "I have to know why you did this."

"Because *I* wanted you."

I scoffed. "You know how delusional you sound? We talked for what—five, six weeks?"

"Plenty long enough for me to know I wanted more."

As she said the words, my eyes landed on a picture frame on the other side of her desk. Bree, a man, and a little baby girl. I reached over, picking it up. "Is this your family?"

"Yes."

I studied them—smiling, laughing, the man with his arms around the two of them. "You stole this from me."

She surveyed her fingernails as if she was bored with the conversation. Her tone was half-hearted. "When we met, I thought you were sweet, something a little different. One hour into our first date, you were the man I wanted to keep around. And usually I find a way to get what I want.

"So when she showed up at your house, I lied. Said you were mine. Because you're too fair. I knew you'd go back to her even if she didn't deserve you." She huffed and looked me up and down, hitching an eyebrow. Clearly she enjoyed the view. "And you deserve the best."

I puffed in disbelief. "And that's supposed to be you?"

"Obviously." She huffed in annoyance. "I can't even fathom how you would compare the two of us."

My fists clenched at my sides. She could say whatever she wanted about me, but she couldn't speak ill of my wife.

"All worked out for the best though." She slowly strolled around her desk to stand right in front of me. "The man I wound up with is rich and adventurous. Very unlike you. However, we have a special little arrangement in our marriage I'd love to tell you all about."

She crossed her arms again, making an intentional show of squeezing her breasts together and giving me an eye-full.

I looked away as heat flew up my spine. Embarrassment churned with my anger making the room feel smaller, hotter. Felt like I'd been caught making out behind the bleachers in middle school. She was a married woman for crying out loud! I shouldn't have come.

She continued, "Our marriage is very *open*, Jack."

Open?

My jaw may have hit the floor. Before I could even find my tongue to respond, she continued. "You are probably overdue some excitement."

This cannot be happening right now.

She reached out to run her fingers down my forearm. "We should—"

I snapped.

"Whoa!" My palms flew out to the sides as my feet quickly put distance between us. "Let's make something crystal clear. The only woman I'm ever going to *be* with is my wife."

Bree had the audacity to laugh. Her head tilted back as she slipped behind her desk, dropping into the seat again. "I had no doubt you'd say that." She gave me a patronizing once over with a tsk. "Yeah, we wouldn't have worked out. Too traditional."

Stunned silence wasn't something I experienced very often. Everything I had marched in wanting to say evaporated from my brain. But I finally formed words, pathetic as they were. "You are disgusting." I shook my head in disbelief. "I must've been blind to keep you around as long as I did."

She perked up. "Now *that* I can agree with. You are most definitely blind." She opened a file on her desk and rifled through the papers. Looked up at me with a plastered smile. "Your loss."

She pursed her lips and tilted her head to the side like the joke was on me.

Then the truth dawned. Bree didn't even value her *own* marriage. Of course she wouldn't care about anyone else's. Looking into her cool and haughty expression, I felt sick for the little girl who would grow up in her shadow.

I had never stopped to consider just how bad off I was after Miranda left. I must've been one depressed, lonely idiot. Standing before her, things were returning to my memory. How she seemed to text and have a lot of male friends. How frustrated she was with my glacial dating pace. How she badmouthed "boring" people. I should've seen who she was.

The apology I wanted? Yeah, that was never going to happen.

Her face was devoid of emotion, stone cold. "Well, unless you've invented a time machine, why the hell are you still standing in my office?"

"Because right now, we are trying to fix what you broke. An entire *family*, Bree. The woman I love thinks I abandoned her because of you. I knew you were a snotty bitch, but I thought you'd give a damn."

She pressed her lips together. "Get out."

There was no use continuing on with her. Some people were past the point of no return. My voice was nearly a growl. "With pleasure."

When I exited her office, I slammed the door behind me.

I stormed out the way I came, hating I had to go to work raging like this. I need to run ten miles. Maybe fifteen. However many it took to run off the tension in my muscles and numb the stress.

I left with only one image burned into my brain— courtesy of my imagination—that repulsive smirk breaking my wife's heart.

What did I expect? Nothing—not even an apology—would make this better. Nothing would ease the ache in my chest. Nothing would change until I fixed things with Miranda. But dammit I didn't know how.

THIRTY-EIGHT

Miranda

I was falling asleep on the couch, trying to read a digital book on my phone, when the front door opened. Jack hung his keys and stooped to take off his boots like he always did. He walked behind the couch and stopped, peering over the back of it.

"I'm awake." I said.

"Good. I know it's late, but can we talk?"

"It's only nine-thirty."

"Okay, I'm going to shower. I'll only be a few."

"Yeah." I sat up. "That's fine."

I was glad Jack was home early enough to talk. I'd been thinking all day long about the conversation we had. Words couldn't express the relief I felt to learn Jack didn't know about the letter. That it wasn't *my* fault all this happened. We truly did the best we could given the circumstances.

But my heart ached to no end. Things could've been so

different. But now, we were here and had to do the right thing for Kacey. The past was the past.

Jack needed to be a part of Kacey's life. We needed to tell Kacey he was his dad.

Surely, Jack would want that too. I hoped my suggestion to co-parent Kacey would encourage Jack to settle outside of court. Things didn't have to get legal. I was willing to stay in Tennessee. Was wiling to do everything I could to make sure Jack was involved. We didn't have to fight over him.

When Jack came back, he was wearing sweats and a hoodie. Cozy clothes no one saw him in. I always loved seeing Jack dressed down like that. It softened the hard lines of his body, giving him a more vulnerable look. He'd go from bullet-proof vest to snuggly bear and it was addictive.

Well, used to be addictive.

I pulled my eyes away. Thinking about snuggling wouldn't do me any favors. He was hard enough to resist as it was. Now that we'd shared an impassioned kiss and learned the truth about the past, my heart was going to need a freaking fortress to stay safe.

I expected him to sit on the opposite side of the couch like he usually did. But he didn't sit at all. He came right up to me and held out his hand. I frowned in confusion, and he gave his hand a little shake, indicating I take it.

I reached up, slowly sliding my fingers into his big warm palm. He wrapped his hand tightly around mine and pulled me to stand. When I was upright, he enveloped me in his arms. My cheek pressed into his sternum as he squeezed. A brief moment of panic overtook me. My arms hung at my side as I fought the urge to push him away.

One of his hands pressed between my shoulder blades while the other ran over my hair, gently smoothing it back, gently running his fingers through it. My eyes fluttered closed as the tickling at my scalp caused goosebumps to run down my body.

Gracious. This feels good.

I relaxed into his hug, my arms lifting to curl around his torso. He smelled amazing. Like fresh manly soap and the laundry detergent I was hating on the other day. I tried not to take a deep breath, yet here I was almost hyperventilating. Unwilling to exhale.

His hands moved to the sides of my head, tipping it up to look at me. His blue eyes looked straight into mine. A pain in my heart formed as I saw the regret there.

His voice, soft and gravelly, was a hum over my face. "Miranda, I never meant to hurt you." His throat bobbed on a swallow. "I'm so sorry."

My breath tumbled. "Jack."

"There's nothing the two of us did wrong. You did everything you could. And I—I just didn't know." He raked his hands down my hair then placed them back on my face. "I promise I would've taken—" He abruptly stopped, changing course. He sighed. "You would've had choices. You wouldn't have needed Chris. I hope you know that."

I nodded. "I know, Jack."

"I keep trying to put myself in your shoes. But even imagining how much this hurt you is so painful I can hardly stand it."

Tears immediately filled my eyes. So painful. He had no idea. No inkling of everything I'd gone through. But Jack had been through so much too.

"I've been thinking the same about you. I wanted you to be a part of Kacey's life. I can't imagine how you feel right now."

He nodded, and we let the suckiness of the situation marinate in the silence between us for a moment.

"We're going to figure all this out." He guided my head

back against him and I relented, rebelliously loving this hug and wanting it to never end. His voice rumbled beneath my ear. "Can I be honest?"

I nodded as his chest expanded with a deep breath then collapsed with a sigh.

"I'm fighting the urge to run out the door and be anywhere but here. I'm sorry I've been gone all week. We should've had this conversation days ago."

I slowly pushed back, willing myself to break out of his embrace. I instantly felt cold. "Yes, we should've."

Jack stuck his hands into the hoodie pocket. "We can talk now though?"

"Yeah." I sat down and he did too. A good safe distance away.

I didn't want to talk about this stuff either, but the stroke of maturity from Jack meant the world to me. He was trying to do the right thing. We'd figure this out. We had to. For Kacey.

"I went to Bree's insurance agency today."

"You did?"

"Yeah."

"She's an insurance agent?"

He nodded.

"What happened?"

"She insinuated that we should hook up."

"You're kidding."

"No, I was shocked. Apparently, her marriage is very open."

"Ew. That's disgusting." I knew he was used to women making themselves available, but that was a whole new level.

He lifted a shoulder. "I called her a snotty bitch."

I grunted, trying to hold in a snort of laughter. The idea of Jack insulting Bree made me way too happy. "Seriously?"

He nodded, a tiny smile pulling his cheeks back.

"Do you feel better after seeing her?"

"No. Not at all."

"I'm sorry."

"Don't say that. It's not your fault."

I nodded. Felt like there were a million things to talk about, but where to begin? We needed to fit Jack into Kacey's life. The idea of piecing our lives back together was daunting.

After a few awkward beats of silence, I opened the can of worms. I was Kacey's mom after all. "We need to talk about Kacey."

Jack nodded but didn't look up.

"I know you have questions and I'll answer anything, but before we get started, you need to know why I didn't tell you the truth three weeks ago when I realized you didn't know." I took a steadying breath as his gaze fixed on me. "I was afraid —rational or not—that you might want to take custody."

His gaze dropped back to his hands.

"And even though you deserve to be a part of his life, I don't want to go to court. On paper, you have everything. And I am the mom on the run with nothing. Nothing of my own. Even the things that were mine I had to leave in Ohio. Kacey's things, too. I was afraid if I told you, you'd want to take him away from me completely, and I have no means to stop you."

"So you were waiting for my dad's inheritance."

"Yeah. Sounds stupid to say it out loud."

"It's not stupid. I do want Kacey."

"I know—"

"I've missed everything with him so far, and I don't want to miss anything else. I'm not going to lie to make you feel better. I've been thinking about joint custody ever since I learned he was mine."

"Joint?"

"Of course joint." He ran a hand over his head. "I wouldn't try to get full custody. Wait, is that what you were afraid of?"

"Well, I'm not in a great place...I thought you might be angry with me—"

"Kacey needs his dad *and* his mom. You are an amazing mother, Miranda. I would never try to take him *from* you. I just want the chance to be there, too."

"Oh."

"I'm doing my best to fix this family. Not make it worse."

Thank you, Jack.

I wanted to hug him as tears filled my eyes. It was a bit irrational. But, I had no way of knowing how he would respond. "Do you think we can do this outside of a courtroom? Surely, you and I can agree on something and not use an attorney. I want you to be a part of his life. It's what I've wanted all along."

"That would be great. I'm not rolling in cash, and would prefer to keep things out of the legal system, too. Let's only resort to legal measures if absolutely necessary, okay?"

"Okay."

"We both want the best for Kacey. That's good common ground and a good place to start."

"Agreed. I think first things first. We should tell Kacey he has a dad."

Jack whipped his head up to look at me. "Has he asked about me?"

I nodded. "Yeah. Recently."

"He doesn't think Chris is his dad?"

"No."

Jack's shoulders sagged on an exhale, and my heart clenched. "Man, I'm glad to hear that. I'm surprised he's asked."

"Well, he watches PBS and most of the kids on the shows

have moms and dads. He once asked why he doesn't call Chris 'dad,' and I had to tell him Chris isn't his dad."

"He must be pretty smart. That seems intuitive for a..." He cursed then lifted his eyes toward the ceiling in frustration. "I don't even know how old my kid is."

"I'm sorry, Jack." The tremble in my voice was impossible to conceal. "I shouldn't have lied."

He gave a quiet, humorless chuckle. "Both you and I are wracking those up, huh?"

"What up?"

"Shouldn't-haves."

"Oh, yeah, I guess so."

"When's his birthday?"

"It's September 5th."

"Jules was right. She said Kacey was too big, too smart to be just now three."

"I should've been upfront from the beginning. It was risky and stupid." I considered telling him Jules confronted me, but even the memory of it made my stomach twist and a lump form in my throat.

"Let's tell him. Tomorrow."

I offered, "Okay, I can do it."

"I'm off for the first time in days. Maybe afterward...I could take him somewhere."

"Sure, we could go—"

"No." Jack averted his eyes, shifting. "I meant just me and Kacey. I'd like to spend some time with him."

"Oh, uh, yeah, of course."

Why did my heart feel like it might stop beating?

"I already feel so awkward as it is...I just thought that might be easier for me."

I held up my hand and waved it across my body as if *no big deal.* Who was I kidding? This was a huge deal. Monumental. My vocal chords felt paralyzed. I faltered for a moment.

"Miranda?"

"Yep." I croaked.

"You don't look okay with that idea."

I gave my head a hard shake. "No, it's really fine. You are entitled to get to know your son without me hovering around."

"Then what's wrong?"

"I've just—we've just never been separated."

"Wait. Not ever?"

"No. Not ever. Since he was born, we've kind of been a package deal."

"Oh, well maybe we could..."

"No!" I stopped him. My voice tightened over that word. I cleared it. "I can have time to myself. Go on a walk. Go shopping alone. Or drink...coffee."

Forms of torture. Every one of them.

I wasn't trying to convince Jack. I was trying to convince myself. Pushing the words out past trembling lips would be the easy part. Letting Jack and Kacey bond without me while I piddled around would be...I hated the thought.

But it was the least I could do for Jack.

The very least.

"Will Kacey be okay away from you?"

"He'd get in the car with the Joker if he said they were going for ice cream."

Jack's lips split in a soft laugh. "We might have to work on that."

"For sure. His situational awareness isn't too great." My next thought was bittersweet. I kept talking, which is typically a bad idea. "Thankfully, his dad is stellar in that area. I haven't been too great at teaching him how to interact with people and his surroundings. We never went anywhere anyway."

Jack's gaze locked with mine. For a few delicious moments, I allowed myself to read Jack's eyes. From the outside looking in, a lot of people saw a big guy who was firm, strong, unrattled. But I knew Jack. Saw a lot of things others didn't see.

He felt deeply. He just didn't like to admit it. Especially to himself. And right then, I was seeing a host of things.

Regret, sadness, longing, excitement.

I pulled my eyes away, knowing Jack could read me just as easily. "He's a great kid. You're going to have a nice time."

I felt his gaze on me as I smoothed the blanket over my lap, trying to find something for my hands to do.

"Are you sure you'll be okay?"

"Totally." I swallowed the stupid emotion forming in my throat. "I need to get past this. It's not like we will all be together forever. He's going to have to get used to the back and forth, eventually."

"Does he?"

My eyes flew back to his face.

Please don't do this.

His voice was gentle like he was concerned I was skittish. "He wouldn't if we...if we stayed married."

"Jack."

"We can both be there. And he wouldn't have to bounce around."

"I want that stability for Kacey, too, but he needs to see his parents happy. That means we need to move forward with our lives. We can't stay like this forever."

"You aren't happy here?"

I picked at a fuzzy on the blanket. I didn't want to look in his eyes and see the sincerity I heard in his tone. Or see the things he wasn't saying. "Yes, I am, but I mean relationally. I don't think him growing up with parents who are housemates is in his best interest." Even though it pained me to say it, I spoke the honest truth. My true desire for Jack. But my voice shook while I did. "You should go on to find a woman who can be a fresh start. Who will be crazy about you. Someone who can give you more beautiful children so Kacey can have a brother or sister." A tear leaked out. "Because I think"—I pushed the sob back in—"I think he'd really like that."

Jack said nothing. The hum of the fan above us was the only noise. He scrubbed a hand up the side of his jaw. "You don't think we can have those things?"

"Kacey was a miracle, Jack."

"What about the surgery? After we sell the lake house, we can pay for it."

"And what then?" I finally looked at him, not caring about my wet cheeks. Not caring what I would find in his eyes. I needed to quell this quickly. "We'd have a child and be...Jack, we can't..."

He squinted.

Of course Jack wouldn't see. He never had.

"We can't stay married for Kacey. We should be in marriages based on love and mutual trust.

"I have never stopped—"

"Don't, Jack."

"I have loved you since the apple crisp, Miranda."

My voice scraped. "Please stop."

"How is that not enough?"

"Because it just isn't. You—you weren't there for me."

My chest heaved. I didn't want to dredge up the past. Didn't want to think about the desperation I'd felt when I'd dropped a vase from a two-story window.

"You always said that."

"And you never listened."

The line of his brow hardened.

I shook my head. "I *really* don't want to talk about this."

"Because you don't love me back." A statement he wanted me to confirm.

How could I confirm or deny that? In some ways, I was intoxicated with Jack. Still so smitten I felt giddy. Which was why our past hurt so deeply. How could someone who loved me disregard me in such a personal way? And why would I keep giving myself to him?

I'd be dumb to keep trying.

There were only so many pieces of my heart I could lose.

When I needed a shoulder to cry on, he didn't pull me close. When I was too lost to get out of bed, his side was cold. When I was drowning in grief, he closed the door. When I felt like my life was ending, he told me to move on.

When I wanted *him*, he gave me freaking flowers.

Flowers.

Because he didn't know how to give himself.

I couldn't face more hard things with Jack. My life was hard enough as it was.

He jerked my thoughts back to his statement. His voice was a tender rasp. "Do you?"

I sighed, "I can't."

He pressed his lips together, brushed his hands down his thighs. Wouldn't look at my face.

"I'm sorry, Jack. We were broken long before Kacey."

He nodded, scrubbing his jaw again. The sadness in his voice gutted me. I closed my eyes, wishing I could protect myself from the harrowing sound of it. "Okay, I'm going to hit the hay. We can"—he stood—"figure out some of the other details later."

THIRTY-NINE

Then

Jack

The sun was coming up, finally lighting the sky around 6 a.m. I worked an overnight shift. Picked it up, actually. Department was a little short-staffed per the usual. I was eager to get home and peek in on Miranda.

My conscience had been nagging me. She didn't seem okay when I left. She'd been in the shower, heading to bed a little early. I asked her a few times if she was alright. She said yes, but offered no other information. After four years of marriage, I was pretty good at reading my wife, but this time, I wasn't getting clear signals.

Or maybe I was and they scared the crap out of me.

My heart was in my boots as I pulled into the driveway. She was probably sleeping, but I'd peek in and make sure she was tucked into bed. When I stopped the truck on the drive and stepped out, something crunched beneath my feet.

I squinted in the early morning light, bent down to look. Glass? A flash of panic raced through me as I jerked my head to check the windows. Had someone broken in? Was Miranda okay?

I turned to take off for the front door when a few huge pieces shifted beneath my feet. I looked down.

Flowers were everywhere.

It was the bouquet I left for her.

My pulse charged into overdrive.

The glass shatter radius had to be thirty feet in all directions. Did this fall somehow? Did she set it on the window sill or something?

I jogged up to the front door and stomped several times on the door mat. When I opened the front door, the sight waiting for me was like a punch to the gut.

Miranda was there, folding laundry into a suitcase. There were multiple suitcases and boxes. Some with clothes. One with books. Her work clothes and apron were on the top of another.

I didn't have to ask. I knew what she was doing.

She was moving out.

She had thrown those flowers out the window.

This couldn't be happening.

My tone was clipped. All the anger and frustration I felt for her boiled to the surface. "What are you doing?"

Her response was tear-filled, bitter, broken. "I—I have to go, Jack."

"Don't do this."

"I have to. I can't breathe here." She stuffed a shirt into her bag. "I am wasting away—I can't be here with you and live like strangers."

My blood boiled. I was so sick of this. So sick of being distant with her. From coming home every night to her anger.

We had talked. She told me she needed me to support her while she grieved. And I tried! Literally tried to give her anything she wanted. She took *weeks* off of work. She laid in bed all the time. She was so depressed she rarely ate. She was on medication.

Like what else was I supposed to do?

We had lost three babies.

Even as I had that thought, my intuition kicked me in the gut. There were more. There had to be. She'd have bouts of lying in bed, extra crying, extra anger. Like the past few days. It was why I brought her flowers.

Either she was having hard weeks, or there were more.

I didn't want to ask "are you having a miscarriage" for fear of triggering her, so I hinted around. Asked a few times if she was okay and took her at her word when she said "yes."

I suggested a few times that Miranda get on birth control so this wouldn't keep happening, but she didn't want to. She said she'd only feel better when she had a baby.

What did I know, anyway?

After the rounds of grief and chaos, things would get better for a while. The ice would thaw and she'd re-achieve some semblance of normal. But then it would blow up all over again. And somehow I was supposed to be the magic man that fixed it all.

To be honest, I was sick of trying to have kids. I just wanted my wife back. I'd be okay—be happy with just her.

I thought she would like hearing me say that. I was *gravely* mistaken. In fact, those words may have been the final nail in the coffin of our marriage.

The wedge between us was wider than ever before. The passion colder. I was crazy about her but done with games. If she wanted to act like I should know everything and punish me for not being there when she refused to even let me in, then fine.

Eventually, I would stoop to begging her to come home. In a matter of mere days, I would be reduced to a miserable, tortured soul, desperate for the woman I loved. But in that fiery moment, the anger and rejection I felt won. I stomped to the bedroom and tossed my gym clothes in a duffle bag.

I slung it over my shoulder as I walked back out the front door. "Try not to pop a tire on your way out."

FORTY

Miranda

Jack slept in a little. I guessed he was pretty tired from extra work and long hours. I set out a coffee mug for him and a sticky note that said "in the garden."

An explanation replayed in my head over and over, fine-tuning with each cycle. How to make Kacey understand who Jack was wouldn't be easy. And he might not even soak in the information. I didn't want Kacey to fail to acknowledge Jack as his dad, potentially making all of this even more hurtful for him.

Not that Jack counted on Kacey to make him feel better. I just wanted to ease the loss for Jack as much as I possibly could.

But the thought of them leaving today had me in shambles. It was so silly. My stomach wound in knots and I shook. I was almost thirty-two years old, for heaven's sake.

The early May sunshine was warm, the dew in the grass cool. The other day, Richard taught me how to search the garden for pests. Flipping over squash leaves to look for squash bug eggs and how to check stems for signs of rot or worms. I found a lot of pleasure in systematically running through the checklist every morning while Kacey played.

The plants were still tiny, but Richard said that's when we needed to be the most vigilant. Said the pests or disease could be present early but wouldn't manifest completely until July. And by then, it would be far too late.

He said we could always spray the garden with pesticides, but it was an artificial and dangerous way to get a harvest. I agreed and chose vigilance instead. Richard gave me a special oil to spray over the plants if I found pests but warned me not to spray the blooms.

I did whatever the man said.

I glanced into his yard, wondering where he was this morning. He was typically out there before us and I enjoyed standing at the fence and sipping my coffee while we talked.

Thirty minutes later, I was rummaging through the shed, looking for paint so I could fix up that old bench.

"Knock knock."

I whirled around to see Jack. Standing there in all of his morning glory. T-shirt stretched across his broad chest, shorts showing off his defined calf muscles, a coffee mug in his big hand.

"Oh, uh, good morning."

"What are you doing?" His morning voice was gravelly.

"I'm looking for paint. Kind of want to fix up that old bench."

"That's a good idea. Do we need to buy some?"

"No." I lifted a can of white exterior paint. "I think this will actually work. White wasn't the color I originally dreamed of, but it will work fine."

Kacey barged in, squeezing past Jack to enter the shed. "Mommy, can we go to the pawk today?"

I glanced at Jack's face. He was watching Kacey with a soft expression. I paused and caught Jack's attention. I mouthed "wanna do this now?" He nodded once.

"Well, Kacey, before we do anything this morning, Jack and Mommy want to talk to you."

"Okay."

"Let's go sit down."

We exited the shed and I sat on the bench next to Kacey. Jack stood nearby, shifting a bit. My heart squeezed for him. He kind of seemed like he didn't know what to do, where to go.

I put my hand on Kacey's tiny little shoulder. "Do you remember how we were watching Clifford and you asked about Emily Elizabeth's mommy and daddy?"

"Uh huh."

"And you asked if Chris was your daddy?"

He nodded.

"Do you remember what I said?"

"Chwis is not my daddy."

"That's right." It was going well. Good thing I practiced.

"Mommy, can we go to the pawk?"

"Maybe later. Right now, I want to tell you who your daddy is." Kacey's eyebrows raised.

I pointed at Jack, who was now eye-level with us, squatting just a couple feet away. "Kacey, Jack is your daddy."

Kacey frowned and looked at Jack. A slow, confused "oh" came out of his mouth. He slid off the bench and walked up to him. My heart stopped beating as I waited. Kacey already loved Jack. But I hoped he wouldn't say or do anything to make this weirder than it already was.

Kacey immediately invaded Jack's personal space, putting

his tiny hands on Jack's big shoulders. "Dack, can *you* take me to the pawk today?"

Jack's throat bobbed. I had never seen Jack truly emotional. He was fighting it back. He blinked a few times, his hand tentatively coming to Kacey's back and patting. "Yeah, buddy, I think that sounds really fun."

Kacey squealed and took a few spins around the yard, doing some sort of half cartwheel thing that made him look like a chimpanzee.

My gaze tangled with Jack's. "That went well," I said.

"Did he understand?"

"We'll know over time whether he did or didn't."

Jack's voice was gentle, soft. "Thank you, Miranda."

An hour later, I had Kacey in his socks and tennis shoes. Jack took my suggestion seriously and told Kacey they were going to the park, getting lunch, and then ice cream.

If Kacey had any reservations about leaving without me, they evaporated. Mine screamed though.

Jack moved the car seat into his truck and buckled Kacey in. Before he hopped into the driver's seat and took off, he approached me. "You sure you're going to be okay?"

"Yes—I need to be."

"I put something in the kitchen for you."

"What is it?"

"Just go check after we leave."

"Okay." Curiosity burned in my brain. But before I could ask more questions, Jack's arms came around me. I didn't hesitate this time, immediately hugging him back.

I didn't even get the chance to enjoy it. It was brief and over before it began. "Thank you for this. Call me if you need me." He turned on his way back to the truck. "Oh, and if you go anywhere, go armed."

I waved them off.

Then made a beeline to the kitchen.

There was a fifty-dollar bill on the counter next to a post-it note with an address. No personal words on it—just an address. I almost dropped my phone, pulling up the maps app as fast as I possibly could.

The address was a Barnes and Noble.

It was the perfect place for me to get lost. Alone. And not miss a single soul.

This was such a Jack move. As long as I'd known him, he excelled in the sweet, romantic gestures department. If only you could build a marriage on those.

But still. I had to stop ugly crying in order to drive.

FORTY-ONE

Jack

"Okay, bud, cone or cup?"

"Cone! Cone!"

"Good choice." We ordered two vanilla cones. Not that Kacey needed the sugar. After running himself into the ground at the park for two hours, he pigged out on chicken nuggets and waffle fries then ran on the indoor playground. Kid had some energy.

Only way I'd been able to call him off the playground was to say it was time for us to eat some ice cream. Miranda was right. It was the trump card.

We settled at an outdoor table. After a few quiet minutes of ice cream, he smacked his lips. "Dack?"

"Yeah, buddy?"

"Mommy said you awe my daddy."

"She's right. How do you feel about that?" He frowned, not catching my meaning. I changed tactics, which I'd had to do repeatedly all day. Major learning curve. "Are you happy I'm your daddy?"

He smacked again, a white beard forming on his face and dripping onto his shirt. "Yes, I so happy."

"Yeah?" I smiled. "I'm happy too. I like you."

He frowned again. "Chwis is not my daddy."

"Yep." Hated that man's name. His mere existence. But I'd heard it a few times from Kacey that day. Learned my son was a bit of a verbal processor.

"Chwis made mommy cwy."

I felt like my heart stopped for a second. Did I hear him right? "What was that?"

"Chwis made mommy *cwy*." He emphasized the last word like I was dumb for not understanding in the first place.

"Really?"

"Yeah."

"Hm. Why is that?"

Kacey shrugged, which was really cute to watch a three-year-old do. "What's a daddy?"

Oh boy. "You know what? You better ask your mom that one. She's better at explaining things." I reached up and touched his soft curls the breeze kept lifting. He was so like Miranda. Big brown eyes, blonde to the roots, a gentle spray of freckles across his nose and cheeks. Absolutely adorable.

I didn't see me at all.

Miranda was clearly a wonderful mom. Even if she cried enough for him to notice, she shielded him. He was centered, happy, undisturbed. I had no doubt he was blissfully unaware of whatever went on in that home.

"You know, you can call me 'daddy' if you want to."

"Okay."

Five minutes later, Kacey started crying because there was ice cream all over him. We dumped the shell of his cone, and I picked him up, holding him at arm's length. We hustled to the bathroom. Kacey stopped crying and split his gut in laughter when I held him up to the bathroom mirror. He said he looked like an "ice cweam monstah."

Man, he was a fun kid.

After trying to wipe him off, I gave up and stripped him down. Kacey was giggling the whole time. Probably on a sugar high.

Kacey was draped over my shoulder, snoring. In nothing but underwear. We came in the front door and Miranda's head popped up from the couch, a huge smile across her face.

Before she could say anything to wake him, I lifted a finger to my lips.

She jumped up and waved me to follow her up the stairs. In their room, she clicked on a sound machine and pulled the covers back. I gently placed him on the bed, tucking the blankets around him.

His head lolled back onto the pillow. That kiddo partied hard and slept harder.

When we were back in the living room, Miranda raised an eyebrow. "Let me guess. You got cones?"

I laughed. Relief flooded me. For the first time, I allowed myself to acknowledge how worried I'd been that it wouldn't go well, or he'd cry for his mom, or wouldn't like being with me. But it went perfect. The relief came out as a laugh and felt really good.

"How'd you know?"

"Been there a time or two."

"Yeah. Lesson learned. Cups next time."

A genuine smile crossed her face as she went around to the front of the couch. She leaned to scoop up a few books.

"I got some books." She lifted them like she was eager to show me. "Two romances from the clearance section and a book on gardening flowers." She dropped them back. "Thank you, Jack. That was the nicest thing you could've done for me."

She was striking. Her hair was down, like beautiful waves around her face. She had a shirt on that was a smidge too short, meaning I got occasional glimpses of skin around her waistline. She had better color than she did a few weeks ago. I wasn't meaning to ogle or stare at her. But I couldn't help it. Dragging my eyes away from my wife was the most pointless and impossible mission.

I'd never tried to hide my feelings, only keep them held back so I didn't scare her away. Every day was proving harder.

At first, I thought we would never come back from the misunderstanding. That notion was zapped so fast. Now, I was pretty sure I'd watch her six while she murdered someone.

I had to find some way to convince her to stay.

I forced my gaze back to her face. "So you had a nice time then?"

"Yes, actually. I think I needed that."

"Of course you did. You've been on duty for three years and eight months."

She dipped her chin, pushed hair behind her ears. "Guess so."

My feet pushed me forward. Couldn't stop them. Couldn't stop my hand from coming to her chin and gently pushing it back up. Couldn't help it when my breathing shallowed looking into her dark irises.

"You've done a wonderful job with Kacey."

She swallowed and moisture pooled in the corners of her eyes. "He's a great kid."

"Because you're a great mom."

She shrugged.

"Really, Miranda. I don't know all the details about your life with Chris, but it's safe to say Kacey is happily unaffected. There is no reason that would happen unless he's had an incredible mother to protect him."

She blinked the moisture away and I let my hand drop.

"Can you show me his bedtime routine tonight?"

FORTY-TWO

Miranda

I sighed as I sat on the edge of the garden bed, propping my cup of coffee against the wooden barrier and starting the checklist. I put on a glove and flipped over the cucumber leaves, systematically searching for eggs.

I wasn't sure how much my heart could take. In some ways, I was finally getting the things I wanted for Kacey, but reality looked nothing like my imagination. I had wanted all these things for years—but not this way.

Last night, I walked Jack through Kacey's nighttime routine. Bath, jammies, teeth, snuggle, book, milk in sippy cup. Seeing Jack bent over sweet Kacey's little head to read Goodnight Moon was everything I hoped for.

To everyone watching, Jack was hardened, rough, insensitive. But to me, Jack was like a giant teddy bear. I had always loved that about him—that he reserved his softness for me alone. Used to anyway.

But now, it was for Kacey. And I loved that.

The thing missing from the reality was *us*. Me and Jack. I was painfully aware I was showing Jack the ropes so we could do it separately. Whereas in my imaginings, we were always *together*.

Togetherness is the only thing I've ever truly wanted. Sometimes, I felt a little self-conscious about the fact I didn't have big goals or dreams. I considered myself a little vanilla. Sweet but boring. My version of fun was curling up and reading a book, doing a craft, or making dinner together. My goal in life was having a happy family—it's the one thing I've wanted and the one thing I've never *ever* had.

For a time, Jack and I were happy. But my dreams were shattered the first time before we returned from our honeymoon. Our marriage wasn't ready.

A flapping screen door jerked me from my thoughts and I looked up to see Richard hobbling. I stood and walked to the fence.

"Richard! Good morning!"

"Well, hey there, young lady." He was moving slow, painfully.

"What happened? Are you okay?"

I went to our gate and opened it, calling Kacey to follow me into Richard's yard. Richard tried to ease into a patio chair and I rushed forward to help him.

"Richard, oh my goodness, are you hurt?"

"No, not really." He clapped a hand against his torso. "This old body's seen worse."

"Well, you weren't moving like this a couple days ago, so what happened?"

"I had a little fall is all."

"You fell?!"

He moved his shoulders, like he was uncomfortable divulging the details.

"Were you able to get up? When did this happen?"

"My daughter-in-law, Cynthia, stopped by to drop off food. She found me and helped me right up. Took me to see the doctor."

"You are lucky you didn't break anything. How long were you down?"

He moved his shoulders again.

"How long?"

"A little while."

"Please tell me."

"About six hours."

"Six hours?!"

That was completely unacceptable! I should have checked on him when I didn't see him out yesterday morning. But then, with Kacey and Jack, and Barnes and Noble, I got busy and didn't come back outside.

"I am so sorry." My eyes teared up. "You poor thing. I am your neighbor! I should've checked on you when I didn't see you out yesterday."

"Oh no. Don't you feel sorry."

"But I do! I am so close!"

I took the man's phone and put my number into it. Told him I would check on him every day. I helped him move out to a chair in his garden. Kacey and I got to work caring for his plants.

According to Richard, he'd be back in the garden after the soreness subsided, but until then, I was delighted to be his hands. Truly happy to learn all the ways he tended his garden —his flowers especially.

He grinned from ear to ear watching me work.

"This is your happy place, isn't it?" I asked.

"It surely is."

"It's written all over your face."

"Everyone needs a safe place. For me, it's here."

Safe place. That struck me.

"While the dew is still on the roses, I come out here. Talk to God, walk around and look at the buds that haven't opened for the sunshine yet. I think of Rose. I pray for you. Pray for my children."

"That's beautiful."

"The world is a crazy place. But a tended garden is a place of peace."

"I feel that." I shrugged, moving the shears deeper into the rose bushes and squeezing. "There's something grounding about coming out, quietly working, taking note of the growth, protecting it."

"Grounding. I agree." He shifted in his seat, wincing. "I actually have a question for you. While you were gathering the supplies, Kacey told me Jack is his daddy."

"Did he really?"

"Yes ma'am. Seemed downright excited about it too."

Huh. That was something. Kacey was telling neighbors. I'd have to tell Jack. It would make him happy to know Kacey was excited.

I said, "Guess I need to explain myself, don't I?"

"No, you certainly don't have to. I figured there was a lot more to the 'friends' claim anyway."

"How so?"

He chuckled, low and slow. "I've had a wife. I know the look in that man's eyes. And yours."

I laughed. "What look in his eyes?"

"Like he wants to drag you back into the house."

"Richard!" I loved elderly people. They could be so unfiltered. "He does not look at me that way." Even as I said it, I knew it was a lie.

"Whatever you say."

I shrugged. "It's a lot more complicated than it looks. We were married before and we got remarried, but not for love." Once I started explaining, everything kind of spilled out. I hadn't realized how much I needed to verbally process all that had happened: Nathaniel's will, Ohio and Chris, how the truth about Kacey came out, how Jack was helping me get the money and start fresh.

"Start fresh?" Richard frowned. "So you're saying after Jack found out you were mysteriously named on his father's will, he decided to marry you so you could, in fact, inherit something which should've been only his. Then he found out he had a child he didn't know about, then wanted to be part of that child's life without taking you to court...and all the while providing for you guys, protecting you from this Chris fella...so you can 'start fresh?'"

I shifted. It was a lot.

"Child, don't be naive. No man would do all that unless he was so in love he couldn't think straight."

I opened my mouth to respond, but nothing came out.

"Hopefully you guys haven't blurred the lines on what's happening when you get your hands on that money. 'Cause if you have, Jack is in for one heck of a broken heart."

I immediately thought of Jack's hands beneath my shirt and in my hair and his lips on my neck and chest. How close we'd been to more. Heat climbed into my cheeks at the memory.

Stupid, stupid, stupid.

I focused harder on the fertilizer I was mixing as tears pricked my eyes. "I—I don't want to break his heart."

"I know you don't, but take it from a man who had a wife for a long, long time. That boy is smitten."

I nodded.

"I think he's a dummy for agreeing to all that mess in the

first place. If he gets his heart broke, he'd have done it to himself, but don't make it worse for him. Sounds like he wants the best for you, which is admirable, I reckon."

I wished Richard would stop talking because I suddenly felt flushed and nauseous. I knew Jack loved me. But hearing Richard state it so plainly made my heart twist in pain.

That boy is smitten.

He continued, "Seeing how life brought you back together—what's holding you back from giving your marriage another go?"

The need to defend my decisions cropped up in me. Flustered, I grappled for words. "You don't understand, Richard."

"Understand what?"

"I was out of options. We were going to be homeless without Jack's help." I lifted a shoulder, needing to explain my reasons, worried Richard might think ill of me. "Jack is a good man—he really is. But I will never be able to trust him again."

Richard hummed, nodded once. "Why's that?"

"Because Jack only knows how to love me when things are good. And a lot of bad things happened in our marriage."

Richard didn't fill the lag in conversation. Just waited for me to explain.

So I did. I sat in the grass beside him and told him all about the children we lost and Jack's absence during it all. How I had to stuff down my feelings so he would even be around me. How I had to pretend to be happy so I wouldn't eat dinner alone. How Jack chose other things over me time and again. And how that dynamic slowly choked out whatever good thing our marriage had.

He clicked his tongue in thought when I fell silent. "Plain as the nose on your face that you love him though."

I swiped the back of my hand against my cheek. I did a decent job keeping my emotions in check for Kacey's sake. He was playing nearby and I tried to protect him from my frequent meltdowns. "I don't think I've ever stopped loving Jack. But...that's not enough. It never has been."

"People change and mature over time. You don't think Jack can do the same?"

"No." I shook my head. "Jack is hardwired to avoid. I couldn't even talk to him about it—every time I tried, he couldn't see. I doubt he'll ever be different." And I refused to be in any more relationships built on happy feelings. They never lasted. People never stayed when it was hard.

Richard hummed. "Quite a pickle you're in, young lady."

A "pickle" was generous. The crux of my conflict was oppressive at best. "Yeah."

"You'd do well to set clear boundaries and talk about them. Often. From the looks of things, you're gonna need them."

And wasn't that the truth? It was impossible not to be swept away by the many many things I adored about Jack. Reminding myself of where we came from and why we couldn't be more was a crucial part of this process—a part I had been neglecting.

I am a train wreck.

Why was life so freaking complicated?

FORTY-THREE

Miranda

Jack put Kacey to bed tonight. I showered and made my way out to the garden to do the nightly watering. Checked the flower shoots in the front of the house and hit them with some water. They were still looking good.

After our long conversation this morning, I helped Richard into his recliner, made him some lunch, and even met Cynthia, who came by during her lunch break to check on him. He told me to dig out some shoots from the irises and plant them in our front beds. I did. Irises in front of the house would be so beautiful.

But the emotional day drained me. So the moment of silence, alone in my garden, came as a relief. My brain went into hibernate mode, and I simply watered, feeling numb from the inside out. The crickets singing and the water hitting the soil lulled my worries.

I was almost finished when the back door opened jerking

my awareness back into this dimension. Jack had worked all day and looked tired.

He strolled out with his hands in his pockets.

"How'd it go?"

"Just fine. He passed out."

"Bedtime is usually easy. He runs until he drops."

"Wish I had his energy."

"Same."

Jack nodded toward the garden. "Why do you always water at night?"

"Because if you water in the heat of the day, the water heats so much it like boils the roots, scorches the plants."

"Hm. Didn't know that."

I tried to smile. Probably looked fake. "Also Richard told me to do it this way, and I'd go to war for him."

Jack chuckled. "He's a good guy."

We talked for a few minutes about Richard falling and how we need to check on him if we don't see him out and about.

When the conversation lagged, I spoke up, dread wrapping around my heart. "Jack, we need to talk about something."

He eased down onto the bench.

"I feel like we need to get back on the same page of where this agreement is heading."

He nodded, his jaw visibly clenching with worry.

"We are well over a month into this. And even though time is flying, a lot has changed." I went down and sat on the edge of the garden near Jack. "I need to keep reminding us where we are headed. That—that I have every intention of signing"—my voice cracked as his shoulders dropped—"divorce papers when we sell the lake house. Because we share history, it's been hard not to get close and feel like this marriage is for real, but we need to remember why we agreed to this. Money." The last word made me want to burst into tears. So pathetic.

He sighed, shaking his head. "I don't get it."

"What?"

"Why it has to be this way. You're fighting feelings, not because you had feelings in the past. But because you have them now."

I couldn't admit to the feelings I was having—because then what? There would be no boundary to protect me anymore. All I could offer was a strong front. And hope it would somehow be enough to keep our hearts in tact when all this was over. So I said, "I don't have real feelings."

He rolled his head back, obviously annoyed. "Come on."

"I don't. Attraction, maybe..."

"Maybe?"

I opened my mouth to respond.

"Miranda, I was married to you for four years. You care about me still. I see proof every time I look at you."

"Of course I care about you! I don't want to see you hurt or anything."

"That's not what I mean and you know it."

"It's complicated."

"I don't think it's complicated. I think you are *making* it complicated." He ran a hand over his head. "I think you're in love and afraid to admit it."

I was an open book once again.

He continued, "Because if you do, it means we have to figure out what the hell happened to us."

I scoffed, agitation immediately flaming to life. "I know what happened to us. You are the only one who is still—after a *million* conversations—confused."

"Alright then. Once more for old time's sake." His gaze bore into mine as we faced off. "Tell me what happened to us."

"Jack!"

"If we are truly broken beyond repair, I want to know why. One more time."

I balked. "It's painful to have to stick up for myself over and over again. You should know what happened to us by now. Plus, why are you pushing for me to stay? It wasn't what we agreed to in the beginning when you proposed this dumb idea."

"Why am I pushing? We have a *child* together. And maybe I'm just selfish, but you know how I feel about you. I didn't initially start out with the motive to win you back, but by the time I was saying those vows at that half-assed ceremony, I knew I meant them."

He continued, "So again. Tell me and I'll try not to be so dense this time."

Anger coursed through me. The fact he still didn't understand proved everything. People chronically tossed my feelings aside. I was only ever treasured in fair weather. No one stayed with me on my hard days or cared to hear my heart when it was broken. Of all the people who *should* have cared, my husband topped the list.

I blurted it, my voice almost rising to a yell. "The *babies*, Jack! The babies!"

"And how are they the reason we can't be together?"

"Because every time my heart got broken, you trampled it."

"What?"

"Yes, Jack. I was dying and you did not care. You came up with every reason under the sun to be anywhere but with me."

"I did care, but I was busy! The department needed a lot of help."

"And the marathon team? They needed your help?"

He opened his mouth to respond, but I was fired up. I kept on.

"And was the gym going out of business without your

dedicated membership? Were Cameron and Jules not happy going downtown by themselves for once? Were the Chicago Bears going to dismantle if you didn't tune in?"

"Miranda—"

"Did you realize that the Nashville Police Department gives you bereavement leave for a miscarriage? And you never took it—not once?"

He cussed and stood from the bench, pacing away, running his hands over his hair. His hallmark sign of discomfort or deep thought.

"You had dinner delivered to me. Or told me to have a girls night, like what I actually needed was a damn pedicure. Or gave me books to read. Or brought home *stupid* flowers. All of those were a substitute for the only thing I ever asked you for."

Silence, long and suffocating, fell. The crickets felt suddenly loud.

When he spoke, his voice was a rasp. "Which was what?"

"How could you not know?"

"Just *tell* me, Miranda."

My fight had drained, and my voice softened. "It was *you*, Jack."

Another beat of silence passed.

I said, "It's why I threw those flowers out the window. I shouldn't have done it and it was rash and stupid, but I was so hurt. They felt like a slap in the face."

He scrubbed his hand up his jaw, head tipped toward the ground.

"You know me. There is nothing I want more than to just have a family, hang out, and be together. I'm literally the most boring person on planet earth…every loss was…" I faltered, emotions catching up with my rampage. "Every loss was a death of that dream. So I was grieving over and over again, while you kept walking away from me.

"The loss didn't affect you. You couldn't see it. You couldn't feel it. It didn't bother you like it did me, so you vanished. My grief was too much for you to handle and be around, so you checked out. I have stuffed my emotions my entire life so people would like me. So they'd stay. I did it for you, for Chris, for my mom. I don't want to do it ever again. Never. The way I feel is important, too."

He finally looked at my face again. "How many?"

"How many what?"

"How many babies did we lose?"

I sniffed, hating the number with every fiber of my being. "Seven."

"*Seven?*" His jaw hung open for a few long seconds. "Miranda, how could I be there if you didn't even tell me?"

"I stopped telling you because you disregarded them every time. It was easier for me to not tell you and suffer alone, than tell you and *still* suffer alone."

He paced further away. His voice was taut, pained. "Maybe things will be different if we try again."

"No, they won't."

He looked at me, wondering how I could be so sure.

"When you found out Kacey was yours, you did the same thing. You freaking disappeared. Instead of *listening* to what I had to say and how I felt. I had to *demand* you to come and even hear my side of the story. But that's how you've always been. You run from big feelings and big problems." Understanding dawned on his face, the hard lines softening, a vulnerable expression edging in. I frowned, trying to sort it out in my own head. "On the one hand, you're overly protective of the ones you love. Do everything in your power to make sure we are okay, but then, when we aren't and you can't deal, you leave. And because of that"—I swiped my eyes—"I don't want to ever face anything hard with you again."

Jack held my gaze for a painful moment. Was it possible? Did he finally hear me? Did he actually see?

Regret filled his expression and his eyes misted ever so slightly. He glanced away.

He understood.

My voice was weak, the fight gone. "Is that answer enough for you, Jack?"

He nodded, pressing his lips together.

"We need to do right by Kacey. We can be parents together. But—that's all it should be, okay?"

"Yeah. Kacey." He turned his head away, making a slow move to exit the conversation.

I watched him walk back to the house, shoulders slumped. My heart broke all over again.

FORTY-FOUR

Jack

As soon as I stepped out of the truck, I heard the air compressor buzzing from down the hill. I felt so uncomfortable. I'd texted Jules, asking if they were home but she didn't respond. Neither did Pat. I even texted Sunny. But, when I pulled into their driveway every vehicle was accounted for.

It was about 4 p.m. I just got off—was still in uniform and everything. I hated to show up unannounced, but if I didn't find someone to talk to, I might explode. Bone-deep exhaustion made me feel achy almost. It wasn't physical—it was something else—something that made me feel like I was steamrolled. I'd done nothing but think about my conversation with Miranda. Done nothing but beat myself up over and over for destroying the greatest gift I ever had.

Her words knocked around in my brain until I wanted to bash my head against the wall.

Every time my heart got broken, you trampled it.

I walked down toward the shop, choosing my brother-in-law's ear over my sister's. I loved Jules, but we had proved a few times over our allegiances were pretty out of whack when it came to each other. A twin's gotta be loyal and we most certainly were—to a fault.

I called Jules the other day and told her everything that happened between Miranda and Bree. Even though Jules was relieved to hear Miranda had tried to tell me, she was still pissed she wasn't upfront from the start of our *fake* marriage—for lack of a better word.

And maybe I should've been more pissed about it, too. But I couldn't bring myself to be upset with Miranda. Right now, the only person I was upset with was myself. My big, stupid self.

Jules wouldn't see the wrong I did. And I needed hard, honest truth. Not something biased by blood. I had a sneaking suspicion if I talked to Pat, he'd shoot straight with me.

I bypassed the house and walked toward the slew of activity in Pat's home-based business, KP Motors. The garage doors were wide open. Two guys in gray t-shirts worked on separate cars. Danny looked smug leaning against the office door, and Pat was right beside him at the workbench, working on some sort of car part.

I'd never asked my brother-in-law for advice before. It was dumb how nervous I was about doing so. But considering Jules' and Pat's history, he was probably the right person.

Honestly, I was so desperate, I'd talk to anyone.

Pat had grease scuffs up his arms, a backward hat on his head. He was hyper focused on what he was doing, so it was Danny who saw me first.

"Jack!" He pulled the vape out of his mouth, moving toward me.

Pat looked up and smiled.

"How's it going?" I held out my hand and gave Danny's a firm shake. He looked healthy, younger. "I do believe those vapes are lending you years."

He gave a gruff laugh, thumbing back at Pat. "That's what this one's been saying."

Pat held his greasy hands up, indicating he'd pass on the hand shake. "Didn't expect you today, Jack. Truck trouble?"

The two guys working glanced over at me, probably wondering what project I had for them. "Nope. Truck's fine."

I didn't say anything else and stood there like an idiot, feeling dumb for walking down in the first place. Maybe I should've settled for talking with Jules.

Pat glanced up the hill toward the house. "Does Jules know you're here?"

"No. I haven't gone to the house yet. I wanted to come down and say hey." My neck prickled with heat.

Say hey? Seriously?

The last twenty-four hours, I'd felt like nothing but a total loser. This moment wasn't helping. I guess I lost my personality somewhere in the emotional jumble.

Pat frowned, trying to figure me out. He wiped his hands on a shop towel. "Everything okay?"

"Yeah—I feel like an idiot. I was hoping to talk to you, but it's still work hours."

"No problem. We are almost done here anyway." He tossed the towel back on the workbench and moved toward the garage doors.

"Pat, I should've made sure you were free. I can come back another time or wait till later."

He clapped me on the back. "Stepping out early is the fun part of being the boss." He looked back at Danny. "Finish that for me, will ya?"

Danny nodded, but he'd already picked up the part.

"Office fridge is stocked. Can I get you something?"

"Actually, yeah, water would be great."

Thirty seconds later, we moved out of the garage into the yard. There were cars lined up alongside the shop. Not haphazard. They were in two orderly lines. Looking down the hill from their house, it wasn't a junkyard. It looked professional. Honestly, the fact he was able to pay two guys to work for him was pretty cool.

I took a swig of my water. "Sorry again for interrupting your work day. I texted but no one responded."

"It's fine. I get pulled away all the time to help with the girls. Things are pretty relaxed here."

"Well, business must be good."

"We stay booked out. I'm not complaining." He took a deep breath and shoved his hands into his pockets. "So, how you doing? Don't normally get a visit from you."

"Man, my world is crazy right now. I'm sure Jules has kept you in the know."

"Got the update last night. I know the situation isn't ideal—but congratulations on the handsome son."

That acknowledgement felt pretty good.

"Thanks. Kacey is a great kid."

"Seemed like Miranda's done a good job with him. How are things going between the two of you?"

A big involuntary sigh escaped. "Not great."

Pat didn't say anything, allowing me to fill the silence.

"I did something horrible." I swallowed, shame creeping in on me for the thousandth time since my conversation with Miranda yesterday. "And I don't know if I'm going to be able to fix it."

There was an arrangement of chairs on one side of the shop. Maybe for clients? We both sat.

"I wanted to talk to you because you helped Jules grieve

and...and I want to know how. After Cameron passed away, she spun out of control. It got worse with every year that went by. She was going to get herself killed if something didn't change. And then she met you."

Cameron was my best friend. After he died, I was afraid I lost my sister forever too.

"I was only returning the favor. Jules saved *my* life first."

"How? What did she do?"

He lifted a shoulder, a gentle smile pulling his cheeks back. "She was just there. Present. At first, I thought she was annoying and presumptuous. But she refused to leave and turns out I needed a reason to live again."

Sounded like a stubborn Jules thing to do.

"So when you returned the favor, you..." I let my sentence trail off, hoping he would fill in the blanks.

He shrugged. "Her big breakthrough was seeing Cameron. She needed someone to hold her up through that. That's all I did. Sit with her. Let her lean on me."

He said it like it was no big deal. But I knew Pat played no small role. He was integral to the changes that had taken place in my sister over the past couple years.

Why did I feel like I was in middle school about to ask a stupid question in front of the entire class? I averted my eyes and rubbed my hand up my jaw. "Did—did she cry?"

"That word's a bit tame."

"It was bad?"

"Oh yeah. Many times. Not just the once."

"She's always been so tough. I've only ever seen her really cry once...maybe twice?"

He hummed like he had some insight.

"What?"

He shook his head. "Jules was *asked* to be tough."

I frowned. "What do you mean?"

"It was expected of her."

His meaning was lost on me.

"Sometimes what folks allow you to see isn't an accurate reflection of who they *really* are." He leaned back in his chair. "Jules gives off an impression of being tough, hardened. But, as I've gotten to know my wife, I've learned she is a very deep feeler. Has mounds of compassion and empathy. But I think it's taken a lot of rewiring for her to accept that's who she truly is. Because her whole life she was asked to be something else. I would guess the same's been asked of you."

"What do you mean by 'asked?'"

"Your upbringing. Your parents." He lifted a shoulder. "I think a child's experience has a lot to do with how they function as adults."

"So you're saying you think my dad asked Jules to be tough."

Pat raised his eyebrows. "Didn't he?"

I thought about that for a moment. It was a simple question—something I never considered. Did Dad ask that of us?

Then I remembered the day we brought my mom home. That was a horrible day I hadn't thought about in a long time.

"Yeah." I nodded slowly. "I say you're probably right."

Pat cycled back to the topic. "So, I think the guilt she felt surrounding Cameron's death really complicated the grief process for her. And complex grief is one heck of a demon. She and I share that in common. Sunny, too." He glanced at me. "And maybe you."

A few things he said struck me. I silently mulled them over. I didn't really think *I* was grieving. Sure, I probably should've let myself grieve Mom more, Cameron more, the babies more.

He lifted his hat off his head and ran his fingers through his hair. "So why we talking about grief? Miranda grieving or something?"

"Yeah." My lungs felt stuffed. "She had been our entire marriage, and I did nothing."

"Grieving what exactly?"

"The family we couldn't have."

"Oh. Infertility?"

"No. We got pregnant easily enough. She couldn't carry them."

"Ah, that sucks."

"We lost seven."

"Seven?" His eyes went wide. "Does Jules know that?"

"No. We got married quickly because of our first. We had plans to make it known after the wedding, but—Miranda lost the baby the day we got home from our honeymoon."

"Ah, Jack. I'm sorry."

"After that, we kept the pregnancies under wraps to see how they were going to turn out first before announcing. Maybe that was the wrong choice."

"Man, that's—that's a lot."

"I don't know if there's something wrong with me, but I couldn't do for her what you did for Jules." Shame crept in. "The sound of her crying was...I'm a coward, I guess."

He nodded.

"I left her alone. I told her the department was short-staffed which wasn't even true. I devised ways to be out of the house." I shook my head, so embarrassed to admit this. "I'd rather be anywhere but home, hearing her cry, watching her heart break and feeling helpless to do anything.

"I don't want to get divorced again. I love Miranda—haven't ever stopped. But now, she doesn't want anything to do with me. She said I walk away when things get hard. And she's right. I do. I don't know why, and I don't know how to fix that about myself."

Silence fell for a few moments before he spoke. "To be able

to look at yourself and know you have to change is a good first step, Jack."

"Any advice on the next one? Right now, I feel pretty lost."

Pat took a deep breath. "Jules—she had to learn there was no such thing as bad or good feelings. Once she let herself feel them—I think that's when she started to heal. Feelings are part of the human experience and none make you a bad or weak person."

Pat paused for a beat. "Sunny is the same way. She grieves something she can't even remember—a sense of loss she carries with her all the time. Because she can't understand it, she feels stupid. She's had to do a lot of relearning, too."

I didn't know much about Sunny's story. She had a nasty one, apparently, but Jules and Pat said it was her story to tell and didn't divulge any details to anyone.

"So maybe that's the next step for you. Figure out why you hate the crying so much and deal with that."

The brief mention caused my mom's memory to storm inside my chest. I'd stuffed it down over and over until it was nearly—but not quite—forgotten. Didn't really want to think of it now and certainly didn't want to share it with Pat.

"Then get to know your wife. Figure out why she ticks the way she does. I don't think I could be the partner Jules needs if I didn't know her past, understand the impact Nathaniel had on her, and stuff. Maybe there are things like that you need to learn about Miranda."

I wracked my brain. "I feel like I know everything about her."

"You might. But just because you know all the clues doesn't mean you've solved the mystery. There's a difference between *know* and *understand*."

Huh.

Solve the mystery of my wife.

He took a deep breath. "Losing seven babies sounds traumatic. Trauma doesn't always make sense from the outside. It literally alters your brain chemistry. Remember that."

All of this felt overwhelming. "Does Jules still have a lot of bad days?"

"Much less than before, but yes, she still has them. We all do."

"What helps you guys?"

"Well, if I'm having a bad day, I usually need to be alone for a while. I process best with silence. Then I need Jules to hear me out—I've talked for hours after those alone times. She's the best listener.

"Sunny is working on processing through bad days. Right now, she tends to shut us out. Will withdraw into books for days sometimes. When she's like that, I try to make a bowl of popcorn and read nearby. Just so she doesn't feel isolated. Sometimes she comes down to the shop and shadows me—I can usually get her to open up if we are working on something side by side.

"Jules typically needs a good cry, but she won't let go and cry if she's alone. She wants to be held. Then she wants pizza and a movie."

He shrugged. "Maybe I'm weird, but I think it's an honor we get to help each other heal. I have their hearts in my hands and I don't take that lightly. It makes life a lot more painful and a lot more complicated, but they're worth it. I'd venture to say Miranda and Kacey are worth that too."

Why did I feel defeated? My response was soft and my gaze dropped to my hands. "Yeah, they absolutely are."

"You know, there might be stuff you need to work out too. Sometimes we aren't what we need to be for other people because we aren't what we need to be for ourselves. Can't help somebody else while you're bleeding out, ya know?"

Was I bleeding out? If I was, I couldn't feel it.

"It wouldn't hurt to talk to someone."

"Is this when you tell me I need a shrink?"

He laughed. "Definitely. All three of us see Dr. Hannel in Hendersonville twice a month, no exceptions. Making it out there for six appointments is expensive and can get a little dicey with babies in the mix, but it's a Moore household requirement."

He pulled out his phone and ten seconds later, mine buzzed in the clip.

"I just sent you his office number in case you're interested."

"Thanks." I smiled. "You know, Pat, I'm glad Jules has you. You're a good guy."

Pat tipped his head down. "Well, Kevin Moore was a good man. Pretty sure I owe him."

Maybe that was the difference between us. Both our families were well off, died young, left fortunes behind. But that's all my dad left behind—money. No one even liked him, least of all his son. He was strict and demanding. In his home, there was no room for error. Jules and I were perfect at everything and I was valedictorian, team captain, and class president because there were no other options. Dad made life miserable if he thought we weren't doing our best, exuding strength, and being successful.

It's why Jules and I finally rebelling and doing whatever we wanted ended our relationship with him. Our accolades were his accolades. Or our lack of, his lack of. When I blew off college and went to the academy, it was a personal affront to his values. Same with my divorce. He took it personally, no doubt.

The only person who ever saw his goodness was Mom. And cancer took her so young. If I thought about it too long, I'd feel sorry for him. Maybe he was a halfway decent human before losing her. I could barely remember back that far. But if I tried, I remembered a few things. Like a fun vacation we took and Dad tossing the baseball with me. Him laughing. Him reading some classics to us at night before we went to bed. Him decorating the Christmas tree with us.

"I really wish I could've met Kevin. Seems like he was a fantastic guy."

Pat smiled. "The best. He deserves full credit."

We talked for a little bit longer. About dad life. Being there for our kids. Twins. Work stuff. I was feeling better. I had an action plan.

Solve the mystery of my wife.

Call this Hannel person.

After a while, I heard a shrill voice.

"Jack?!"

I looked up the hill to see Jules coming down, pushing a double stroller. "Hey sis!"

"I texted you back. How long have you been here?"

I stood and gave her a hug. "About an hour, I guess. Been talking to Pat."

"Aw. You guys are bonding."

I pulled out some sarcasm. "Aren't we precious?"

She patted my cheek, playing right along. "Yes, you are!" Jules turned to Pat and he pulled her down on his lap. She looked in his face, lowering her voice. "You didn't tell him, did you?"

"Of course not."

"Should I?"

"Up to you, baby."

I was squatting down, talking to the girls. "Wait. Tell me *what*?"

Jules was beaming. It was written all over her face.

I felt my jaw dropping. "No way."

She nodded.

"You've got to be kidding me, sis."

"You're not even going to give me the pleasure of actually announcing it?"

"Sure, go ahead."

"We are pregnant!" She squealed a little at the end.

"Jules, your twins are like eight months old! Was that an accident?"

"Ew. That's kind of personal"—she curled her arm up and around Pat's shoulder as if it drove her point—"but no. It wasn't."

"Wow."

"Pat's thirty-six. We wanted one more before he turns forty." She laughed.

Pat squeezed her a little tighter, and she leaned into him.

"Congratulations you two."

Pat's face looked a little apologetic. I glanced at him, trying to telepathically communicate. I didn't want to ruin Jules' moment. Didn't want Pat to feel guilty she shared the news. "Seriously, congratulations."

Even as I said it, something shifted in me. I was happy for them, but once again, I felt jealous of Jules. Jealous I had a *wife* at home who didn't want me to pursue her anymore. Who had lost so many babies our marriage ended.

We made a little small talk about the baby coming then I checked my watch. I had a long drive home and a lot of thinking to do.

"I'm going to go."

Jules stood, hugged me. Pat shook my hand. "You've got a family to get back to now."

"Yeah, guess I do."

"Jack?"

"Yeah?"

"One last thing—if it were me..." He shrugged and shoved his hands in his pockets. "I wouldn't let her get away again."

I mulled over our conversation the whole way home.

Then

My rock thunked into the lake, a sharp contrast against the solemn quiet of the day. I looked to my dad, whose dark brows slanted over his blue eyes, wordlessly voicing keen disapproval. I wanted to get it right, but the technique was beyond me. "How do you do it again?"

He sighed and stooped toward the ground, dragging his fingers over the gritty soil. When he dislodged a smooth stone, he crouched next to me. I didn't want to look him in the face, but knew if I didn't, I'd get in trouble. His gaze burned into mine.

"Are you watching?"

I stole a glance back at Mom. She sat in the bench rocker, folded into herself. It was a warm day, but she had a shawl wrapped tightly around her shoulders as if fighting off the bitter cold. She gave me a gentle smile. I tried to smile back.

I jerked my attention back to Dad and nodded.

He slowly bent his pointer finger along the edge of the stone, and moved his hand to the other side of his body. He demonstrated a sharp flick of his wrist before actually releasing the stone into the water. When he did, it skipped four times.

"See that?"

I nodded again, stooping to drag my fingers over the soil just as he had done. I found the perfect rock. Smooth, round, and a little bigger than Dad's was. Confident this was my moment, I curled my pointer finger around it and crossed my arm over my body, just as he had done. I practiced the flick of my wrist once, twice. I looked back at Mom. Was she watching?

She was. She smiled again and gave me a weak nod.

I let the rock fly.

If all of my dad's expectations for me could be summed up in a rock, it was that rock. The stupid thing hit the water with a graceless splash, rustling the surface of the lake. A turtle on a half-sunken log jumped back into the water at the disturbance. My face heated, and the one thing Dad hated most of all heated the back of my eyes.

I took a deep breath.

His voice was gruff. "Jackson, it's not that hard."

My feet stepped back from the lake. I didn't want to try anymore. The urge to run to Mom coursed through me. I wanted to be with her. Should've been with her in the first place.

But a cool rock was thrust into my hands, and Dad stood behind me. He grabbed my right index finger and forced it around the rock. "We are going to get this right." The lake blurred. I blinked hard.

I stiffened when his fingers dug too firmly into the flesh of my forearm as he demonstrated the motion half a dozen times. If there was a way I could escape, I would've. My gaze wandered over to Mom.

He followed my gaze. "What do you want from her?"

I lifted a shoulder, feigning indifference.

He sighed and released me. I stumbled forward a step. His gaze traveled up the bank to Mom too, and his voice swelled with emotion. "You aren't always going to be able to run to her."

I knew that. But the words were like a knife.

"She's going to be okay," I insisted.

"Jackson." Dad shoved his fingers through his graying hair. "Have you heard anything we've been saying?"

I lifted a shoulder again.

He dropped to my eye level and squared my shoulders to face him. "Son, no. She's not going to be okay."

Tears were threatening, hotter than before. Mom had been in hospice, but we'd brought her home. To my nine year-old brain, that meant she would be okay. Words leaked out around the lump in my throat. "But she came home."

He cursed under his breath, and his voice wobbled. His brows slanted deeper. "You don't listen to anything." His grip tightened on my shoulders. "We brought her home because she wanted to be here. With us. Not in some room somewhere."

I shook my head in denial. "She's sitting outside. She's feeling better." A hot tear burned a trail down my face despite my efforts to swallow it back.

"Hey, nuh-uh, none of that."

I reached to dry it, but Dad swiped it away with a rough hand.

"We are going to be strong. For her. For your sister. For each other." I could tell he was trying to keep his voice level, but his teeth were clenched and his fingers were hurting me. Was he angry at me? He lightly shook my small frame. "We aren't going to cry, okay?"

I nodded and bit the inside of my cheek.

"Life is full of loss, Jackson. Crying right now is only going to upset your mother. We have to—"

Mom scolded him, "Nathaniel."

Dad shook his head and stood up, pacing away from me. "He needs to learn."

I squatted and drug my hand over the surface of the dirt. Feeling, not seeing, the tiny bits of gravel scraping the pads of my fingers.

"He's going to learn all too soon." Her voice was frail, her skin so white looking.

The bench groaned as Dad sat next to her and slipped his arm over her shoulders. She shifted, sinking into his chest. Their voices carried to the edge of the water.

"He needs to grieve, Nathaniel."

He said nothing.

"You're being too hard on him. You're always too hard on him."

Still nothing from Dad.

"Promise me you'll let him grieve. No tough guy stuff when I'm gone."

The bench groaned as they rocked. A breeze lifted the hair on my head and cooled my hot, damp cheeks. I watched as a motor boat zoomed by, just outside the no-wake zone. A wave lapped the tip of my boot, and I stuck my hands in, letting the dirt wash from my fingers. One of my tears mixed with the murky water.

A strange feeling unfurled in my chest—a burning and aching. She *couldn't* be leaving. My knees pressed into my sternum as I squatted lower to the ground and ducked my head down, hiding my now-flowing tears. Kept pretending to look for a good rock.

Dad lowered his voice and said something to Mom. But the quickened tide drowned out his answer. Then his special watch beeped. He scooped up Mom and walked up the hill to our house. The nurse would be waiting for her. Regret pricked as I watched them disappear through the back door.

I should've been sitting with her.

When they were out of sight, I dug my fingers into the

tender soil and tugged at a big rock. The kind only good for one thing—splashing. I stood and chucked it as far as I could. It hurt my shoulder pretty bad, and a sob ripped out of my throat so suddenly I startled.

But once the first sob escaped, there were more. One after the other. I was crying, flinging rocks, aiming for the docks across the lake. After fifteen minutes or so, the turtles were gone, the ripples had vanished, the sun was setting, and my shoulders were on fire. I wasn't sure if I was upset because my shoulders hurt, or Mom was leaving, or Dad would be the only parent I'd have left.

As all those realities hit me, the last of my energy drained, and I sank down onto the shore. The wet sand soaked through the seat of my pants.

I took a few deep breaths. Tried to get control. Maybe he was right. It was better not to cry. Certainly hadn't made me feel any better.

FORTY-FIVE

Miranda

I was washing the dinner dishes when I heard Jack's footsteps plodding down the stairs. He had just tucked Kacey into bed and was on his way out the door for a night shift. Dinner was awkward. I felt weird around him. We hadn't talked since almost a week ago, when I basically blamed him for everything that went wrong.

I'd been thinking about that conversation ever since.

Maybe I was too hard on him.

I saw him infrequently. He worked, slept, ate, and spent all his free time with Kacey. Which was good. It's what we agreed to. But I couldn't ignore the pinch distance created in my heart.

Because I tried not to hover over Kacey and Jack, I had bouts of alone time. I was in the midst of a decent fantasy read which was nice, I guess. I'd also picked up another virtual assistant job which added a few work hours to my week. And as always, I kept busy with Richard. Mostly kept busy trying not to stress myself to death.

I didn't worry about Kacey when he wasn't with me because Jack was doing great with him. He had to learn a few things the hard way. Like making sure Kacey took bathroom breaks. Kacey would get so excited he'd have accidents—which happened on Jack's watch right in the middle of a playground. But overall, he was learning on the fly and doing a really great job in the dad role—which of course didn't come as a surprise to me at all.

And Kacey was thoroughly obsessed. He waited at the front door for Jack and cried when he had to leave. Something about watching him cry as Jack pulled out of the driveway was the knock-out punch to my remaining emotional strength. The fact I had a garden to maintain was the only reality that saw me through.

I felt like Richard—secure with the plants. Silly, I suppose.

But there was no other place I could go where my heart could know a moment's peace. The dynamic of living day in and day out with all the things I wanted but could never have crushed me. So I found things to do in the garden until my neck and arms were tanner than they'd ever been in my whole life.

Jack walked into the kitchen, dressed and ready for work. "You about done in here?"

"Yep." I rinsed the last pot.

"Dinner was really good."

"Thanks. I've always wanted to try chicken cacciatore. It turned out." I placed the pot on the drying rack, turned around to face him, and leaned back against the counter.

His brow furrowed. "But you hardly even ate."

Jack was worried about me. I shrugged off his concern. "I wasn't real hungry."

"You're anxious?"

I shrugged again.

"There's a new bottle of wine in the cabinet."

"Jack, it's—" I sighed. "I'm really fine."

He nodded as I shifted, smoothing the front of my damp shirt.

His eyes trailed down my body, making zero effort to conceal his longing. He swallowed, a strange look crossing over his face like he was debating whether to speak his mind.

"Why are you looking at me like that?"

Then a slow smile pushed back his cheeks and he gave a soft huff of amusement. "Because you're gorgeous...you don't even realize. At work, I can barely stay focused. Can't think of anything but my wife."

Wife?

Heat flew to my cheeks. I wore a fitted t-shirt that had a big wet spot on the front from dish duty. My hair stuck to my neck from being in the garden earlier, and there was still dirt on the back of my shorts, which, come to think of it, I'm sure he noticed. "You're insane. I'm a mess."

His gaze burned my skin. "My kind of mess then."

I couldn't breathe. Jack was looking at me the way he had hundreds of times before. If we were for real married, he'd be caging me against the counter top right about now.

"Saying stuff like that just makes this harder."

"But it's how I feel."

I sucked in a shallow breath. "We've been over this Jack. You and me are about Kacey now."

"I need to talk to you about that."

"Alright then."

"I've been thinking about the conversation we had. You were right. Everything you said in the garden. I'm starting to see how I hurt you and"—his chest expanded with a deep breath—"I'm sorry, Miranda. I can't change everything that's happened, but I am trying to change me."

The hope that instantaneously blazed to life in my heart was silly. Premature at best. Unfounded at worst. I did my best to squelch it. Hoping for change would only complicate things. If I returned to Jack's arms it would be my own fault when my heart was broken again.

I tried to keep that front and center in my brain.

He continued. "I realized something. I was wondering if I love you too much. Wondering if I needed to chill out, tone it down, maybe even let you go. But the truth is—I don't love you *enough*, Miranda. I still love myself more, which is why I do dumb stuff like walk away when you need me. Because that protects me from things I don't like facing."

I blinked a few times.

"But that's not love." He moved around the counter.

I placed a hand over my heart.

"I don't have all the answers and I don't know how to fix my severe allergy to negative feelings, but I'm working on it. For you and Kacey. And for me." He stepped closer. "But there is something I need to be upfront about. Something you need to know."

The look in his eyes made it hard to inhale.

"As long as you are in my house, under my roof, I refuse to lay off. I'm always going to be working on loving my wife. You don't have to reciprocate. You don't even have to like it. Because whether you want it or not, I'm going to make you see how much I love you."

He stopped two feet away and braced one hand against the edge of the countertop behind me. He leaned in and used the other hand to cup my cheek. His voice was hoarse, quiet. "I have no intention of hiding how I feel to make this easier for us."

Freaking air. Where is it?

I sucked in a shallow breath, turning my head to the side. I didn't have the courage to look into his eyes. "Jack, we didn't agree to this."

"It was a stupid agreement and you know it. We weren't capable of doing this without feelings involved."

"I—I don't have feelings." Flimsy. We both knew it.

He dragged the back of his hand across my cheek, and I shivered. "Whatever you say."

He pushed away. Precious oxygen finally filled my lungs.

"I've got to head out. Put something on your dresser for you." He shot me a confident smile. "I'll see you tomorrow morning? Maybe we can have a cup of coffee."

I nodded, helpless to do anything but agree.

I let myself take him in. Big, powerful shoulders, perfect teeth, piercing eyes, towering stature. He was gorgeous, too. The difference between the two of us was he knew it.

He flipping *knew* it.

He was assured of his capability to leave me gasping for breath as he walked out the front door, unfazed. If he was of the mindset to woo me, it was going to take a truck-load of fortitude on my end to withstand him.

Did I have it in me?

I sighed. Unlikely.

When I was sure he was pulling out of the drive, I scurried up the stairs and crept into the bedroom where Kacey slept to see what Jack put on the dresser. For a woman dead set on resisting advances, I was far too eager. I fumbled around in the dark, and finally found it.

It was a jar of some kind with a sticky note on the top.

I sped into the hall so I could see.

The note had a simple question mark on it. That's all. No

words. Just a question mark. I peeled the note off to read the jar.

It was sugar scrub. An audible growl escaped my lips before the tears of frustration pricked my vision.

For real, Jack? Why are you doing this?

He was asking me if I remembered. Yes, I remembered full well. If I thought I couldn't breathe downstairs standing next to Jack, I was practically turning blue now. The realization *he* remembered the sugar scrub and was *thinking* of it stole the air from the room.

I loved sugar scrub. It made my legs so soft. But, our routine was a little...well, Jack was the one who had always applied it. We'd both hop in the shower, and he'd gently massage the sugar into my calves and thighs. By the time he would finish, I would be so turned on. It led to more. Every time without fail.

I placed a hand on the door frame to keep myself upright.

Good grief. What was Jack doing?

He was trying to make me fall in love with him again. If only love was the issue! I'd been gone for Jack since he sat at my table in the twos, sipping tea and watching me screw up every ticket in my section.

Love wasn't the problem.

How could he still not see?

FORTY-SIX

Miranda

A couple days later, I went out to do the nightly watering. I tucked Kacey into bed and left a plate of food in the fridge for Jack—he got held up and wouldn't be home until 8 p.m. or so. I hummed to myself as I turned the spigot handle and tromped through the backyard.

I hit the bottom of the tomato plants with the stream and their aroma released into the air. I could get drunk on that smell. When I finished the watering, I cut off the water and returned to the garden, deciding to pull a few weeds while I was at it. It was easier to weed the garden when the dirt was wet. Plus there was still plenty of light.

I got lost in my thoughts. For some reason they turned to Chris. I wondered where he was. If he was looking for us. If he missed us. Then my brain kept imagining scary scenarios where he kidnapped Kacey and me. I tried to shake them, but the fears persisted.

It was dumb to stress like I was. Chris had probably realized we weren't coming back and found some other woman to persecute with his impossible standards. Surely, he didn't care enough to actually hunt us down. That kind of crap happened in movies, not real life.

I thought of Sherri. Our communication had slowly tapered off. I hoped she was doing okay.

"Hey."

A weed flew into the air as I jumped out of my skin.

"Whoa!"

"Jack! You scared the crap out of me."

"Sorry. I said your name."

I took a deep breath, shaking my head. "I must've been lost in thought." A nervous laugh spilled out of me. "My heart is pounding."

"Some thoughts."

"You're telling me." He was already showered and dressed in shorts and a t-shirt. He must've gotten home right when I walked outside. I changed the subject, ready to get Chris and Sherri out of my head anyway. "How was your day?"

"Uh, tough."

"Oh no." I knew his tone. "Something bad happened."

"Yeah." He didn't say anything else. Jack was not usually very quiet. He liked to talk and silence meant something was wrong.

After a few moments, I asked, "Want to talk about it?"

He scrubbed a hand up the side of his face. "I'm—not sure I honestly can."

My voice was soft, almost drowned out by the crickets coming to life. "I'm sorry, Jack."

"That's okay. I'd rather focus on you anyway." He flashed me an assured smile. "Tell me about your day."

I told him what we did and about a couple silly things Kacey said. But our day wasn't very eventful, so in a few moments' time, the conversation lagged again. Jack knelt on the opposite side of the garden and began pulling some weeds, too.

Finally, he said, "Tell me something."

"Like what?"

"Something about you."

I gave him a surprised frown. "That's pretty vague. What do you want to know?"

"How about pregnancy? Or birth or something? That's an entire part of you I know nothing about."

I felt hesitant to discuss something that personal. Jack should've been a part of the whole process, so it was awkward. But, I mean, Kacey was his son. It made sense he'd want to know all the things. I tried to keep my response light. "Oh boy. What a topic."

"Maybe keep the details of Chris out. I've had a bad day as it is."

"Well, it would please you to know that Chris was in the waiting room as my friend during Kacey's birth. Along with a co-worker of mine I was close to. I did the actual birth alone."

His gaze drilled into me as he took a deep, quiet breath—the only evidence was the expansion of his chest. "Were you afraid?"

A sting in my eyes pushed in unwelcomed. "Yeah. I was terrified." I cleared my tightening throat. "Jack, this is a big conversation. I might—it could make me really emotional."

He reached for a weed inside the squash plants. "Unless you object to sharing, I'm all ears."

He might change his mind in a few minutes when I started blubbering, but how long had I wanted to have this conversation with Jack, anyway?

"Pregnancy was hard. When the doctor told me it was viable and the baby looked healthy, he ordered bed rest. Which was a problem because I was a waitress. That's when I came home and...we know how that went. Anyway—I didn't want to take chances of losing Kacey, so I went to quit my job. Chris was my boss at the time. He—well, never mind, I can skip that part..."

"Wait. Don't skip it."

"You said no details about Chris."

"I'm curious now. Go on."

"Okay." I tried to remember where I was. Jack hadn't pressed for too many details about Chris. Probably because he knew he'd blow a gasket. I'd been careful not to say too much—but it was time he knew some things. "He had a duplex he owned and allowed me to move into it for a really cheap rate. He knocked the normal rent way down."

"I thought you lived with your college friend at that point."

"I did, but she got engaged and moved literally a few months after I got there. Left me high and dry. Obviously, I couldn't afford rent by myself."

He grunted.

"So I moved into Chris' duplex and lived there while I did some kind of remote tech work on my phone. It wasn't much pay, but it was enough to make the low rent."

"Were you sick?"

"Sick as a dog for a while. I was miserable until I was almost four months pregnant."

Jack's shoulders worked as he picked a few more weeds. I was done on my side, so I perched on the garden barrier, talking. "I did nothing but lay in bed and do a few exercises here and there. I was determined to make sure our little guy made it."

Jack's gaze snapped to mine.

I think the *our* caught him off guard. As it did me. My brain had to fumble for words to find my bearings again.

"When I was nine months pregnant..." I let my words trail off. "Are you sure you want to hear all this right now?"

He nodded. A gruff "yes" came from his bent head and rigid shoulders.

"There was a small kitchen fire at the duplex over the kitchen stove. I wasn't there thankfully. I was depositing a check and picking up groceries.

"I was just so happy all my stuff didn't go up in flames. The fire stayed small and was put out very quickly. There were enough damages though that an entire wall needed to be rebuilt. The insurance claim covered everything and when the reno started, I had to move out.

"I had nowhere to go. And yes, my credit was terrible because of that dumb card I forgot about. Chris opened the doors of his personal home. I walked into that situation for a lack of options. I couldn't work to make my own way, I had no friends since I did remote side-gigs for income, and I had a baby coming in a month. So, I went with him.

"He said he'd get the duplex unit back up and running as quickly as he could. But when it was finally finished a month later, he said he was having financial trouble and needed to rent it to someone at market price.

"So, I had to stay with Chris. He assured me he'd help me find something else. But weeks rolled into months. Chris had to move several times and always packed us up with him. I never questioned why he moved so often, although, looking back...I kind of wonder if he was in some sort of trouble?"

I shrugged. "I don't know. I didn't question much of anything. I was so depressed I could hardly care for Kacey. I had scary thoughts that made me feel like a terrible mom. I was so anxious. Making my own way would've been impossible. Chris knew my emotional state and he took advantage of me. Started asking me for things and made me feel guilty if I said no. Like he'd done so much for me—how could I refuse?"

The garden was weed free and twilight was edging in upon us. But we sat on the edges of the garden, neither of us making a move to leave.

"What type of stuff did he ask you for?"

That's when my eyes started burning. "Little things at first. Make dinner. Clean the house. Run this to the bank for me. Watch a movie with me. Have a romantic dinner with me. It just"—I swallowed the lump forming—"things just escalated from there. I ended up being his girlfriend and I wasn't even sure how it happened. There were a lot of little compromises that...stacked up over time. I was not in a place to make smart decisions anyway. Saying no and holding boundaries...I couldn't do it. I was struggling postpartum, felt..." I shrugged, letting my explanation be good enough.

I sniffed, hating the wave of emotion washing over me as I remembered those horrible early days with Kacey in Chris' home. I was grieving the loss of everything I ever wanted. Jack, a home, security, family. Especially Jack. A few tears trickled down my cheeks.

"That bastard devised the entire situation, didn't he?"

I nodded, my voice weak. "Yes, I think he did."

"You didn't love him?"

"No. He was not lovable."

"Cruel?"

I shook my head. "Cruel makes me think of being chained up and starved or something. Nothing like that. It was mainly his words—I don't know how he did it, but he made me feel like crap every time we talked. And it wore me down. I did what I had to do to not feel so bad all the time."

"That's cruel in my book."

I swiped my cheek with my glove, realizing belatedly I probably left dirt on my face. "I was weak. Pathetic, honestly. I should've stood up for myself."

"No. You were abused and preyed upon, Miranda."

I shrugged. "I was supposed to be telling you about birth—I'm sorry."

His voice was soft, reassuring. "Don't apologize. Tell me whatever you want. I want to know everything about you."

I sniffed, shifting away from Jack. "Kacey was born via c-section."

"Really?"

"Yeah, Kacey was in distress for some reason and they opted to give me a c-section, especially due to my uterus. They didn't want to take chances."

Jack asked me some questions and I explained the caesarian section process, how it felt, what recovery was like.

He asked, "Was it crazy when they handed him to you?"

I smiled even though I tried not to for Jack's sake. Talking about this was wildly courageous of him, and I was doing my best not to say or do anything that might make it harder for him to swallow. "It was unreal. I was so happy, but terrified. I knew I'd be taking a baby home alone and I was—I felt my inadequacies."

"You've done an incredible job."

"Thank you."

"So, what did you crave while pregnant?"

The shift to a lighter question eased some of the tension in my legs. "Um, that's an easy question! I was a very typical pregnant lady. Ice cream."

"Is that why Kacey is an ice cweam monstah?"

Jack's imitation of Kacey's "r" made me laugh.

Really laugh.

I gasped for a breath. "Yeah, guess so." We laughed for a few minutes about Kacey's various antics. It warmed my heart how much Jack already learned about our son, how in tune he was with him.

He asked, "Do you have any pictures you could show me of him as a baby?"

Poor Jack. He deserved so much more than old pictures.

I took a pained breath. "I have a few. Mostly in a scrapbook I left at Chris' house."

"Oh. What's his last name?"

I squinted. Why would he need that information? "Bernstein."

A firefly lit up a few feet away.

I said, "It's like completely dark. Sorry for talking so long."

"Don't apologize."

"Hopefully, it was a decent enough distraction."

He stood and we slowly walked back to the house. He crossed his thick arms over his chest. His words were taut, forced out. "There was a shooting today in a bad neighborhood."

"Oh no."

"One of the victims was—a little boy. Looked a smidge older than Kacey."

My fingers reached over and slipped into the crook of his elbow.

"The image sticking with me is the parents." I looked over but couldn't see much of his expression in the darkness. "If it had happened in April, it wouldn't have bothered me like it did today."

In April. Meaning, before he knew he was a parent.

"I kept thinking of Kacey, and how I'd feel if I lost him and —and I hardly even know him."

We stopped at the back door and he faced me, uncrossing his arms. My heart squeezed with compassion. It was so easy to focus on only what I'd been through. What I'd lost. But Jack's life was anything but pain free. He was still trying to grapple with unexpected fatherhood. Desperate to comfort him, my fingers moved, sliding down into his hand without permission.

"Thank you for telling me." I squeezed.

"I'm trying to practice." He squeezed back.

We were pushed close together on the threshold of the back door. Jack reached up, running his thumb over my cheek bone a few times. "Got some dirt." After a moment, his eyes left his task and freely roamed my face. The pressure of his hand against my cheek caused a thrill to run through my core. If only he didn't look so sad, so heavy.

We stood, staring at each other in the gentle light from the window panes. This is why I couldn't be near him. Looking into his eyes, all my grounds for resisting us faded. I was pulled into the deep blue by an angry riptide. I couldn't find ground if my life depended on it.

When he pulled me into a hug, I melted into him. His arms and firm chest immediate comforts. He murmured into the top of my hair. "If I can't convince you to stay, you won't ever go back to him, right?" The edge of worry I rarely heard in his tone sent shivers down my spine.

"No, we won't ever go back."

"You promise?"

"I promise."

He nodded, his breathing out of rhythm. Jack was anxious and it hurt my heart. I pushed back and looked in his face. "Do you need a distraction, a wind-down from your day?"

"What do you have in mind?"

"Kettle corn and a movie this time?" I scrunched my nose, worried my offering wasn't good enough.

He whispered, "Will my wife be there?"

The question made my bones feel like jelly. "I—I'll be there, Jack."

"Sounds perfect then."

FORTY-SEVEN

Jack

I had a connection—a buddy who frequently dug up info as favors for fellow officers. He owed me a few, so I cashed in. Wasn't legal, but no one needed to know.

My friend dug up everything there was to know of Christopher Bernstein as easily as browsing a Sunday paper. Where he lived, his number, his many home addresses, his business degree, and his *whopping* criminal record. Miranda probably had no idea he was a thief. There was an active warrant for his arrest for a couple years, which is why he moved frequently. He *managed* rental properties for a company for a while. Got fired and his boss filed a report about Chris' money mishandlings. The only property Chris owned was his car. His charges were white collar—all fraud related.

He was a full-fledged con, which would explain how he had so easily ensnared Miranda. He was likely smart and charming. And she was so sweet, so generous.

As soon as my buddy filled me in on all the details, I

contacted Chris and arranged a meet to pick up their things. Told him to meet me in a grocery store parking lot in Cincinnati, Ohio with *all* of it or I'd be knocking on his front door.

He didn't agree for free.

He whined over text that he would have to borrow a friend's truck. I tossed more cash into his pile to make him comply. Whatever. I wanted my family's things at any cost. And a chance to give him second thoughts about ever paying Nashville a visit. I was sick of looking over my shoulder and worrying he might find them while I was on duty.

The last thing I wanted to do today was take time away from Miranda and go to Ohio on my day off, but they left everything they ever had there. Her pictures, her beloved scrapbooks and craft supplies, her bookshelf and novels, clothes, special things I knew meant something to her. Not to mention, Kacey's toys and the scrapbook she made just for him.

Pat had volunteered to accompany me which I was thankful for. We talked a little on the drive, but my brain was preoccupied. Time with Miranda was slipping through my fingers. The days flew like they never had before. I worked, slept a little here and there, played with my son, and tried to warm up my wife.

My long shifts stole from the moments we had left. I felt myself growing desperate—frantic almost—to convince Miranda to stay after we sold the lake house. Funny, here we were, seven weeks into this agreement and the stupid lake house was the least of my concerns. Don't get me wrong. The money was going to be great, but it felt like the pathway back to Miranda. Not the real prize.

We had been in touch with Mr. Haskins and were set to sign papers and receive the house on the sixtieth day of marriage. June fifth. Two days after Miranda's birthday. An all-cash buyer was lined up, meaning the sale would be swift. We could close remotely by signing digital documents and money would be wired within forty-eight hours.

Divorces, on the other hand, take a while. We would be married longer than two months, even if Miranda didn't agree to stay. But once she got the money...I wouldn't be able to keep her under my roof. She would have the means to leave. To go anywhere, buy a house, and start a new life.

The possibility followed me like a looming storm cloud. Threatening to ruin the best do-over I ever had. And it pressed in by the day. Miranda was stand-off-ish. She loved me. I saw the evidence in her eyes every time I looked at her. The love between us had never waned.

But she didn't trust me. She didn't want to give me another chance. She wanted to get out of this situation as quickly and as unscathed as she could.

A lot of my advances were met with a brick wall. And I had moves. Good ones. I knew Miranda like the back of my hand. The post-it notes, small gestures, and physical advances were things she would've responded to in the past.

But she wasn't responding. Not at all.

She was ignoring them.

Dr. Hannel said "building trust takes time." It made me want to smack him. I didn't have time.

I flipped on my turning signal at the store's entry and immediately saw him at the very back of the lot. He'd unloaded all their things on the concrete around him. Boxes, a toy bin, and a kid's mattress. Boxes were untaped per our agreement.

There wasn't much. It was enough to fit into my truck bed —no problem.

Honestly, I was surprised the dimwit followed through on the plan. I guessed for Chris, money talked.

I pulled up beside him, double checking the wad of cash in my back pocket. With each passing second, adrenaline poured by the gallon into my veins. My muscles twitched with anticipation at the upcoming fight. I nearly trembled with rage. Seeing Chris face to face—and allowing him to live to tell the tale—was going to take a level of strength I rarely exerted.

I absolutely planned to throw a couple punches at the guy because he couldn't do a thing about it. He wouldn't be calling authorities, considering the warrant.

Ideal scenario.

He was leaning against the tailgate of the truck. I'm not the best judge of handsome, but it pissed me off to no end that the man was halfway decent looking. Not sure why that accelerated me toward my breaking point.

I guessed he was about 5'11", brown hair, medium build.

My jaw ached and sweat beaded on my neck already.

"You ready for this?"

I grunted. "Can't wait."

"Looks like he did what you asked."

"Seems like." I jerked the keys out of the ignition. "You're going to keep me from killing him, right?"

"Yep."

"Good." I opened my door, subconsciously adjusting the glock on my hip. Ohio was an open carry state, so my weapon was in plain view.

I stepped out of the truck, slamming the door behind me.

I spoke in the tone I used at work. Clipped, hurried, commanding. "Christopher Bernstein?"

A slow nod was the only response.

"Are these their things?" I nodded toward the haphazard line of moving boxes.

"They are." He looked me over, probably sizing me up. Couldn't judge—I was doing the same. Chris' build was like

Pat's—lean, swift. If a brawl ensued, he'd have me on speed. I boxed with Pat a couple times, and when I nailed him, he was down for a minute. But, he was scrappy and quick. Chris crossed his arms over his chest, unimpressed. "You got the money?"

"Yes. But we load first." I pointed to the boxes and said to Pat. "Check them." Pat flipped open the flaps, making sure we had the things we came for. Books, toys, some kitchen equipment, and most importantly—her scrapbook stuff.

Chris waited impatiently as Pat looked through boxes. I didn't dare bend over or take my attention off him. Had no idea what this loser was capable of.

He was eyeing my weapon. "Miranda never called me back."

"She doesn't need to. She and Kacey aren't your concern anymore."

"Arent my concern? I've been taking care of them for years."

"Taking *care*?" I scoffed. Raised my voice. "You attacked her!"

His tone was cool. "I didn't hit her. She fell."

"Willing to stick to that in a court of law?"

He said nothing.

"Yeah, I didn't think so. If you don't want me to drag your ass to the nearest police department, you better shut the hell up."

"On what basis?"

I stepped closer. "How about your outstanding warrant?"

"Wait." The color drained from his face as he scanned the surrounding parking lot. Looked over his shoulder toward the main light. "How would you know about that? Are you a cop or something?"

"Police Sergeant with Nashville PD, precinct twelve."

"Her ex was a *cop*?!" He cussed.

It pleased me immensely Miranda had never told him I was in law enforcement. "I know plenty of people. Wouldn't take but one phone call to get you cuffed."

His face pulsed red with anger. "This was a set up!"

"Nope. I just want their stuff and I'm out of here. If you're smart, you won't move."

He leaned back against the truck, scowling and murmuring profanity. I bent to grab a box, keeping him within my line of vision. As I heaved a third box into the bed, he muttered something that zapped the last of my in-tact restraint.

"I should've let her and her bastard go to the streets."

I whipped my head around. "What was that you said?"

He spat the words, cool and unintimidated. "Good riddance. She's an ungrateful bitch."

It was like I was being remote controlled. Possessed zero power over my appendages. My fists were in his collar and I slammed him against the side of the truck so hard he winced. But then he smiled, enjoying the ruckus. I pressed into his upper sternum, listening to his air *whoosh* out. "Say it again. I dare you."

His words were squeezed. "Good luck in bed. She's a boring—"

That's when I jerked him off the side of the truck and let the first punch fly. Clocked him square in the jaw. Felt the impact zing up to my elbow. My anger had a target and I aimed again, following him as he staggered backward.

A random car pulled up and rolled the window down. "They okay?"

Pat called back, "Nah, they're fine. Just solving something the old fashioned way."

The guy laughed and drove off.

When he gained his footing, my second hit landed right in his diaphragm. He grabbed his midsection and doubled over, moaning. His back hit the concrete. It took two seconds for me to kneel over him and deliver more punches to his nose and an eye.

Chris got two hits in. Somewhere on my face but I hardly registered them. Less than a minute later, Chris' face spewed blood and he wasn't fighting back.

Strong arms locked around my shoulders.

"Jack!" Pat dragged me off him. "That's enough!"

Blood pooled in my mouth and I spat before yelling down at Chris, who was moaning on the ground. "You aren't allowed to even *think* about my wife like that." I wound a foot back to deliver a kick, but Pat's arms were still dragging me off. My boot barely missed Chris' ribcage.

His chest heaved. "*Ex*-wife." The lunatic had the audacity to correct me?

"*Current* wife." I lifted my left hand. Ring in full view. "If you ever show your face in Nashville or contact my family, plastic surgeons won't know what to do with you."

It took two more minutes to get everything into the back of the truck and secured with ratchet straps. Chris laid on the ground the entire time. When we were finished, I dropped the cash on the asphalt next to him. His whopping five-hundred bucks. I thought about withholding it and just driving away, but I didn't want to give him a reason to hunt me down.

He slowly stood and flipped us the bird on the way out. I smiled.

Flipped one right back.

FORTY-EIGHT

Miranda

The snap-pea crunched in my mouth. They were still warm from the vine in Richard's garden. The last of the season now that temps were pushing past eighty degrees. Every bite was perfect, and I made a mental note to add snap-peas to the list of early spring crops I wanted to try next year.

I grabbed another from the mixing bowl on Richard's patio table and dragged it through the shallow dish of hummus I'd made. We were talking about it the day before. He had never even heard of hummus, so I made a special batch just for him.

He loved it.

My skin tingled from two hours in the sun. These days, I was helping Richard in his garden quite a bit. In fact, I was in Richard's garden so much, I tended my own garden after I put Kacey in bed most nights. I didn't mind. I loved caring for Richard and Rose's plants. He taught me so much, and I adored his company.

I didn't realize how hungry I was for a friend. I never

thought I'd find one this way, but wanted to soak in every moment as his next door neighbor. When I inevitably moved out at some point, I'd still come to visit him.

I knew gobs about Richard's family. He showed me pictures of each and every grandchild multiple times. Told me story after story.

He apologized once for talking about them too much. But I really didn't mind listening. Almost felt like I could live the family life I never had through him somehow. Hearing about his sons' accomplishments, his favorite memories of Rose, and the funny things his grandchildren did made me feel part-of in a small way.

"You know," he said, still chomping on a pea. "Rose always wanted a daughter. So did I. Wish she was still here to meet you. Would'a taken to you just as quickly as I did."

"Aw, Richard. I wish I could've met her too."

"She would've nabbed you up, treated you like her very own." He gave a soft, tired chuckle. "Wish you were one of ours." He leaned back in his chair and patted me on the bottom of the chin. "You better keep coming to see me after you move 'cause this right here is a smile I'll miss."

Being welcomed in, invited, wanted. It was a feeling I rarely experienced, but craved. Its absence was a chasm in my spirit. Every decision I made in my life backfired, pouring salt into the wound. Into the emptiness I always carried.

Warmth flooded my eyes. "I'll keep coming. I promise."

He stood from his chair, taking a few wobbling steps as his back muscles unraveled. "Stay put."

He returned clutching a straw hat. I didn't have to ask who it belonged to. It was clearly a woman's. Rose's.

"This belonged to Rose." He eased back into the chair and lifted the hat to eye level. Tipped it. Like he was imaging it on her head. "She had pretty hair. It spilled out from under this hat and shimmered. It was gray before she lost it. I liked her gray hair better than her brown. She wore this every day in the garden because she'd lose track of the time and get blister-like burns on her neck."

He shifted and placed the hat on the table beside our bowl of snap-peas. "You remind me of Rose a bit. Loving, feminine, good listener, eager to help, green thumb."

I frowned at him on that last point. I was hardly a green thumb.

He nodded at the hat. "Put it on."

"You want me to try it on?"

"Yes. Come on now."

Doing such was sacred. I wanted to protest. I couldn't wear Rose's hat. But I glanced up at Richard's eager face. Refusing would disappoint him. So, I smiled, pulled my ponytail free, and put it on.

He looked at me and the slow smile pulled a million lines into his face. A little moisture gathered in his eyes, and he rubbed his knee and looked away. "Yes ma'am. You remind me of my Rose quite a lot."

"Oh, Richard. You miss her so much."

"That I do."

I grabbed the rim of the straw hat and lifted it off my head.

"Don't take it off. I want you to keep it."

"Keep it? Richard, I couldn't...this is something special. Something you should keep."

He shook his head, determination written across his face. "No, Miranda. Special things are meant to be given away. Rose gave everything away and that right there is what made her so wonderful. She'd want you to have it."

"You don't want to keep it for you?"

"Rose gave me plenty." He tapped the spot over his heart.

"What about your children?"

"She gave them plenty too. Plus, they don't really garden. It'd bring me joy to see her hat in the sunshine again."

I smiled through my tears and placed it back on my head. My "okay" was almost silent, muted by the tension in my throat.

We sat in silence for a few moments, watching Kacey run around the garden with his cars.

"You wanna know the difference between you and Rose?"

"Tell me."

"Rose knew how to forgive."

I felt my head move backward a few inches as his words hit me from out of left field. What the heck was that supposed to mean?

"I pray you'll still be my friend after I speak my mind, 'cause I'd feel downright heavy-hearted if I didn't say something."

My heart dropped to my stomach. On the heels of such a wonderful moment, he was going to lecture me.

"Look at your garden."

I did. Thankful for a chance to turn my face away.

"You're doing a fine job keeping it up. You're doing all the things most folks don't like to do. Keeping an eye out for problems, pests, being patient, trouble-shooting. You're protecting your harvest before harvest time even comes." I chanced a glance back at Richard. He was nodding, looking at his own garden now.

"You know, we were two youngins when we got married. I didn't have the faintest idea what to do with a woman. And I learned real slow. She was patient with me. Taught me. Loved me while I made messes. I took to gamblin' when I was in my twenties and she stuck with me. Could've left. Probably should've. But Rose was committed to tending our marriage."

I felt like I was going to be sick. I knew where he was going with this and mentally kicked myself for sharing too much of my story.

"Rose was a dyin' breed. Folks these days want immediate reward and most things in life don't work that way. Especially relationships." He glanced into my eyes and I averted mine, feeling stupid wearing Rose's hat now.

"Seems to me you've got a man over there who loves you to pieces and is willing to do whatever it takes to do things right this time. Correct me if I'm wrong...Jack was good to you in every other way."

He paused, waiting for me to confirm. I wanted to lie to bolster my stance, but I couldn't. I thought of all the ways Jack had loved me. No, he wasn't perfect. He had flaws. He was bossy, outspoken, and sometimes put up walls. But he *was* kind, committed, tender, and generous. I blinked, forced the words out. "You're—you're not wrong."

"But you don't want to give him that chance because you're afraid to put your heart on the line while you work together. That don't seem right to me."

He was seriously calling me out?

He continued, "I know things were tough, and I ain't discounting tough. Lord knows grief's a marriage killer. I get that. But now, you're together. A second chance was dropped in your lap. And instead of grabbing it by the horns, you want to protect yourself."

"I'd be stupid not to protect myself." I took a deep breath, searching for calm. I shook my head, convincing myself his words stung because they were untrue.

He hummed. A hum of insight.

"Right?"

"Well, I don't reckon I agree."

"Okay." I tried to hide my irritation. I was confused enough as it was. "Then what would you do in my place?"

He nodded once. "The work. The tending."

"Can you just *tell* me what you mean in plain terms?"

"Forgive him. Try again. Fight like hell."

I wanted to do that. I really did. I wanted to be like Rose. But the mere idea of laying all my biggest insecurities bare before Jack caused anxiety to sweep throughout my body.

Why am I so afraid?

Wouldn't forgiveness and trying again just result in more broken hearts? Richard just didn't understand.

I pulled the stupid hat off my head and put it on the table.

The low hum of an engine jerked my attention toward the street. Jack was home. He'd left at 4:30 a.m. and was probably exhausted. I was thankful for a reason to exit the conversation.

"We need to get back and start dinner."

I called Kacey and instructed him to gather up his cars as a meltdown pressed against my throat.

We said our goodbyes and headed toward our gate when Richard said, "Don't forget your new gardening hat."

I turned back and grabbed it with a fake smile.

FORTY-NINE

Jack

Miranda walked, chin tucked, from Richard's backyard into ours. Kacey trailed behind her. I waved, but she didn't look up. Before she disappeared behind the house, I called out, "Miranda! Kacey!"

Kacey whipped his head around then bounded toward me. "Hey, buddy!"

He tackled my legs. "Hi, Dack!"

I faked a mad voice. "Hey now." I grabbed him by the waist and lifted him, flipping his legs into the air and over my shoulder. "We talked about *Dack*."

He giggled uncontrollably into my chest, limp as a rag doll. "Oh, I keep fowgetting!" I ran a spider hand up his back and he squirmed and kicked, correcting himself. "Daddy! Daddy!"

It still brought the biggest smile to my face even though he'd never said it without being prompted. I kept it lighthearted, but knew the day he said it all on his own would break me.

I flipped him upright and settled him against my hip. "Want to see what I brought?"

"Yes! Yes!"

Miranda made her way around the house. The moment she saw the truck bed, she paled.

My heart plummeted into my tennis shoes, suddenly worried I overstepped. I thought she'd be happy.

I pointed into the truck bed so he could see. Kacey screamed, almost bursting my eardrums. "My toys!" He jerked, trying to scramble to them. "Slow up, Kacey. I'll get them out."

I set him down and he ran to Miranda. "Mommy, Dack brought my toys!"

"I see." Her monotone reply set me on high alert.

How is she not happy?

I looked at her face, she clearly wasn't. As a matter of fact, she looked ill. Flustered, restless, obviously teary-eyed.

She came to the back of the truck while I loosened a ratchet.

Worry lines on her forehead sent my brain into a defensive position. Swallowed it down the best I could, searching for something less combative to say. "You don't look happy."

"I—you—" She shook her head, gathering thoughts. Irritation caused my neck to tingle. "You shouldn't have done this, Jack."

"Why on earth not?"

Be cool, man.

"Because!"

"*Because* isn't really an answer. Why shouldn't I have done this for my wife and son? These are your things. Doesn't seem like enough after doing nothing for four years."

I took a deep breath, turning away to hide the depths of my agitation at her response. Hadn't this woman figured out that I loved her yet?

When I looked back at her, her eyes immediately fell to my mouth. I'd cleaned the blood off my chin and hands, but there was still some on my shirt. My bottom lip was split on the side and the surrounding area was a little purple. She jerked my chin towards her, surveying it. "Oh my *gosh*. Did you and Chris fight?"

Despite her horror, I smiled. "Oh yeah."

"That looks awful!"

"You should see him."

She released my face, frowning. "You're doing too much for me." She turned and looked back to Richard's garden and tucked her head again. "I—I wish you would just stop."

Stop?

The wind left my sails. Felt my shoulders sag.

"I was trying to do something nice, Miranda."

"You're treating me like we are..."

Her words trailed off, her lips frozen in speaking position, as the worried expression melted. Her gaze locked on something beyond my face.

Ah. The ring.

She blinked several times and her lips trembled. "Jack, why are you—"

"Come on, Dack! Get my toys!" Kacey screamed.

"Just"—she waved me off, turning her head so I wouldn't see her tears spill—"let's just get all this out."

Way past Kacey's bedtime, Miranda's soft voice called down the stairs. "Jack?"

I sat up, jerked out of my slight doze. I'd been watching a

baseball game on mute with subtitles—kind of dumb. It was a recipe for spending the night on the couch, but sometimes I just needed a silent distraction.

"Yeah?"

"You up?"

"I'm sitting on the couch."

She came down, her footsteps nearing the back of the couch. I tipped my head backward. "You good?"

"Just wanted to talk to you for a minute."

I straightened up a little and clicked off the TV. She'd avoided me ever since I got home and insisted we not unpack anything. Said we shouldn't waste the time.

Felt pretty low the rest of the day.

"Everything okay?"

She prepared to sit on the opposite side of the couch as I patted the cushion beside me. She paused, a flash of indecision crossing her face. For a moment it looked like she'd come sit beside me. Her feet moved, but she held back and sat far away.

"Look, Jack. I need to clear the air."

I nodded, said nothing.

"First of all, I'm sorry for being a jerk. You—" She looked everywhere around the room but at me. "You driving to Ohio to get our things might be the nicest thing anyone has ever done for me. I reacted like I did because I felt guilty. I was upset about something else, and then you were being so nice to me and I felt like I didn't deserve it."

She rubbed her hands down the front of her pajama pants. She looked so huggable in the plaid flannel pjs and white t-shirt. If things were well between us, she wouldn't stand a chance looking that cute.

"So, thank you for doing that."

"You don't have to thank me."

She quickly swiped a knuckle over her eyelashes. "Yes, I do. How did you even find him?"

"I know people."

She sniffed. "How on earth did you get Chris to agree to this?"

"Money."

"You paid him for my things?"

I nodded.

"Jack, you shouldn't..." She stopped, shaking her head. "No, thank you. I don't know why you did, but I'm glad. Kacey was on cloud nine all day. He fell asleep holding one of his Peterbilts."

She lifted one shoulder, screwing up her face. "I'm almost afraid to ask, but is Chris still...alive?"

I laughed a little. "Yeah, unfortunately."

"I'm surprised."

"Pat was there. He promised to keep me out of prison. But I got a few punches in."

"Have you iced your lip? It's puffy."

"Yeah, a few times. It looks worse than it is, I promise."

"Okay." Her gaze cut around the room as she shifted. "Uh, do you think he'll be looking for us?"

I thought for a moment about the things he'd said about Miranda and how easily he'd given up her things. Answered as honestly as I could without disclosing those hurtful details. "No, I don't think he will. He got the message loud and clear."

"The message?"

"That we're married. That you're mine. That if he tries anything funny, he's a dead man."

We sat there. Quiet and staring. Correction: I was the one staring. She was looking at the fan, the dark TV, the cushion edge she was picking at.

She gently scraped at a fuzzy on the couch. "The second

thing I need to talk to you about is..." She chanced a glance at me. "Your old ring. I didn't even know you kept it."

"What about it?"

"Why are you wearing it?"

"Because I'm married."

"Jack, but—we aren't married like that."

"I am."

She sighed. Long and defeated. "Please listen. I don't know how I haven't been clear enough with you. But I'm moving out when the money comes. I'm not going to unpack boxes and get all cozy and tucked in, when I know we are leaving." Her shoulders were rigid. She held her chin high. But her voice trembled. "Then I'll see an attorney. I'm not going to consider this"—she wagged a finger between the two of us—"real because we have butterflies."

"I'm not wearing a ring because I have butterflies."

"Aren't you though? We are attracted to each other so let's throw caution to the wind and make all the same mistakes on repeat, right?"

I sat up and placed my elbows on my knees, getting riled. "I have no intention of making all the same mistakes."

"Well, for me, the mistake is trusting—" She waved a hand. "Forget it."

"No, finish what you were going to say."

"It doesn't matter."

"How you feel absolutely matters." I sat silently waiting for her to finish.

She looked at me and blinked a few times. Silence swelled between us like a balloon. Until the pressure popped. She made a choking noise as she sniffed. Then the tears came. Uninvited and breaking the dam. She covered her face with a hand, and spoke between stifled sobs. "Sorry—Jack. I need to go to—bed." She stood to go. "But you should—take the ring off, okay?"

She moved around the couch and I jumped up and grabbed her hand. "You're *not* leaving like that."

She resisted my leading her back to the couch, trying to pull her hand back, but I persisted. Wrapping my hands around hers and finally settling her back down on the couch right next to me this time. She did her best to hold herself together, but failed. The tears came, whether she liked it or not. She said, "I'm sorry. I know you hate this."

She apologized like four times as she pushed back under the onslaught. I held her hand. Helpless to do much else. Her battle against her emotions was an attempt to protect *me*, and I didn't know what to do with that exactly.

The truth hit me in the gut like a punch.

I'd made her feel like she wasn't acceptable this way. Hadn't I?

Just like Dad did to me.

My fingers squeezed hers.

My voice cracked, gravelly, like I hadn't used it in years. "Miranda, you can cry for a little bit if you need to."

She tsked and rolled her eyes to the side. She didn't say the words, but her response said *yeah right*.

When she calmed, I said, "I want you to tell me what you were going to say earlier. You said 'for me, the mistake is trusting' then you stopped."

Her cheeks bunched as she swallowed. Something about her in white. She was gorgeous. Her blonde hair spilled over her shoulders and smelled so good. It caught the distant light from the foyer lamp, almost glistened like gold.

I whispered, withdrawing my hand to give her a little space. "What you were about to say is the reason a marriage I want is going to end. Please tell me."

She shrugged. "Just trusting people is all. I trust too easily and get hurt."

"What do you mean? You're saying that like there's more to that statement than just me."

Pat's words reverberated in my brain. *Just because you have all the clues doesn't mean you've solved the mystery.*

The woman before me had lived an entire lifetime prior to our paths ever crossing. What she meant was important, pivotal. I'm definitely not the smartest guy, but I had a sharp ear and was a quick learner. I was *going* to solve her.

She drew air through her nose and let it out, puffing her cheeks. "The people who say they are there, aren't. And no, I don't just mean you. The mistake I make is thinking that people actually care about anyone other than themselves. I've been pushed aside more times than I can count."

I wished I knew what she meant. She'd said her dad left when she was a kid. But it seemed bigger than that. "Are you talking about your dad?"

"I don't know. I'm not even sure I have it sorted in my own head."

I nodded. "Okay."

"I'm really tired." She stood. "Think I'd rather just go to bed right now then dive into all this."

I stood too. Before she could escape, I pulled her back by her elbow and wrapped my arms around her. She stiffened against my chest, definitely didn't hug me back.

I leaned, dropping my cheek to the top of her amazing hair. "I don't know how to be all the things I'm supposed to be for you, but I'm not going to quit till I figure it out."

She started relaxing. Felt her hands move at my thighs. I rubbed the middle of her back in a slow circle, pulled her closer with the other hand.

"I'm stubborn. You know that. I'm not giving up on us."

Her hands came to the small of my back. Gingerly, like she was afraid of getting tangled up.

"I'm not wearing a ring because I have butterflies. Don't get me wrong, I definitely do. It's pretty crazy how bad they are." Wasn't that the truth. This woman could wreck me with a single glance. I pushed her back a little and she looked up. Those big brown eyes waiting for what I might say.

I continued slow. Wanted her to hear every word. "I'm wearing it because I love you. I'm not sure how many times I'll have to say it for you to believe me."

She drew her bottom lip between her teeth.

"If you want to end things, fine. Just know every time we cross paths, every time we pass Kacey back and forth, every time we text or call, every time our lives intertwine...I'll be there, and this chapter—Jack and Miranda—doesn't end. Not for me."

Her poor bottom lip was losing color.

I cupped her chin with my hand, swiped my thumb across her lip. She released it, and the pink flooded back in. A millimeter of her tongue came out, putting moisture back into her lips. Man, if only things were different. I wanted her so much I could hardly breathe.

My voice was hoarse with concealed desire. "Sleep on that, okay?"

She nodded and I watched as she slowly made her way back up the stairs. My hand came to my ring finger as I twisted the symbol of our union. To the rest of the world, I was taken. Even if she refused to take me back.

FIFTY

Jack

A few days went by. Miranda did her best to keep her distance.

But, overall, that mission was doomed to fail.

Because, see, I knew something about her she refused to admit—that she *wanted* to be around me. She could hide it from the outside world and keep up the charade with herself. But she couldn't lie to her husband. I saw her. She lit up when I walked into a room. She was eager to share. She watched me when she thought I didn't notice.

I never stopped noticing. Not for a second.

She was too easy to engage. Too easy to make smile. Too easy to hook into conversation. Too easy to fluster when I pressed in close.

When I teased her about it, she dug her grave with excessive vehement protesting.

We couldn't help it. Falling into a rhythm together was as

natural as the sun and moon rising and falling. We'd always talked like two old souls. Our first date was five hours long for crying out loud. We were polar ends of a magnet. Pulled together despite feeble attempts at dumb boundaries.

Miranda tried to keep up walls, but convincing her was a piece of cake. I didn't have to twist her arm to get her to sit with me. When I offered we watch something, she'd put up a distant front for about thirty seconds then "reluctantly" agree. She'd go to the kitchen for popcorn then settle back on the couch a little closer than she was before.

Which is why when I told her I asked the Moores to babysit Kacey so I could take her out for the evening on her birthday, she responded with the whole *Jack, that's a terrible idea* bull crap. But then agreed less than half an hour later.

Our two months were up in two days. I'd be lying if I said I wasn't nervous. This was my last ditch effort to convince her to stay. Unfortunately, convincing her to go out for her birthday and convincing her to stay married to me forever were whole different ball games. A small voice in my gut said this gesture was too much, but I followed my plan anyway. Needed to go big or go home.

I pushed the thoughts away and turned my sights on my woman, who sat in the passenger's seat looking pissed because I forced her to put on a blindfold about five minutes ago.

For now, she was my focus. I'd worry about our longevity later. If all this ended in flames, I wanted to soak in every second. Memorize each moment so I could torture myself until my dying breath with memories of the woman who stole my heart.

Miranda had her arms crossed, her lips pressing together in frustration. I'd nearly run off the road a few times. Calling her a distraction would be downplaying reality. She'd gotten dressed up. Her pale yellow maxi dress had tiny crisscrossing straps in the back. Bare shoulders showed off the tan from her hours outside with a tank top. Her hair had one loose braid wrapped around the back of her head. The rest of it hung over one shoulder.

"Why won't you just tell me where we are going?"

"Because I'm afraid you might jump out of the moving truck if you figure it out."

Her mouth dropped open in surprise. "Jack!" she whined. "Please tell me we aren't doing something like a couple's massage."

I laughed. "No, obviously not." I hummed. "Wish I would've thought of that."

She smirked in irritation again. Soft country tunes played on the truck radio. I wasn't a huge fan of country, but Miranda was a Nashville girl and lived for it.

We finally hit a gravel drive and she corrected her posture. "Where the heck?"

"Chill."

Two minutes later, I put the truck in park. "You have to keep that thing on. I'm not ready."

I slammed the door before she could answer and grabbed the stuff I needed out of the truck bed. Last time, I was more prepared and did this ahead of time.

Went as fast as my feet could take me. Pulled plastic wrap off the tray, set out a few blankets, strung some twinkle lights over the canopy, and set out our wine glasses. The whole scene was less perfect than the first time I brought her out here, but it would have to do.

I went back to the truck. As soon as I opened the door, her protests filled the night.

"Did you cheat?" I demanded.

"No, but I'm about to." She lifted her hands to the blindfold and I swatted them down.

I chuckled and leaned in to unbuckle her. Then, without waiting for permission, I scooped her up into my arms. Shut the truck door with my foot.

She squirmed for a few moments, whining again, but quickly settled against me as I walked, her hand stilling against my chest. I looked down at her.

She was biting that bottom lip again.

At the top of the dock, I set her down and moved to untie her blindfold. She took in the sight and immediately turned back to me. Her voice was a gentle chide. "Jack, this is..."

She let her words trail off.

It was a recreation of the night I proposed to her. The night she told me she was expecting the first time. I knew it was a lot. The setting sun made the spot romantic. And the whole set up was a nod to our beginnings.

This could be a new beginning. But I didn't verbalize that.

I pushed her down the dock as it swayed under our feet. "Come on. Don't make it weird."

"This is beautiful."

"Yeah, nice spot. I'm still buddies with the guy who owns the property."

"That's cool."

I made the dock as cozy as I could. A few blankets, two throw pillows, one charcuterie tray in the middle. She eased herself down onto the blanket. Any discomfort she felt would fade in a matter of minutes. We would do what we always did—have an incredible time together.

"Oh! Is this what we're having for dinner?" Her voice was shrill with excitement.

"Yep."

"That looks so good!"

She settled onto the blanket next to the board. I sat on the opposite side.

She looked up at me and our gazes tangled, a beat of awkwardness setting in. Last time we were here, we'd made out in the lake and took things all the way in my truck bed after. Hopefully, that memory wouldn't cause her to clam up.

"I know this is too much. But I just wanted to spend a quiet evening with you."

"It's sweet, Jack. Thank you."

And just like that, the awkwardness faded. Thirty seconds later we were digging into the charcuterie board, discussing the meat and cheeses. I'd hand-picked and flavor paired everything myself. Down to the pinot noir we were drinking.

Every few seconds, Miranda would try another flavor combo and hum in satisfaction. I couldn't stop smiling. I knew she would love it.

"What is that again?" She pointed to a cheese.

"Gruyere."

"And this?"

"Fig jam."

We enjoyed the food in silence for a while. She was so engrossed in dinner and the sunset and the lake around us that I was watching her completely undetected.

She looked at me and the quiet space between us was full. Pushing and pulling. Longing and resistance mounding together. Her eyes dropped to my lips.

I winked to break the moment and looked away.

If I didn't look away, I'd smother her before she could even object. And as much as I wanted to crush her against the dock, I wouldn't make the first move. She'd have to give.

Another moment of silence passed and we listened to the

tiny waves lapping the shore behind us. The dock dipped with the gentle tide. The pink and orange of the sunset had completely melted into purple hues, darkness covering us, minus the twinkle lights and the lit windows from houses across the lake.

I slid the charcuterie board out from between us as Miranda finished and stretched out, looking into the sky. Stars were appearing in the edges of the sky—the furthest from the disappearing sunlight.

I refilled both of our wine glasses.

Images of us together the last time we were here played in my brain. The way she'd pulled off her dress and jumped into the water…I cleared my throat, knowing I needed to talk. Needed a distraction. When I spoke, my voice was low. Scraping my vocal chords. "Tell me something."

"This again?" She laughed as she turned toward me, propping on an elbow.

"Yep. Anything you want."

"I don't know what else to tell you about me."

"How about your summers with Tag? Tell me about those."

She sipped her wine to stall. "I love Tag."

"I know."

"Feel like he was the only person who cared if I was happy when I was little."

She started talking. Telling me about how they'd ride horses, muck stalls, climb trees, and swim in the disgusting pond. She told me how they'd gotten into trouble a hundred times and about her Granny who was kind and loving even though she could hardly control them.

She didn't stop talking for a long while. When she finally did, her wine was gone and she was laying on her back, looking at the stars in their full glory.

"Why did you spend summers in Texas and not with your mom?"

"Because mom and Trent didn't like changing their schedules all summer for me."

"Why?"

"Well, Mom did whatever the man she was currently with told her to do. And Trent didn't like me. Didn't like the inconvenience of a child." She shook her head. "I was upset about Dad leaving and acted out a lot. I think they thought life was easier without me. Then it kind of became a routine. I'd come home from the last day of school in May, pack my bags and get in the car. Wouldn't see them again until August and barely even talked to them throughout the weeks I was gone."

"And your mom was okay with that?"

"She cared a lot more about the men in her life than she did about me. Dad, a couple boyfriends, Trent."

"Have you talked to her?"

"No. Not really. Haven't seen her since Kacey was a baby. We text every once in a while, but it's how it's always been. Strained. Awkward. She's unconcerned with my life and my struggles. Only cares about her own."

"I'm sorry."

I made lots of mental notes. I'd heard most of this before, but a lot felt like new info. Or maybe I was just listening in a new way. "Have you told me this before?"

"Maybe. Not sure."

"Did you feel like they dropped you off because you were difficult?"

"For sure. I hated Trent, was angry at my dad for jetting. Thought my mom was a doormat. I was moody and impossible." She shrugged. "I don't know. It kind of felt like she just pawned me of on Granny instead of helping me."

She didn't have a place. A belonging growing up. She was

stuck between so many different people and realities. That knowledge hit me for the first time ever.

Is that why she was so obsessed with togetherness? With making a home and having a family? Not sure how I'd never put two and two together.

She looked up at me and I realized how close we were. Throughout the conversation, someone had subconsciously closed the distance. Probably me. She was lying on her back and I was propped up on an elbow, looking over her.

"I hate that you didn't have anyone for so long."

She rolled to her side, propping up on her elbow. "It all worked out. I'm okay."

"Are you?"

She shrugged. "I think so."

"I'm glad you didn't stay in Texas. That you're here—with me."

I let my eyes trail downward. I couldn't help it. The way she was propped up drew my eyes to the twists and turns of her curves. I knew every slope and angle of her body. Something my brain wouldn't ever let me forget. The strap on her dress was falling to the side.

I swallowed hard, willing myself to look back at her face.

When I did, she was looking at me the same way. Eyes trailing downward, a firm swallow, then back to my face.

My heart pumped hard, felt my skin heating.

What I was feeling, what I wanted, was not one sided.

Her gaze settled on my lips again. And mine to hers.

She wanted to kiss me. And the knowledge kept me on the edge of our precipice. Silently begging her to push us over the brink. I wouldn't do it even though every cell in my body was begging me to.

She needed to want us enough to take the risk.

And I'd chase every crumb she threw me.

I whispered, "You want to kiss me."

She said nothing. Wet her lips.

"Do you?"

"Yes." She said softly.

The energy in my body built to a low buzz in my gut, made my breathing go weird.

"But that doesn't change anything." She tried to look at my face, but her gaze kept rebelling, dropping to my mouth repeatedly. "I—I won't toy with you, Jack."

I scooted a couple inches closer, our knees touching. I slipped my fingers into her hair, needy for some kind of contact. "Toy with me. I can handle it."

"Jack."

"Let's indulge our fantasies. Just for a minute."

"What—what do you know about my fantasies?" Miranda wasn't breathing right either. Her breath bathed my face in uneven puffs.

A tiny smile pulled at my cheeks. "A lot more than you might think."

She said nothing, an invisible force moving her face a few millimeters closer to mine.

My voice was a painful rasp. "You want to remember what my weight feels like. What I taste like. How I make you lose yourself."

Hers was barely audible. "Jack."

"Is that close?"

She knew she was stripped bare. Knew she couldn't lie. Knew she'd look dumb trying. So she nodded. Slow and resolute.

"Do it then. Just a kiss. You have my word."

Her tiny hand slid up my torso, feeling the ridges of my body beneath the fabric. The motion lit me on fire. My eyes fluttered closed and I shuddered at her firm touch. Her fingers made a path, slipping up and around the back of my neck.

She closed the last few inches, her hot mouth meshing with mine in a frantic lurch.

And I was lost.

FIFTY-ONE

Miranda

The façade I worked so hard to uphold shattered in a single moment. In a lapse of weakness, I was in Jack's arms. Kissing like he might evaporate before I could experience him.

Our bodies fused, my hands wildly memorized, and my mouth clung to his with a desperation I couldn't remember suffering before.

I could no longer say "I don't want this." It was feeble before. But now, the claim would be the brunt of all Jack's jokes.

Because here I was, leading the charge.

I simply could not stop myself.

When he had the audacity to beg me.

Beg me.

As if I needed begging.

He'd invited me to live my fantasies—just for a minute. If

only I could do everything I wanted in sixty short seconds. We were making good time, but not *that* good.

How could I say no?

Toy with me.

This was a no strings-attached kiss. A simple memory I'd deposit in a bank already overflowing with them. A treasure among many I'd pretend was fool's gold. Not worth anything but the thrill.

I had my hands in his hair, forcing him deeper into my kiss. He groaned and hauled me up against him, his hands tracing my back. They ran the length of it, down my thighs and up to the bare skin at my shoulders.

I was fully open for him and he for me. I threw my leg around his waist. His lips tugged on mine, firm and demanding. With every passing second, we each made demands. Demands for more time. More skin. More heart.

And more us.

Jack kissed me with a fervency and level of desperation I'd never felt with him. His body quaked under my moving hands. I was destroying him and for some reason the knowledge fueled me.

This was not just a kiss.

And we'd long surpassed a minute.

The realization should've caused me to slow, to backpedal. But he asked for this. And I wanted this moment. I lifted his shirt and he arched his back, allowing me to pull it over his head. I tossed it to the side, giving my fingers the freedom to feel him again.

I wasn't sure where I snapped and how I lost the handle on my control. But I would be forever unsated. Always empty without him.

How had I let "just a kiss" escalate to this? How could I be afraid to give myself to someone I craved? It was instinct to give my body—but my heart?

Richard's words from a few days before rolled around in my memory, bursting into our moment, uninvited.

You're afraid to put your heart on the line while you work together.

I tried to silence my stupid thoughts. But they raged, clanging between my ears. I wanted to put my heart on the line. I did *so* much. Could I? What if we broke again? Would I survive? I didn't know.

I backed off, a painful moan escaping as our lips separated. "Jack." My voice was heavy with desire. I forced my eyes open. "We can't—"

I pushed away from him, taking a deep shaky breath. His hands encircled my waist. Starving eyes and flushed cheeks gave him such a vulnerable look. His hard bare chest heaved under my palms.

I took another deep breath, gathering my wits. Then I scolded him. "You—you said just—a kiss."

He stared at me for a long moment, a frown and a smile at war on his face. He spoke as a laugh peppered his words. "You're blaming *me*?"

"Yes!"

Jack laughed, his fingers gently squeezing my sides. That sexy laugh probably traveled across the lake. He ran a hand over his face trying to gain some composure. "Miranda, I'm—" He stopped, laughed again and muttered a cuss word. "I'm not the one on top right now."

Embarrassment sank into my chest like an arrow and my cheeks flamed with red. I was plastered all over the front of him, while his back was on the dock. And I was blaming *him* for taking things too far!

"Shut up!" I shrieked, as I drove the heel of my hand into his pec, simultaneously attempting to scramble off.

But Jack was fast. He caught my wrist and pulled me down as one of his strong legs curled around one of mine. In one fluid movement, he turned, bringing my back to the dock. Now, he was over me.

He smothered his laugh with another kiss. One that started, deepened, and ended in a single motion. He pulled back, a stupid smile stuck on his face. "I'll happily give you something to blame me for if you want."

I squirmed, trying to get free of his gaze. But Jack's leg was still wrapped around mine like a vise and he had my wrist pinned out to the side. I needed to move because my whole body was screaming at me to kiss him again.

I stilled, my attention pulled into his blue gaze like a magnet. He braced himself with his forearm alongside my shoulder.

His smile was so cocky, far too pleased. His laugh had diminished to a low, throaty chuckle. "I knew you wanted to kiss me."

"It was a pity kiss!"

Jack didn't even respond. He died laughing, his head hanging low next to mine. I felt myself laughing too. Did I purposefully make a joke? Didn't know what the heck was going on with my emotions.

He laughed through his words. "If *that* was a pity kiss, I'd pay some big bucks to have a real one, Miranda Barkley."

Every cell in my body ached to pull him closer, to make him transfer his weight into mine. I didn't trust my appendages. They might move without permission. So, I laid stock still, trying to resist.

His warm breath bathed my throat. "Miranda. I am crazy about you." He spoke between gentle kisses to my neck. "You *own* me." His kisses traveled to the spot beneath my ear. He paused then whispered so low the hum of his voice tickled. "I wish you could see how much I love you."

My spirit shattered into a million pieces. Jack had laid his heart on the line for me over and over again. And still worried I didn't see it. I hated the fears that had slowly resurrected walls around my heart throughout the years. Hated the way I'd handled my hurts. Why couldn't I be more like Jack—blunt and honest? Willing to follow a hunch and take a risk despite the odds?

I was too tired to keep fighting. Maintaining a wall of protection was so freaking exhausting—especially when Jack worked to tear it down every chance he got. I swallowed hard, needing to tell this poor man I saw his love and all his sacrifices, but that I just didn't know what to do with them. The words pushed through the emotion clogging up my throat. "I see, Jack. I know you love me."

"Kacey too. Both of you."

What would it be like to reciprocate? To put all my vulnerabilities up on full display? To give the only man I'd ever loved another chance? I loved him so deeply it pained me. But I'd done my best to ignore and hide the truth. Because if I put it out there—what then?

He brought his mouth to mine once more, prodding me open so he could fully kiss me. He didn't have to ask me to kiss him back. Because he—his arms, his voice, his heart—was home. He always had been. I fell limp under his touch, my arms and legs paralyzed. Useful for nothing else but to remind me he wasn't a dream. To remind me the warm dock still pressed into my back.

Even as my brain dredged up the million same old reasons I should hold my ground, my spirit gave way, crumbling under his bold tenderness. Every woman has her breaking point, and here—with Jack pressing me down, kissing me, confessing his love—was mine.

My numb fingers woke up, finding purchase on his chest. I pushed him gently as the truth escaped, barely audible, against his lips. "I love you too."

He stilled, pulling his head back to search my eyes. His brows knit, surprised by my admission. A moment of silence passed as we stared straight into each other. The moment full, tense. No more hiding behind empty words. Jack's throat bobbed as he finally released my other wrist. His voice was serious and intense. "Then why do you still want to leave?"

My voice shook. "Because I'm afraid."

"We have the chance to take our marriage back. Make it be what we always wanted."

"What if we break all over again? I won't be able to handle it, Jack."

"But if we don't—we'll be together for our *son*. We can have everything." Jack shifted his weight onto one arm so he could bring a hand up. He pushed his fingers into my hair, squeezed, and dropped his lips to my forehead. I tried to ignore the goosebumps racing down my arms. "If we get divorced again, you're going to eventually realize it was the biggest mistake of your life."

I wanted to be brave enough.

"Listen, I am willing to do *whatever* I have to do to be good enough for you." He pressed a chaste kiss to my lips. "I'll be who you need this time."

"Jack—"

"What can I do? I have to convince you to stay."

"Trust me, Jack, it's not that I don't want to. I'm—I'm confused." I ran my fingers through my hair, letting my arm flop down to the dock in frustration. "I don't want to agree to something because I feel pressured. I just need some space, I guess. Space to figure out what I want."

"But you—you do love me?" The hope filled lines in his brow made me want to burst into tears.

"I haven't ever really stopped. I've been heartsick over you for four years." My hands slipped up his arms and to his broad shoulders. "But I don't know if I'll be ready to take the chance again. You might get sick of waiting on me to make up my mind."

His leg uncurled from mine, his chest collapsing with a sigh. "I'll wait as long as it takes, Miranda. As *long* as it takes." The intensity of his promise made me shiver. He did a full push-up. "And give you whatever you need." Space—the thing I asked for—rushed between us, feeling cold and empty, defying the warmth of a June night.

FIFTY-TWO

Miranda

"Richard!" I called out as I stepped into his back yard during Kacey's naptime.

"Well, hello there, young lady."

"I need to talk." I swiped my eye with the back of my hand.

He frowned in concern as I plopped in the opposite patio chair. "What's wrong, child?"

He seemed tired. I hoped I wasn't bothering him, but at the moment, I didn't honestly care if I was. I needed someone.

"I was trying"—I sniffed—"to look up apartments for Kacey and I. Money should come within a week or so. I could leave. I could, but..." I allowed my words to trail off as I groped for an explanation that would do justice to how I felt.

Richard filled in, nodding slowly. "But you don't want to."

I covered my face with my hands. "I don't know *what* I want. I don't know *why* I'm so afraid."

He adjusted, sitting back and offering his full attention.

I took a deep breath, reining in my racing thoughts. I'd

been up all night reliving the conversation Jack and I had on the dock and replaying our steamy kiss like an addicting song on repeat.

"It sounds weird to say this, but Jack has always felt like—like home. Do you know what I'm talking about?"

"Sure do." He gave a soft chuckle.

"I'm sure Rose felt like that."

"That she did."

"I want to fight for that feeling, but I am"—my lips trembled and I ran a hand over them—"so scared to get my heart broken again. I was…in a really bad place for a long time after I lost Jack. I don't know if I can do it again."

Richard grunted and shook his head with a small laugh.

"What was that for?"

"You're talking about a broken heart like you can avoid it."

"Can't I?"

"No, I don't reckon you can. Seems like you're pretty tangled. Will moving out and signing divorce papers really make you feel better?"

It should've been a simple question. But I stared blankly at Richard as a humming bird flew past our heads. I watched as the little guy hovered over the red feeder a few feet away. "I—I think it's safer that way."

"I don't. Tearing you two apart's gonna hurt no matter which way you slice it. A pick your poison situation."

My voice froze. Pick my poison?

"You staked it all at the very beginning. You're no fool though. You knew what you were doing."

"I don't understand."

He shot me a droll look. "You're afraid you'll break your heart, Jack's heart, and your son's heart if you try again and fail. But that's happening already."

My mouth opened, but I couldn't say anything.

"Look at you. You're all tore up. You're in love with him and trying to prevent the inevitable."

A choking sound came from me as I wrestled my emotions down. "I do love him. But love isn't enough to save a marriage."

A few deep creases in his forehead appeared as he frowned, taken aback. "It isn't?"

"No, Jack and I have always loved each other. But, at the end of the day, it's not enough. We need something we don't have. Something we weren't able to give each other."

He shook his head, resolute in his conclusion. "No ma'am. That's where you're wrong."

"I don't understand."

He pointed to my garden. "Look out there."

I fought the eye roll, knowing a parable was coming.

"Those plants are at the brink of harvesting time, ain't they?"

I nodded.

"It'd be a real shame if you plucked 'em out."

I hesitated. "Yes. It would."

"They've survived the most vulnerable, tender phases and lived to tell the tale. The harvest is gonna be just fine. It'd be downright silly if you pulled them up today and threw them in the weed pile because you thought they were useless. They're alive and well. What they need is maturity."

"Richard, just tell me what you mean."

He rolled his eyes. "Your love is immature, Miranda."

Part of me took offense at that, feeling like a middle schooler being lectured about relationships. But the other part screamed at me to listen. Told me he was likely right and if I had a lick of sense, I'd pay attention.

He continued, "Some folks think you either got love, or you don't. Rose and I found it ain't that simple. Love grows. Love strengthens like a muscle. You give some then give more over time. It ain't just a feeling. It's a skill."

"A skill?" I had never heard it called that before.

"Love is something you practice, child. Something you break your back working for. Leaving will break you. But so will loving. It will hurt you to love patiently. To forgive over and over. To sacrifice."

A slow smile spread over his face. "But it'd be a crying shame to miss out on the harvest. Once Rose and I figured out love was something we gave each other and not a feeling we had, we became a unit that loved deeply. Not just ourselves, but many." His eyes misted. "Our harvest was so big, we had plenty to share. My Rose was especially skilled at giving love away. Right deft at it."

The mental image of a pantry stocked from floor to ceiling with old fashioned Ball jars filled my mind. An abundant harvest. Something real enough, big enough, that many felt its power.

The special things are meant to be given away.

He stood, wobbling for a moment before slowly making his way into the house, using the wall to support his journey inside. "Stay put."

I silently hoped he wouldn't bring out another hat. When he returned, he handed me a simple, laminated card.

It was handwritten in beautiful cursive. Flowers and greenery laced the edges. I scanned the words, recognizing the pattern as wedding vows. But they were unique, had a real voice behind them. "Did Rose write these?"

"She did."

"These are beautiful. She wrote her own vows?"

"Yes."

"She hardly knew you, Richard, right?"

"Didn't matter. She knew this was what she wanted to say to her future husband."

"Wow."

"She didn't just say them once. She made that card, said them over and over. When we had a fight, she'd stick them in my lunch bag before I went to work. Fixed us right up every time."

I puffed a breath. "She sounds unreal."

"She felt too good to be true more times than not."

I tapped it against my knuckles, looking away and into our gardens. "Her love was mature, huh?"

"Yes ma'am. It surely was."

I sighed, a smidge of hopelessness setting in. "I'm not sure I have this in me."

"You're stronger than you think."

I shifted in my seat, crossing my legs under the table. Something new stirred within me. Something warm and fresh. Maybe hope. I asked slowly, unsteady. "I want to try. Where would I even start?"

"Forgiveness. True love doesn't keep records."

I nodded. "He's never asked me to forgive him."

"Well, the way I see it, you can sit around, watch your life and opportunities pass you by, waiting for the man you love to say a few magic words...or you can just forgive him. You don't need to be invited. Forgiveness happens in the heart whether someone even realizes they need to be forgiven."

"Does forgiveness mean I have to forget everything that happened between us?"

"Not at all. Just means you stop punishing him for it. Stop letting your heart hold on." He tapped his chest as he squinted at me. "I know I'm an old man and my vision is not too good anymore, but from everything I can see, your heart really needs to let go."

I instantly recognized it as the truth.

I admitted, "My heart wants him to beg me for forgiveness. Does that make me a horrible human?"

"Not a horrible human. Just human." He shook his head. "You just need some rewiring. If you want relationships in your life to thrive, you got to operate for *their good*, not your own."

"That's exactly the opposite of everything people say."

"Yep. And it's the reason sixty-plus year marriages will die with my generation. Forgiveness, love, commitment—they're all sacrifices. Painful ones sometimes. Folks don't like pain."

I let my eyes wander into Richard's garden. How true that was. I did not like pain. And I have been through so much. That was the hang-up for me. Fear of more pain. But Richard was definitely right. Leaving now, walking away from Jack right now, would hurt too. My eyes teared up at the very thought.

I asked, "How will I know if I've truly forgiven Jack? I want to."

"It's a good question." He clicked his tongue a couple times, thinking. "I reckon you'll know when you're more concerned about whether you're loving him rightly than whether he's loving you rightly. You'll know when you stop wishing he'd make it up to you."

That struck a chord in me. Had I unintentionally punished Jack for not being what I needed? Is that why I didn't tell him about the babies? I mean, yes, it was because it was painful. But I also felt like he didn't deserve to know. A sob pressed into my throat and I swallowed it down with a muted squeak. "I need his—his forgiveness too."

"Then lead."

"Lead?"

"In forgiveness. It starts with one. If you have wrongs to right, make them right."

A moment of silence fell over us as I pondered his challenge. "I wish I was like Rose."

"She was a woman to model. You can be. Growth happens one day at a time. Put the work in and you'll be just like her."

"I'm so selfish, Richard."

"Well, news flash. You ain't going to stop being selfish. Just got to learn to recognize it and nip it straight in the bud." He crossed his arms across his chest with a faraway look in his eyes.

"Does marriage—loving someone—ever get easier?"

He thought for a moment, pursing his lips. "I would say there are easier seasons, but overall, no. Take it from someone who was married a long time. Love ain't romance. It's grit."

Grit.

So courage and character. Two ways I fell short.

"That sounds so hard."

"Maybe. But it's a lot more rewarding than chasing butterflies."

Jack's words reverberated in my memory.

"I'm not wearing a ring because I have butterflies."

Jack was in it for real. In it to cultivate us. He didn't have all the tools and all the answers, but he was trying. He'd come to the conclusion that our little family was worth the backbreaking.

But it takes two.

And right now, I was the one lagging behind. The one on the fence. The one who doubted the risk would be worth it.

Jack understood something I was just now coming to terms with. A few weeks ago, he'd said, "*I don't love you enough.*" He understood it was a muscle. That love would start imperfect and strengthen over time. Even Richard and Rose had to grow.

Everything in my heart and mind was falling into place. Like Richard had tipped the line of dominos. The *one* thing I had always wanted since I was a child—a place to belong and be loved and accepted through the worst days—was something I wasn't willing to provide for Jack. I only wanted it for myself. I left our marriage when it was difficult.

Maybe I was more like Jack and my mother than I knew.

We all had the same problem. No one wanted to do the hard things. No one stayed through the fire.

I had so much to think through. So much to rework in my heart. We sat in silence again as I sniffled.

What if trying again changed everything? What if we could be the family I always wanted? I'd have to risk my heart, but...I wanted to.

I wanted to love my husband that way.

My husband.

A realization hit me like a waterfall. Jack was my husband already. I had his heart and he had mine. Whether we liked it or not, there were no take-backs. I didn't walk away intact the first time. I certainly wouldn't now. Leaving would gut me. Timeline didn't really matter.

Might as well try.

I sucked in a deep breath. I forced my voice above the whisper in my throat so Richard could hear me. Blinked back tears. "I need to tell Jack I forgive him and want to stay."

Richard smiled. "It's not hard."

"Words seem weak though."

"Show him then."

An idea hit me. Something I could *do* for Jack. A picture painted in my mind's eye. A scene. A quiet moment between the two of us. I needed to work out the details, but the idea definitely had potential.

What would Jack say? Would he be happy?

I gave my head a hard shake. Of *course* Jack was going to be happy. I'd lost count of the times he'd announced how he felt. How real it was for him. I wanted to prove I was in this, too. For better and worse.

Until harvest, whenever our harvest might be.

I said, "I think I know what I could do for him, but it might take a few days to get it, and my heart, ready."

I told Richard my idea. Said it sounded silly, like it wasn't big enough.

But he said, "Love is quiet, enduring. Something simple and poignant will do just fine."

"I need to go. Kacey will wake up soon."

Quiet, enduring, simple, poignant.

All things I wanted for us. I stood and moved to his side of the table. I leaned down to kiss his forehead. "Thank you. You have no idea what your friendship has done for me, Richard."

"Well, I love you, Miranda. You're a special young lady."

A sharp intake of breath filled my lungs, and I wrapped my arms around him. My voice was taut with emotions rolling through my heart. "I—I love you too, Richard."

FIFTY-THREE

Jack

My day was long, hard. Heavy stuff on the job. Heavy stuff at home. Had to deliver a death notification to a middle-aged woman. Took a rookie with me. Combo made my suck day ten times worse.

The kisses with Miranda last night should've left me soaring. But I was in a post-high crash. She'd said in no uncertain terms that I needed to give her some space.

What if she decided she didn't want this?

Would I ever be able to kiss her again?

The questions haunted me all day. Made me miscall a few reports on the speaker.

I wanted to believe we had a chance. But I'd pushed hard. Too hard. Maybe she was done with me long ago and had just endured the time together and tried not to break my heart while we were forced to live under the same roof. I'd made a giant jerk out of myself by pushing for what I wanted, instead of listening to what she wanted.

She'd tried to tell me a few times to lay off.

But I ignored her and maybe destroyed my last chance.

I planned to go home, shower, and crawl into bed. I didn't want to see Miranda and be fake. Pretend like I was okay, when everything inside was screaming I wasn't. These were the feelings I'd conditioned myself to run from. As much as I wanted to just disconnect, exercise for four hours, or stay at work, I at least had to go home.

Somehow, I'd have to balance being there and being honest. I'd keep my word and not pressure her. She deserved better than to be pushed around.

Miranda must've been tucking Kacey in when I got home because the house was quiet. I slipped into my room, showered, and pulled on my sweats and a hoodie. I was a little hungry, but hunger felt like a poor reason to risk seeing Miranda before I got my nerve up.

If she wanted to leave, we needed to interact as little as possible. I doubted I could be around her without crumbling into a beggar. The thought of my house going back to the way it was...

That *was* a feeling I'd keep running from.

I kept the lamp on and settled onto my pillows, staring straight up, watching the fan spin. Took about fifteen seconds watching the thing go round and round for me to zone out and remember Miranda in my arms. Remember how she felt, tasted. How hungry she was for me.

A soft knock on my bedroom door caused me to jolt out of my daydream.

"Jack?"

"Yeah. Come in." I pushed into sitting and leaned back against the headboard.

She stuck her head in. "You sick?"

"No."

She stuck a plate of food through the small opening. "You didn't come get a plate."

"You can come in. I don't bite."

She stepped in sheepishly. "I know. I didn't know if you wanted to be alone."

I shrugged. I did, but she was irresistible. She had her cozy clothes on. Gray leggings that made her legs look incredible. The Schrute Farms hoodie. Sloppy bun.

I found myself smiling and patting the bed next to me.

Surprisingly, she climbed up. My bed was huge. King sized almost due to necessity. But she came up, left about six inches between us, and handed me the plate.

"Oh, man. This looks delicious." Caeser salad and grilled chicken.

She studied me. I didn't have to look to confirm. I felt her eyes all over me.

She spoke, quiet and slow. "Something bad happened, didn't it?"

"How'd you know?"

"Your face."

"Good guess." I shrugged. "I try to leave it in the truck."

"You don't have to leave your bad feelings in the truck. You should talk to someone about work stuff."

"I do, actually. I've been seeing a therapist."

Her brown eyes went wide. "For real?"

"Yep."

"And you guys talk about work stuff?"

"A lot of stuff."

"I'm"—she faltered—"really impressed, Jack. How long has that been going on?"

"Three weeks or so. I've seen him twice."

"Every other week?"

"Yeah, that's the goal."

"Well, if you need someone to talk to on the in-between times, I'm here." She pulled her legs up, crisscrossing them on the bed. Those big eyes were as sincere as ever. I wondered how long she'd be "here" to talk to.

"Thanks." I situated the plate on my lap and stabbed at some lettuce. This was what I was bad at. Talking. Being honest when it was ugly. I took a deep breath, trying to gear up. "We had to basically scrape a body off the road today. Then I had to do a death notification with Porter, one of the rookies. The wife was...hysterical." I lifted a shoulder. "Most calls—even the crazy ones—feel pretty routine, but stuff like that kind of sticks with you for a while."

"Of course it does." Her hand came to my forearm and gave it a gentle squeeze. "Thanks for telling me."

Silence settled. Her sitting beside me on the bed felt strange. She shifted uncomfortably before shifting to face me. "I've been wanting to show you something. I've been putting it off because it kind of brings up a lot for me—but I've been wrong, really wrong, not to share it with you before. It's a wrong I need to make right."

I swallowed my bite and leaned to place my dinner on the nightstand. "Sure."

She left and returned a few moments later with a scrapbook I recognized. She crawled up and placed the book in my lap then turned to go.

"Where you going?"

"I thought I'd let you look at it alone."

"Stay."

She shook her head. "That's okay."

"What's in here?"

"Stuff I can't look at without getting pretty emotional." She crossed her arms over her chest and gave a kind of silly smile, trying to hide tears that were already pressing in. She backed toward the door, accidentally hitting the door frame with her behind.

"Miranda."

She stopped.

"Please stay."

She opened her mouth to respond.

"I am trying my best to get better at being okay with tears. Let me practice?"

She swallowed and took a slow step back toward the bed. I beckoned her with my hand and she climbed up on top of the covers. Slow, wide-eyed. She looked at the book then back at me. Like she was trying to decide if she should protect it. Like I might toss her treasure against the wall or something.

"Together?" I leaned, gently bumping her shoulder.

She nodded. Her chest rose and fell. She was fighting a panic response. And so was I—for totally different reasons.

"Is this book about the babies?"

"Yes." Her answer was quiet, already swelling with emotion. "I made this because...I didn't want to forget them."

Forget.

That single word mowed me down. For a moment, I groped for my next move as my mind whirred. The word sent me into a momentary tailspin and I couldn't put my finger on why.

I gave my head a hard shake and channeled my attention to the scrapbook. It was large, plain black, with white paper pages slipped into protectors. I flipped it open and Miranda sniffled beside me.

The first page was simple. There was a date, a red flower, a green gemstone, and a *name*. It felt like someone placed a cement block on my shoulders. Why did I not know she named them?

August Joy.

I ran my finger beneath the calligraphy.

"Was this what you named our first baby?"

She gave a tiny nod.

"That's—really beautiful." I touched the flower and gem. "Are these birth flower and birthstone?"

"Yes, a gladiolus and peridot."

I flipped the page. An ultrasound picture. I couldn't really make much out on it, but I was certain she could.

A burning desire in my chest to flip through these pages as fast as possible nagged me. I could look but not really. Just get it done to appease her. But her gentle sniffling beside me tapped my brakes. Made me remember why I was in freaking therapy.

She needed me to do this. Really do this.

And I probably needed it too. I forced myself to slow down, to look at every piece. To ask questions. Even if I didn't want answers. Even if I wanted to pretend I'd never let my wife lose these tiny humans alone.

A warmth pricked behind my eyes and I pushed it back.

Sucked in a deep breath.

I touched the black and white photo. "Can you—show me what you see here?"

She pointed out the date of the ultrasound and the gestational weeks. "This right here"—she moved her finger about an inch and half, tracing a white spot—"is the baby. Still really small at that size, but you can make out the head."

"I see."

"You were there for this ultrasound."

"I remember." I touched a sticker on the edge of the page. "What is this piece of fruit here for?"

"Oh, that shows how big a fetus usually is at nine weeks."

"The size of a grape?"

"Yeah."

I chanced a glance at her. Her cheeks were moist, but she was smiling. The next page had fragments of her boarding pass for her homebound flight, a picture of us on our honeymoon. A *"forever my joy"* in calligraphy. It was her memorial of the loss.

She had scooted closer to me, her torso against my elbow and her shoulder against mine.

We turned the pages together, her explaining every piece.

December Peace. May Grace. January Blessing. October Mercy. March Hope. November Love.

There were blueberries, limes, plums. Even an apple and avocado. On every third page, there was a beautiful phrase in calligraphy. A personalized inscription coinciding with the name of each one.

The last one read. *"With all my love."*

There was no way I'd be able to feel these losses as personally as she had. But I *was* feeling them. Couldn't remember a time in my life I'd fought tears so hard.

Or maybe I was feeling for Miranda.

The journey through her memories was like being forced into her shoes. And it hurt. I hurt for her and hurt for our babies, more than I ever thought I could.

Felt like my heart was pumping slow, laboring under the weight. Because the worst part was…I understood.

For the first time, I understood how I'd abandoned my wife. I got why she left. I saw it. Plain as day. A few times, I'd told her I understood. But I didn't. Not like this.

I destroyed our marriage single-handedly.

When I flipped past the last ultrasound, all the birth flowers from the previous pages were arranged together like a bouquet. A bouquet of loss and pain. But when I looked at Miranda, she was still smiling. She was pressed against me, her face leaning on my shoulder. Her finger tracing the edge of the page.

"I think these are beautiful."

I nodded once.

"I don't know a lot about flowers, but I'm always able to pick these varieties out now if I see them in real life."

I swallowed. She needed me to say something, but words were inadequate. What my wife had created for our children was...sacred. Hauntingly tender.

And so very Miranda.

"Miranda"—I cleared my throat, blinked a few times—"this is...very special. It shows what an amazing mom you are."

"Turn the page."

I did, hoping I wasn't about to get another gut punch.

It was wishful thinking. A deep, involuntary breath filled my lungs at the picture of Miranda with a big, rounded belly. I wasn't able to catch many details about the picture because my vision started swimming. I pressed my lips together, *hating* this feeling.

Miranda must've seen my struggle. Because her hand slid into the crook of my arm and squeezed. "Jack, you don't have to keep looking if you don't want to."

I had to relax my jaw to answer. "I want to."

There were four pages of pictures about Miranda's pregnancy. Medical report clippings, "it's a boy" in calligraphy, hospital information, and more. Several gorgeous pictures of her littered the pages. "Who took these?"

"My friend, Charlotte, from work. She just took them with her iPhone. I know they aren't very good."

I shook my head. "They're perfect, and you are beautiful."

"Charlotte took some time off to help me after the birth too. She was a real friend."

I turned to find pictures of Kacey as a newborn all over the page. On Miranda's chest. On a weigh table. Wrapped in a striped blanket. So many.

I looked up and away from the book, leaning my head back on the headboard with a steadying breath. I hadn't cried since I was like nine. Didn't feel good about starting now.

Miranda's hand slipped up to my shoulder. "Are—are you okay, Jack?"

My swallow hurt, and I kept my eyes closed. "I don't know, honestly."

"I understand."

I tipped my head back down to finish flipping through the pictures. Now, I had a mission. Get to the end. Quickly.

But when the end came, there were about thirty photos tucked loosely between the pages.

"I stuck those in there to make some more pages with, but I haven't worked on my scrapbook in a long time."

I picked up the photos, straightening the stack. They were all of Kacey. Growing, changing, learning, achieving.

A tear leaking out onto my face felt like hell. I swiped it off, muttering a cuss word. "He's a—" I couldn't even finish. Emotions made my voice feel like a rusty wheel. Like a faucet knob that had calcified.

What would I say anyway? A beautiful child?

That didn't even begin to scratch the surface.

Another freaking tear came out and I cussed again. I handed Miranda the stack of pictures with shaking hands. Didn't want to see any more of what I'd lost.

When my hands were free, I ran them over my face, pressing the moisture into the pads of my fingers. Miranda laid her head against my shoulder.

"I'm sorry, Jack."

"You have no reason to be apologizing."

I slipped an arm around her shoulders and pulled her into

my chest. Her head bounced up as I took an almost violent inhale. I ran my hand over her head. "I'm sorry I wasn't there."

"It's not your fault."

She was absolutely wrong. All of this was my fault.

I said nothing.

"We're both here now. That's what matters."

We sat in silence for a few minutes. My tears had dried but something had settled into my heart like a death sentence.

I did this to her. To Kacey. To us.

I had abandoned her long before she left.

My presence now didn't change a damn thing.

I wanted to drive my fists through a wall as hot, raw anger pushed out the grief. I was the idiot that caused this mess.

I withdrew my arm and she sat up.

"Thank you for showing me."

She gave me a sad smile. "Thanks for looking."

Thanks for looking? She was thanking me for giving a crap, which proved just how big of a clueless asshole I'd been in the past. I *did* care about her, but had failed to demonstrate it to the point that my wife was *thanking* me for flipping through the pages of a book she'd made with pieces of her soul. Like just viewing it was some big sacrifice on my part.

Man, I'd screwed up.

I'd screwed up so big I understood why Miranda didn't want anything to do with me. Why *would* she? I had trampled the most tender parts of her. Her miscarriages weren't a body malfunction to her. But I treated them that way. Like a sucky period.

I inwardly cursed myself.

I'm a smart guy. Why hadn't I treated our babies like what they were? Treated my wife like a grieving *mother*?

"I'm, uh, pretty tired from today."

"Okay. I know it was long."

"It was."

She moved to scoot off the bed.

I wanted to say something. Wanted to enter into this pain with her. Wanted to make up for lost time somehow, someway, but I was being crushed under a thousand pounds of regret. And I didn't know what to do with it. There was no answer. No time machine. No way to make it right.

She hesitated at my door like she wanted to say something, but she didn't. The door softly shut behind her.

Reality flashed before me like a blinding light I was forced to stare into. This marriage would end just like the first had.

And it was all because of me.

Miranda would walk away from an insensitive piece of garbage, and I'd give her my blessing.

She deserved better.

Far, far better.

FIFTY-FOUR

Jack

My wet t-shirt clung to my back. I was pretty disgusting because I'd run about four miles. I hadn't meant to. But after Miranda left my room, I abandoned my salad on the nightstand and ran hard. Probably would've demolished a wall if I hadn't. Miranda watched me go out the front door. I didn't miss the flicker of fear in her eyes.

I pushed past my normal speeds. I puffed out my breath, closing in on the baseball fields and playground about five blocks up from our house.

Indecision crouched in on me. I needed to talk to someone, but it was getting late. I slowed my pace as I ran into the park's lot. Jules would listen. I unclipped my phone from my shorts and almost jammed my finger hitting pause on the dumb song playing in my headphones. I needed silence. Needed to think through the awful feeling pressing into my chest. I couldn't remember ever feeling this way. I couldn't put my finger on exactly what it was. There was regret...and something else.

Something worse. Something causing my breath to shallow and my throat to constrict.

I paced the lot, battling the thoughts in my head.

After my breathing had slowed, I sent Jules a text: *You up?*

It took about fifteen seconds for my phone to start ringing.

"Hey, sis."

"Jack, what's wrong?"

I snorted. Backing out of the impending conversation wasn't an option. That ship sailed as soon as I pressed send.

"I'm sorry to bother you. Know you're probably busy."

"No, Pat and I are just chilling on the couch right now. There's something going on for you to text me past nine o'clock."

I sighed. "Yeah—yeah, I guess so."

"You're scaring me."

"It's nothing like that. I just—did Pat tell you about the conversation we had?" If there was a way to avoid telling her the gritty details, that'd be great.

"No. He was so annoying and didn't tell me a thing."

Of course.

I sighed. Where would I even start? I dropped to sit on a park bench and propped my elbows on my knees. Jules and I had developed a much stronger relationship the past few years, but it was still hard talking. To anyone.

Words pressurized in my chest as I toyed with saying them or not. The reluctance was so strong, I squirmed in indecision. But finally words leaked out, slow and painful. "I really need someone to talk to. I'm not sure why it's so hard for me to be open. There's a lot I've never told you about Miranda and I."

"Oh, no."

"Yeah."

"Is it bad?"

"Humiliating, Jules."

"I'm here. You know you don't need a filter with me. I won't say anything until you're done."

"Okay."

"Pat's right here. Want me to move to the porch?"

"No, it's fine. I know you'll tell him anyway."

She scoffed like she didn't know what I was talking about. "I'm all ears, Jack."

Everything poured out. The babies, the extra shifts, the stupid marathon team, the flowers Miranda threw from the window, the conversations Miranda and I had, and my conclusion. I talked for forty straight minutes.

She sniffled off and on.

"What I did is unforgivable. I'm starting to think it would be better for her...if I let her go. Let her and Kacey have their own lives and I'll just be—every other weekend dad, I guess."

"Is that what you want?"

"Of course not. But at some point, I need to do what's best for her and stop pushing to get what I want."

She hummed in understanding.

"What should I do, Jules? We sign papers to receive the lake house in the morning. It won't be long before she has everything she needs to walk away."

Pat murmured in the background.

"Pat has something to say."

"Okay."

"Hey, man. Don't settle for every other weekend dad. Kacey needs you as an active part of his life."

"We've talked about co-parenting. But that requires me seeing Miranda all the time, knowing I can't be more. I—I don't think I'm strong enough to do that."

Pat said, "Life has a funny way of making you use what you know. You've learned a lot about Miranda, about yourself and how you messed up. Co-parent. Embrace the suck of that.

You'll have an opportunity day after day to prove how far you've come."

I groaned in frustration. "That's going to be so hard."

Jules tried to encourage me. "But Kacey deserves that. Regardless of how things work out between you and Miranda, your son needs his dad."

"I want to be there for him."

"Time can change things. You never know."

Two beats of silence passed before I changed direction. "Sis?"

"Yeah?"

"Do you…do you ever think about mom?"

"This is going to sound horrible, but not really. We were nine. It's been twenty-five years."

"Do you think Dad handled her death well?"

Her sigh said it all. "No, I don't."

"What do you remember?"

"Mostly the weird stuff he did. Like take her pictures down. He immediately packed all her things away. He'd get really frustrated and overwhelmed when we had a hard time. He couldn't handle his pain and ours. I think that's why he shut her memory out. It was easier for him to cope that way."

She continued, "I've talked to Dr. Hannel about this. I think the dysfunctional way Dad dealt with Mom has played a part in why I had such a hard time after Cameron died. I was not able to process my pain. Like, at all. Dad wanted us to pretend we were fine so we did. Oddly enough, pretending is still my go-to way of coping."

"That makes sense."

"Maybe that's why you struggle to be emotionally available for Miranda. It's not like we had good examples of that."

"I think I'm more like him than I realize. Any time I needed him, or cried, or had a bad day, he got distant with me. I see Dad in the way I handled Miranda."

"Oh, Jack."

"And that makes me so freaking angry at myself. *That* is what makes me feel like they're better off without me."

Pat chimed in. "No, they're better off without old Jack. Changing and being something different is a choice you can make. If you check out because it's hard, you're doing the same thing to Kacey that your dad did to you."

I cussed, letting my forehead drop into my palm. "Yeah, I see that, too."

Jules said, "Love does hard things. That used to scare me, but it doesn't anymore. You can do the hard thing for them, because you love them. If that means showing up, being present, and waiting...do it."

A beat of silence passed before Jules asked, "You keep talking about Miranda's grief. What about yours?"

"I'm okay." The sting in my eyes and taut voice betrayed me.

"It's okay to not be okay. You've lost a lot, too."

"I know." I rasped.

She was full-fledged crying. "I can hear it in your voice, Jack. You don't have to be so—so strong all the time."

I let out a breath at that. Was it true? Then why did I feel like such a failure right now?

We exchanged I love yous then I ended the call with shaking hands. I let my head fall into my palms and stared straight at the ground. A circle of white caught my attention under the bench.

A baseball.

I picked the ball up, rolled it in my hands for a second. It swam, the red stitches melting into the white, blurring in the light of the street lamps. I stood, suddenly propelled to my feet. I chucked the stupid ball as far as I could, over the fence, into the diamond.

A stabbing ripped through my shoulder. I gripped it, grunting in pain. A rusty and aged sound leaked out. The first of many. The combo of pain teleported me back to the lake's shore.

I sunk back onto the bench, holding my shoulder and allowing myself to do something I hadn't done in twenty-five years.

FIFTY-FIVE

Miranda

A soft knock at my door jerked me out of my almost-sleep. I raised my head from the pillow, wondering if my mind was playing tricks. When soft footsteps receded down the hallway, back to the stairs, I jumped up and ran to the door. Jack wouldn't have knocked unless it was really important.

I cracked the door and whispered. "Jack?"

He stopped and turned back.

"You okay?"

Soft light from downstairs filled the hallway. He was still in his running clothes. Drenched from head to toe. His eyes were...pink?

"Not—not really." His voice was hoarse.

"Did something happen?"

He shifted, his restless hands looking for a place to rest. " I just needed to say..." His words trailed off as he ran his hands over his head. "That I am sorry. I have made a total ass of myself. I have tried to force you to want this. Want us. But that scrapbook... I see now, Miranda. Truly and fully."

His chest expanded and collapsed on a deep, painful-sounding breath.

"While seven of my children passed away, I was nowhere to be found."

"Jack—"

"And because I'm an idiot, instead of realizing I ruined the best thing that's ever happened to me, I've been pressing, pushing, and acting like I still have some sort of chance here."

I swallowed, tears coming to my eyes. I didn't mean to hurt him with the scrapbook. "It's okay—"

"Don't. It's not okay." He shook his head, almost angry. "I have zero expectations for you to ever forgive me, so I'm not even gonna ask. But I just need you to know how sorry I am."

I reached out to touch his arm and he stepped back. He said, "Don't do that. I know what you do. You're going to have compassion on me because that's who you are. It's obviously not who I am... And you deserve a lot better. So, I am going to stop forcing myself on you and be the best possible dad I can be for Kacey. Because I love him. And I love you, but if you don't believe that..." His voice broke. "I—I get it."

He went on and I wished he wouldn't. My heart was breaking for him. "I—neglected the most tender part of who you are and left you the exact same way all the other people in your life did."

A sound, something reminiscent to a cry came from him, but he wrestled it down. "It took that scrapbook for me to realize I would have an eight-year-old if things hadn't happened the way they did."

He ran his hands over his head again, his sigh filling the silence once more. "I'm sorry, Miranda."

He took a quick step forward, wrapped his hand around

the back of my head, and pressed a gentle kiss, damp with tears, to my forehead.

"Jack, you—"

He shushed me and whispered against my head, "*Shhh. Stop.*"

Then he left.

FIFTY-SIX

Jack

To say he wore me out was an understatement. Kacey ran circles around me. It was my day off and he'd gotten it into his head that I needed to take him to a trampoline park he saw on a commercial. We went after his naptime and jumped until we dropped. Then I pounded down dinner at a restaurant like I was a teenager again. So did Kacey. Had to buy the kid another container of nuggets.

Miranda spent the afternoon out. Running errands, getting some work done.

Before we'd scattered for the day's activities, we had a hurried video chat with John Haskins and digitally signed trust documents. We officially owned a two-plus million dollar mansion. Felt surreal.

I had a hard time keeping my chin up that day. The previous night had done a number on my emotions. Felt pretty embarrassed. Other than our quick chat with John, I hadn't even seen Miranda to gauge how well she took my late-night display in the hallway. Even our morning coffee didn't overlap because she and Kacey had rushed out early to accompany Richard on a Lowe's trip. Which meant I spent the first half of the day fretting and trying to find something to do.

Maybe Miranda was avoiding me—wouldn't really blame her for that.

Now, as I drove home from the trampoline park, Kacey fought to stay awake in the backseat. But he needed a bath before bedtime. Really bad. On the last minute stretch of the drive, I reached into the back seat and squeezed his knee. "Come on buddy, hang on. We're almost there."

His head lolled to the side and his little mouth fell open.

"We have to get you in the bath..."

My words tapered off as I turned onto our street. Emergency vehicles lined the road in front of our house. A cop car, a firetruck, an ambulance. As I got closer, I realized. They weren't at our house. They were at Richard's.

I took the fastest shower I ever had in my life then paced the living room, my heart feeling like lead. The vehicles had cleared out, which I was glad about for Miranda's sake. I'd skipped Kacey's bath time and just stuck him onto my bed for the time being. I didn't want to wake him, because...well, tonight wouldn't be the right night for bedtime troubles. Sleeping sweaty wouldn't kill him.

The task before me loomed large, overwhelming. Doing this kind of thing on the job sucked. Usually equated to a very bad day in my book. But this time, it would be my wife. And she was through and through a lover. Miranda didn't give pieces of her heart. She gave it all. She loved hard, loved deep.

And she gave Richard her heart. In totality.

I was about to wreck her.

My stomach twisted and lurched, the chicken and fries feeling heavy. Every time I turned on my heel, I'd glance at the window, wondering when I would see her headlights flash through the drawn blinds.

But finally, they did. I took a steadying breath. I shouldn't overwhelm her as soon as she walked in. We'd talk for a few minutes then I'd tell her.

I unlocked the front door for her.

"Hey!" She hurried in and dropped her purse and Hobby Lobby bag over the back of the couch. Once her hands were free, she turned to me and reached. Her arms came around my torso.

I hugged her back, confused on why she'd pull me into her arms, but too distracted to ask questions.

She pushed back and looked up into my face. "I would've done this last night but you ran…" The words died on her lips. Her hands dropped to her sides and she took a step back, a serious expression pushing out the bubbly one. "Jack? What's wrong?"

"Something—something happened, Miranda. You might want to sit down."

She paled. "Where's Kacey?"

"Kacey's fine. He's on my bed."

I gently led her by the elbow to the front of the couch. Pulled her down next to me. I shifted to face her. She was already breathing hard and tears brimmed in her eyes.

"You're freaking me out, Jack. What happened?"

"When we got home, there were a lot of emergency vehicles in front of Richard's house." Her lips trembled and she shook her head from side to side. "He passed away a few hours ago."

"What?"

"I'm so sorry." My voice cracked.

"That—that can't be. He was fine. Just earlier today." Her voice picked up pitch. "I saw him. I wore Rose's hat and—and we were laughing. He—he was fine!"

"Miranda, they aren't sure what exactly happened, but they think he had a stroke. Probably a complication from the fall he had recently."

"Jack." My name escaped her lips with a sob. She covered her face with her hands. "Please tell me this is a bad dream."

I reached over, letting my hand rest on her knee. "I wish it was."

She stood, wobbling a hair, backing away from me. "I got to—" She sobbed once. Violently. Her voice strained around words. "Got to get Kacey in bed." She sobbed again and covered her mouth.

I stood too. On the job, we delivered death notifications in person because people need the compassion of earth-shattering news delivered face to face. We were trained to be strong, present, but unaffected. This—watching someone you love suffer—was a whole different animal. One there was no manual for.

"Miranda."

Her journey to my bedroom door deteriorated. She stopped, bent at the waist, and a cry, like a long high-pitched groan, came from her. My feet moved toward my wife before my brain decided what to do. I slipped my hand around her waist.

And she crumbled.

Onto the rug. Falling to pieces.

She sobbed, her cries muted by the floor. I gingerly rubbed her back, feeling awkward.

Before, this would be the moment I tried to force her to be okay, reassure her with empty words, plug my ears, and run.

But I couldn't leave. This time would be different. My love for her anchored me. I hauled her up and into my lap, cradling her like a baby. She clutched my shirt and turned her face into my chest. Miranda's entire body shuddered with her tears for a long time. I squeezed her close, resting my head against the top of hers. After a while, I scooted toward the back of the couch, leaning on it so I could hold her better.

"Jack," she cried. "He can't be gone."

I said nothing. Just kissed her forehead.

"I love him so much."

"I know you do."

She whimpered. I tipped my chin to look down at her. Her beautiful brown eyes were red, starting to swell. Her cheeks were splotchy pink, her lips twisted. "My heart is breaking."

So was mine. I kissed her forehead again, knowing that action did little to fix anything. But it was the only thing I knew to do. Only thing I knew how to offer. And it felt grossly inadequate. Pathetic even.

But as pathetic as my response was, I *was* responding. And I wasn't having to grit my teeth through it. I wanted to be there for her and couldn't imagine walking away.

The realization was monumental.

Last night, I'd let myself feel things I'd buried. Which made Miranda's feelings a lot easier to swallow. I closed my eyes against my own surge of emotion, taking a deep breath of her hair.

If only this hadn't come too late.

But Pat's words from the night before hit me, encouraged me to keep on: *You'll have an opportunity day after day to prove how far you've come.*

I didn't deserve for her to stay. But *I* would stay. I would be the anchor I should've always been. Be the one she could count on when everyone else walked away. Not because I wanted to manufacture the outcome, but because this precious woman in my arms deserved it.

She cried for a long time on the foyer floor. I'd only let go once to fetch her some Kleenex. Eventually, her crying slowed and all her energy went to hiccups. I brushed hair off her face. She wiped her nose with her seventh tissue. There was a little damp pile on the floor next to us. When she spoke, her voice was froggy. "I'm sorry, Jack."

I shook my head. "Why are you apologizing?"

She shrugged.

"You've got *nothing* to be sorry for."

She nodded then asked a feeble question. "Was he alone?" A renewed sob pressed in. "Please tell me he wasn't alone."

"No. Cynthia and Bob were with him."

"Thank goodness." She relaxed in my arms. She sniffed. "I'm going to be so sad without him."

"I know you will."

"He was the greatest friend I've ever had."

"I know." Why did I keep saying that? It was stupid.

She cried for a few more minutes. The tears had lost some momentum now. Her arms laid limp by her sides. "I'm so tired. I don't even know if I can move."

"Don't then. I got you."

I slipped my arm behind her knees, the other behind her back. She gasped in surprise as I lifted her off the floor. She settled her head on my shoulder as I walked to my room.

"Your room?"

I eased open the door, my voice falling to a whisper. "Kacey is in here."

She needed to go to the bathroom so I placed her on her feet in front of the sink and clicked on the light. She stood, her bun flopping to the side, face puffy. Our gazes locked through the reflection of the mirror.

Something shifted in her expression. "Are you...are you staying in your room too?"

"If you want."

She nodded once, slow, and I shut the bathroom door.

I hurried up the stairs to grab her toothbrush and pajama bottoms. Two things I knew she wouldn't want to sleep without.

When I returned and softly knocked on my bathroom door, she opened, dabbing at her eyes again with toilet paper.

"Here."

She gave a sad, grateful smile. "Thank you."

I went to the kitchen to make her a glass of ice water. When I came back, she was under the covers. Right next to Kacey. I set the water and a box of Kleenex on the side table and crawled in on the other side. Kacey was sprawled out between us.

I laid in the dark, hurting for my wife. Her soft sniffling started up again. What else could I do for her? I didn't know. I wished I did. I had fumbled this part of our life together over and over.

A bit of time passed before Miranda sat up. Ice clinked and she blew her nose. Before she settled in again, I reached over Kacey and caught her arm. She froze and whispered, "What?"

I didn't answer. I gently led her down and around Kacey. She followed my gentle tugging until she had crawled to my side of the bed. I lifted the covers and she slipped in beside me.

There was nothing graceful about it. She flopped into my arms, melting into tears all over again. This time, she stifled them so she didn't disturb Kacey. I encircled her in my arms. Her head pressed against my chest, her tears leaving a wet spot on my t-shirt.

This. This was what my wife needed from me when she had grieved our children. Images of her crying like this, curled in a ball all alone, while I was off running or watching a stupid game or doing some other dumb crap made me so angry at myself I could hardly draw a full breath.

But I rubbed her back, pressed her close. After a while, she slid her hands up and around my neck, stretching out against me. "Thank you," she whispered. "For just holding me."

Something else Pat told me hit my brain like a kick: *"She needed someone to hold her up... That's all I did. Sit with her. Let her lean on me."*

Emotions swelled in my chest. I'd had so many opportunities to hold my wife like this, but opted out. I reached up, sinking my fingers into the loose roots of her bun. "I'm here."

If there was a millimeter of distance between us, she scooted into it, sealing us together. She lifted her face to mine, pressing a warm salty kiss on my lips. It shocked me into perfect stillness. Was the last thing I expected. I wasn't sure why she offered a kiss, but I wasn't going to argue. A few seconds later, I kissed her back, keeping things as gentle and tender as she wanted them.

It was short, chaste. Appropriate for the moment.

I loved her.

Please forgive me, Miranda.

I wanted to beg her, but I promised I'd stop pressuring her. I gave my word.

She pulled away and tucked her head against my thrashing heart. In a matter of minutes, she was breathing heavy and sleep found us entwined.

FIFTY-SEVEN

Miranda

Richard's memorial service was three days later. I met all his wonderful children. They were in their late forties and fifties and their children were my age. Lots of them recognized my name because Richard had apparently talked about me. I got so many phone numbers and was overjoyed to learn many of them lived close by. Two of Richard's granddaughters wanted to do coffee soon. They had children Kacey's age and he fell in love with them, too.

His granddaughter, Evie, said, "If you were family to Richard, you are family to us." I choked back an onslaught as Evie hugged me and wiped tears from her own eyes. When she let me go, Jack's hand came to the small of my back. The light pressure held me steady.

Apparently, the biggest holiday of the year for this bunch was the Fourth of July at Bob and Cynthia's house. We accepted the invite. This huge, loving family sucked me and Jack right in. Exactly like Richard had.

There were lots of tears, but also laughter. Each generation following Richard was full of life and joy.

A harvest.

A beautiful, bountiful harvest I was one-hundred percent certain was due to Richard and Rose. It made me cry all over again every time I allowed myself to feel the magic, the radiance, and the hope within the room.

I thanked Richard a hundred times in my heart. Hoped he could hear how grateful I was. I thanked Rose too. For loving Richard so much he had love overflowing for me. For letting me be a recipient of all they had to give. For letting me have the special things they were so intent on giving away.

Jack's hand never left mine. Every time I introduced him as my husband, I'd feel him glance down at me. Trying to sort me out. Trying to figure out if I meant what I said. I did mean it, and I couldn't wait to tell him.

During the reception, one of the older men, I forget his name, said, "How long have you two been married?"

Jack answered. "Two months."

The man laughed. "Oh, newlyweds! No wonder you two look the way you do."

When I realized why the man said that, my cheeks started to burn. Jack's extreme attentiveness to me must've garnered some notice. In fact, I could only remember two brief moments during the whole thing that Jack didn't hold my hand, touch my back, rub my shoulder, or put an arm around me. And I was well aware of the dumb look on my face when I looked up at him. I tried to have a more neutral expression. But I couldn't help but beam at him. He was so handsome and I loved him so much.

For the first time ever, he made something emotional easier to face. I had so much to tell him. So much to share with him. I couldn't wait to talk to Jack about our future. But, I'd had to hit pause. After I lost Richard, I needed a few days. Time to be sad, to think, to find my bearings.

At home, Jack gave me space when I asked for it and suffocated me with a hug when I asked for that too. My asking was growth. I told him what I needed, and he didn't shy away.

Ever since our conversation in the hallway, Jack wasn't sure what to do with himself. He looked to me for cues. He only gave what I asked for and only repeated what I praised.

Every day, I would go out to the gardens. First Richard's. Then mine. I picked his veggies and left them inside the house for his family. They liked that. It helped them out, and I was happy to find a way to serve them. I picked his green beans and made them a casserole. And a tomato pie. And some fresh cucumber salad. I left vases of fresh-cut flowers inside the house. Cynthia and Bob thanked me a hundred times for caring for all of Richard's plants.

Then I tended our garden. The harvest was just starting to come in. Red crept into the green tomatoes, a few squash and cucumbers had already been picked. My flowers were filling out and looked really nice. Beet greens were full and the kale needed to be clipped back. My basket wasn't overflowing, but it wouldn't be long. The foundation was strong and the harvest was promising.

Being out there made me feel better. I cried a lot, but mostly, I just felt thankful. In his final days, Richard gave gifts that would span way beyond his lifetime. Maybe even beyond mine.

When I wasn't gardening, I kicked around with Kacey and Jack. We went to the park, watched some movies. Just had quiet days. Jack only got one sick day off. I understood. He couldn't just sit. And I didn't need him to.

Plus, when he wasn't home, I was working on my project. It wasn't much, but it did require a little of my time.

It was probably best we didn't spend too much time together. Because as the days went by, I burned for him. I needed to tell him how I felt. Soon.

Jack was sad, maybe even nervous. And I couldn't keep him there if I knew what I wanted. We had signed papers to sell the lake house right before we came to the funeral. Money would come within a week and Jack wasn't certain what I was going to do. He didn't ask though. He was pretty quiet overall. I could tell he was thinking a lot. And so was I.

He never pushed to talk about us during that time. Even when I crawled into bed with him. Funny. I was *sure* he meant for that to be a one night thing. But one of us would tuck Kacey into his toddler bed then we'd sit on the couch and kind of end up falling asleep in Jack's room somehow.

Each night, I gave him a sweet, gentle kiss. He didn't push for more, which I appreciated, but I knew lying next to me without pressuring was no small feat for him. Heck, it was a feat for me. The third night, he didn't pull me close. Just put a hand on my arm and kept his distance. I knew why. I can't be completely certain, but I think he even moved to the couch after I'd fallen asleep. Because when I stirred in the night, his side was cold.

On the forth night, I told Jack I didn't need to come to bed with him. I was certain I couldn't sleep next to him because I wanted him and felt how much he wanted me.

Making love on uncertain terms wasn't my gig. Despite the tension humming between us, I wasn't willing to sell out. That step was very big.

I wanted to say everything the way I'd planned to say it first. My plan would mean something to him. I just knew it would.

Before I went upstairs for the night, he double-checked to make sure I was okay. Asked if I needed anything. Made sure I wasn't going to go up and cry alone.

I promised him I wouldn't.

But it was a lie, because as soon as my bedroom door shut behind me, I burst into tears.

Happy tears.

Because somehow my husband had gone from running from my big feelings, to making sure he wasn't missing out on them. I knew it wasn't easy for Jack, but he was literally bending over backward to hunker through the storm with me. It was an unexpected change that made our future all the more promising.

I pulled myself together and slipped into the upstairs bathroom, shutting the door behind me. I turned on the fan so my voice wouldn't carry. The phone call I needed to make was part of my project, and I didn't want Jack to overhear.

I checked the time. Only 8:30 p.m. Surely, it wasn't too late to call Jules. My hands shook. I doubted there'd be any confrontation, but her icy blue eyes were seared into my brain. When they babysat Kacey for my birthday, there hadn't been any obvious animosity between the two of us, but unfortunately, that knowledge wasn't enough to calm my nerves.

I dialed her number and pressed send.

"Hello?"

"Jules, hey, this is Miranda."

"Oh! Miranda! Is everything okay?"

"Yes. I'm sorry to call you so late."

"No, it's fine. Pat and I usually stay up way too late. I'm"—she hesitated—"really glad you called."

"Oh?"

"Yeah, not to hijack your call, but I've wanted to apologize to you. I was hard on you that night at Jack's and didn't know the whole story."

"You had every reason to be hard on me."

"I could've at least given you the chance to explain."

"There would've been no way to explain in that short time. It's really okay. I know you were just looking out for him."

"Yeah, we are pretty protective."

I hadn't planned on getting overly personal with Jules. But the next words out of my mouth felt natural, and I wanted to share them. "Well, you should know, I didn't strike up this deal with Jack because I want to be rich or anything. I was just trying to get—"

"It's okay, Miranda. I know. Jack told me about Chris. I hope that's alright with you. He and I talk a lot more than we used to."

"Of course. I'm glad you have each other." Slight embarrassment crept into my heart. Jules probably thought I'd fumbled things so badly.

"Listen, I hope it's okay for me to say this, I wouldn't feel right not saying something—from one mom to another—I'm sorry for all your losses." Emotion swelled in her voice and my heart squeezed with a host of feelings. "I can't honestly wrap my head around it."

I swallowed hard, trying to hold it together. For my babies to be acknowledged felt—good. A hard type of good.

"Thank you, Jules." I cleared my throat. "Means more than you know."

"I hope you and Jack are able to work everything out."

My voice squeaked. "I love him. I won't hurt him again."

A sniffle on her end threatened the flimsy dam holding back my own flood. "You have—no idea how happy I am to hear that. Have you told him?"

"I told him I love him, but I need to tell him I want to stay. Actually, that's why I called. I—I have something, uh, special planned for Jack."

"Oh!" Her tone did a one-eighty. "Does your sweet boy need a babysitter again?"

I laughed. Jules and I used to be friends. She was a little on the wild side, but I'd loved her to pieces. Would we find friendship as moms now? My motherhood thus far had been so isolated, I'd never had a mom friend to hang out with. I smiled so big. "Yes, he does."

She squealed. "Oh, I'm so excited! Just tell me when."

"Is tomorrow afternoon too soon?"

"Not at all."

"I can drop him off around 3 p.m. and get him…I don't know, after dinner?"

"No, no! Just leave him overnight."

I backpedaled, "Oh, uh, I don't—I don't think that will be necessary."

She scoffed, her tone turning a bit suggestive. "Well, I don't know what you have planned, but if you're making any kind of commitments, it's gonna be necessary."

Her confidence made me draw a shaky breath. "You think he'll be happy?"

"Are you kidding?! Happy is not even the right word!" She made another excited noise. "Girl, let us keep him overnight. Pat can take him down to the shop to look at all the cars, we'll get a pizza, make pancakes in the morning, play outside. If he likes to swim, we can go down to the river. We all think he is the sweetest kid!"

A night alone with my husband. I put a hand over my stomach which fluttered out of control.

I hoped she couldn't hear how breathless I got. "Are you sure, Jules?"

"Positive!"

We talked details. When I hung up, I was in full freak-out

mode. By this time tomorrow, I'd be in his arms for real. Not holding back ever again.

If everything went according to plan.

FIFTY-EIGHT

Jack

My work shift started early. I was in by 4:30 a.m. and if all went well, would be leaving twelve hours later. Which was perfect because I had a two hour appointment at five. Wouldn't be home until after dinner.

When I called to tell Miranda not to wait dinner on me, she seemed upset. Didn't say why, but I definitely heard something in her voice. It bothered me all day. Maybe she was having a hard time and missing Richard. Worry started to eat at me.

I'd brought street clothes and changed at the department after my shift, so I would be more comfortable for my appointment. I thought about canceling, but the guy had slipped me into the schedule kind of last minute.

Close to six, Miranda texted: *Eta?*

What in the world?

"Hey man, what time you think you'll be finishing up?"

The guy didn't look up. "Probably twenty minutes or so."

I texted her back one-handed: *6:45ish?*

She sent a thumbs up.

As soon as I paid him, I jetted.

I thought about her the whole way home. Felt a little uneasy. Did the money come or something? I hadn't checked my account. Were we about to have a sit-down? Miranda was usually very chill when I worked late.

I came in the front door with my duffle slung over my shoulder. Three things hit my brain at the same time—the smell, the sound, the sights. First of all, whatever Miranda had baked caused the entire house to smell like cinnamon. My mouth started watering and I realized how hungry I was. Next, soft music—the Lumineers—was playing. One of my favorites. Thought that was funny, because Miranda only listened to country music if she was alone. And finally, the lights were dim. There were two candles on the coffee table.

I called out, "Miranda?"

Nothing.

"Kacey?"

Nothing.

I hung my keys on the hook and kicked off my shoes. I figured Miranda must be in the backyard. Before I went that way, I opened my bedroom door to toss my duffle in.

A candle was lit on my dresser and the bedsheets were turned down.

Adrenaline raced through my veins, my breathing immediately going shallow.

I went to my bathroom and flicked on the light. Miranda's sugar scrub was on the sink and there was a little tiny heart drawn with a marker on the mirror.

What in the...

Where was Miranda? I quickly exited my room, shutting the door behind me, feeling like I'd seen something I wasn't supposed to.

My heart beat was tangible, noticeable. I puffed a few breaths as I scanned the rest of the house for the woman, growing urgent.

"Miranda?"

I traveled so fast toward the back door, I almost missed a scrapbook propped open on the kitchen counter. I pulled to a stop when I realized the note card next to it had my name. Along with two words.

"Flip through."

I glanced through the kitchen window, wishing it had a view of the garden.

This scrapbook was all black with the word "us" on the cover. I instantly recognized it. She started this scrapbook when we were dating. Tiny mementos portrayed all the fun we had over the years and the places we went. Each photo was dated and labeled in an artistic way I would've never been able to pull off myself.

I'd always told Miranda she should do craft shows or something. She had a way of making something as simple as paper look incredible.

Won't lie though, I didn't spend a ton of time viewing old pictures. I flipped quick, singularly focused on the purpose of all this. Was she trying to remind me of our history?

The pictures of us morphed into pictures of Kacey. All the loose pictures I'd seen a few nights ago were now glued to the pages.

My pulse was still sky high, and I just tried to get to the end so I could find my wife. My gaze darted to the kitchen window again.

I suddenly stopped flipping, realizing the pages had gone

blank. There were frames and paper clippings, but no pictures. I leaned closer, reading a few labels.

The current page had a big empty frame with the label, "Kacey's fourth birthday," which wasn't until September.

I flipped back a page. Another empty frame was labeled "family pool day." Another "Daddy and Kacey." Then there were two whole pages with the title "family pictures" dated for tomorrow.

I turned back to the first empty page. Right front and center, there was a large empty frame. The label said "vow renewal" and today's date.

My breath tumbled out in a rush. Where was she?

I abandoned the scrapbook, believing I received the intended message: there was a future for us.

My heart kicked against my ribcage.

I moved toward the door as fast as possible without breaking into a jog. When the humidity of the summer evening hit me, I saw her.

She'd dragged our tiny patio table and two chairs out into the yard, situating it near the garden. A vase of fresh flowers sat on the table. And it looked like she'd repainted the bench.

And she was...

I swallowed hard, all the details of the scene falling into oblivion. She was seated at the table. Her blonde hair cascaded down her back in waves. Looked like gold in the softening evening sunlight. She wore a flowy white dress, the edges of it draping off the side of the chair into the grass. Sleeveless, meaning her shoulders and neck, in all their glory, were in full view.

"Miranda."

Her gaze snapped toward the door and she jumped to standing. She smiled nervously.

I wasn't smiling. I didn't think I could smile.

I moved toward the table, numb with awe of her. As I got closer, I realized just how wonderfully the dress she was wearing accentuated her curves. Her chest was exposed in near perfection and a slit in the dress rose almost to her hip.

I stopped a couple feet away.

"Jack."

"Miranda."

We stood there for a few beats, just taking each other in.

"Jack, I need to get stuff off my chest. So just listen."

I said nothing. Tried to calm the chaos in my chest.

"I want this. I want us."

I sucked in a breath.

"I'm sorry it took me so long to figure it out." She ran her fingers through her hair. "In the hall, you said you wouldn't blame me if I never forgave you. Well, I've spent a lot of time not forgiving you. And all that has done is hurt us." She choked up. "But I need you to know that I do forgive you now."

She ran a hand over her stomach. "When we were married before, I expected things from you I wasn't even doing myself. Like, I wanted you to communicate, be patient with me, and understand me." She lifted a finger to her eye, carefully swiping under her mascara. "But, I wasn't patient with you. Or communicating with you about how hard I was grieving. I even kept some of our babies to myself because I was angry."

She took a deep breath and looked me straight in the eyes. "I'm learning that fumbling—messing up—is just part of this crazy process. That we will accidentally hurt each other. But real love—the mature kind—grows together through those things."

"Jack," she said, her voice strained with tears. "I didn't hold on for us. I should've been in freaking counseling. I quit because the striving hurt. I wasn't willing to keep fighting and...it cost us so, *so* much."

I started closing the distance.

"I know you're not perfect, Jack. I'm not dumb enough to believe in fairytale endings, but I want to work for us. If we practice loving and forgiving, it gets easier and the reward gets better. I want that with you, Jack." She gave a half laugh through her tears. "The pain *and* the gain, I guess."

I stopped right in front of her. She looked up at me. "But, if we are going to have all that, I need *you* to forgive *me* first. For giving up on us. For leaving when crap got hard."

My eyes roamed her full cheeks. A layer of tears pooled on her bottom eyelid. I lifted my hand and brushed one off her cheek as it fell. "Miranda, it wasn't all your fault. Neither one of us were willing to do the hard thing for each other. I ran too."

"Well, forgive me for my part. Please, Jack." Her quiet pleading tugged on my heart.

"I forgive you. I already have."

She nodded, her shoulders falling with relief. "I know. I needed to hear it."

"I'll say it again then." I slipped my hand into her hair and let my fingers gently drag through it while I spoke. "I *forgive* you. We lost time, but we won't lose any more."

I pulled her into my arms and she squeaked with emotion. I leaned down, kissing the top of her head. "I love you, Miranda."

Her words were muffled into my chest as she squeezed me. "I love you, Jack." She pushed back, looking up again. "You know how you said you meant our wedding vows?"

I nodded.

"Well, I didn't mean them. I don't even remember what the heck we said. I was just trying not to faint."

I chuckled. "I remember."

She turned back to the table and picked up a little card. "I wrote some vows. I want to say them to you."

Miranda was unbelievably sincere. With everything she did in life. My chest tightened. She wanted to read vows to me? I'm not a good judge of romance, but vows were a bold move, leaving me feeling a bit breathless with anticipation.

I nodded for lack of words.

"Can we sit so my neck stops breaking?"

We moved to the chairs, her settling in the one opposite me— too far away. *Way* too far. Had to do something about that.

She smoothed her dress. "I feel so cheesy."

"Here, let me make it worse." I grabbed her hand, pulling her out of her seat and leading her to my lap. I grabbed the back of her knee and directed her to sit, straddling my legs, facing me. She laughed, only inches from my face now. "Oh my gosh, this does make it worse."

I couldn't laugh. I loved this woman more than my next breath. The slit in her dress fell open, bearing one of her legs in totality. I slid my hand up her thigh and back down. Her eyes fluttered closed on an inhale.

But she recovered quickly and swatted my hand. "Now, you can't be doing that. I won't get through this."

She held the card up. Took a deep breath to start, but didn't start. She pressed her lips together and blinked a few times. Tipped her head to the side, like she was trying to move the moisture around in order to see the words. She whispered, "I'm going to cry, Jack."

"You can cry."

She took a steadying breath again. "I, Miranda Leigh Barkley, give my heart to you, Jackson Nathaniel Barkley."

Heat pressed behind my eyes.

"I promise to love you in all seasons of life." She sniffed. "To grow with you through every storm. I promise to protect your heart. To keep a watchful eye over things that would steal from our love. And to purge myself of selfishness that would choke out our reward."

Her sweet lips trembled. "I promise to nourish you and help you be everything you are meant to be. When things are hard, I promise to stay. To mess up. To learn with you. To change with you. And to mature with you."

"May our love be ardent, faithful, and unending. May our love be so deeply rooted, it outlasts us. From this day forward, my heart will be your only home. And yours, mine."

She put the card down and looked at me, waiting for some type of response. I closed my eyes, that feeling pressing in on me. My eyes filled as I plucked the card out of her hand. I held it up, my voice a rasp of emotions I rarely felt. "My turn."

She pressed her lips together, tears amping.

"I, Jackson Nathaniel Barkley..."

Not sure how I made it through them. With each line, Miranda cried and the swell of emotions grew in my chest to the point I felt like I might pop. I blinked to see the words on more than one occasion. Her hands rested on my shoulders. By the time I finished, she had scooted closer, practically gripping me with her legs.

"...and yours, mine."

I placed the card on the table behind her.

Silence fell over us. Crickets sang out. Darkness edged in on the sky. Her hands slipped up the side of my face and she placed her forehead against mine. One of her thumbs gently brushed a single tear off my cheek.

"I love you, Jack. Not as I should, but I'll get better."

I kissed her gently on the lips. "We have a strong start."

She brought her lips to mine. They were soft, sweet. This kiss felt different than the ones we shared before. Before, we were desperate. Desperate to convince the other. Desperate for as much as we could get before it ended.

But this was tender, meaning-packed. We knew we had a lifetime.

FIFTY-NINE

Miranda

I slowly ran my hands over his shoulders and down his arms, squeezing his muscles every few inches. When I made it to his forearm, he winced, grunting in quiet pain.

I reared back, confused as to how I hurt him.

I looked down, trying to figure out if I pinched him or something. What I saw made me stop breathing. I grabbed his hand, jerking his arm toward my face.

My voice wobbled, "Jack?"

He said nothing.

"What is this?"

Flowers were inked into his arm. The arrangement was still pink and puffy, the design smaller than my palm, but so intricate I could pick the types out immediately. Gladiolus, holly, lily of the valley, carnation, cosmos, daffodil, chrysanthemum.

An abrupt sob escaped my lips as I counted.

There were nine flowers total.

Two at the bottom were bigger than the rest. I pointed, careful not to touch it again. I cried, "What—what are these?"

"A morning glory for September and a rose for June."

The question squeaked out. "For Kacey and me?"

He swallowed, nodding.

I broke.

My emotions shattered into a thousand pieces. I straight up ugly cried. The acknowledgement was too much. I trembled under the weight and joy and pain of our losses. Our family of ten hit me like an avalanche and I melted in his arms. "Jack," I forced through the wave of tears. "Why did you do this?"

His hands came to my face, pushing the tears back. "Because I wanted you to forget. It was easier for me. But I'm not going to make that mistake again. This is my attempt to bear pain with you. To remember what we've lost and where we came from. And to protect the blessing of what we have."

He did this before he was even certain I would take him back?

I threw my arms around his shoulders, crying into his neck. His hands rubbed my back for a few minutes as I struggled to regain control. I gasped for air several times. "That is the—the most beautiful thing I've ever seen."

He held me as I looked at his tattoo for a long time, naming the blooms and fawning over the artist's excellency. It was a memorial for me. For *us*. For the family we wouldn't know and for the family we did.

We talked for a few more minutes until I stopped actively bawling my eyes out.

I dried my cheeks for the hundredth time. "I was going to take a picture of us for the scrapbook, but I am a wreck right now. And we'll have to use a flash which will make me look shiny."

"Take one anyway, so we can remember this." Jack retrieved his phone from his pocket and we had a mini photo shoot with me in his lap. I was smudgy and blotchy in all of them, but we were so happy, it didn't matter. We took pictures of Jack's tattoo and even took selfies of us kissing—like teenagers who just made it official.

I loved this man. I *loved* him.

Finally, we put the camera and the words aside. His arms encircled me and we allowed the heat of our kisses to spiral. I'd been deprived of Jack for far too long as it was. The fact we'd been separated and lived to tell the tale was nothing short of miraculous.

So, I dove into him. The tenderness of the moment catching fire and melting into—*finally*—unrestrained passion.

Jack's hand moved up my thigh and his fingers slipped under the hem of my dress. His other hand pressed into my back until I whimpered. His tongue swept into my mouth as I ran my hands over his head and down his arms. He felt like a dream.

We were unleashed. Desperate for more. Aching for skin. Demanding and taking. Giving and surrendering.

His hands followed each of my curves—touching and getting reacquainted with the contours of his wife. I allowed my head to fall back. Jack shuddered, his lips instantly finding my neck and chest with a deep groan.

Something from the depths of my conscience nagged me as his hot mouth moved across my throat. I didn't want to care, but common decency said I probably should. My voice was hoarse, nearly painful, as I jerked my awareness to something other than him. "Jack?"

"Hmm."

"There's like two houses that have a view of our backyard."

"What houses?"

I puffed a breathy laugh. "Want to take me inside?"

His fingers flexed on my ribcage. "Is this the part where I take you to the shower and use the scrub you put on my sink?"

My head snapped upright. "You weren't supposed to see all that! It was a surprise."

He looked up, his slow smile borderline wicked. "Trust me. Seeing it early ruined nothing."

"Then yes, this is that part."

Jack stood, effortlessly toting me in his arms. I clung to his muscled back and chest. I breathed in the spicy scent at his shoulder, letting my lips find his neck, his jaw, and the spot under his ear.

"If you want to make it to the house, you better quit," he growled.

I laughed, relishing in his strong arms holding me up, the speed of his pace, and the way he clumsily groped for the door knob.

"Wait!" I shrieked. He halted mid-kitchen. "I made you an apple crisp." My smile was suggestive, devious. I batted my eyelashes, enjoying the impatience on his face. "Don't you want to eat some first?"

His eyebrows drew together and he quickly ran his teeth over his bottom lip. "Let me work up an appetite first, and I'll eat the whole thing."

I laughed again, my arms clenching around his neck.

He flew through the living room and into his bedroom, pausing between the bed and the bathroom door. He looked between them and back at me. His blue eyes were wild, starving.

"What first?"

"Bed."

He smiled then tossed me down.

SIXTY

Jack

Two whole hours.

My patience was wearing thin.

I climbed back on the bed and dropped beside Miranda. Her face was scrunched against the pillow, her hair tangled under her cheek. She was so peaceful, I hated to wake her. But time was ticking. We had to pick our kid up at twelve-thirty, which left us a little less than three hours.

I arranged everything perfectly. I was freshly showered, breakfast was hot, coffee was fresh, I tidied the room from the night before. Everything was ready for her and I was sick of waiting. I pressed my lips to her forehead, then her cheek, her nose, her chin.

"Miranda."

She drew in a long sleepy breath and hummed.

"Wake up." I kissed her lips.

They moved under mine just a little. Her eyes fluttered. I drew back so I could watch her come to.

She opened her eyes, squinting at the late morning sunlight.

"Good morning," I whispered.

"Good morning."

That morning voice.

A slow smile spread over her face. "What time is it? I must've really slept in."

"Going on ten."

She took a deep breath and brought her hands over her head in a full stretch. The sheet slipped to the side, revealing the sexy nightgown she fell asleep in. She rubbed her eyes. "I never sleep like that."

"I wore you out last night."

She gave a half-awake chuckle. "No kidding."

I ran my hand over her hair, smoothing it back. "You've got some bed head going on."

She smirked. "My best look."

I nodded. "Absolutely. This is the most beautiful I've ever seen you."

She smiled then sniffed through her nose. "Something smells amazing."

I let my shoulder hit the bed beside her, clearing her line of vision to my dresser across the room, where breakfast sat on two trays.

She tipped her head. "Breakfast in bed?" The sleepiness was melting from her eyes, a fire taking its place. "Jack, that's very romantic."

"Figured you'd be hungry."

"I am!" She sat up, adorably eager. "What'd you make me?"

"I made you waffles, eggs, some bacon, and fruit salad. Obviously, coffee."

Her eyes grew wide. "My dreams come true!"

She fluffed a pillow behind her back and rubbed her hands together as I carried a tray over. I almost laughed out loud. How long was it going to take the woman to notice?

I placed a bed tray over her lap. She started chattering about the food and took a sip of her nearly white coffee. Her eyes rolled back like that sugary cup of crap was the best thing she ever had. She had a few bites of egg and waffle while we made small talk—mostly reminiscing over the previous night and discussing the family photo shoot that afternoon. Miranda had booked a photographer for us and everything.

She was driving me nuts. I'd prepped a surprise for her and she wasn't noticing. I kept having to fight back my smile. Just when I thought I might have to drop a hint or force her to slow down, she snapped a piece of bacon in half then dropped it back on the plate with a gasp.

"Jack!"

I let my smile loose. She finally saw.

She held her left hand out and waggled her fingers around. Her face turned a little red as tears brimmed in her eyes yet again. She'd teared up all through our love making last night and every time we'd talked. Even in the shower. She was so happy. I think she told me a thousand times.

She bit her lip. "I had no idea you still had my ring."

"I wasn't going to get rid of it."

"Did you put this on me while I was sleeping?"

I nodded, turning so I could fully see her face.

"Thank you."

"If you want a new one, we can do that."

"No freaking way. I love this ring."

Somehow I knew she would say that. I grabbed her hand, kissed it and her ring. "Don't take it off then, *wife*."

"Never again, *husband*. I promise." She leaned toward me

and kissed the smile off my face. We got sidetracked for a couple minutes before returning to our breakfast.

After she ate to her heart's content she pushed the tray aside and ran to my closet, jerking a few hangers out. She held them up, whipping out a bossy tone. "You're wearing this today."

"Oh, we get to pick each other's clothes now?" Her face was already deadpan, reading my tone. "If that's the case, don't change."

She waved down the front of her body. "*This* is what you want me wearing in family pictures?"

I tsked, scrunching my nose. "Yeah, probably not."

I braced myself on the nightstand with one hand, easing my tray to the floor with the other. When I sat back up, I patted the mattress beside me. "Don't you think it's a little early to be getting dressed?"

She glanced at an invisible watch on her wrist. "It's almost ten thirty."

"We have plenty of time."

"Good. Because I need to do some laundry before we go."

I shook my head, stifling a smile.

She rolled her eyes around like she was mentally counting through her to-do list. "And unload the dishwasher."

"Miranda."

She crawled back onto the bed, a facetious smile breaking across her face. "And unpack some boxes."

"*Miranda*."

"What?" She giggled, flopping back down on her pillow.

I pushed up onto my forearms, "We are *not* doing laundry right now."

"Really? What else should we do?" Her playful voice faltered as I pressed a kiss against the tender skin of her throat.

"This might be a—show don't tell situation." I grabbed her

hips and dragged her across the bed, situating my gorgeous wife beneath me.

She feigned exasperation. "Oh, this *again*?"

"Yes, *again*."

"You aren't sick of this yet?"

I laughed. "Not in the slightest."

Her coy charade evaporated as desire lit in her eyes.

I trailed kisses down for a few moments before she grabbed my head and brought it up to hers. "Kiss me, Jack. Kiss me right now."

We tangled. In a blend of passion and tenderness. In another sweet relenting. Our union would forever be an outworking of knowing and being known. Of loving and being loved. Of our broken history and promised future. Of forgiving and offering forgiveness.

She had sent my heart into a free fall long ago. Fast and hard. No brakes to slow the descent. No pads to soften the blow. My heart was hers. Always and forever hers.

And I was lost.

We were on our way to Pleasant Gap to pick up Kacey when Miranda looked up from her phone and cussed—loud.

I startled, tapping the brakes. "What?!"

She stared out the window, a dazed look on her face. "Jack?"

"Speak! You're freaking me out!"

"We are *millionaires*." She squeaked out the last word.

"For real?"

"Yeah," she turned the phone toward me, like I'd be able to read it while driving. Her jaw hung loose. "Money came."

"Holy cow."

We let that sink in for a few beats. I was shocked, honestly. Knowing it was coming was totally different than having zeroes in your account. It'd be one hell of a tax season.

"Why do you think your dad included me in his will?"

It was something I'd considered many times. It might have been a flex of values. Or maybe a final way to stick it to me. Our strained relationship went to pot after Miranda and I split. He always told me he would never support a divorce. At the end of the day, that seemed the most logical explanation—proving how seriously he took marriage.

My dad wasn't a person to model, but his loyalty to mom beyond her lifespan was honorable, albeit misguided and martyr-like. "You know what? I don't really know. Don't care to be honest." I reached over, squeezing her thigh. "Nicest thing he ever did for me."

She beamed at me. "I'm thankful."

"Me too." Because the nature of our relationship had been undetermined, Miranda and I never discussed the money. "So, what are we going to *do* with it?"

"Um, vacation! Duh!"

I laughed. "Well, obviously we can go on vacation." I quickly imagined spending a week with my wife and son somewhere tropical. "Okay, *definitely* vacation."

"Bora Bora?"

"I don't care. You pick. Somewhere with white sand and blue water."

She squealed. "Oh my *gosh* we're going to Bora Bora!"

"We also need to see a financial advisor."

"*Pfft!* That's boring."

I shot her a look.

Her shoulders dropped an inch or two. "You're right. I probably need one."

"We *both* do. That's a lot of money and we need to be

smart. There's no reason that money shouldn't still be serving us when I'm retired."

"True. Okay, but let's not ruin the moment." The excitement had flooded her face again. "We will talk retirement with the advisor. Right *now*, let's talk wish list."

I couldn't help but smile. "Alright, fine. Wish list."

"What do you *want* to do that you wouldn't ever be able to do without it?"

I knew what I wanted. But debated whether to say it or not. Because the choice was ultimately hers.

"Jack, I know what I want. And it's a big ask. I mean big, big."

"Shoot."

She told me about her Ohio neighbor named Sherri and her husband Ed. How sick Ed was and how Sherri worked really hard to keep paying for their house and medical bills. They'd sold their home in the country, poured every penny they had into a new life close to the Cincinnati hospital and were barely keeping dinner on the table.

Apparently, this Sherri woman was the sole responsible party for getting my family out of Chris' clutches.

"Jack, can we—can we pay off their mortgage? I asked how much they owed. It's $125k."

The first thing my wife wanted wasn't even for herself. The ask shouldn't have surprised me. She would always give big. Love big. Ask big. Life had tried to beat that out of her, but it was still there—on full display.

"I think that's a perfect way to say thank you." Our agreement made Miranda tear up.

She swiped under her eyes. "Okay, your turn."

I hesitated. It was probably too soon to discuss something like this.

She narrowed her eyes at me. "I think I know what you're going to say."

"What?"

"You say it."

I swallowed, deciding to dive right in. "You can say no. But I think you should get the surgery. We should try for one more."

She nodded silently for a few long moments. "The surgery isn't guaranteed to work, Jack."

"I know."

"What if we lose another?"

I lifted a shoulder, trying to be careful not to disregard in any way. "We've learned a lot. My gut says we'll survive this time."

Her smile was slow and hope-filled. "Mine says the same."

We decided to call and make a consultation about it—at the least. And just go from there. See how it played out. We ran out of time to finish a wish list but we'd cycle back later.

We pulled into the Moore's driveway, and my son sat on the porch swing, his feet dangling off the side. When we parked in the driveway, he jumped up, tripped and fell, then bounded through the grass toward our open doors, unfazed by the fall.

"Mommy!" He screamed when she scooped him into a hug. Kacey struggled from Miranda's arms as his eyes landed on me, practically flinging himself through the air. "Daddy!"

Daddy. Unprompted.

He plastered himself to my chest, molding into a perfect fit over my shoulder. My eyes heated and I quickly took a step back toward the truck, taking a moment to just hold my boy. No every other weekend dad stuff for me. This little guy was mine—every day. I blinked rapidly, trying to discourage the tears as Pat and Jules came down the front walk.

He squeezed me as tight as his tiny little arms could, wiggling closer. "Daddy, I missed you!"

The last week had worked over my emotions more than the last twenty-four years combined.

I swiped my cheek then patted his tiny little back. "Yeah, buddy, I missed you too."

He pushed back, looking straight in my eyes. "Awe we going to have fun today?"

"You bet."

Jules and Pat beamed at us. When Jules caught my gaze, her expression morphed into a *you got some didn't you* look which made me roll my eyes with a smile. But I mouthed "thank you" and she waved me off.

Pat grabbed my hand, shook it hard. "Congrats, man. One heck of a family you got there."

Wasn't that the truth. I glanced at them both, noticing how the sun reflected off their hair and how the dimples deepened on their faces.

We all talked in the drive for a few minutes, and Kacey ran back in to hug Sunny, Winter, and Woods goodbye. As I buckled my kiddo into the backseat, I let myself entertain the idea of one or two more beside him.

Miranda gripped my hand as I slid into the driver's seat. Looked over her shoulder at Kacey then back at me. Tears brimmed in her eyes. Heck, mine too.

The fulfilled silence said everything words couldn't say. This family was all either of us had ever wanted. And the reality was so much better than I ever dreamed it could be. Maybe the way we got here—as painful as it was—somehow made this better. Made this stronger.

I lifted her hand then kissed it then I threw the truck into reverse.

The Barkleys' best days were yet to come.

EPILOGUE

Four Years Later

I'm listening to all my favorite sounds. The breeze making the wind chime tinkle. The cows braying across the street—something must have gotten them riled. The coffee pot brewing just past the screen door—it's not our best habit, but Jack and I enjoy an afternoon cup now. Must be a parent thing.

But my favorite sound rises right from the backyard.

Voices, laughter.

I want to sit on the deck and listen all day.

Every now and then, I catch a glimpse of my precious family around the bushy tomato plants. Right now, they are harvesting. Gathering up what will probably be one of the last big hauls of the season.

This garden looks nothing like my first.

Mostly, because we have a lot more space. We left behind Jack's house in Nashville and moved out to Pleasant Gap. Jack started policing here—said he was ready for a little town.

Something quieter. It didn't take long for Jack to become a well-loved officer in the small community. A few officials are encouraging Jack to run for Sheriff next term.

I hope he does. He's the perfect man for the job.

I like to think that the strength of his character, his heart for people, and his love of justice is just one way the Barkley family is overflowing. One way we are a bounty for all.

We decided to get a house with a couple acres so I can garden to my heart's content. Which means our garden grows enough to keep a family full year-round. I grow dozens of varieties and have a flower garden, too. We have a pantry with Ball jars lining long shelves. I run seed drives every spring at the Pleasant Gap community center. And I host classes on our property Tuesday and Thursday nights. People come into my safe haven with a paper and pen.

I guess Richard was right. I am a green-thumb.

Rose's hat shields my face from the scorching sun. It reminds me of the choice I have to make every single day for the rest of my life. So I wear it all summer long. Hang it in clear view during the winter.

The coffee finally clicks off, and I head inside to pour myself a cup. I pour Jack a cup too and stick it in the freezer. He'll add ice when he's ready.

A laminated card sits above the kitchen sink, propped against the window sill. By this point, it's got some wear and tear on it. It's gone into lunch boxes, been taped on mirrors, leaned against truck consoles, and slipped into my harvesting basket. Whoever reaches for the card is being the mature one. Sometimes it's me. Sometimes it's Jack.

The tactic is nothing short of magic.

These days, the card stays on the window sill more often than not, which I think says a lot about us.

I stroll into my happy place and find my seven-year-old picking heirloom tomatoes. He holds up a fat one and we admire it together. Jack is cutting cucumbers off the trellis. I stop to enjoy the pulsing muscles in his shoulders and forearms as the shears snap and he tosses the veggies into a basket.

He catches me staring and flashes me a slow, knowing smile. "What are you looking at?"

"You know," I say, soaking him in.

He forces his gaze away so he can finish picking. He doesn't have to help in the garden, but he likes to. He knows I'm happy when we're all out there together. Thirty seconds later, he plops the basket down on a gardening table and moves toward me. "If you keep looking at me like that, Kacey is going to have to babysit for a few minutes."

He places a warm kiss on my lips. His leaning motion bonks Levi's head into my face. I giggle and Jack rubs Levi's dark hair. "Oops. Sorry, buddy."

I smile at the two of them. Inside the baby carrier, Levi is a speck against Jack's broad chest. We all are. In fact, I'm constantly amazed Jack's chest is big enough for all three of us to crowd in. And he pulls us close, holds us tight—often.

Our second miracle came right before we gave up hope. Levi Richard Barkley. Our violet. He's eight months old and growing like a weed. Kacey adores having a little brother. He keeps asking for another, but after Levi, we permanently closed that door.

I marvel at the ink on Jack's forearm. There are thirteen blooms now, because the surgery wasn't as successful as we'd hoped. I'd be lying if I said it wasn't heartbreaking. I grieved hard. Still do sometimes. There were and are dark days.

But now Jack is here, and I never face them alone.

We're bound, abundant. Strong in our love.

It's interesting looking back. At one point, I would've said those blooms broke us. And maybe they did. For a time.

But not all broken things are beyond repair.

AUTHOR'S NOTE

Not all relationships are worth fighting for.

As soon as Jack materialized in *Hold Back the River*, I knew I wanted to write a marriage reconciliation for him. I treasure the sanctity of marriage and hope that comes across in this story. But an important distinction needs to be made. Sometimes, the only appropriate response in a relationship is to *leave*. Which is why I added Chris.

If you find yourself in a violent or abusive relationship, please call the National Domestic Violence Hotline at 800-799-7233. Or visit www.thehotline.org to learn about the forms of abuse, your local resources, and what to do if you're stuck in an abusive relationship.

Not everyone has a neighbor like Sherri—but that doesn't mean you're alone.

ACKNOWLEDGMENTS

I find it humorous I can write a one hundred and thirteen thousand word novel, but here, in the acknowledgements, is where words will fail me. Writing this book was a team effort, and I thoroughly believe it would still be in progress without the incredible support system I have.

To my editor—JD Rogers. You are brilliant and made my story better. I'm thankful for a writing friend like you and thankful to benefit from your expertise. To many more stories.

To Emily—thanks for reading over and over, listening, helping when I wrote myself into a corner, inspiring the "my wife" moments, and for cheering me on when I got cold feet. Thanks for threatening to hunt me down and end me if I backed out of certain plot points and for holding me to a level of confidence. This story pushed me outside my comfort zone in multiple ways and you've stood behind me.

To Christen—we really should petition Goodreads to allow you to add the same book to your list five times. Thanks for combing through this book over and over to find the fragments of plot changes I left behind. You saved me days of stress I can't even begin to describe. Thanks for starting that one voice message with "okay, first of all, don't freak out" and thanks for the last minute Bree makeover.

To Summer—thanks for letting me steal your apple crisp story. The way you tell it is adorable, and I hope Miranda and Jack did it justice.

To Dad—thanks for reading my manuscript at every stage.

To my teams—betas and advance readers. You guys are the fun part of this process. Thanks for screaming about this story from the rooftops. And as a special shout-out—my second-string beta team absolutely came in clutch, single-handedly saving the day.

To my readers—every time you open my books, you bless me. Thank you.

To Austin—we've been dashed on the rocks and lived to tell the tale. Thank you for fighting for our love. Thank you for your ardent belief in me. I love you.

ABOUT THE AUTHOR

Ashley Dill is a mom of four living in the Upstate of South Carolina. Ashley started writing when she was sixteen years old and still enjoys waking before the sun to share her stories. When she's not writing, she stays busy homeschooling and helping her husband with their family-owned tree business.

Join my newsletter to receive exclusive content.

Contact Online

facebook.com/ashleydillauthor
instagram.com/ashleydill_author